The Impossible Enchantment
and Other Tales of Faerie

The Impossible Enchantment
and Other Tales of Faerie

by
the Comte de Caylus

Translated, annotated and introduced by
Brian Stableford

A Black Coat Press Book

ISBN 978-1-61227-809-4. First Printing. November 2018. Published by Black Coat Press, an imprint of Hollywood Comics.com, LLC, P.O. Box 17270, Encino, CA 91416. All rights reserved. Except for review purposes, no part of this book may be reproduced or transmitted in any form or by any means, electronic or mechanical, including photocopying, recording, or by any information storage and retrieval system, without permission in writing from the publisher. The stories and characters depicted in this novel are entirely fictional. Printed in the United States of America.

TABLE OF CONTENTS

Introduction

The first twelve stories in this volume are taken from *Féeries nouvelles* first published anonymously in 1741, allegedly (but falsely) in The Hague, and subsequently attributed to the author whose full name is nowadays said to have been Anne-Claude-Philippe de Tubières-Grimoard de Pestels de Levis, Comte de Caylus, Marquis d'Esterhazy, Baron de Bransac (1692-1765) but who only used the title Comte de Caylus for purposes of identification and was known to his relatives and friends as Philippe. The next five are taken from *Cinq contes de fées*, published anonymously in 1745 without any indication as to its publisher or place of publication.

The remaining two stories translated herein were published by the widow Duchesne in 1775 in a small volume, *Tout vient à point à qui peut attendre, ou Cadichon, suivi par Jeannette, ou L'Indiscrétion, contes par feu le comte de Caylus*, ["Everything Works Out for Him who Can Wait; or, Cadichon," followed by "Jeannette; or, Indiscretion," tales by the late Comte de Caylus], which contains a preface that must have been written with the intention of publishing the volume while the author was alive, probably in 1760 or thereabouts; although it is unsigned, it confirms that he was the author of the two previous volumes, and also referred to his exploits in Egyptology in a fashion that rendered his identity recognizable.

It is possible that the three volumes in question do not contain the full set of the Comte de Caylus's endeavors in the genre of *contes de fées*, but the preface to the last volume implies that they do, and the other stories featuring fays that have been sometimes been attributed to him by various speculative bibliographers are probably not his. The catalogue of the Bibliothèque Nationale notes that *Cinq contes de fées* had been speculatively attributed before 1775, by the assiduous

7

chronicler of the works of female writers Josephe de La Porte, to Madame de Villeneuve, the author of "La Belle et la bête" (1740; tr. as "The Beauty and the Beast") although La Porte was very hesitant in that suggested attribution, and the point is only worth mentioning to illustrate the difficulty that contemporary bibliographers routinely had in identifying the authors of anonymous works published without a license from the royal censors. Although he was a famous and very well-connected man, with a considerable reputation as a scholar, Caylus thought it politic to publish many of his works anonymously, devoid of the benefit of the royal prerogative that was necessary at the time for licit publication, with false title pages often claiming publication outside France, although they were certainly printed in Paris. The bulk of the fiction attributed to him, including all the stories translated in the present collection, was reprinted under his name in a twelve-volume set of *Oeuvres badines complettes* [Complete Playful Works] compiled in 1787 by Charles Garnier, and that became the definitive compendium of his illicit works, although the accuracy of Garnier's bibliography is inevitably open to slight doubt.

It is not always easy to see from the viewpoint of today what might have deterred the royal censors from granting the *Oeuvres badines* a license for legal publication—probably discouraging the author even from submitting them to that filtration—but there is enough veiled eroticism and political satire in the *doubles entendres* of which Caylus was fond to alarm men who always had the stern representatives of Church and State looking over their shoulder. Many royal censors were impoverished writers who needed the income that the position in question provided, and who were therefore very careful in the exercise of that profession, although many of them published works of their own illicitly, some of which were far more scandalous than the amiably tongue-in-cheek works attributed to Caylus. The case of his *contes de fées* is, however, somewhat different from that of the more licentious works collected in *Oeuvres badines*, because, in spite of their relative inoffensiveness, the entire genre was still in bad odor at the time, for reasons that went back to the late 1690s, when the coterie of female writers who had invented the genre in salons appended Louis XIV's court had been broken up by his police and its three most prolific writers forced to leave Paris, Mademoiselle de La Force being exiled to a provincial nunnery, Madame d'Aulnoy simply being banished, and the Comtesse de Murat ending up in a state prison, for crimes that were never explicitly specified.

Philippe de Caylus came from an aristocratic military family, his father having been a general and his mother the daughter of a vice-admiral. His orphaned mother, Marthe-Marguerite de Mursay (1673-1729), had been brought up by the redoubtable Madame de Maintenon, who regulated Louis XIV's court for many years, and who appears to have been secretly married to him. Her significant memoir of that court was edited for posthumous publication by Voltaire. None of the members of the salon coterie who invented and popularized *contes de fees* is mentioned in the memoir but the absence might well be significant of diplomatic avoidance rather than ignorance. She is credited with a tale of that kind herself, published in the extremely elusive *Nouveaux contes des fées allégoriques* (1735), several of whose inclusions were probably written long before, although they include the oft-reprinted novella *Boca, ou la vertu récompensée* by Françoise Le Marchand, of whose salon Caylus was probably a member. We can, however, only speculate about the possible influence that Madame de Caylus might have had on her son's liking for *contes de fées* in general, and the works of the Comtesse de Murat in particular.

Caylus had a distinguished military career himself between 1709 and 1714, but abandoned it after the death of Louis XIV and devoted himself thereafter to antiquarian studies, especially studies in Egyptology, in which academic pursuit he was an important pioneer. His antiquarian studies would have familiarized him with the work of Françoise Le Marchand's father, Joseph-François Duché de Vancy, a member of the Académie des inscriptions. Caylus carried out important research on ancient painting techniques, and was very active himself as an etcher, leaving behind a rich legacy of engravings as well as his prolific writings. He acquired a posthumous reputation for riotous living, but that was greatly enhanced by a set of licentious fake memoirs published in 1805 and by scathing comments by contemporaries who did not like him, the most oft-quoted of whom was Denis Diderot. It is not necessarily the case that a liking for *doubles entendres* implies a licentious life, and there is no real reason to doubt Caylus's respectability, at least in terms of what passed for aristocratic respectability in the early eighteenth century.

Caylus was one of the major writers of the "second wave" of *contes de fées* produced in the 1730s and 1740s, when the publication of unlicensed works became a flood, far too abundant for effective suppression; the concentration of the legal authorities on works thought genuinely dangerous (including many works now considered classics, penned by *philosophes*) left a large population of works that were not actively pursued, but which still had to be published anonymously for safety's sake and sold "under the counter" rather than openly displayed. Almost all the notable *contes de fées* of the period were published in that fashion, although some works explicitly intended for the consumption of children, in the tradition established by Charles Perrault, and subjected to rigorous self-censorship, could still obtain prerogatives.

Among notable unlicensed works in the genre, Caylus's first collection had been preceded into print not only by *Boca* but also by Mademoiselle de Lubert's *Tecserion ou le prince des autriches* (1737: tr. as "Tecserion; or, The Prince of Ostriches") and the incomplete collection headed by Madame de Villeneuve's "La Belle et la bête"—not to be confused with the heavily abridged plagiarism that became far better known—and had probably read both of them. If the stories in the present collection were written in the order of their production, he seems to have begun with the intention of parodying the genre, but soon became carried away by its impetus and began a much more intense and elaborate exploration of its themes and potential, having become firmly hooked on its charms even before getting half way through that first story. Like Lubert and Villeneuve, he took his primary inspiration from the pioneering works of the Comtesse de Murat, the finest productions of the first wave of *contes de fées*, especially *Histoires sublimes et allégoriques par Madame la Comtesse D*** dédiées aux fées modernes* (1699), and like them he tried to take up where Murat had been cruelly forced to leave off, in trying to develop further the narrative strategies, key themes and imaginative inventiveness of the genre. Like Lubert, with whose work Caylus's has a marked affinity, he had a flair for the bizarre that continually edges into the surreal, and he never entirely forsook the spirit of parody in which he had apparently commenced.

By the time the second wave of *contes de fées* found the market space that had been denied to it for a genre following the deliberate destruction, with prejudice, of the female coterie that had invented and sophisticated the genre, the genre had been supplemented, and to some extent displaced, by a species of mock-Oriental fantasy pioneered spectacularly by Antoine Galland's *Les Mille et une nuits* (1704-1717) which featured tales of a similarly fanciful sort, often written in a similarly buoyant spirit, but which used a different lexicon of fantastic images, drawn from Arabic literature. That genre was fused with its predecessor in Charles Mayer's classic 41-volume *Cabinet de Fées, ou Collection choisie des contes de fées et autres contes merveilleux* (1785-1789), but Mayer was only acknowledging a process of overlap that had begun even before the first wave entirely petered out in the later work of the author who became posthumously known by the (entirely fictitious) name of "Madame d'Auneuil," collected in *Les Chevaliers Errans et le Génie familier par Madame la Comtesse D**** (1709).[1] Caylus wrote a collection of *Nouveaux contes*

---

[1] The *contes de fées* of the author in question are translated in *The Tyranny of the Fays Abolished and Other Stories* by Comtesse D.L., that being the signature attached to her first

11

orientaux (1743), which is distinct from his collections of *contes de fées*, but the creeping overlap between the two genres is already evident in some of the stories in *Féeries nouvelles* and the subsequent collections, in which the male counterparts of fays are not called *enchanteurs*, as in the first wave stories, but *génies* [genii, in the sense of spirits], a term extensively employed by Galland as a translation of the Arabic *jinni*, which gave rise in further translation to the bastardized English term "genie."

Prominent among the motifs that Caylus picked up from the Comtesse de Murat and elaborated somewhat is the notion that the community of fays has a kind of parliament or legislative council which regulates their activity, although he might have taken that more directly from "La Belle et la bête," where the activities of such an assembly shape the background subplot. That notion is closely connected with the distinctive use by Caylus of the term *Féerie* [Faerie] as a proper noun as well as a trivial noun meaning "enchantment," so that it comes to refer, more portentously, to the Art of Enchantment, or to the polity of the fays, and, on one late occasion, to a kind of parallel world in which fays and other supernatural beings live, as it often came to do in later phases of the evolution of *contes de fées*.

It is unarguable that the *fées* themselves—which I translate as fays because the common English translation as "fairies" is awkwardly misleading—were already in their period of decadence in the 1740s, and the Comte de Caylus is the author

---

collection *La Tyranie des fées détruite, nouveaux contes, dédiez à Madame la Duchesse de Bourgogne par la Comtesse D.L.* (1703). More elaborate accounts of the evolution of the genre in the context of salons hosted by Louis XIV's female courtiers can be found in the introductions to *The Robe of Sincerity* by Marie-Jeanne L'Héritier de Villandon, *The Land of Delights* by Charlotte-Rose Caumont de La Force and *The Palace of Vengeance* by Henriette-Julie de Murat, all published, like the present volume, by Black Coat Press.

12

who seems most aware of that decadence in his works, the scathing sarcasm and casual bizarrerie of which often show traces of a kind of quasi-apologetic contempt, and his work also has an overripe exuberance that is closely associated with the attitude that he is trafficking with absurdities that are already past their sell-by date. That rhetorical stance is also, however, partly derivative of the fact that Caylus was the leading male practitioner in a genre whose other leading practitioners were almost all women, and the contemptuous edge of his work also reflects a kind of unthinking sexism that was deeply endemic in the society in which he lived.

The work in the present collection is various, including such exercises in earnest allegory as "Le Palais d'idées" (tr. as "The Palace of Ideas")—which seems to be trying to make a serious point about the psychology of amour, although it is probably not one that many readers would have recognized—and such forthrightly conventional moralistic fantasies as "Bleuette et Coquelicot" (tr. as "Bleuette and Coquelicot") and "Jeannette, ou L'Indiscrétion (tr. as "Jeannette; or, Indiscretion"). The curious "Fleurette et Abricot, cadres" (tr. as "Fleurette and Abricot: A Frame Story"), which poses as the frame story of an imaginary collection of tales set in a land where the art of faerie has determined the people must change sex every year on their birthday, also aspires to the status of a Voltairean *conte philosophique*. The real strength of Caylus's *contes de fées*, however, is in the longer and more distinctive stories, and in their phantasmagorical elements.

The longest of all Caylus's *contes de fées*, the ebullient "Le Prince Courtebotte et la princesse Zibeline" (tr. as Prince Courtebotte and Princess Zibeline"), covers an enormous amount of colorfully diverse narrative ground at a rapid pace, while the stories that are the most impressive inclusions in his first two collections, "L'Enchantement impossible" (tr. as "The Impossible Enchantment"), "La Princesse Azerolle ou L'Excès de la constance" (tr. as "Princess Azerolle; or. Excessive Constancy") and "Bellinette ou La Jeune vieille" (tr. as "Bellinette; or, The Young Old Woman], achieve a spectacular abundance of hectic bizarrerie. Although "L'Enchantement Impossible" is more heavily dependent on motifs borrowed from Murat than any of the others, it benefits greatly from its brief but spectacular climactic battle to move into unexplored narrative territory in a cavalier fashion. "Azerolle" similarly makes use of the vengeance of a nasty fay as a productive plot lever, but complicates it intriguingly by juxtaposing her with two other fays whose benevolence is compromised. "Bellinette" reverts to a more straightforward contest between good and wicked fays, but enhances its plot with some intriguing allegorical episodes. All three of the stories are slapdash, obviously improvised as the author went along rather than being planned, but their improvisation is so buoyantly inventive as to compensate abundantly for a certain lack of coherency. Caylus did not seem to be able to maintain that cavalier spirit later in life, and his imaginative reach does not have quite the same effect or charm in the belated "Cadichon ou Tout vient à point à qui peut attendre" (tr. as "Cadichon; or Everything Works out for Him Who Can Wait"), although that story still retains an admirable bizarrerie in parts.

It has to be admitted that Caylus is a rather casual writer, and his work gives the impression not only that he was making up his stories as he went along but that he might have been dictating them to an amanuensis at high speed rather than writing them steadily in his own hand, but that imprudently informal methodology has rewards as well as penalties, and if, as the author admits in his humorous "advertisement" of his first collection, some of the stories could have done with being tidied up somewhat, most of them have a reckless brio that that is very appealing. No other writer of *contes de fées*, of his or any other period, gives the impression so strongly of dabbling in the genre purely for fun, and he was clearly enjoying himself in the process, even if he does take time out occasionally to add a literary flourish, to make a shrewd observation, or insert a serious argument. Because of that, in spite of its manifest literary flaws, his work remains very entertaining.

The first twelve translations herein were made from the two volumes of the 1756 second edition of *Féeries nouvelles* that are reproduced on the Bibliothèque Nationale's *gallica* website. As indicated in the footnotes, several of those stories have been translated into English previously, most of them rather freely, the majority appearing in *The Green Fairy Book* (1892) by Andrew Lang. The remaining stories were translated from a version of the ninth volume of *Oeuvres badines*, reproduced on Google Books

Brian Stableford

Advertisement

Most authors who want to have the honor of being authors in spite of themselves usually complain that someone has stolen their work.[2] If the author of these tales made the same complaint, it would be well-founded. The manuscript really has been stolen, and it was me who did it. I do not claim because of that, to be regarded as a thief; I am merely a wholesale plagiarist—which appears to me more honest to be one in detail, like so many others.

Some of these tales could have done with a few changes, and the last one is unfinished.[3] I would have proposed to the author that he put the final touches to it, but I feared that instead of doing me that kindness, he might have made me give the whole thing back, and it seems to me that although it is good to be an honest man, there is no point in stealing things

---

[2] Because it was impolitic for authors in the 1730s to sign their unlicensed works, they routinely denied having written them if the legal authorities took an interest, or, if that proved impractical, claimed that the books had been published without their knowledge. The most famous instance of the latter strategy occurred a year after the publication of this note, with regard to *Le Sopha* (1742; tr. as *The Sofa*) by Crébillon *fils*—a royal censor himself—who used it as an excuse in order to be allowed to return to Paris after being exiled when he was found to have written it.

[3] I have omitted the unfinished story from this volume of translations; it is identified on the contents page of the second volume of the origin as "Hermine, fragment," although the story itself—which breaks off in mid-sentence after less than 5,000 words of a story that seemed to be shaping up to be much longer—carries the title "La Belle Hermine et le Prince Colibri."

only to give them back. The consequence, dear reader, is that you will have the things as I took them; if my action remains unpunished, it will engage me to do better—which is to say, to steal more.

Adieu, buyer, read on—and if you get bored, which I do not anticipate, take it from me that you are wrong.

PRINCE COURTEBOTTE AND PRIN-
CESS ZIBELINE[4]

There was once a king and a queen who were extremely stupid, but who loved one another prodigiously. There could not have been anyone in the world, except for the flatterers in their court, who would not have said that their love was proof of their mutual stupidity.

Such as they were, they were monarchs, and for that, everything goes well, and everything is good, all the better because, in the time of Faerie, princes had no affairs more essential than those of getting along well with the fays and the genii, giving them cakes, a few meters of ribbon and other bagatelles of that kind. It was necessary, above all, to have a little memory, in order not to forget to invite fays and genii, good or evil, to a queen's childbirths. They were also obliged to take great care not to discontent those who liked doing harm. With those sorts of attentions, everything was settled, and a realm was well governed. Since the times when Faerie went into decline, kings have begun to govern by themselves; nowadays, they all have intelligence, a knowledge of affairs, and capability; and, in particular, they strive to know the human heart.

The queen became pregnant. She employed the entire time of her pregnancy compiling a list of all the fays that it would be possible for her to assemble. There were a large number of whom no one had ever heard mention. All the king's subjects were ordered, on pain of death, to give the names of all those who were known to them, and people took great care to write their declarations. But of all the bodies of the realm that were consulted in that important matter, none

---

[4] The abridged version of this story reproduced in translation in Andrew Lang's *Green Fairy Book* (1892) is entitled "Heart of Ice."

were treated with as much consideration as that of wet-nurses and nursery-maids, and that was only just, because of their great knowledge and their profound erudition. They were, therefore, admitted to the Council, and gave all their advice, with the details, diffusions and obscurities for which they have been well-known since time immemorial.

The term of the labor arrived and the list of all the names that it had been possible to collect were filed—albeit in small handwriting—a large folio volume, for which a large stand had been set up on a podium at the foot of the queen's bed, so that the whole thing resembled a lectern.

At the moment when it was least expected, the good queen was gripped by pains; it was between midnight and one o'clock precisely. The king was asleep at the time, but she gave birth so promptly—even though it was her first child and no fay had assisted her—that the good king, who had been informed as soon as the pains began, and who was sleeping in a room separated from the queen's by a simple partition, only just had time to put on his shirt and slippers and come running, while still asleep. In spite of that diligence, he found the queen giving birth. He ran to the lectern and ran up the steps so rapidly that history reports that he lost one of his slippers in the process.

What a task for an idiot! So there he was, perching in front of his huge book, holding his gavel in his hand. There he was, shouting at the top of his voice: "I implore and beg you, Fay So-and-so, Genius So-and-so, to honor me with your visit, to come and endow my child." He was in so much of a hurry and was so prodigiously emotional that he did not pronounce three names as they were written.

On the other hand, the queen shouted herself hoarse, crying: "Someone bring me my cakes; someone arrange my presents; take this key and open that cupboard," and a thousand other things.

In sum, it was impossible to hear anything in that bedroom.

Fortunately, the time of those sorts of invitations was limited, or the queen's attestations, which were always fertile in futile and oft-repeated orders, would never have finished, and nor would the king's reading—him being the greatest mumbler there ever was—before their little boy was ready to be weaned; for it was a prince that Heaven had given them, an article of joy that contributed more than a little to making the king lose his head.

Although the time of the invitations should not have lasted more than half an hour at the most, the king employed two full hours reading from his big book, whatever anyone could say to him, and he only reached the third page. Finally, it was drawn to his attention that several fays and genii were waiting for him in the great hall of the palace, and were becoming impatient at not seeing anyone to do the honors and welcome them. He ran, in the indecent attire that I have already mentioned, made a hundred apologies to all the fays he found in the hall, and asked for their protection.

Almost all those assembled were touched by his extreme submission and promised him not to do his son any harm; they all assured him that he would live to a ripe old age and that a time would come when he would enjoy all the happiness imaginable. But during the king's reading, one black fay, whose name he had written in capital letters in the fear of forgetting it, and of whom no one had ever heard, having been one of the first named, had also been one of the first to arrive in the hall. Annoyed at having had to wait, and piqued at not having been greeted as she descended from the large coconut in which she had come from the depths of Guinea, she said between gritted teeth: "Read on, your son will be no larger; read on, he will only be a shortass."[5] She would doubtless have continued the litany of defaults that she wanted to give him if the good

---

[5] The equivalent English colloquialism is "shortarse" which is far more common than its Americanization; a literal translation of Courtebotte would be "short-boot," but that is not what the term is intended to imply.

Guerlinguin, who gave the realm and the royal family a particular protection, had not come running of her own accord, without waiting to be summoned, and begged the black fay to moderate her ill humor, which she did, with difficulty. In the end, they received all their presents, went to visit the queen, and each returned to their own affairs.

When they had all gone, Guerlinguin approached the queen's bed and said to the king: "You haven't done anything properly, everything has gone awry; why didn't you deign to consult me? But fools are always suspicious; you didn't even invite me—me. whose generosity you know so well!"

"Oh, Madame," said the king, throwing himself at her feet, "did I have time to read as far as your name? Look"—he showed her his bookmark—"I was still at the beginning."

"I'm not piqued," she told him, "at not having been invited; I don't pay any attention to such trivia with people I love; otherwise, I wouldn't have saved your son from so many misfortunes, But I have plans for him, I have to take him away from you, and you'll only see him again *all covered in furs*."

At that phrase, which the king and queen could not understand, in a climate as warm as the one in which they lived, they dissolved in tears. Guerlinguin told them not to be afflicted, that she had been good enough and kind enough to allow the king to be brought up by his father and mother, who had spoiled him, to such a extent that he was nothing but a fool, but that she did not want the same thing to happen to their son, and that they ought not to embarrass themselves with anything but governing their realm wisely.

After that she opened the window, put the little prince in a basket, and, giving herself a kick up the backside, she glided through the air as if she were on skates.

The king and the queen were penetrated by an inconceivable dolor; they found themselves separated from a son whom it had taken them such a long time to make. They were preoccupied by the last words that Guerlinguin had spoken. "You'll only see him again," she said to us, "all covered in furs." They consulted everyone in order to find out what it meant, for advice is the prerogative of those who have no part to play and know nothing, but all those consultations were unable to inform the interested parties. It was therefore opined, and they were easily persuaded, in view of the disposition they were in, that the furs must be a terrible thing.

In consequence of all their advice and reflections, therefore, the king and the queen made the wise decision to be so afflicted that everyone would feel sorry for them. Utterly sad and unemployed as the king and queen were in their palace, they could not resolve to give their son little brothers or little sisters.

Let us return to the little prince. The fay took him home with her. She lived in a lovely country house. When she arrived, she took away from a healthy and vigorous young peasant woman the child she was nursing, and substituted the little prince for him; she fascinated her eyes so that the peasant woman still believed that he was her own child. She brought him up in the local farmyard, but as he grew older, the fay took him into her company more often, in order to cultivate in him the gifts of nature.

The wise fay was convinced that a simple and natural education with regard to the mind, and a hard and fatiguing one with regard to the body, were the most essential gifts that she could give the young prince, but the attention she wanted to give him was not only limited to that. She resolved to form him by means of obstacles, mental trials and a knowledge of human beings.

Courtebotte did, in fact, need all the talents of heart and mind, for as he grew older he did not grow in stature; by way of recompense he had a pretty face, and was robust in his short stature; few men were seen more muscular and more vigorous than him. Since early childhood he had exercised his courage in the forest, and had formed troops of children of his own age several times, who had always deferred to his command, so true is it that almost everyone does in childhood what they have to do at a more advanced age. The years fortify the inclinations, good or bad, but their principle is always indicated in youth.

Courtebotte was not unaware that the name he bore, although he did not know any other, was a nickname that had been given to him, but in order to console himself for that he had promised himself a hundred times to become illustrious and to render himself commendable. The fay informed him often by means of his dreams that he must soon quit a place where a birth as low as his was a sort of reproach to the elevation of his heart.

That was not the only means she employed to inspire him with everything necessary to bring the greatest adventures to a conclusion. She imprinted him forcefully with patience and boldness, the combination of which produces a cool head, and she assured him many a time that as long as he was virtuous, he could not fail in anything in distant countries; and to convince him further, when she summoned him, she only talked to him about the crowns acquired by men of his kind, and the reputation they had acquired by virtue of their valor and good conduct.

With his head filled with all those ideas, his heart naturally noble and magnanimous, and his stature very short, he arrived one day in a large town not far from the fay's mansion, the ardor of a hunt having taken him that far. He was mounted on a fine chestnut horse, of which the fay had made him a present shortly before. He was simply dressed, and had no other weapons and a bow, arrows and a spear, but that equipment, although a trifle primitive, had a marvelous grace in association with his person.

He arrived at the moment when all the inhabitants of the town were going to the main square to hear what some foreigners had to say. Their cortege, their costume and their bizarre vehicles, unfamiliar in the region, attracted curiosity. Everyone therefore came running, because, needless to say, there are idlers everywhere.

Courtebotte ran too, and found himself very close to the foreigners. They preceded the proclamation they were going to make with the noise of various martial instruments. When the fanfares had finished, a venerable old man with a beard tucked up behind his ears read in a loud voice:

"Let all the world know that whomsoever can conquer the Mountain of Ice will posses not only the precious Zibeline, the most beautiful of beauties, but also all the Estates of which she is to be the queen.[6]

"Here," he went on, after that proclamation, "is a list of all the princes who, struck by her beauty or that of her portraits, have perished in trying to bring the proposed enterprise to a conclusion, and of those newly engaged for the conquest."

Courtebotte then felt himself animated by the most violent desire that the idea of glory has ever excited in a heart. He hesitated, however, reflecting on his estate and the scant resources that he had.

In the midst of the agitation caused by all the thoughts that had just assailed him in a host, the old man who had just spoke, after having prostrated himself three times, uncovered a kind of litter and displayed to the entire assembly the portrait of the beautiful Zibeline. Courtebotte was so impressed by it that, cleaving through the crowd, and no longer considering anything else, he demanded to be inscribed.

The foreigners, perceiving his smallness and the simplicity of his costume, did not know whether to accept his proposition or refuse it.

"Give it to me," he said in a loud voice, "so that I can sign. Do you know who I am?"

They obeyed, but as he was animated by amour for the portrait and anger against the foreigners, he did not have time to choose another name than his own and signed "Courtebotte." At that name, coming after so many princes, the laughter of the foreigners was violent.

"Rogues," he said to them, "give thanks to the portrait whose care has been confided to you. But for that…."

---

[6] Zibeline is the French term for the animal known in English as a sable.

He did not say any more; moderation took hold of him again. He drew away from them, promising them to make them see who he was, but only after having learned the name of Zibeline's country and the time it would require to reach it, in order to attempt the adventure.

In spite of his great courage, Courtebotte found himself filled with all the doubts that such an enterprise might have caused anyone but him. As he was well-known in the town, however, and had signed his own name, which the trumpets had repeated a thousand times, to the great hilarity of everyone, and his little friends came to congratulate him on his great enterprise, he had no doubt that rumor of the event would soon reach the fay's mansion; he did not dare, therefore, to go back there and present himself to the peasant woman he believed to be his mother, especially having subscribed to the hope of a kingdom and a beautiful princess.

He bid adieu to his little friends and embraced them, assuring them that they would only see him again as a king and Zibeline's husband, or that he would die trying. He departed without worrying any more about everything that was being said in the vicinity about his enterprise. There was much talk of it in the provinces, after which there was much talk of it in the court, and the court in question was that of the king, his father, and the queen, his mother, who were unaware of the part they played in the jokes that were being made about Courtebotte, and which they were making themselves. The poor monarchs in question lived in the manner that I have already described.

Courtebotte left the town on his fine chestnut horse, deep in thought. It is not astonishing that he had profound reveries; the memory of Zibeline's portrait preoccupied him, and the difficulty of the journey weighed on his mind; but amour, on the one hand, and the shame of returning to the fay's mansion, on the other, made him decide firmly to make the journey. He read the notice that the herald-of-arms had given to him, and did not find it very clear. It was conceived in these terms:

Four hundred leagues from Mount Caucasus, in the northern mountains, you will receive your orders and instructions for the conquest of the Mountain of Ice.

A fine instruction for a man departing from a region in which Japan is found today! However, he orientated himself in accordance with the knowledge of geography that the fay had made him learn from Robbe's *Geography* and continued on his route.[7]

He carefully avoided all towns, in order to avoid at the same time all the jokes he had heard made about his name. As he had not traveled much, he did not understand mockery yet. He therefore slept in forests, and thought he could sustain himself on a few fruits that he would encounter on the way; but the fay who protected him and who wanted to help him without diminishing his courage by confidence in marvels, blew him nutriments while he was asleep, so that when he woke up, he found himself increasingly refreshed and well. She still wanted to follow the plan, which she had made a long time ago, of making him pass through all sorts of ordeals.

One day, when he was following a forest path, as usual, he was attacked by one of those monsters of which America is full. It was like a cross between a tiger and a leopard. The battle was fierce, and Courtebotte triumphed over the monster in the end, but not without difficulty, for it cost him the life of his horse. That loss was dear to him, but the ardor of his courage sustained him in that adversity.

He continued his route on foot, and finally arrived in a sea port. He found a ship there that was setting forth shortly for the coast he desired, and he still had enough money to pay for his passage. It set forth, but after a few days of navigation a tempest blew up that caused its shipwreck. He was the only

---

[7] Jacques Robbe (1643-1721) was Louis XIV's royal geographer. His treatise on geography was published in 1678. The practice of intruding anachronistic academic references of this sort into tales set in "the time of the fays" was introduced into the first wave of *contes de fées* by the Comtesse de Murat.

survivor of the entire crew and passengers, and came ashore with great difficulty on a desert island.

There, he had time for serious reflections; however, his great heart would not allow him to be beaten. He lived on hunting and fishing—at least, he convinced himself of that, although it was more probably the secret assistance of the good Guerlinguin.

One day, when he was walking rather sadly on the sea shore, he saw a ship that was sailing in his direction. He made signals to request help, but the closer the ship came, the more extraordinary it seemed and he was unable to perceive people on the vessel. Finally, it came under full sail to run aground. Hazard and luck enabled it to encounter a mud bank, on which it came to rest very fortunately. Courtebotte was then within range to examine the vessel more closely; he saw that the masts were green trees full of leaves, that the rails were composed of little trees in hedges, and that, in sum, it strongly resembled an arbor.

Surprised by that, and by the solitude of the ship, he leapt aboard, and only found men reduced to a frightful state. They were motionless, and had almost become trees. Some were stuck to the deck of the ship by the legs, others by the arms, depending on the action in which the maneuvering and communication of the ship had surprised them.

Gripped by the compassion that such a spectacle could cause, Courtebotte tried to detach the wooden limbs at retained them with the iron tip of one of his arrows. He succeeded in that, and carried them to land one after another. He tried a few fermentations of herbs on their wooden legs, and did so with such success that in a few days, they were in a condition to act and maneuver as before. One can easily imagine that Guerlinguin worked hard on that cure.

Either by virtue of inspiration, or simple reflection, Courtebotte had all the timbers of the vessel rubbed with the same plants that had worked so well on the sailors, and that help was very necessary, for without the care he took, the ship would soon have become a forest. The gratitude of the poor sailors was infinite; he easily obtained from them that they would take him where he wanted to go, but they could not give him any answers to the questions he asked about the condition in which he had found them except that, passing within sight of a heavily wooded coast, a wind from the land had assailed them, so violent that the air had suddenly been obscured by the thick dust, which had doubtless communicated a vegetal virtue to everything aboard, except metals. They had found themselves getting heavier, then they had lost sentiment, and gradually, unable to avoid it, the wood had overtaken them and attached them to it.

Courtebotte reflected on such a singular event, and, wanting not to neglect anything of what had happened to him, and might be useful or curious, he picked up a fairly large quantity of that powder and put it in a box, which he conserved preciously about his person. The fay, who had produced that marvel, contributed a great deal to that inspiration; the crew of the ship had no difficulty leaving the desert island, and set sail in the finest weather in the world.

After a month of navigation they sighted land, and resolved to disembark there, not only to ask for directions but also to take on water and refreshments, of which they were beginning to run out. Courtebotte embarked on the launch that they put into the sea.

As they drew closer to the shore they did not see any people, but they had no doubt that the cost was inhabited, because they perceived movement. Someone was making signals to mark their discovery, and they could also distinguish clouds of dust—thin, in truth—converging on the place where they were about to land, which clearly proved that precautions were being taken.

When they came within visual range, they discovered large barbet dogs posted along the coast, which were standing guard, and others formed into troops.[8] Those in the lead came forward proudly to investigate the launch, and, seeing that Courtebotte did not greet them which the vile word: "Fire!" and, on the contrary, said to them: "Good day, my good dogs," they immediately began wagging their tails, and uttering barks that signified their contentment. They did more and offered their paws; they asked him if would care to follow them and abandoning himself to their conduct. Not only did he understand everything I have just said, but he also understood that they did not want any of the crewmen to accompany him, and that they were granting that mark of confidence to him alone.

Curiosity determined Courtebotte's decision; he therefore ordered his men to wait for him for a fortnight, after which they could continue on their way even if they had not had any news of him. He recommended them, however, to be very careful of the island's inhabitants during his absence, to live in peace with them, and to make their provision of water and everything necessary to them with the consideration that one has for friendly people.

As for himself, he abandoned himself to the mercy of the good animals, and half a league from the coat, he discovered a fairly large village, which was composed of the prettiest and cleanest huts in the world. Before arriving there he encountered carts drawn by horses and other animals destined to that usage by human industry. He was surprised by the cultivation of the land, and to see at every step, everything that the most exact civilization can present, without perceiving anyone other than barbets.

---

[8] Although the term barbet now refers to a specific dog breed, in the mid-eighteenth century it was used more generally to refer to any large woolly dog of a kind often employed as sheepdogs or retrievers; in the latter capacity, several descendant breeds became known as "water dogs." The specific definition of the "grand barbet" contained in Buffon's *Histoire Naturelle* was only published in 1750, sometime after the publication of the present story.

30

When he arrived in the village he was served refreshments. In the meantime, two horses were harnessed to an Italian carriage driven by a large barbet, as the best postillion might have done.

In that carriage, Courtebotte traveled about ten leagues, sometimes traversing villages and encountering carriages like his own driven by barbets, in which he saw other barbets, which saluted him with great politeness. Eventually, they arrived in a large town; he had no doubt that it was the capital of the land.

All the inhabitants were at their doors, on the walls and in the streets; they had been notified in advance by a courier of the confidence that the stranger had in them and of his arrival in the town. Courtebotte was infinitely satisfied by the exclamations and caresses with which he was received.

When he had traversed several narrow streets, well-paved and well-planted with trees, he arrived in a large esplanade, on emerging from which he traversed a large courtyard in the midst of two thousand barbets, which were lined up. They were nearly clipped, had moustaches, and almost all of them had pipes in their mouths, as one sees in our homeland when one takes them for walk.

The courtyard was overlooked by the king's lodge, brilliant with gold and azure. When he was a short distance away, Courtebotte got down, in order to show respect, and found the king lying on a rich carpet of Persian fabric, surrounded by little dogs occupied in chasing away flies. He was the finest and most handsome of barbets; he had astonishingly delicate eyes, a mild and intelligent physiognomy and a very agreeable stature. When he had seen Courtebotte, he made him a hundred caresses and offered him his paw, in recognition of the confidence he had testified to him. Then he made a sign for the entire court to advance and show reverence to the stranger. The entire crowd was composed of barbets of the smallest species, they all had polished manners, and the bitches could not have been more modest.

After a few moments employed in compliments of that sort, the king made a sign for everyone to retire, and summoned a Secretary of State, to whom he dictated a compliment, on the dolor he felt at not being able to make himself understood vocally, the canine language not being easy to understand. As for writing, it had remained the same as that of humans.

Courtebotte replied to that compliment with the politeness that it merited, and begged the king to satisfy his curiosity, especially regarding the surprising things he saw in his court and his Estates. That speech brought sad ideas to the king's mind; however, after he had given a few moments to the reflections that took possession of him, he told him, again through the ministry of his Secretary of State, that his name was King Biby, that a fay who was a neighbor of his Estates, named Marsontine, had been touched and impressed by the form that Heaven had given him at birth, that she had done everything possible to engage him to love her and marry her, but that he had never been able to resolve himself to do either, because if the attachment he had to the Queen of India, by whom he was ardently beloved.

In the end, the fay's amour had been converted into fury, she had metamorphosed him and had reduced him to the condition in which he saw him. In order to redouble his misfortune, she had taken away the usage of speech, while she had left him all the other faculties of the human mind. He would easily have consoled himself for his own misfortune if the fay, in order to afflict him even more, had not exercised the same tyranny on all his subjects.

By virtue of that speech, Courtebotte easily understood everything that he had seen in the kingdom that was singular, and expressed to the king the sympathy he felt for the misfortunes that had just been confided to him. But as he was naturally avid for glory, and keen to testify it, he immediately and urgently offered his aid and swore that he would not find anything difficult to oblige a prince who seemed to him so likeable, and to extract him from the deplorable state in which he saw him.

The handsome Biby replied to him that his misfortunes were beyond help, since the malevolent fay had said at the cruel moment of his metamorphosis: "Yap and be covered with fur until the time when Amour and Fortune have recompensed Virtue."

"You can see," he added, "that that is to be condemned to remain a barbet all my life."

Courtebotte agreed with him, but made advantageous use nevertheless on that occasion of the common bond that links all the unfortunate, in saying to him elegantly: "It's necessary for Your Majesty to be patient."

Touched by all the compassion in Courtebotte's words, Biby wanted to show him that the reason for his misfortunes merited his attachment, by showing him a portrait of the Queen of India painted by Largillière.[9] He almost caused Courtebotte an infidelity—it seems to me that our hero easily received great impressions from paintings. At any rate, Courtebotte applauded the king's attachment and the choice that he had made. He was no longer surprised by the coldness with which he received the provocations of the prettiest bitches of the court, and easily understood how wrong it was that all the ladies accused him secretly of impotence.

In his turn, Courtebotte related his own story, and the great designs by which he was animated. Biby gave him some very useful enlightenments as to the route he ought to take, and made him a present of a marine chart of which his people had once made use, and which had always been kept in the archives.

The two princes had no difficulty in swearing an eternal mutual amity, for they felt it veritably. Biby wanted to escort our hero back to his ship. Courtebotte found all the sailors delighted to see him again, and not at all anxious for his per-

---

[9] Nicolas de Largillière (1656-1746).

son, but they had been heaped with presents and refreshments that had been brought to them every day on the king's orders.

It was with dolor that Biby separated from Courtebotte, but he insisted on giving him a squire of whom he was fond, and whose value and capacity he knew, in order to accompany him in his journey. He instructed the dog to send him word carefully of everything that happened to his friend the prince, and ordered him to attach himself to his new master as he always had to himself. The squire's name was Mousta, and he quit the king with inconceivable regret, but promised to acquit worthily the employment with which he had been honored.

The wind then being favorable, Courtebotte's ship set sail. The chagrin that Biby felt at his departure was expressed by a general howl that he had ordered all the troops lined up on the coast to utter. Gradually, as the wind picked up, the coast was lost to sight.

The navigation was fortunate; they reached the land for which they had set sail without having experienced any of the disgraces by which sea voyages are usually accompanied, and found themselves two leagues from the port where they wanted to moor; but, the weather not being very assured, Courtebotte begged the captain of the ship to put him ashore. It was sufficiently indifferent to him where he landed, having no business to do in the city and not being in a condition to make any expenditure. He separated from the worthy mariners with some regret on his part and a great deal of chagrin on theirs.

Our hero was thus disembarked two leagues north of the city, with no other company than Mousta, his squire. After having walked for some time, abandoned more than ever to providence, he arrived in a charming meadow. It was bordered by a wood, the coolness of which invited him to take some rest.

He had no sooner sat down than a little she-monkey came to settle beside him, pulling faces and making the prettiest grimaces in the world. At first he did not pay any attention, but she repeated them so frequently that, in the end, he was struck by them, and then made every effort to render him her master, Before allowing herself to be captured, however, she set out her terms—which is to say that she made him promise that he would follow her wherever she wanted to take him.

Courtebotte agreed to that, and the she-monkey immediately leapt on to his shoulder and murmured his ear: "We have no money, my poor Courtebotte; we're not thriving in our affairs."

"Alas, what can one do?" he replied, rather sadly. "It's necessary to suffer and not complain. I'm sorry for you, my darling monkey, because I can't give you sugar or a biscuit

"Since you're so hard up yourself, and so compassionate to others, I want to take you to the Golden Rock; but it's necessary for you to order Mousta to wait for you here."

Courtebotte did as he was ordered.

The monkey leapt down to the ground and said: "Follow me." She went into the wood then, and preceded him, leaping from tree to tree, sometimes waiting for him, sometimes calling to him.

After having walked for about an hour, he found himself in a part of the forest where there was a large clearing, which allowed the sight of a little green meadow at the foot of a mountain. The little meadow was only interrupted by a rock about eight or ten feet high and five or six broad.

When he was close to that boulder of sorts, the monkey said to him: "Strike that rock, which seems so hard, with your spear."

He did that, and the force he employed broke off several shards, which only had a surface layer of rock, which enabled him to see that the whole interior of the mass was gold.

Then the monkey said to him: "What you've broken belongs to you; I give it to you; take whatever you wish."

He took one of the smallest fragments, and thanked her for her generosity. Then the monkey was transformed into a beautiful tall lady, who said to him: "Courtebotte, always be as virtuous, laborious and moderate as you are at present, and you can hope to succeed in the most difficult things. Go, the little piece that you have is sufficient for you, since I am giving it the virtue of multiplying itself in accordance with your needs. But I want you to know the risk that your moderation has enabled you to avoid."

She led him into the wood then, which he found full of men and women whose faces were pale and their bodies emaciated, who were running back and forth, searching the ground, looking up in the air and lending an ear to the slightest sound, sometimes saying prayers and sometimes uttering imprecations, who were imploring the blackest divinities to enable them to find the golden rock.

"You see the trouble they're giving themselves," the fay said to him, "but all their efforts are superfluous, they will die in penury; they will never enjoy the golden rock, but will end their days like many others who have preceded them—which is to say, by breaking their heads in despair."

The fay had taken him back to the place where she had found him; then she disappeared, and on his return Courtebotte received thousands of caresses from Mousta, who was waiting patiently where he had left him.

After that, he took the road to the city, and reached it without any further adventure. He rested there for a few days and obtained directions carefully of the route that it was necessary to follow to reach Mount Caucasus. He also asked many questions about Princess Zibeline, but could not inform himself fully, except on the route to follow. He was still so far away from the Princess's Estates that he only heard confused rumors about her.

He bought horses, a few slaves, and, in sum, everything necessary for his journey. All the purchases he made were simple and not gaudy, but sound and sturdy. The little piece of gold furnished everything he needed abundantly, without diminishing.

He traversed the Caucasus easily; after that he no longer heard talk of anything but Zibeline; foreigners were heading toward her court from all directions; but in hearing talk of her beauty and intelligence, he also heard talk of the number of his rivals and their power. This one had an army, that one treasures, another had in his retinue everything the arts could furnish of the useful and the agreeable. As for him, poor Courtebotte, he only had a great determination to succeed, his dog and the ridicule of a name that still served to call attention to his small stature. As he was inscribed under that name on the list of ambassadors, it was not possible for him to give it up and take another; he therefore made the decision not to worry about it any longer, and I think he did the right thing.

After walking for two entire months he arrived in the city of Trelintin,[10] the capital of the Estates promised to Zibeline. He spent a few days informing himself of the customs of the land, researching the character of his rivals, asking questions about the Mountain of Ice and gathering information about the enterprise that he was about to undertake.

This is what he learned regarding the last item, for about the Mountain, as no one had ever come back from it, people could only talk conjecturally.

Farda-Kinbras, Zibeline's father and the king of a large part of the North, had married Birbantine, the daughter of a neighboring king. The convenience of the Estates was in accord with that of humors and persons; in sum, hazard made a good marriage on that occasion, so good that it turned the heads of the two spouses, who were stupid enough one day when they were on a sleigh to defy fate to be contrary to them, so much did they experience the love for one another with which they were smitten.

"You shall see the contrary," said an old woman who chanced to be there, whom the rigor of the cold was engaging to blow on her fingers.

---

[10] The nonsensical word *trelintin* was familiar in Paris at the time when the story was written because it featured in the chorus of more than one popular comic song; it is an approximate equivalent of the English *tra la la*.

The king wanted to punish the audacity of that insolence, and leapt down from his sleigh, but the queen, milder and more moderate, stopped him. "Don't get annoyed, Sire. Perhaps she's a fay."

"Yes, undoubtedly she is one," said the old woman, acquiring a firm voice, growing and becoming gigantic, and making a fiery chariot out of her little foot-warmer, a huge dragon from her staff, a golden umbrella out of her rags and two rockets out of her clogs. "Yes, she is one," she repeated, "And you'll see what the fruit of your amour will be, and sometimes remember your presumption and the fay Guarlangandino."

The king and queen prostrated themselves before her, but she was already far away, flying northwards, her chariot and her rockets leaving nothing behind them but a long fiery trail.

Farda-Kinbras and Birbantine were deeply ashamed then, but what could they do? There was no remedy for their anxieties.

Not long after that adventure, the queen found that she was pregnant, and brought Zibeline into the world, who seemed beautiful the moment she appeared in the light of day. All the fays of the North presided over her birth. The king's Estates were so vast that more than a hundred fays had their residence in his kingdom; he had taken great care to invite them all, and had confided Guarlangandino's threat to them. She did not appear at the feast, and she did not come to receive her present, although she had been invited with the greatest attention, and urgently. After having left all her sisters tranquilly to endow the little princess with all imaginable talents and virtues, however, while everyone was at table and the king could not contain the joy that he felt at having seen the gifts of the fays concluded without any opposition, Guarlangandino slipped into the palace in the form of a cat.

She easily obtained entry into the little princess's room, hid under her crib, and as soon as the midwives and the nurse had turned their backs, she stole the beautiful little Zibeline's heart, while leaving her the faculty of living. After that fine coup, she left the palace as easily as she had entered it, only harassed by a few dogs and scullions. She found her carriage, which was waiting for her in the main square, and shut herself away, with the booty she had just collected, in the Mountain of Ice near the Arctic Pole. She imposed so many difficulties on being able to make its conquest that she counted on enjoying all her life the wretched condition to which that poor court was reduced.

The fays left after dinner without suspecting anything; in consequence, the king and the queen thought they were perfectly safe. Zibeline, who was as beautiful as the most beautiful day, learned everything with an indescribably facility, but no sentiment whatsoever was ever observed in her; intelligence performed all its functions, but the heart did not say a word. How could it? It was in the Mountain of Ice.

Zibeline, it is true, increasingly had the admiration of all those who saw her, with regard to beauty; she was not unaware that a princess ought to know how to dance, so she danced, but she only did so methodically; one did not see in her dancing the fortunate turn, the I-know-not-what, that only the desire to please can give. She had a beautiful voice, so she sang, but she never rendered the sentiment of the words. She pronounced the word *amour*, and all those that follow it, as she would have pronounced the words of a foreign language that she did not understand. Was what she did with her beautiful voice really singing? I appeal to my reader. It was the same with everything she did.

In spite of the admiration and flattery of an entire court, in spite of paternal blindness, a defect as essential as the one the princess possessed was perceived, for, after all, when one does not love, one cannot be loved for long. In spite of that principle, our princesses have always imitated Zibeline at the commencement of her life—but not with regard to amour, of course.

In order to remedy such great inconveniences, one runs to consult the fays. Farda-Kinbras invited them, and convened a general assembly, in which he exposed his grievances, and ended up imploring them to examine his daughter again.

"Certainly," he said to them, "you have left your work imperfect, and I can assure you that something is lacking. I don't know exactly what it is, but what I'm saying is certainly true."

They all assured him that they had not forgotten anything of what they owed to the king, their friend, as he had always professed himself to be. After that compliment, they went to visit Zibeline, but when they went into her room they all cried: "Oh! It's a miracle! It's a prodigy!"

The entire court, and the princess herself, in spite of her great intelligence, thought that those exclamations were addressed to her beauty, but after the others had gone out, the fays told the king and queen that they had just seen something supernatural, that their daughter had no more heart than they had in their hand.

Farda-Kinbras and Birbantine began uttering loud cries at that news, and implored the entire sacred college to remedy that inconvenience. Then the oldest of the fays opened her psalter, or grimoire—for she always wore it hanging from her side, on a beautiful silver chain, from which her key was also suspended—and discovered that the privation of heart was an operation by Guarlangandino. Right away, she discovered what she had done with the princess's heart, and the difficulties that she had attached to the Mountain of Ice.

"What remedy is there for our misfortune?" cried the king and queen dolorously.

"You'll be troubled for a long time," she said, "and will certainly suffer from seeing and loving an idol like Zibeline, but if it's possible to see an end to her indifference, it's probably only by promising her, along with your Estates, to the man who has enough valor and conduct to merit her by making the conquest of her heart. Send her portrait all over the world, and promise what I've just said to you. She's beautiful enough, and the dowry is good enough, to determine all the princes in the world to risk their lives for her deliverance."

Immediately, they sent portraits and ambassadors in all direction, similar to the one that Courtebotte had encountered.

He learned that more than five hundred princes, not to mention their pages and squires, had already perished in the snow or in the ice, and that new ones were arriving every day from every part of the empire, a number difficult to count.

After having made all these reflections, and not having made any decision other than to follow the impulses of his heart, Courtebotte decided to have himself introduced to the court. His arrival has not made any great noise, his equipage being almost as succinct as his height, and the magnificence of all the princes then to be found at the court almost eclipsed that of Farda-Kinbras, to whom the title of the Magnificent could not be refused.

Courtebotte, dressed quite simply and scarcely heightened by his stature, bowed to the king with as much intelligence as good grace, and asked him, as was customary, for permission to kiss the hand of his daughter, the princess, as a man who counted on liberating her or perishing in the attempt. When he had declared that his name was Courtebotte, the king, accustomed as he was to representation, could scarcely retain his hilarity, even though our hero had taken the liberty of adding the title of Prince to his name; he was so far from home that it was forgivable. That example from remote times had not been one of the last to be followed subsequently.

At any rate, Courtebotte, as an intelligent man, seeing that the king was, as they say, splitting his sides while trying to retain himself, and that the princes, his rivals, by whom he was surrounded, had, by contrast, no such restraint and were laughing scandalously, addressed the king and said: "Sire, let Your Majesty relax and burst out laughing; I am very glad to be able to amuse him; but if these gentlemen take me for the butt of their jokes I shall be able to straighten them out." And, choosing with his eyes the one who seemed the most conceited, he decided to take him to task.

That was Prince Fadasse, one of the great heroes of whom the Romans were fond, proud of his ancestors, intoxicated by his long face and charmed with his long silky hair

Courtebotte therefore said to him, while staring at him proudly: "You, my tall sir, do you think yourself no more ridiculous than my name? I challenge you to combat, armed as you please."

Fadasse accepted the challenge, sniggering with pity at the temerity of his adversary, and the duel was arranged for the following day. On leaving the king's apartment, Courtebotte was taken to Zibeline's. He was struck by her beauty, and had difficulty holding back the emotion that she caused him. These are a few of the near-compliments that he paid her:

"I have come from the ends of the earth, attracted by the beauty of your portrait, Madame, in order to offer you my services. I bring you an infinite good will, but the ridicule of the name that I bear, which is, in truth, not one of the most elegant, has already embroiled me in an affair in your court. Tomorrow I must fight a tall rascal of a prince; I beg you to honor my combat with your presence, and to prove to the entire world that a name is nothing of consequence, and that, in sum, you admit Courtebotte as your knight."

The princess smiled, for she had intelligence, and told him politely that she accepted him with pleasure. He asked her then whether she was not protecting his adversary, Prince Fadasse

"Alas," she said, "I don't protect any of them; all those gentlemen importune me, and their folly is insupportable to me. I find myself to be very well as I am; why do they talk all day long about saving me? I don't understand what they want from me at all. *Amour*, they say, *sentiments*, and a thousand other things even more platitudinous, which I can't remember."

Courtebotte had too much intelligence himself not to sense, at that moment, that, in desiring to please a person who only has intelligence, it was necessary not to lament any more than to display sentiment, but that it was necessary above all to declare himself, to obtain confidence and advance by pleasing. He therefore replied without contradicting her, and turned the conversation in the direction of his rivals, searching for a few points of ridicule, especially regarding Prince Fadasse. Zibeline was grateful for that, and even helped him to find a few, with the result that, from the first moment, Courtebotte became the person whose conversation she enjoyed most in all the court.

The entire city and the court were occupied with the combat, the spectacle of which was arranged for the following day. The king, the queen and the princess took their places in the amphitheater. In the lists, Prince Fadasse had the most beautiful and most magnificent armaments in the world. He was followed by twenty-four squires and a hundred palfreymen, each leading a horse by hand. Courtebotte entered on the other side, with no weapons other than his spear, simply but tastefully dressed, only followed by Mousta, his barbet, who was leading a horse with great perfection.

The comparison of the two adversaries made the entire assembly laugh, and Mousta attracted all gazes. When the judges of the camp had taken their places and the trumpets had given the signal, Fadasse's squires left the lists and Mousta did likewise. The two champions charged one another furiously. Courtebotte, whose skill and agility were infinite, avoided the thrust that the prince aimed at him and found the means to prove that he did not want his life, for the masterly blow that he dealt him was delivered to his horse, which fell dead on the spot.

Courtebotte leapt lightly to the ground, disengaged Fadasse from beneath his horse, and told him that he did not want the advantage he had had. Furious at his adversary's restraint, Fadasse drew his sword, but Courtebotte shattered it into a thousand piece, and said to him afterwards: "I respect everything that is attached to Princess Zibeline too much to kill you; go and thank her for the life she is giving you."

The squires returned to the camp, and Mousta leapt down from his horse in order to catch his master's and hang on to the stirrup; jumping back on to his own, they emerged from the career very seriously, to the sound of trumpets and the acclamations of the people.

The king and the princess sent felicitations to Courtebotte in the little house that he had chosen for his habitation, and offered him an apartment in the palace. Courtebotte did not delay in going to thank them, and only mentioned the combat with the moderation of a gallant man, and a man made for victory.

The princess asked him why he had been so lightly armed. Courtebotte replied that he had not acted thus by virtue of any scorn for his adversary, but the weapon of which he had made use was the most comfortable for him. Then she asked him questions about Mousta; she desired to see him and stroke him. Courtebotte assured her that he was at his post—which is to say, in the antechamber with the squires. A young slave received the order to go and tell him that Princess Zibeline was asking for him.

Mousta did indeed present himself with the respect and the manners of a barbet familiar with a court and its customs. He was made to do a hundred thousand things, each more surprising than the last; in the end, the princess could not help asking Courtebotte to sacrifice him to her and make her a present of him. Courtebotte consented to that joyfully, not only out of politeness, but also because he foresaw that he could not have a more reliable and more faithful spy with regard to Zibeline, the king and the entre court.

The combat and the noble and casual fashion in which he had acquitted himself therein, earned Courtebotte a great deal of consideration.

Meanwhile, the king was informed that an ambassador of a neighboring and very powerful king was at the frontier, and was asking permission to come to the court in order to discuss an important affair. It was King Brandatimor who had sent him. A courier was dispatched to him right away, and orders were give for him to be received with all possible honors all along his route, for that king's Estates were contiguous, and he was, moreover, a king renowned for his personal valor, the good quality of his troops, and, in sum, for everything that can render a king terrible.

The ambassador preceded his numerous equipages in a fast carriage, with his letters of credit. His name was Arrogantin. He saw the king incognito, and presented him with a letter in rather nasty fashion, of which I am assured the terms were as follows:

Brandatimor to Farda-Kinbras
Greetings.

If I had seen one of the portraits of the beautiful Zibeline before yesterday, I would not have suffered such a great number of adventurers and petty princes getting themselves frozen and chilled in order to merit her. Personally, I have no fear of competitors as soon as I have declared myself, as I am doing in requesting your daughter in marriage, and I am sure they will not persist in their pursuits. Arrogantin therefore has my order to marry her immediately on my behalf, for I do not believe all the tales that have been told by the travelers that you have sent all over the world to spread your nonsense regarding the Mountain of Ice. If it were true that she has no heart, that would not embarrass me at all, being certain that I have enough to make her one. I embrace you, my dear father-in-law.

The reading of that letter embarrassed Farda-Kinbras greatly and displeased him infinitely, as well as Birbantine, and the vanity of the princess was offended in the highest degree by the arrogance of the style and the turn of the demand. All three of them, however, resolved to keep that negotiation secret until they had decided what course of action they could take.

Mousta was present at that conversation; he had witnessed the impression that it had caused and did not fail to inform Courtebotte by means of a note. The news animated him with fury. The description of the letter nearly put him beside himself; however, he made the decision to contain himself, and meditated for a long time on the expedients that might be found to evade a demand made in such a brutal fashion; but he racked his brain in vain.

In that agitation he ran to see the princess; as they were both occupied with the same thought, and they were both revolted by the arrogance and indolence of Brandatimor, the conversation fell of its own accord on that subject and the revulsion that errors of the heart and the mind cause everyone, but especially those who are the victims. The conversation became heated, and Courtebotte seemed so well informed of the present circumstance that the princess was astonished by it, confessed to him everything that he already knew, and asked for his advice.

Courtebotte, who had not yet decided anything, advised her to defer the response for as long as possible, and assured her that the superb entrance that Arrogantin was promising with so much emphasis and so little modesty might serve as a pretext for eluding it at least for a few days.

Zibeline approved of that small resource, feeble though it was, for she feared Brandatimor infinitely. She therefore advised the king and the queen to postpone their response until after the ambassador's entrance, and that was indeed what they decided to do.

Arrogantin received that short delay with considerable impatience, but he told them that on the day after the arrival of his equipage, which would take place in a few days, he would give the entire city and all the petty princes with which it as inundated, an idea of his master's power and treasures.

Courtebotte, in despair and infinite perplexity, seeing the day of the entrance imminent, out of ideas, implored the intercession of the good Guerlinguin urgently. He often thought about her—for his heart was not ingrate—but he had made a firm resolution only to importune her on great occasions. This one seemed to be of that number; he therefore invoked her, and, the night being assailed by the agitation of his mind, he saw her in person in a dream. Courtebotte," she said to him, "you have conducted yourself well thus far; continue to be laborious and virtuous, and you will find good friends when the occasion arises; make the success that the ambassador's entrance will have valuable to Zibeline."

Joy woke Courtebotte up; he tried to throw himself at the fay's feet, but could not perceive any object and feared momentarily that he had only experienced a sort of contentment by the illusion of a dream. He was hopeful, however, and without mentioning to the princess all the amour that he felt for her, he urged her, for an event that was about to happen, to use words that do not say yes or no. To the question that he asked her as to whether she would be very obliged to someone who could deliver her from the importunities of Brandatimor, she assured him that the obligation she would have would be infinite. He pushed the question further; he wanted to know what she would desire in that fortunate mortal, and she assured him that it would be to love nothing, to be like her.

A lover has a great deal to suffer when he has such words to support from everything he adores, so they tore poor Courtebotte's heart.

Arrogantin's carriages arrived, and with an arrogance worthy of his master and himself, he only wanted to make use of what he had brought with him. He therefore demanded his audience for the next day; it was granted to him, and all the inhabitants of the city took their places at daybreak in order to see the magnificence announced with so much haughtiness and vanity. The benevolent Guerlinguin took care of furnishing the assembly with pleasures, for she fascinated the eyes of all the spectators and charged Illusion—the divinity that has all too much power over the human race—with punishing the pride of Brandatimor and serving Courtebotte indirectly.

The livery therefore appeared to all those who saw Arrogantin's entrance to be rags and tatters that vagabonds would have been ashamed to wear; all the horses that the ambassador and his retinue thought sprightly and prancing were seen as pitiful meager nags that did not have the strength to drag themselves; the fine harness made of gold had no other effect than the collars of plow-horses ornamented with old sheepskins, and all the pages had a perfect resemblance to the most wretched chimney-sweeps. The trumpets and all the other instruments rendered the sound of onion flutes or combs over which pieces of paper have been placed, and the file of the fifty carriages was regarded as fifty ramshackle carts would have been.

Arrogantin appeared in the last of them, with the arrogance of a brutal prince, of whom he believed himself a worthy representative. What threw a greater comicality and ridiculousness over the entire entrance were the faces and the proud stances that satisfied vanity gives, and which the ambassador and his retinue had, for the illusion only pertained to attire and ornaments, it allow the men to be seen with the airs and fashions appropriate to what they believed to be their surroundings.

The catcalls and jeers of all the people were proportionate to the singularity with which they saw all the equipages. The king, who had been alerted long before the arrival of the ambassador—for he was walking very slowly, at a pace appropriate to his dignity—rightly believed that it did not befit his own to receive an ambassador by whom be believed himself to be insulted to that degree. He therefore had the doors to his palace closed and refused the audience.

Arrogantin, who could not imagine the reason for such a refusal, his magnificence equaling his arrogance, was easily transported to fury. He expanded himself in insults against the king and against an entire people who were hurling all sorts of pleasantries at him, and the little people, authorized by the refusal on entry to the palace, responded to the magnificent insults that he uttered and the terrible threats that he made, sent the ambassador and his cortege away with a barrage of stones and ordure, by which he was nearly overwhelmed, and from which he had great difficulty escaping.

Arrogantin departed immediately, not without employing his powers to make a declaration of the most terrible war that had ever been made, and I have heard it said that that was the first time that the threat of putting everything to fire and blood was employed.

A few days before that beautiful embassy, King Biby had sent one of his couriers to Courtebotte with a letter full of amity, offers of services and curiosity in his regard. Courtebotte replied to all his good will as was appropriate; he told him about everything that had happened, and, especially, did not neglect to tell him the story of Arrogantin and the terrible war that the event had ignited between the two kings, Farda-Kinbras and Brandatimor. He gave the letters to Biby's courier on the very evening of the adventure, and had him depart immediately, with an order to make as much diligence as possible. He could not finish his letter without asking his dear Biby for the aid of a few thousand of the most determined and battle-hardened barbets, promising to neglect nothing for all that might be necessary to them, and making him the judge of the need that he had for such help.

The king, the queen and the princess could not understand the procedure of Arrogantin, or, rather, that of Brandatimor; the former had presumably not been acting without orders, and the evidence of scorn they had received appeared to them, with reason, not to be in accord with the demand that Brandatimor had made for their daughter, the princess.

Preparations were swiftly made for the war, and all the other princes who were at the court offered their services, requesting the most important positions in the army. Courtebotte was not one of the last to testify his willingness, but he only asked to be aide-de-camp to the general appointed to command the army. That was an old relative of the king, a very gallant man celebrated for his victories.

When the army was assembled, it marched for the frontier. It arrived in time to oppose the one that Brandatimor had assembled furiously, in the determination to make the conquest of Zibeline and her Estates, and avenge himself for all the insults made to him in the person of his ambassador. All that Farda-Kinbras army could do at the commencement of the campaign was to be on the defensive and oppose the furies of a brutal and outraged king.

Courtebotte acquired the esteem of the officers and soldiers, and that esteem only rendered him milder with his equals and more submissive to the generals. He defeated the enemy troops every time he encountered them and obtained small commands; in sum, fortune seconded his good conduct and his valor, and it is easy to imagine the jealousy of his rivals.

Eventually, Brandatimor, who wanted to satisfy his fury at any price, found the means to engage in a general battle. It was terrible, but in spite of the valor of Farda-Kinbras's troops, and the aid and activity of Courtebotte, the battle was lost and the general was killed. Courtebotte saved the lives of several of his rivals, including that of Prince Fadasse. He did more, for, after the death of the general, he was the one who enabled the army's retreat; he saved its debris and threw troops into all the places that might be attacked. A hundred times during the retreat he turned to face the victors, and constrained them to stop a hundred times. In sum, sometimes by personal actions and sometimes by virtue of the fashion in which he posted his troops, he impeded the progress of the victory.

The rigors of winter arrived, and suspended all hostilities. Courtebotte returned to the king, whom he found in an infinite consternation, and who could imagine no better expedient than to entrust command of the army to our hero. He begged him to accept, and nothing was any longer done in the court without his advice. Greater authority only attracted more friends to him. The amusement of his intelligence pleased

Zibeline's; he saw her frequently, but in the matter of the heart he only made the feeblest progress.

The winter passed, during which Courtebotte conducted himself as I have just described, while formulating the plans of the campaign that was about to commence. In the meantime, he received news of King Biby. It was such as he desired, since it informed him of the departure of twelve thousand of his finest troops, all of whom had volunteered to come and fight and aid his good friend Courtebotte. Biby also invited him to send his orders over the frontiers, where General Barbesalle would receive them, either for refreshment quarters or for those of assembly.

Charmed to have such considerable help, Courtebotte resolved to employ it usefully. He therefore asked Barbesalle to keep his arrival secret, to thin out his troops and distribute them over the frontier in allied or enemy garrisons, at his discretion, and agree with him the means of reuniting them when necessary.

Courtebotte received his orders for the campaign and a free hand for anything he wanted to do. He arrived on the frontier and arranged a rendezvous with Barbesalle. They held a great conference by means of writing. Barbesalle was really a great man of war; not only was he very valiant but he also had a very expedient intelligence, and our hero asked him to spend a few days with him incognito.

The only thing in favor of the army of Farda-Kinbras was the confidence it had in its new general. By contrast, the enemy army had the presence of a king who commanded in person and whose amour and vanity were in revolt; it also had the memory of its previous victory. Courtebotte decided to accept the battle that was offered to him, but he only made that decision after having agreed his strategy with Barbesalle. In consequence of the council they held, the grand barbet detached aides-de-camp to give marching orders and rallying instructions to all the barbets in their various quarters, and being informed of the general's dispositions, the barbets showed a determination proof against anything. Courtebotte therefore accepted the battle and presented a front to the ene-my, which he was obliged to extend considerably, because his troops were much inferior in number.

Brandatimor was counting on a complete and certain vic-tory; everything, in fact, ought to have assured him of it: the ardor of his troops, the superiority of his forces and, most of all, the vanity that a king already victorious can have.

When the signal for the charge had been given and the troops were ready to come to grips, all the barbets, who had received their orders, and whose dispositions it had been easy to make without their being suspected or remarked, leapt sim-ultaneously onto the rump of each cavalier of the first line. They were not content to put the squadrons in disorder by the surprise that their action naturally caused the horses; they also leapt at the throats of the cavaliers, unhorsing a great number, and guided the horses of which they were thus rendered mas-ters, into the flanks of the battalions, which were easily put in disorder. Barbesalle, with a thousand of the most determined barbets, broke through the king's defenses.

It was not difficult for Courtebotte to profit from such a great advantage; he won a complete victory. He combated personally with Brandatimor, and took him prisoner in spite of his fury. That prince, whose destiny no one lamented, died suddenly when he arrived at the foot of Zibeline's throne, to which Courtebotte sent him; the death was attributed to a revolution of pride.

After the victory, Courtebotte sent the barbets back to their homeland, with letters for Biby singing their praises and expressing the great obligations that he had to them. For their return journey he begged them to observe the same precau-tions that they had taken in arriving. He only retained fifty of the youngest and most determined, which he chose for his personal guard, along with the grenadiers. But what proves that valor, and even temerity, do not always cause those whom Nature honors with those sentiments to perish, and, on the contrary, that less of them perish, is that on the great day, no more than four hundred barbets were killed.

Courtebotte employed two months in ensuring for Farda-Kinbras the conquest that he had made of all of Brandatimor's Estates. After that, he returned to the court, covered in glory, to adore Zibeline, who received him with the simple joy that the victory and success of our little hero could give her, but without experiencing or expressing the slightest emotion of the heart in any fashion.

No one knew about the essential aid that the barbets had contributed to the victory, so Courtebotte and the troops received endless eulogies. The general received them with an even greater moderation than usual, since he was not unaware to whom he owed his victory.

While Courtebotte was ensuring the king's conquests, Fadasse and the other princes hastened their departure in order to undertake the conquest of the Mountain of Ice, which the war had suspended. They had seen such good conduct on Courtebotte's part, and so much valor and so much resource in his intelligence, that they thought they ought not to allow themselves to be preceded by a man like him. They departed, therefore, with an infinite urgency.

On his return, Courtebotte learned of their departure with great chagrin, and although it was for the interests of the princess that he had delayed the execution of his great enterprise, that same princess, who did not know the merit of sacrifices, did not feel the slightest gratitude to him; far from consoling him for pains that he only experienced for the glory of her arms, he only received from her those eulogies departing from intelligence, which only flatter vanity without expressing anything to the heart.

Courtebotte was too amorous and had too delicate a heart not to feel all of Zibeline's coldness keenly. It was, however, necessary for him to accept being praised coldly by the most beautiful mouth in the world. As for the eulogies he received from the king, they were proportionate to the obligations he had to our hero. All the poets celebrated exhaustively a man who had given them, by his conquests and his victory, the most beautiful field for poetry, but there were few poets in that number to exalt the majesty of his height.

At any rate, Courtebotte, occupied with his amour and his project, asked a thousand questions of the faithful Mousta. It was in vain that he looked at it from every possible angle, searching for some glimmer of hope. Mousta could not tell him anything about the sentiments of the princess other than what he had already determined only too well for himself. By means of asking all those questions, however, at least he experienced the consolation of being perfectly sure that Zibeline's heart was absolutely indifferent, for the first idea of lovers, when they are not loved, is always to imagine that the heart of the object they adore is prejudiced by passion for another. They are sometimes right, but that was not the case with Zibeline

Unable to resist the desire to attempt the adventure of the mountain, animated by amour and glory, Courtebotte decided to depart. The king and the entire court did everything possible, not only to delay him, but even to prevent him from doing so, for everyone was in despair at seeing him expose himself to a peril to which so many princes and heroes had already succumbed. However, Courtebotte was unshakeable in his resolution.

To console him for the delays that were demanded of him, at least he learned that Fadasse, all his great retinue, and the other princes who had exposed themselves to the adventure not long ago had met the same fate as those who had preceded them and had perished in the ice. That recent example might have deterred anyone by Courtebotte, but, on the contrary, he felt his desire redoubled by that news. He therefore took his leave of the king and queen, whose dissolved in tears as they bid him adieu. Then he kissed the hand of the beautiful Zibeline, who gave it to him with the same coldness with which she had offered it to him on the day of his arrival. He kissed it, that beautiful hand, not without experiencing an infinite emotion.

The king was present at that adieu, and all the court, men and women alike, especially the latter, shrugged their shoulders indignantly on seeing the coldness of the princess, so much had Courtebotte captivated everyone's inclinations. Finally, the king made a speech, saying to him: "Prince, you have constantly refused everything that I have wanted to offer you. The greatest kings on earth would have been tempted by it, but at least you will not refuse one gallantry that I want the princess to make you."

That gift was a mantle of marten fur, which the princess ordinarily wore. It was admirable against the cold, but the beauty of the fur heightened Zibeline's splendor admirably, and it was not without reason that it was her favorite attire. Courtebotte was honored and charmed by the king's proposition. The princess added a polite compliment to it, and Courtebotte departed with that superb fur, and a small faggot of various sorts of wood, only accompanied by two of the most handsome barbets one could ever see, who were the captain and lieutenant of the fifty guards that he had retained from King Biby's troops. Out of modesty, he had never wanted the entire company to appear at his side; he had always kept them cantoned in various quarters in the city, and only ever had the general staff of the little troop with him. He had arranged a rendezvous with the others on the frontier, and had ordered them to make their way there in ones and twos, in order not to attract attention on the way.

What an equipage for a man who had just added a great kingdom to the one from which he was departing, adored and respected by everyone! Several persons of the greatest importance not only wanted to escort him but also to accompany him; he implored them to leave him with his horse, a briquette with which to make fire, his half-dried and half-green faggot, and his two dogs. He was obeyed with difficulty, and in spite of the simplicity of his equipage, he was received throughout the extent of the kingdom with an infinite magnificence, and evidence of the love and consideration of the people, certainly

more pleasing for great men than the monuments erected solely by flattery to honor princes.

Finally, he arrived at the frontier—which is to say, at the
last inhabited village—and it was there that he left his horse in
a stable, in case he was fortunate enough to return from an
enterprise in which so many others had failed.

A few paces beyond the village he found himself walking on snow, without being able to perceive any other object
as far as the eye could see. Those immensities of snow have a
sort of beauty in themselves, but it is a beauty full of horror.
He found the forty-eight barbets with whom he had arranged a
rendezvous waiting for him in battle order. He greeted them,
and pronounced a few sounds that he had learned from the
captain and Mousta, but as he had bought a writing-desk,
whose ink had fortunately not yet frozen, he wrote a message
of thanks that the captain read to his troop. They all assured
him of a fidelity proof against anything, and they set forth on
the march.

The beginning of the route was partially frayed; at any
rate, it was not difficult to follow, for there were no others
than the one heading directly northwards. When they had gone
far enough to repose, Courtebotte, whose reflective intelligence left nothing behind that might be useful to him, and who
had been meditating the project for a long time, made use of
the kind of projection powder that he had collected in the forest ship that had run aground on the desert island. A small
pinch of that powder vivified all the branches of his small faggot; they grew momentarily, ripe fruits succeeding the flowers
in an instant. By that means Courtebotte found aid against
hunger.

Not all the branches he had sprinkled grew leaves and
fruits; those of dead wood increased so abundantly in that
condition that, with the help of the dogs, he had no difficulty
making a ring of fires, in the middle of which they settled
down. By the aid of those fires, the snow and ice melted, often
allowing them to see the bare ground. That was their encamp-

ment of sorts, and the fashion in which they not only spent that first night, but all the others along their route.

That was not the only good fortune they had. A few barbets sent out to explore discovered, a short distance from the fires, a horse laden with provisions, especially biscuits. They came back to fetch flaming firebrands, gradually unfroze the poor animal, and took it to Courtebotte. As excessive cold renders all substances incorruptible, they also unfroze the provisions, which were a great help to them.

It was in that fashion that Courtebotte traveled for six months. Sometimes, he and his dogs lived on truffles and admirable potatoes, which they were able to find in the ground they uncovered, sometimes on chestnuts and other fruits of every species, which grew beyond their needs, and sometimes on the provisions they encountered, like those I have already mentioned. Furthermore, the branches of fruit trees and those of dead wood never ran out, for they took care to cut a small branch off each of those they left at their last shelter and take it with them.

Courtebotte had forbidden, on pain of death, the unfreezing of any of the men with whom the route was filled. They had great difficulty supporting the horror of the subjects that were presented to them continually, including all the figures of men and horses, which the cold had conserved so well in their entirety that not only were they recognizable, but one could still make out on their faces the frightful emotions by with their souls had been afflicted at the moment of congelation.

For three months, Courtebotte and the troop continued their march. For a long time they had been able to perceive a mountain that was distinguished by its height from all the others by which it was surrounded; it was, in fact, the desired objective. Finally, they arrived at the foot of that very mountain, the steepest imaginable. Its steepness would have rendered it impracticable from the outset without the aid of the fire with which Courtebotte formed esplanades in order to repose and routes along which to advance.

57

The palace that crowned the mountain was immense in its extent and superb in its structure. All that architecture can have of the great and the correct was executed in frozen snow. What a habitation! What solitude! And what surroundings for a young heart!

With very well-managed heat—for if he had not brought great precaution to it, he would have been immersed by the melting of those superb slabs—he succeeded, after having traversed courtyards, halls and immense apartments, in reaching the foot of a throne, on which he perceived a cushion of snow, and on that cushion a diamond whose glitter was prodigious and whose whiteness surpassed all that of the palace that surrounded it. These words were inscribed above the throne in letters of ice:

Mortal whose courage and virtue have rendered him the possessor of the heart of Zibeline, enjoy in peace the happiness that you merit so perfectly.

Courtebotte went up the steps of the throne ardently and seized the diamond that contained all the sentiments of the most beautiful princess in the world. Then, like those whom a violent desire bears to the end of a career, which only the agitation if their senses has allowed them to travel, but whom exhaustion no longer permits to make further efforts, he only just had time to thrust the diamond into his bosom before he fell, unconscious.

The good dogs did not abandon him; they carried him out of the palace and brought him round.

Possessor of the heart of Zibeline, by which he was a thousand times more delighted than the honor of having brought such a fine adventure to a conclusion, he had no difficulty quitting the Mountain of Ice and the beautiful palace, a part of which he had been obliged to destroy by means of the heat he had had to employ in order not to succumb to the cold. So true is it that men, when they are animated by passion, destroy the most beautiful monuments, and nothing in the world can resist their industry.

He resumed exactly the same route that he had followed in order to arrive. All those who had risked their lives for love of Zibeline touched him with compassion; he therefore ordered his barbets to beat a path over the snow with great exactitude, to extend it as far as they could, to warm up, and, in consequence, to reanimate, everything animal they could find that might be alive. His orders were carried out, with the result that he brought back all those who were believed to have been lost—and, in fact, would have been, without his aid.

When he arrived at the frontier, what had been in him only the effect of compassion produced what the most powerful vanity could have sought, for he had in his retinue more than five hundred sovereign princes, not to mention vassals, squires and all their followers. He arrived at the village where he had left his horse, therefore, and entered it, with a cortege such as no prince on earth had ever had before, and no other, I believe, ever will have. The recent obligation that all those composing that cortege had to our little hero formed a charming society, but it is necessary to say everything: Courtebotte lived with them in a fashion so simple that they adored him. It is certain that the moderation in question merits a eulogy, but this is not the place in his story for me to insist on it further. He was the master of Zibeline's heart; when one has what one has desired with so much ardor, it is very easy to be mild and to have an agreeable humor; the happiness we enjoy easily bears us to compassion.

At any rate, scarcely had Courtebotte recovered his horse and traveled a few leagues on the earth, so to speak, than he encountered the faithful Mousta, who had come in the hope of meeting him. Mousta was unaware of the great success that his enterprise had had; the excess of his attachment for Courtebotte, and above all the change that he had noticed in the person of Zibeline, had obliged him to quit the court in order to come after his dear master, in order to find him or to perish in his turn in the ice. In sum, he had done so well that, if he had been lost to the palace, the princess would have been inconsolable.

Courtebotte therefore learned from the faithful squire, whom he made to write incessantly, that Zibeline, for a certain time that he specified for him—it was precisely that of the conquest—had been sad, that it had been remarked that she was ill-humored, and that she had even become difficult to serve. Mousta added that she often talked about him; in sum, he went into detail with Courtebotte that brought his joy to a peak.

Having not been able, by virtue of his canine estate, to obtain complete confidences, Mousta had only been able to assemble minutiae and bagatelles, but as nothing is trivial for a lover in great haste, Courtebotte read every last circumstance with avidity. Mousta had been struck by all the evidence of particular amity he had received from the beautiful Zibeline, the genre of which had become quite different from previous ones.

Courtebotte received a courier from the king and queen; he had been dispatched as soon as his success became known, and the princess sent her compliments by way of the courier.

Two days from the city, the king's carriages came to meet Courtebotte; all the people already regarded him as their master and wanted to render him the honors due to him in that quality. Not only did he receive them with modesty, but even with reluctance. He ordered Mousta to go to Zibeline a few days before his arrival, and the joy with which he was received by the princess is inexpressible. Whatever merit the faithful barbet had, Courtebotte had given him, and that had rendered him dear for some time.

Finally, our hero arrived in the great city of Trelintin. I shall pass over in silence the magnificence of the reception that he was given, in order only to attach myself to individual sentiments. On arrival, Courtebotte wanted to kiss the hands of Farda-Kinbras and Birbantine, but both of them did him the honor of embracing him, telling him that they regarded him as the master in their estates and the possessor of their daughter.

Courtebotte told them that on that matter, he had many things to tell them. Then he went to see the princess, who blushed on seeing him, and, for the first time in her life, could not find anything to say. The elegant silence of amour was expressed mutually, and was accompanied by everything it can have of the most agreeable.

Finally the prince drew from his bosom the large diamond that he had taken from the Palace of Ice, and, as he put it in Zibeline's hands, he said: "Here, Madame, is what I have not yet purchased by sufficient perils, nor sufficient labors."

"Alas, Prince," she said, "you have only conquered it for yourself, and if I accepted it from your hands it would only be to have the pleasure of rendering you its new possessor."

The king and queen entered at that moment and interrupted their conversation in order to ask him all imaginable questions, and often asked the same things again to which he had already replied several times. But as there is always a favorite remark for an event; that day's, which was, I believe, uttered by more than a thousand people, was: "You must have been very cold."

The king had only come to see his daughter in order to take Courtebotte to the Council and declare him to be both his son-in-law and his successor. Courtebotte followed the king without knowing his intention. When he found himself in the presence of all the grandees that had been assembled from all the Estates of the realm, he took the liberty of interrupting the king at the beginning of his speech, and said to him in a loud voice:

"If I had been able to foresee Your Majesty's generosity I would have anticipated it, but since the exactitude of keeping his word has caused him to act with so much haste. I will declare to him that I am unworthy of all the bounty with which he wishes to honor me, by virtue of the misfortune of my birth."

Then he related everything he knew about it, not hiding the fact that he was the son of a peasant. When he had pronounced the word, the sky suddenly darkened, thunder was

heard, and lightning flashed. The din of that storm was succeeded by a great light; it was the good fay Guerlinguin, who
descended from her chariot at the window of the council
chamber. She was in full dress—which is to say, in the most
brilliant apparel of Faerie—and was carrying under her arm
the prettiest barbet in the world. She addressed Courtebotte,
saying to him: "I am content with your moderation, and above
all with your good faith." Then, turning to the king, she declared the birth of the prince, and related the story of his life.

She said to Courtebotte: "Your virtue has brought you to
the culmination of your wishes, not only in the matter of
amour and glory, but also in the matter of amity, since you are
going to see King Biby and all his subjects resume their natural estate, which they owe entirely to you. I have made you
pass through all the proofs that contribute to the formation of a
just and great king; I have put you in a state to find resources
within yourself. I have enabled you to know amity and to experience not only the pleasures it procures but also the veritable aid that it alone can provide in the course of life. That, I
believe, is the best education that can be given to a man who
must command others. Now, it only remains for you to put
into practice on the throne the virtues that you have shown
while you thought you were only a obscure individual, I know
that that is a point that is not without difficulty, but I have
hope in the goodness of your heart."

Then a chariot was seen to arrive drawn by eagles,
which, on the fay's orders, had brought the king and queen
from whom Courtebotte had received birth. They embraced
their dear child with infinite emotions of joy, and found him,
as Guerlinguin had predicted, all covered in furs. While they
were also caressing Zibeline and clutching her hands forcefully—for I have noticed that it is a caress that fools gladly
make—chariots of every species guided by an infinite number
of fays were seen arriving from the four corners of the earth,
appearing over the horizon at every instant.

"Sire," said Guerlinguin to King Farda-Kinbras, "I have
given a rendezvous in your court to all the fays whose urgent

affairs are not occupying them indispensably; I thought that you would not disapprove of that and that you would be glad to host the Great Ball at which we ordinarily meet once every hundred years."

The king responded to that favor appropriately. Peace was made between him and Guarlangandino, and it was the king and that fay who led the great dance. Marsontine returned King Biby to his original form, and all his subjects experienced the same favor; the prince in question then appeared as handsome a prince as he had been a barbet, and he married the Queen of India the same day, to whom one of the fays' equipages had been sent.

In sum, no wedding was ever celebrated with so much splendor as that of Courtebotte and Zibeline. They lived happily; their children divided up all their kingdoms; and Courtebotte, in recognition of the marten fur of which the princess had made him a present for his journey, gave the name of zibeline to the most beautiful martens, in order to distinguish them from the others, and that nickname has been transmitted to us.

ROSANIE[11]

No one in the world is unaware that all fays, although they live for several centuries, are subject to death, and to all the infirmities of the animal whose form they are obliged to assume for one day a week. It was in such a circumstance that the Queen of the Fays unfortunately perished.

The eulogies of the deceased were pronounced; in accordance with custom, a general assembly of the fays was convened, and proceeded with the election of a new queen. After much debate, all voices united around two among them. One was named Paridamie, the other Surcantine. They were celebrated for their talents and commendable in their capability. Their merit seemed so perfectly equal that, in spite of the enlightenment of the ladies making up the assembly, it was not possible to make a choice and give one preference without committing an injustice.

In the end, in order to bring everyone into agreement, it was agreed that whichever of the two could produce to human eyes something more singular than her competitor would be recognized from that moment on as the queen. Before separating, the members of the assembly decided that the admiration that was caused to humans would not have for a principle the upheaval of the elements, not all the tumult that has become so commonplace in stories of Enchantment. They declared authoritatively that they did not want transported mountains, nor any other metamorphosis of that species.

In consequence of those resolutions, Surcantine formed the project of bringing up a prince whom nothing could render constant, and Pardamie undertook to show mortals a princess who would subjugate all those who saw her for an instant. The time that they were to employ in the execution of their work

---

[11] Like the previous story, this one was adapted by Andrew Lang for publication in the *Green Fairy Book*, as "Rosanella."

was unlimited. The realm was placed in the hands of four of the oldest members of the association, whose great age distanced them from all ambition.

Pardamie had long had a great depth of amity for King Bardondon; that prince was endowed with talents and intelligence, and his magnificent court was the model of gallantry, politesse and probity. No court similar to his had ever been seen, and Queen Balanice was also a charming person. It is very rare that two spouses of such simultaneous perfection are seen on a throne.

From that beautiful alliance only a single daughter had come, whom they loved madly; her name was Rosanie, a name that it had not been difficult to give her, since she had come into the world with a charming rose on her breast. At the age of four, she had already said surprising things, and several courtiers not only knew them by heart but repeated them incessantly.

In the middle of the night that followed the aforementioned fays' assembly, Queen Balanice uttered a piercing scream, which woke King Bardondon; for, in spite of the elegance of their court, the good sovereigns did not have separate beds. The queen told all those who ran to her aid that the pain of which she had given evidence had no other foundation than the illusion of a dream.

"It seemed to me," she added, "that my daughter had suddenly become a bouquet of roses, and while I was examining the flowers, with as much curiosity as tenderness, a bird—which was charming, in truth—swooped down upon me and snatched them away from me. Will someone go, though," she continued, "to see how my daughter is."

Someone ran to her apartment—but what became of the king, the queen and the entire court when they learned that Rosanie was not in her crib! The more research that was carried out in search of news, always futile, the more inconsolable the queen became. Bardondon was no less afflicted, but as a firm man, he was able to repress his dolor.

The king proposed to Balanice that they go to spend a few days in an isolated country house they had had built not far from their capital. She consented to that gladly, because dolor is the friend of retreat.

One day, when they were reposing in the middle of a star formed by twelve convergent pathways, they saw in each of them a peasant woman coming toward the place where they were sitting; their gentility, their youth and their cleanliness attracted their gaze. The closer they came to Their Majesties, the more the latter found that they merited attention. Each of them was carrying a very agreeable basket, with which she seemed to be very occupied. They put the baskets down at Balanice's feet, and said to her: "Charming Queen"—for one never speaks otherwise to a queen, no matter how ugly she is—"receive this consolation in your misfortune." After that compliment, they disappeared.

The queen opened the baskets hastily, and found that each one contained a little girl about the same age as the one that was causing her affliction. That first sight reanimated her dolor, but in the end, the graces of the pretty children gradually calmed her, and ended up consoling her entirely.

Nursemaids, chambermaids and wardrobe maids were summoned immediately; servants were sent in search of dolls and toys, and boxes of candy and jam were ordered. It was perceived that all of them had a tiny but perfectly colored rose on the breast.

The queen had too much intelligence not to appreciate the difficulty there would be in finding twelve pretty names all at once for the twelve little girls; she was too familiar with the ways of the world not to foresee that the matter would require a considerable time, especially taking into account the number of days we see a woman spending in choosing a name for a single lapdog. She therefore made the wise decision to distinguish them by the names of colors that she attributed to them, and in which she ordered that they should always be dressed. Her order was carried out, and when they were in the queen's apartment they formed the most agreeable as well as the most singular flower-bed.

As they grew older, they were found to have, firstly, an infinite depth of intelligence, which the advantages of an admirable education ornamented pleasantly. It was also seen that they were very different in character. So, losing the names Flax-gray, White, etc., they acquired by just entitlement those of Gentle, Lovely, Pretty, Lively, Caustic, Delicate, Obliging, Cheerful, Serious, Agreeable, Fine and Difficult.

It can easily be imagined that, on seeing their charms born, which were well above any description, the amour was also born of all the young men of the court and that of foreign princes attracted by the rumor of so many beauties; but the queen's daughters—I am assured that it was her who originated that denomination in her household—were as sage as they were pretty, and amour was absolutely unknown to them. Thus, they did not enable unfortunate passions: an example which, I have heard it said, the daughters of queens that succeeded them have not always imitated. So many different characters, all sustained by the solidity and charms of intelligence, removed from all hearts not only indifference, but also the passions that appeared the most vivid. Such were the twelve prettiest creatures that it was possible to encounter on earth.

In order to form the inconstant individual to which she was engaged, Surcantine cast her eyes upon a king whose was a germane cousin of Bardondon. He was aged seven or eight when the fays regulated the succession to their crown. She had endowed the young Prince Mirliflore—that was his name—with all the talents of mind, but neglected nothing to increase them further, or any care to embellish his face and supply all the seductive graces that make so many dangerous male lovers and unhappy female ones.

Not only did his face become singularly agreeable, but his mind, simultaneously mild and lively, produced with as much facility as charm the frivolous things that amuse and seduce women so perfectly; casual attire and adornment suited the charms of his figure equally; the most beautiful hair in the world ornamented his head; his seductive mouth from which the most flattering speech emerged incessantly without insipidity, was ornamented by the most beautiful teeth in the world. He also had a seductive voice that went straight to the heart. His beauty was masculine, and it was impossible to have more aptitude for all bodily exercises. He had a natural valor that the lovable women by whom he had always been surrounded had further increased—for the women of those times preferred courageous men a little more than they like them today.

It was also for the education of the charming Mirliflore that Surcantine invented novels; it is necessary not to believe that something that maintains valor and tenderness in the heart simultaneously could have been invented by humans.

The fay inspired the young prince with the best sentiments in the world in all respects, except with regard to women; she represented to him the languors of a veritable attachment, while depicting the pleasures and vivacities of coquetry, so flattering for self-esteem. In sum, she combined all the seductions with which she had been able to ornament him with the false sentiment that our young men know only too well today, and which convinces them that the more women they have had—even without loving them—the more commendable they are.

At the age of eighteen, Mirliflore no longer found anything in his father's court that he could sacrifice to his inconstancy. He departed, therefore, and in all the lands to which he went he experienced the power of his charms and was able to employ seduction successfully. He made countless women unhappy, but as self-esteem was able to get him out of anything, however afflicted those he doomed might be, they at least had the consolation of having been preferred.

It was amid that host and that disorder of pleasures that Mirliflore had spent his life when he arrived at the court of his great-uncle, King Bardondon. What a pleasure it was for a coquettish man, accustomed to please, to find it ornamented by a hundred beauties—but what became of him when he perceived the twelve prettiest individuals that Nature had ever formed!

For their part, they all sensed a great liking for him, and that equal liking on their part redoubled the embarrassing situation in which he found himself. Finally, he reached the point of not being able to be without them for a moment.

Gentle engaged him by charming words, which the vivacity of Lively made him forget. Cheerful charmed him, but he was no less sensitive for that to the solidity of the discourse of Serious. Fine piqued his appetite, and Delicate made it blush. He consoled himself with Obliging for the jokes he had to endure from Caustic. Lovely occupied him with gazes that Pretty immediately stole. Finally, Agreeable seduced him, while his vanity was teased by the desire to please Difficult.

Such a situation rendered the handsome Mirliflore insensible to all the other beauties of the court; the flirtations, the notes, the gazes and the sacrifices, all the things that had previously been his delights and his sole occupation, were no longer able to animate him; he felt amour for the first time, although twelve individuals were the object of it, and even Surcantine was mistaken in regard to that sentiment. That attachment for such a large number appeared to her to be the perfection of the inconstancy that she had undertaken to produce. She was therefore triumphant, and Paridamie did not say a word.

Mirliflore's father wrote to his son, but in vain, that he desired his return; it was with the same futility that he proposed to him a very advantageous marriage. The prince could not accept any of those propositions; nothing in the world could engage him to separate from his twelve sovereigns.

One day, when Balanice was giving a fête in the gardens, and the prince did not know to which one to pay attention, some bees were heard buzzing. The beautiful young women, in fear of being stung, all ran away in a panic in order to avoid them, and, in consequence, were separated from the company.

Then the insects increased in size, and quickly became large enough to lift up the dozen beauties. Their screams and those of the spectators were lost in the air.

That astonishing adventure caused the entre court to experience a very sincere affliction. As for Mirliflore, after the first moments of a despair that made everyone fear for his life, he fell into an excessive languor.

Surcantine hastened very diligently to help him and extract him from a state so little in conformity with the education she had given him. She brought him three manuscript novels that she had not yet had the time to have printed, but he did not even deign to open them. He threw away the portraits of the prettiest women, which she presented to him and of which he would once have made a pile, like a trophy to his vanity. In sum, Mirliflore, sad, somber and only loving solitude, caused anxiety for his life.

One day, when he had abandoned himself entirely to his sad regrets, he heard cries of joy and admiration coming from all directions. His curiosity was not excited by that, but the astonishment that everyone was expressing was surely well founded. A crystal chariot could be seen advancing slowly through the air; the sun's rays rendered the vehicle dazzling; an infinite number of damsel-flies whose naturally shiny wings produced a marvelous splendor, were carrying thousands of garlands, which formed a theater of flowers. Six more damsel-flies were harnessed to the chariot; a young woman was guiding them with an infinite skill and grace with roseate ribbons.

That procession, or, rather, that pomp, was as brilliant as it was elegant, but the entire spectacle, excited even more admiration as soon as it was possible to distinguish the Beauty who was descending from the heavens. Paridamie was sitting beside her. They both set foot on the ground at the bottom of the great stairway of the palace and went up to the queen's apartment. They finally arrived there, in spite of the crowd that surrounded them; the doormen had infinite difficulty in making way for them, and the respect owed to the palace did not impede the exclamations that were made about the beauty by which everyone was dazzled.

"Great Queen," said the fay, "here is your daughter, whom I am bringing to you, the same Rosanie who was stolen for you while in her cradle."

After the first transports of a joy similar to the one that Balanice felt, she said to the fay tenderly: "And shall I not see my twelve daughters again? Am I separated from the forever?"

"Soon you will no longer ask me that," the good Paridamie replied, but she pronounced those words in a tone that made it obvious that no more questions were to be asked. Then she disappeared from the queen's apartment and, flying away in the chariot at lightning speed, was soon lost to sight in the sky.

People ran to announce those events to Mirliflore. Everything that was reported to him regarding the beauty of Rosanie did not make the slightest impression on his mind, and it was very difficult to persuade him to come to render a visit to his beautiful cousin; politeness and decorum were the only things that determined him to make that effort.

He was struck by all her beauties; his delicacy had even reached the point of reproaching him for that fact that he still found something beautiful in the world after the loss that he had suffered. Beauty alone has never made anyone inconstant, but at every moment of conversation he discovered in the character and intelligence of Rosanie, sometimes a charm, sometimes a grace and sometimes, in sum, one of the seductions that had enchanted him in the twelve individuals whose loss he was regretting.

All in all, he found in Rosanie's character all the various charms, as he was struck by all the features that her face retraced for him simultaneously. Could a lover as enlightened and as tender as Mirliflore be mistaken? All the other recognitions, what the fay had said, and even everything that Rosanie said, were only weak proofs by comparison with those that

71

amour pronounced. Mirliflore, more amorous than he had ever been, easily obtained his beautiful cousin in marriage.

At the moment when he made his request, Paridamie appeared, triumphant; she was in the most beautiful of the chariots destined for the Queen of the Fays, for she was already the queen. At the mere sight of Rosanie, Surcantine had abandoned her pretentions. Paridamie rendered a very exact account of the greatest miracle of Faerie, which she had produced; she related the fashion in which she had raised Rosanie and how she had separated her twelve characters in order to render them perfect more easily, and to destroy Mirliflore's inconstancy at the same time, in a fashion that he did not suspect, and yet was certain at the moment of the reunion of such a great number of rare talents.

The wedding was celebrated, and Rosanie's charms had such a powerful gift of seduction that that even Surcantine wanted to give the newlyweds a wedding present. Rosanie felt as much amour herself as the twelve beauties had experienced. As for Mirliflore, he was constant all his life—well, who wouldn't have been?—although his reign and his life were of very long duration.

PRINCE MUGUET AND PRINCESS ZAZA[12]

There was once a king and a queen who gave away everything they had, because they were the best people in the world and they could not allow anyone to suffer. Their neighbor King Bambou, knowing that they had no more treasures, entered their lands with a large army and took possession of them. The poor king, having nothing with which to defend himself, or to subsist, was obliged to don a false beard and go on foot with his wife, the queen, carrying under her arm, with a great deal of difficulty, little Muguet,[13] their only son, who was three years old, and whose face was charming.

Those unfortunate sovereigns at least had the good luck in their misfortune to avoid the pursuits of the malevolent King Bambou, who wanted to put them to death. They traversed the desert, and found themselves, after incredible fatigues, in a beautiful valley cut through by a stream, the freshness of which maintained admirable meadows.

While they were considering the beauties of Nature, which alone has the right to charm us veritably, they heard a voice that said: "Fish, and you will find."

Those words made all the more impression on the mind of the king because he had loved fishing all his life, and always carried fishhooks in his pocket. That precaution then became very useful to him because he attached them to the end of a desespoir[14] that the queen had fortunately conserved, and in a trice caught several large fish, with which he made a

---

[12] Andrew Lang's version of this story, in *The Green Fairy Book*, is entitled "Prince Featherhead and Princess Celandine."
[13] *Muguet* is the French term for the flower known in English as the lily of the valley.
[14] *Desespoir* translates as "despair" but this usage presumably relates to an obsolete double meaning.

very good meal, for the poor royal family had only eaten wild fruits and roots in the wilderness. Sensible to that small assistance and touched by the beauties of the location, they made a shelter of leafy branches to protect them. They collected leaves and moss, of which they made a good bed.

Everything is relative. That little habitation soon seemed to them to be full of delights. However, they found that their happiness lacked a flock, and the queen thought she could guard sheep with the little prince while the king went fishing, for the fish continued not only to be very abundant, but were of a ravishing beauty, and the colors of their scales were as vivid as they were brilliant; they often found harlequins among them. That was not all; they were easily domesticated, and the king, having perceived that particularity, noticed that they learned to talk and whistle more rapidly than any parrot.

That discovery caused him to make the resolution to go and sell some of them in a town not far from his retreat. He did that, and seeing that there were no fish of the same species in the market, he displayed his own, and pointed out that what they could do and say, assuring people that they were young, that he had only been teaching them for a short time, and that their talents could only be augmented.

Such a singular thing would have succeeded anywhere, but it could not fail to have a great effect in a town where luxury was so highly regarded, so everyone hastened to buy the king's fish. He was given all that he asked for those he had brought, and he was even made to promise that he would come back with more. In a short time the fish became fashionable; people put them in large crystal vases full of water, which were suspended like cages in apartments; their beautiful colors appeared clearly, and they could easily be matched to the furniture.

With the money the king obtained for his beautiful fish, he was able to buy a flock of sheep and embellish his retreat with all kinds of necessary things. He sensed soon afterwards the charms of the life he was leading, and no longer regretted his beautiful kingdom.

The Fay of the Beech, touched by the situation of the unfortunate royal family, resided in the valley to which hazard had led them; she was the one who had made the voice audible that had advised them to fish, and who had take them under her protection, because she liked children very much, and little Muguet, who never wept, became prettier every day. It is very easy to please afflicted people by sympathizing with their misfortunes, so, without initially admitting that she was a fay, she made the acquaintance of the fisher king and the shepherdess queen, who did not take long to conceive a strong amity for her, and even entrusted the handsome Muguet, their only hope, to her.

She took him to her palace, and that was with great pleasure on his part, because she gave him tarts, cakes and cream incessantly; at first she employed those means to make herself loved, but afterwards she took advantage of the liking he had for her, and made use of it to inspire him with sentiments appropriate to his birth and to give him the knowledge necessary to all men, but even more so to a prince.

In spite of the fay's caution, however, vanity carried Muguet away and corrupted the good sentiments that nature had established in his heart, and when he reached the age of fifteen, he had no appetite for rural life; the neighboring town, where luxury and laxity reigned to excess, seduced him. Yielding to all the charms of inconstancy, he made as many conquests as he had the design of making, for he was charming. The king and queen were very afflicted by that mode of life, but they did not know how to oppose it, for, just between us, the Fay of the Beech was a little too good.

Meanwhile, she received a visit from Saradine, one of her companions; the latter was so angry that she could hardly speak.

"My God, what the matter?" the Fay of the Beech said to her, mildly.

"You can judge for yourself," she replied "You know that, not content with having endowed Zaza, the heiress to the Isle of Roses, with everything a princess can hope for in order to please, I brought her up personally, with infinite care. Would you believe what she's done to me? No, I'll never get over it. While giving me more caresses and amities than usual, she made me promise to grant her a favor. Her manners seduced me, and I confess that I swore. In sum, this is what she asked of me; 'You've heaped me with generosity,' she added. 'I'm overwhelmed by your gifts, but I implore you to take them away from me; for, after all, if I have the good fortune to please you, I don't know whether it's my own doing, and I'll be in the same situation all my life with those I encounter. See, then, what a distaste your generosity, for which I'm not ingrate, has spread over my life.'

"I've done everything I could to change her mind, in vain," Saradine continued, "but my efforts have been futile. Am I not right," she went on, angrily, "to make her suffer as many pains as I counted on procuring her pleasures and satisfaction? After having performed the ceremony necessary to take away all my gifts, I've come to repose with you and seek in your solitude and dissipation of which, I confess, I have great need. But fundamentally, what have I taken away from that Zaza, whom I still love, perhaps? Nature has formed her beautiful and given her so much intelligence that she only needs herself in order to please. I wanted to begin," Saradine went on, "by making her experience bodily pains, and I transported her to this desert, where I've just left her."

"What! Without any aid?" the good fay asked.

"Yes, said Saradine.

"Well, give her to me," said the Fay of the Beech. "I don't see any harm in what she has asked of you; it's necessary to punish vanity and correct it by amour; there's more intelligence in her procedure that one ordinarily finds in all these little fools that we have the generosity to endow."

Saradine accepted the proposition, and left the Fay of the Beech in the forest.

Her first concern was to get rid of everything that might inconvenience the beautiful Zaza, and form a little path before her that would take her, beneath charming shade, to the habitation of the fisher king and the shepherdess queen.

They were surprised to see her, but they were even more touched by the deplorable state to which the brambles and the thorns had reduced her before Saradine had taken care of her. Although the charms of a face always increase interest, the more one has suffered, the more sensitive one is to the suffering of others. The good sovereigns were sitting on the edge of the stream; they were letting the greatest heat of the day pass and resting from the morning labor while awaiting a repast appropriate to their present condition.

The king went toward Zaza, who dared not approach; the candor that reigned over his face and a few polite simple words he pronounced, full of interest, which only the customs of society can teach one to pronounce, soon reassured her, and when he had taken her into his cabin, she accepted the meal and shelter without difficulty.

Zaza told them everything that had happened, without any disguise. The king was charmed by her intelligence, and the queen thought she had been very bold to dare to contradict a fay.

"Your generosity, Madame," Zaza replied, "prevents me from regretting what I have done; for after all, what I have merited thus far, I only owe to myself, and my conduct and my gratitude will enable me to obtain even more in the future, by virtue of the care I shall take to please you, if you permit me to stay here for a while."

Such a discourse charmed the king and the queen equally; they regarded Zaza as a gift from Heaven, and as a consolation for the pain caused them by the almost continuous absence of Prince Muguet. He was incessantly in the town, where the fay maintained him in a magnificent house with all possible comforts. Zaza, therefore, established herself in the cabin, and, sharing the cares of the household with the queen, she was soon extremely beloved.

She was introduced to the Fay of the Beech, to whom she told her story—which the latter knew as well as anyone, but made a semblance of being informed of it. Yielding to the liking she had for amiable youth, it was not difficult for the fay to make herself loved by the girl; she often invited her into her retreat, or her palace of foliage, which was formed of the oldest and most beautiful trees in the world. The interlacement of their branches formed several apartments of several floors, if which Honoré d'Urfé's Temple of the Goddess Astrée is only an imperfect copy, but which sentiment will always render preferable.[15]

Every day the fay showed her some of the rarities that she had assembled for her amusement, but Zaza preferred to all the other places the Cabinet of Romance. It is true that the room in question was very agreeable; the rarest morsels were to be found there, in a charming order, which form the basis or the greatest ornament of fiction, such as the sword of Lisvart, the lance of Roger, the Model of the Bow of Faithful Lovers, and a perfectly beautiful painting of the glory of Niquée—in a word, all the finest books that the imagination has be able to create in order to please and amuse. They charmed Zaza; but as she wanted to be perfect, she also instructed herself with all the tales of enchantment she could find.[16]

---

[15] Honoré d'Urfé's pastoral novel *L'Astrée* (1607-27; initially in four volumes with a fifth added subsequently by a different hand; tr. as *Astrea*) was a greatly influential work, the enormous length of which, its portmanteau structure and obsession with faithful but severely-tested amour set a pattern for many works that came after it, including the novels of Mademoiselle de Scudéry, and contributed significant elements to the conventional apparatus of *contes de fées*.

[16] The "Romance" to which this paragraph refers was the literary genre established in France in the twelfth and thirteenth century, initially in verse and subsequently in prose, thus pioneering prose fiction. Many of its elements were deliberately adapted into the apparatus of *contes de fées*. The adaptation was somewhat indirect, the elements in question having already been adapted and re-emphasized in pastiches of French

Not content with taking her into the Cabinet of Romance, she often enabled her to go into another, where, showing her the greatest rarities, she said about each piece that it was for the man who would marry her. Sometimes, it was a beautiful golden hat, sometimes a ship that traveled under water, a hunting horn made from a single ruby, two candles of blue wax that were not consumed, diamonds that produced others, and a thousand other things, as beautiful as they were singular, the list of which would be too long.

How could one not love madly someone who added to the charms of society the hope of making so many beautiful presents? For the beautiful Zaza did not doubt that those rarities would one day be her wedding presents. It is true that the Fay of the Beech had never said anything more positive to her, but why would she have shown them to her if they were not destined for her. There would have been impoliteness and harshness in the fay's procedure.

However, she was only acting in that manner in order to punish her more essentially. In order to succeed in that, she cast her eyes upon the handsome Muguet. I have already said, I think, that he had acquired as much distaste for the country as liking for the town that I mentioned. Luxury and pleasures were sufficient to occupy fully a young man endowed with beauty but who, very attached to his face, believed himself to be even more perfect.

Some people might perhaps criticize the Fay of the Beech for her indulgence, but she loved the young prince and only wanted to correct pleasures by means of the pleasures

---

Romance produced in Spain, Portugal and Italy. Thus, among the cited examples *Lisvart de Grèce* is one of several "continuations" of the enormously popular Spanish Romance *Amadis de Gaula* (c.1500), which enjoyed great success in its French translation, in which *l'arc des loyaux amants* [bow of faithful lovers] and Niquée [Niquea] are featured; the lance of Roger [Ruggiero] is featured in the French translation of Ariosto's *Orlando Furioso* (1532).

themselves. That remedy is far milder than it is reliable. But in sum, out of generosity, she had not imagined others, Muguet, the model and example of our young fops, wanted to be everywhere, to know everyone, to be reputed to have had all the pretty women and to be able to put them in a catalogue that he drew vanity from augmenting. Such fine projects prevented him from going to visit the fay, much less his parents. The country bored him, he said, and those excessively simple good folk did not understand his language and did not admire the stories he told them about this pretended prowess.

He was most occupied with those beautiful reflections, common to youth, when the Fay of the Beech judged him appropriate to mortify the beautiful Zaza. She often mentioned him to her as a charming young man, whose birth, equal to hers, might make him a suitable match for her, if their sentiments found themselves in conformity. She announced Muguet's return a few days before he arrived.

Zaza prepared herself for that sight by a thousand attentions to her adornment, and although she had no doubt of her success, she was agitated by a thousand ideas, all of which promised her an assured conquest. But the Fay of the Beech, who had no doubt that the prince, by virtue of taste, novelty or vanity, would be inflamed for her at first glance, had found a means of moderating it, for she had extended over Zaza's person a gauche manner and a deterioration of her facial features, which would only appear to the eyes of the handsome Muguet.

He came into the Palace of Foliage, even more agreeable than the fay had depicted him, but, having scarcely glanced at Zaza, he asked the fay a hundred questions and told at least as many stories. The princess was astonished by the slight effect of her charms, and, by virtue of a chagrin that is only too natural, and makes itself felt in a moment, she responded to a compliment that he only paid out of respect for the fay with a great deal of disdain. Her disdain was futile, however, and was not even noticed.

Piqued, Zaza did not doubt that the charms of her intelligence would merit his attention, but, although she took great care to manifest them, that last resource was no more useful to her. Does one know intelligence at a certain age? Beauty makes a hundred conquests for every one made by intelligence, which usually only serves to conserve them.

The prince's responses were polite, but they were not accompanied by the vivacity that produces the desire to say something as agreeable as what one has just heard, nor the surprise and the fashion of listening that discover even in silence the contentment that that one inspires.

Several visits confirmed Zaza's misfortune, for the prince had touched her heart, and in spite of all the ridicule that she had found in him without difficulty, she had not been able to resist the charms of his face. After having said to herself everything that we read in novels, and that one can say in such a situation, she regretted a thousand times over the gifts that she had not wanted to conserve.

For his part, Muguet was surprised by the eulogies that the fay, the king and the queen continually made regarding Zaza's face. They served to confirm his idea of the poor taste that country people had; and to prove the opinion that he had of them, delicately, he continually made them portraits of the beauties of the town whom he loved, had loved or counted on loving. Those speeches were as many dagger blows for Zaza, who often witnessed them.

The fay, however, also wanted to correct his commerce with so-called flighty women. She was surely right, for they almost always render a man unsupportable, and veritably ridiculous. In order to succeed in her design, she sent him via a stranger, who delivered his message with a great deal of mystery, a package containing a portrait of Zaza as she really was, accompanied by a letter that read: *This beauty, very intelligent, a brand new heart, would fulfill the desires of the handsome Muguet, but his inconstancy is redoubtable.*

That note made less impression on the prince's mind than the portrait did on his eyes. He often explained, unable to help it, that he had never seen anyone simultaneously so beau-

81

tiful and so pretty. "It isn't possible," he added, "that such a physiognomy could be deceptive and that the mind does not respond to so many charms."

After those initial transports, he recovered himself, and ran all over town in order to avoid the ridicule of being in love with a portrait, and to rid himself promptly of all the idea that it had been able to provoke in him; but he no longer found in the beauties the thought the most piquant the attractions that he had obtained therein. *This one*, he said to himself, *does not have that delicacy in the eyes, that one does not have as much grace in her smile, that one's nose is not as well-fashioned.* In brief, everything he perceived did not resemble the portrait, which preoccupied him in spite of himself.

The town soon became importunate to him, and because he no longer knew how to occupy himself or to snigger at the trivia of which commerce with women of the world is usually composed, he appeared less likeable to them. The abode of the Fay of the Beech and his parents' retreat began to appear more agreeable to him.

The fay made a semblance of not perceiving that change; wanting, on the contrary, to treat him as she had always done and contribute to his pleasures, she assembled in her palace all the women that the prince had loved and gave them a great dinner, at which Muguet, who did the honors alone, played a very embarrassing role. The sight of so many objects, some of whom he had quit on bad terms, others he had turned to ridicule or sacrificed, of whom he no longer saw any but their bad side, made such an impression on him that a feast had never seemed so annoying to him, for he was the object of tender, discontented, piqued, jealous, ironic, insipid or stupidly animated gazes. That company, consisting of twenty women who, at any other time, would have been his triumph, then became a source of remorse and reflection, which led him to more distaste for his past life.

Meanwhile, the unfortunate Zaza, in the home of the fisher king and the shepherdess queen, was humiliated— which is to say everything about a pretty woman. She believed that absence would eventually destroy sentiments for which she could no longer pardon herself, but what can oppose a passion that resists scorn?

Muguet, giving himself to the retreat and beginning to experience its advantages, caused the rebirth in Zaza's heart, not of hope, but a least of curiosity, for she wanted to know what had caused the change in him. The more she examined him, the more she saw the appearances of amour. Well, who knows it better than those who feel it? But she thought she also recognized the appearances of sentiment, and was pained to see that she was far from inspiring it. None of the prince's actions could be taken for the timidity that often delays the consolations that love has at the moment of giving.

Zaza, meek and timid—for a woman only becomes proud and haughty by virtue of the submission and deference people have for her—wanting at least to see the prince, sought opportunities to talk to him; and for his part, far from avoiding her conversation, sought it. He could not conceal his love from her, but acknowledged that he dared not admit it to himself, so much did it make him blush. That confession, which the princess could not attribute to herself, was infinitely sensible to her, but after all, as she was accustomed to overcoming her dolor, she let nothing escape that might reveal the unfortunate state of her heart.

One day, when the prince was asleep at the foot of a tree, she approached him quietly in order to enjoy undisturbed the pleasure of seeing him, How surprised she was when, perceiving a portrait beside him, she recognized it for her own; and although, on examining it, she was not overly content with it, joy and the seizure of a unexpected hope almost burst forth. But when she remembered the fashion in which he lived with her, his distraction and the tender ideas he had in her presence, of which she was not the object, she fell into a further embarrassment. Everything that relieves jealousy being a pleasure however, and no longer being jealous of all the care that he gave to the portrait, she no longer thought about anything but means to make him declare it.

83

Her efforts were futile; the more she thought about it, the less she understood how it was possible that the prince adored her portrait, while having at the same time such a great indifference for her. He acknowledged, however, that she had a great deal of intelligence; often, he even desired that the object for which he sighted had a character similar to what he admired in her. That was very little reward for such a great amour, it must be agreed.

The sight of her portrait had, however, made her bolder, so she ventured one day to ask him the name of the fortunate princess by whom he was preoccupied.

"Alas, I'd like to be able to tell you," the prince replied, sadly.

"Well, Sire what prevents you?" said the tender Zaza. "What can you fear?"

"Since it's unknown to me, alas," said Muguet, "but I won't remain for long in the trouble I'm in, and if the world contains her, she won't escape my research."

Extremely surprised, Zaza wanted to doubt what she had heard, but in the end, the desire to please always being accompanied by patience and mildness, she implored him to show her the portrait, and in order to obtain that, she did not hide from him the circumstances in which she had already seen it. The prince consented to that, and Zaza, having examined it for some time, said to him as she handed it back to him that it was nice enough.

Such faint praise was misinterpreted by the prince, who could not help saying to her: "I confess, Zaza, that I had thought your intelligence above the prettiness common in woman." He continued, hotly: "Do you think that that splendor, combined with so much sweetness and grace can be found anywhere else?"

"I think, Sire," Zaza replied, blushing, "that that princess ought to be content with her painter."

"Which is to say," said Muguet, "that you think it flatters her."

"Undoubtedly," said Zaza, lowering her eyes, "but she is nevertheless recognizable."

"What!" cried the prince. "You know her?" He threw himself at her knees. Please," he said, "get me out of trouble. Know that I shall owe you life if I can see such a perfect object thanks to you."

"Well, Sire," said the princess, her eyes bathed by tears, "was I not right to tell you that it was flattering? Why do you want to oblige me to admit it to you?"

The prince needed all his politeness then not to make any response. Thinking as he did, any response would have been shocking. But, seeing that Zaza attributed the portrait to herself, and not wanting to let her see the extent to which he thought her blinded by her vanity, he stood up in a cold and reserved manner, without proffering a single word, and never had a lively conversation concluded so abruptly, because, for reasons easy to imagine, Zaza, for her part, had no thought of sustaining it.

After having withdrawn, the prince departed a few hours later. That departure put the princess in despair, for, after all, she could not believe that she was loved, and the absence of the prince made her see with so much horror the places that had witness the scorn to which her charms had been subjected, that she resolved to go away.

She left without expressing her gratitude to the king, the queen and the fay, unable to determine herself to make a confession of her woes, which interested her self-esteem too much to require confidants.

When she had walked for some time, overwhelmed by her dolor, she saw a little house in the distance, toward which she directed her footsteps, slowly—for she was extremely fatigued. The closer she approached it, the less considerable the building seemed; in the end she distinguished an old woman sitting on the doorstep, who was looking at her with a rather surly expression.

"I'll wager," she said to her, when she was within ear-shot, "that this is one of my beggars, whom idleness engages to travel the region."

"Alas, Madame," Zaza replied to her, weeping, "a sad destiny obliges me to ask you for shelter."

"Well, didn't I say that she'd beg me for something? From shelter she'll come to supper, after supper she'll need money to continue her journey. Truly, truly, if one could find a dupe every day, I wouldn't want to live any other way, but personally, that's not me. You build, you buy provisions, is that for you? No, it's for passers-by; I'll wager that a youth like that has more money than me. I'll have to search her." She got up, leaning on her stick.

"Alas, Madame," said Zaza, "I wish I had some; you'd give me great pleasure by accepting it."

"But you're very well dressed," the old woman continued, "for the life you lead."

"What!" said Zaza. "You think that I'm asking you for alms?"

"I don't know what you're doing," replied the old woman, "but I know that you aren't bringing anything. Anyway," she continued, still looking at her garments, "what do you want from me? Shelter, isn't it? All right, that doesn't cost much, but from there you'll come to supper; no, no, I won't hear that, for at your age one has an appetite always open, and what's more, you've been walking, and I'll wager that you're dying of hunger."

"Alas, Madame," Zaza replied, "when one is chagrined, one isn't difficult to nourish."

"Well," she said, her face clearing slightly, "If you promise me to be very sad, you can spend the night with me, I agree to that."

Then she had Zaza sit beside her, and, struck by the beauty of her garments—which were, however, quite simple—she said to her, still with astonishment: "Skirt on top, petticoat underneath, look how much all that has cost you; wouldn't it have been better to keep something, to eat your own expense rather than ask it of others? If one were sure of finding it, as I said, that would be very convenient, but these days no one gives anything away, everyone sells everything, and they're right, for one never knows what might happen, times are so hard." She added "Those clothes are very expensive."

"Alas, Madame," the princess replied, "they didn't cost me anything, and I've never known what money is."

"What have you learned, then, if you please?" retorted the old woman. "Oh, I see, you're one of those little damsels of the world, who scorn the household, and whom a lover has doubtless abandoned."

"No, Madame," Zaza replied. "I'm more to be pitied, and more virtuous than you suspect, but," she continued, dissolving in tears, "since my condition can't touch you, and if my services might be useful to you, you could...."

"Me, services," said the old woman, "It would be necessary to pay for them, and I'm not too good to serve myself. A servant would cost too much money, a servant wouldn't leave me anything, and she'd eat everything."

"Madame," Zaza said to her, "reduced to the most deplorable fate, I wouldn't ask anything of you, I'd relieve you in your difficulties; I'd do, in a word, everything I could to live in a place as remote as this one."

"It's to trap me," said the old woman, "that you're saying that you'll serve me for nothing. However, I concede that you can do it—but how can you want my servant to be better dressed than me? That isn't possible. There's a remedy for everything, though. I'll give you other clothes, if you want to give me yours. Let's go, that's what we'll do, I won't look at it too closely, and I'll take you into my service, for, after all, I'm very old, and some accident might happen to me."

Poor Zaza, who was only seeking a shelter from all gazes, consented to everything, and the old woman, having fetched a small package, came to help her undress, saying "How that's lined! Oh, great gods, what fullness," And, measuring the skirt with her arm, she cried: "There's at least four skirts in that one. You'd never have been able to walk with all that paraphernalia, my child, nor turn around in my house."

As she said that, she folded up all the clothes, for which she had a veritable consideration, very neatly, and Zaza put on the rags that the old woman had brought her.

When she saw her thus dressed, she said: "You're a marvel, and I like you much better in those clothes. What's your name?"

"My name is Zaza," replied the sad princess.

"Well, Zaza, "see how honest I am. How many people nowadays would be capable of not keeping their word and sending you away! Agree, at least, that I'm a good woman."

"Alas, Madame," Zaza replied, "how could I regret it? Am I not, at present, in a condition more appropriate to the situation of my heart?"

The old woman, attributing her insensibility to the chagrin she was experiencing, did not allow herself to be impressed by such scant attachment to things that she valued so highly—for she counted on having gained clothes for the rest of her life.

When the time for supper came she went into her house, not wanting Zaza to follow her, and came back, saying: "Let's sup now." The she gave her a tiny morsel of black bread and served two plums on a very clean little board.

"Come on, let's eat," she said. "Do you know that I'm having twice the usual? You've given me an appetite, if you please." Then she took one and divided it and said: "Let's share this one." Which she did. "As you're the newcomer," she added, "you'll have the side with the stone, but don't swallow it, because I collect them with great care, and you can't imagine the good fire that I make of them in winter. So take it from me—it won't cost you anything—that it's always necessary to buy fruits with stones in preference to all the others."

Scarcely sensible to this good advice, Zaza ate her little piece of bread and drank a little water, without touching her half of the plum, which the old woman very carefully took back in order to keep it for her breakfast. Charmed by her procedure, she could not help saying: "I'm very content with your services, Zaza. If you continue, we'll live together for a long time, and you won't have any reason to repent of it, for I'll teach you things that few people know. For example," she said, "do you see my house? It's me who built it; can you guess with what? It's with the pips of all the pears I've eaten. Everyone throws them away, but God doesn't make anything useless, and when one has patience and intelligence, you can't imagine everything one can do."

Insensible to such advice, Zaza made no reply.

As soon as the sun had set, the old woman said: "The evening air gives one a appetite. Furthermore, calm is danger-ous. Let's go to bed early; that's my custom, and I stay in bed late, one dissipates less there, and in consequence, one doesn't need so much reparation."

Zaza spent the whole night in a cruel agitation, and when the old woman wanted get up, she said to her: "I've under-stood you well, you've had a good night and I'm sure you have no desire for breakfast."

"Alas, no, Madame," said Zaza. "Don't you need any-thing?"

"To stay in bed," she said to her. "Try to sleep; it'll do you god. For myself, I'm going to do the housework; I don't trust you enough yet to let you do it; everything's familiar to me and I've never broken anything. That's how it's necessary to be. Tomorrow, I'll go to town; it's market day, and I'll bring back a sou's worth of bread to see us through the week."

She said a hundred more things of that sort to poor Zaza, who did not listen to them, and having got up, went into the beautiful desert to lament her misfortune; but as a diet as terri-ble as the old woman's would surely have ruined her health, the Fay of the Beech, who only wanted to diminish her pride, sent her aid whose source she could not determine. It was a beautiful white cow, which came to caress her, and, following her incessantly, returned to the old woman's house with her.

When the latter saw it her joy was extreme, but, soon dreading that those to whom it belonged would come to reclaim it, she said to Zaza: "Let's milk it anyway. We'll drink a little of the milk and keep some for tomorrow and make cheese with some. Milk is so good, it's a pity it's so dear."

With those fine reflections, the cow was milked; they made it a little shelter at the foot of a tree with dry grass, and the old woman could not weary of admiring the good fortune by which they had found such a beautiful animal.

Zaza had been living in that sad dwelling, which was not susceptible to any variety, for some time when, one day, as she was dreaming on the edge of a stream while her beautiful cow was grazing, she saw a young man in the meadow. She got up promptly and was trying to run away when the handsome Muguet—for it was him—perceived her in his turn. He ran toward Zaza with all the more urgency because he recognized her, not as the Zaza whom he had scorned, but as the original of the portrait the adored.

The Fay of the Beech, thinking that Zaza's vanity had been sufficiently humiliated, wanted to employ the same remedy against Muguet, who had no less need of it; the fay returned her veritable features to Zaza, and, at the same time, deprived Muguet of the beauty that had been the source of his inconstancy.

Muguet threw himself in front of Zaza in order to prevent her from fleeing. One can imagine the speech that he made to an object with which his heart was filled, and which he had found after infinite research. He employed terms so humble and so touching that Zaza consented to listen to him out of compassion.

Muguet wanted to go with her, but she forbade him to do so. She only gave him permission to come to the same place occasionally, in order to share her solitude. Unhappy and scorned amour is ordinarily submissive; he obeyed her, but he did not fail to come to the meadow every day in search of the woman he adored and to try to soften her.

"How happy I am," he told her, "to have found you. I am already too delighted with my fate to dare to lament it; decide it, you are its sovereign."

It was in the course of one of these conversations that Muguet, who had attached himself to meriting Zaza's confidence, learned with a extreme dolor that she had disposed of her heart.

"I cannot," she said to him one day, "receive your prayers. I have loved, and I still love, to my misfortune, a flighty, inconstant prince full of pride, who only loved himself, who was only sensitive to false appearances, and whom good fortune had rendered ridiculous. Women had spoiled him, and he was, in consequence, incapable of knowing amour. To complete my woes, he scorned me."

"But it's a fop that you're describing to me," said the prince. "Can it be, with the intelligence that you have, that such a man seduced you?"

"It's only too true," said the beautiful Zaza, shedding a torrent of tears."

Thus, the prince, penetrated, said against himself everything that the idea of a rival presents to the mind. "How," he added, "with the beauty with which you are ornamented, were you able to find an insensible man? If amour had accorded me the happiness of touching our heart, I would have sacrificed the entire world. I have traveled the world and renounced all pleasures merely by virtue of seeing a portrait. How humiliating that confession would once have been for me, but you are more beautiful than your portrait. I have seen you, I will never separate myself from you."

"What! My portrait?" said Zaza, with a heartfelt vivacity. "Has Muguet sacrificed it in a fit of jealousy?"

"He will not quit life without that precious portrait," said the prince then, with the eloquence of a heart penetrated by amour, "but how do you know my name?"

The embarrassment of Muguet and Zaza would only have been augmented by their discourse, if the Fay of the Beech, who had tested their hearts sufficiently, had not permitted Muguet at that moment to appear to Zaza's eyes under his true features, such as the beautiful princess loved him. All the reproaches he had lavished on his past ridiculousness, all the bad things he had said about himself, and, more than that, the degree of amour that he had attained, had destroyed the vanity that had been the sole obstacle to his happiness.

Who could describe the pleasure they felt? Those stories are beyond expression.

Both content and charmed, they took the path to the little house where Zaza had been received; it was then that she reproached herself for the rags in which she was clad; she became anxious about it, but the prince was not thinking about it, and when he perceived it, he was touched, flattered by all that she had suffered.

It did not take them long to reach the old woman's house. On seeing them arrive, she cried: "It's rightly said that if you plant girls, boys will come. What you're doing is fine for a girl," she said to Zaza, "but I don't want all that commotion in my house; you can't expect to come back in, truly, truly, that would be a fine thing."

"But my good woman," the prince said to her, "you can't think so."

"Yes, indeed truly, I think so; it's for having thought so that I won't think otherwise. But look at that beautiful beard, with his 'good woman.' Who do you think you're talking to?"

Muguet was annoyed for the moment, seeing the injustice of the old woman and the insult she was offering to Zaza, so he left her to settle the quarrel; but she did not come out of it the better of the two, for what cries, tears and oaths were not exhaled as soon as she pronounced the word *clothes*.

However, the princess insisted, for since she was beloved, her rags were insupportable to her. Meanwhile, the old woman screamed as if her throat were being cut. "That's what you get for rendering people a service. They rob you, they take your property; to hear them, wouldn't one think that they were right? If I weren't so far from help, thieves wouldn't come to abuse my weakness, as they do." Finally, she swore by all the gods that she did not have her clothes, that, on the contrary, touched by compassion for Zaza, who had none, she had given her own to her, which everyone would recognize easily, since she had always worn them.

Eventually, however, after many false oaths, she softened slightly, when the princes said to her: "But I'm not asking for the clothes for nothing; I count on buying them from you."

Then the prince threw her his purse, which she promptly picked up, saying: "I'll go and see whether, by any chance, I might be mistaken."

Before going into the house she retraced her steps and asked the prince and princess whether it was really true that the purse was hers; not content with that question, she made them both swear that they would never demand it from her. "For, you see," she said to them, "you're much stronger than me, and what would prevent you from taking back your money if you were dishonest enough to do it?"

They swore to her everything that she wanted, and the old woman brought back some of what she had taken.

After having dressed in the old woman's house—where the latter kept her in sight in the fear that she might take something—Zaza reappeared to the eyes of her lover a thousand times more beautiful than anything he had ever seen. After a delightful conversation, they needed to eat, for, unfortunately, "one cannot live on air or amour." It was then that the old woman recommenced her complaints.

"To nourish people of that contentment!" she said, weeping.

But whatever she said, as the prince had no more money, and he was beginning to get annoyed, fear made her give him a little bread and six plums, which each cost her a dozen sighs; they combined with that the milk of the beautiful cow, and in spite of their necessity, our lovers ate very little, for the avidity and contentment of their gazes filled their souls entirely. In the midst of oaths and the most tender assurances, they satisfied their reciprocal curiosity.

The princess told the prince everything that she had experienced in the home of the Fay of the Beech, and her narration took a long time because of all the interruptions by the prince, who sometimes detested his blindness and sometimes begged for a pardon, which it was necessary to obtain before allowing her to continue.

When the princess had finished an account that was interesting in itself and delightful by virtue of everything that accompanied it, the prince told her that the embarrassment in which she had put him by revealing her sentiments, the justice that he rendered to her intelligence, and the desire to encounter an object so necessary to his happiness had obliged him to depart, that he had run all over several kingdoms like a lunatic, sometimes alone, sometimes with his equipage, always maintained by the Fay of the Beech; that he had not had any other occupation than informing himself about beauties who were causing a stir in society; that his research had been futile; that nothing had responded to the idea that the portrait had given him of grace and beauty; and that it always appeared to him that no one said enough about any women to persuade him that she might be the one by whom he was struck.

"Because," he added, "the greatest eulogies were united in regard to Zaza, to whom I was sent back with a unanimous voice, but as I had judged her so differently, I always said, I confess, 'What prejudice!' and 'How could anyone say that if they had seen the individual I only know in a painting?' No one said anything different. Finally weary, and even more desperate, I resolved to abandon myself to hazard, and to travel the countryside. These deserts have enchanted me by their natural beauty, and I shall consecrate my life to them, since I have finally found you. How I shall love you, since I loved a portrait so much, which no longer gives me any pleasure since I have seen you."

"That portrait flattered me too much for me to be recognized in it a year ago; today my beauty destroys it," said the princess. "What reasons for me to be alarmed! But I see that my heart attaches me to you; it is stronger than intelligence and reflection. Let's not think about it anymore. In any case," she continued, "you can surely see that we can't stay here; apart from bliss, we have no resource." ·

The prince agreed easily, and in order to remedy that inconvenience he proposed that he go in search of his equipage in order to take them to the abode of the Fay of the Beech, tell her about their adventures and rely on her generosity.

In that resolution the prince was about to depart when they saw two small chariots arriving through the air, one of jasmine and the other of honeysuckle, which were to take them to the dwelling of the Fay of the Beech.

Before their departure they heard the screams of the old woman on seeing the beautiful cow disappear. They learned subsequently that she had died of hunger and lassitude, always trying to pick up the gold coins that the prince had given her, which, by virtue of a punishment of the fay, incessantly dropped out of the bag that contained them.

The Fay of the Beech came all the way to her perron to meet the princely couple. She embraced them a thousand times and said to them: "That lesson was necessary to you, to you, Zaza, in order to cure your pride, and to you, Prince, to cure your inconstancy and your vanity."

Then the fisher king and the shepherdess queen arrived with Saradine, for the good fay had summoned them. Saradine pardoned the beautiful Zaza, who embraced her a thousand times. The more she found her embellished, the more it appeared to her that she had suffered too much. She returned the Isle and Empire of Roses to her, promising them her protection. For her part, Zaza assured her that she would always merit it.

The Fay of the Beech told the king and queen that their subjects had killed the tyrant Bambou, and were waiting for them in their kingdom with great impatience; but, being accustomed to a simple and delightful life, they abdicated gladly in favor of their handsome Muguet.

The fays took charge of introducing the royal couple to their beautiful realms—which, fortunately, were neighbors—

and establishing them on the throne, which they did with the greatest magnificence, after they had heaped them with all the beautiful presents that filled the cabinet. Muguet and Zaza lived happily, for they were constant.

TOURLOU AND RIRETTE[17]

There was once, in a hamlet, a young boy named Tourlou. His face was as agreeable as it was interesting, and his character was lively and animated.

A young girl, almost the same age, shone in the same hamlet; her name was Rirette. It was impossible to be prettier than her; her mildness was imprinted on her face, but that mildness was only marked by all the brilliant features that ordinarily denote vivacity.

Such were little Tourlou and young Rirette. Their parents were separated by the old hostilities so common in the heads of old people, which they conserve more out of habit than for any reason.

Since early childhood Tourlou had sought out Rirette and Rirette did not enjoy herself when Tourlou had not come to meet her. Their occupation was guarding their flocks. That was one of the first concerns of humankind, which even the most ambitious men of the world cannot imagine without regretting it.

Although young, therefore, they were very soon entrusted with what their parents had that was most dear, but that was not without forbidding them to meet one another. It was not the desire to do something that prohibition always inspires that made them desire to see one another; their natural penchant always took them to the same places, and without ever having experienced any other sentiments, or having known the slightest distraction in their hearts or minds, Amour, whose name they did not even know, had no more enthusiastic and zealous subjects than Tourlou and Rirette.

The Fay of the Meadows was interested in their fortune from their earliest childhood, solely because of the attraction

---

[17] Andrew Lang, in *The Green Fairy Book* substitutes the names "Sylvain and Jocosa."

that pretty faces always inspire. The older they grew, the more they inhabited the places of her empire, and they became dearer to her every day. The sentiments of the good fay were of the kind that loves to give effective proofs, which are ordinarily unsuspected. She always enabled them to find, as if by chance, either in the hamlet or the pastures, what they desired for one another, because they had no personal desires for themselves. It was enough for one of them to encounter the attentions if the fay for the other to share them instantly; they were thus reciprocally ornamented by everything that they were given, and what they had desired to give.

Independently of those little presents, the Fay of the Meadows loved, as I have already said, to please and oblige them; she always took care, therefore to enable them to find the best little cakes or preserves, and often candy, for their midday meal.

When they had reached a certain age, the fay wanted to make herself known to them. One day, when they were taking the air in the shade of a florid living hedge, they perceived a tall lady dressed in green, simply but gracefully coiffed with flowers. They saw her turn her steps in their direction; they got up, bowing politely with the intention of evading her, but the beautiful lady overcame their surprise and embarrassment by means of the mild and flattering words with which she accompanied her approach. She told them that they were the prettiest people in the world, that she had loved them for a long time, and that, in order to give evidence of the amity she had for them, it was her who provided them with the good snacks that they found every day, sometimes in one place and sometimes in another.

"But to give you proof of what I'm saying," she added, "today, for example, you haven't found anything. Always be good, love one another well, and I'll bring you a meal. Then she gave them a little basket filled with even better things than they had eaten thus far.

Their thanks were proportionate to the generosity of the presents. The fay quit them shortly thereafter, bidding them adieu and recommending them only to talk about her when there was no one else present. "You'll see me often," she added, "but remember that I can see you even when you don't see me."

That visit was not the only one she rendered them; she took pleasure in seeing them, and occupied herself with the task of forming to virtue the best-born hearts in the world. She saw with joy, by virtue of the candor and simplicity of their responses or their requests, how naturally amiable their hearts and minds were.

The more the sage fay loved Tourlou and Rirette, the more she wanted to ornament the minds of her pretty pupils. She made use cleverly of the sentiments they had for one another. In order to succeed in her project she often told them little stories, which all had a purpose. They sensed themselves that reading and writing are a great relief in the shortest absences of what one loves. Sentiment, therefore, taught them to read and write with an incredible promptitude. The first words that they traced and gave one another to read were: *I love you*. Tourlou wrote Rirette's name everywhere, and also read his own name written by his beloved.

Music and poetry then became familiar to them. They had no other master than the author of their desires. The depiction of the delightful life that they spent in innocence, the story of their petty events and the detail of their first amusements were the first exemplars, as they were the first principles, of the eclogue, but they made so many that they have often been imitated. Intellect has spoiled everything in that genre, by taking the place of the simplicity of sentiment.

Rirette was convinced by examples that found nothing to combat in her heart the sagacity and virtue that are necessary to a young person of her sex, and Tourlou too, vigorous as he was, was obliged to agree that virtue is one of the strongest bonds of amour.

When their minds were well-formed with regard to agreeable things and talents, the Fay of the Meadows wanted to demand of them, and accustom them to, a slight attention, not for her—because they loved her wholeheartedly, and when one loves one is always attentive—but for something else.

"I require," she said to them both, one day, "that you give your concern to something that is dear to me. You know the spring that I call my favorite, and which merits that name, both by its freshness and by the clarity of its waters. Promise me that every morning, before the sun's rays have been able to warm it, you will have the attention of cleaning it, removing stones and anything that might trouble its purity. I shall attach to that innocent concern a proof of your amity for me. Know too that the happiness of seeing one another, and that of never being separated, depends absolutely on the exactitude with which you fulfill the engagement that you have made with me."

In order to testify to the gratitude and amity that they felt, and, above all, wanting never to be separated, they did not think that charge considerable enough. They represented the little difficulty they would have in acquitting a task so easy to carry out, the recompense of which was so considerable, but the fay only demanded that condition.

For a long time the cleanest spring was incontrovertibly the favorite. Our lovers envied one another the happiness of rendering their first cares to it and the pleasure of having satisfied before the other the proof of all their sentiments; but excess of amour and delicacy have often led to faults being committed.

One morning, when they had both anticipated Aurora, and she discovered in the most beautiful spring day all the flowers that she had just enabled to bloom, our lovers, enchanted by that aspect, which related so well to everything they loved, were each convinced that they had enough time, one to assemble a bouquet and the other to make a crown for the object of their love. The multiplicity of flowers presented them with the wherewithal to satisfy the whim in a moment, but sentiment renders difficult things intended for the person one loves; one flower appears more beautiful than the one that one has just picked joyfully as the rarest in the meadow, another attracts the eye by virtue of the novelty or charm of its odor.

In that choice, so simple in appearance, which only ought to take a moment, the moments flew by and the sun's rays alerted them to their fault. They ran to the favorite ardently, but they found it already gilded by the star that there were engaged on oath to anticipate. They arrived at precisely the same moment, but by different paths, and they perceived that it was seething in the most frightful manner.

A wide river, terrible in its breadth and great rapidity, came to swallow up before their eyes the favorite, which had been so precisely recommended to them. The terrain that bore our two lovers withdrew to either side and became the banks of that redoubtable river, whose width barely permitted the sight to distinguish an object on the other side.

That event happened with so much promptitude that our lovers, uttering a cry of dolor, only just had time to show one another the crown and the bouquet. A simple glance expresses many things when the heart is attentive, and that tender exclamation only served to redouble their woe.

Tourlou tried swimming twenty times over in order to rejoin his dear Rirette, or at least to see her at closer range, but an invincible force always brought him back to the bank from which he had set forth. Rirette found several boats, and even several trees that the river had dragged away by virtue of its rapidity, but the efforts she made on her part to rejoin her lover were no more fortunate than those he had made.

They followed the banks of the river, therefore, with infinite difficulty, in the hope of finally being able to cross it. The nights were terrible, but the light of day at least brought them the pleasure of perceiving mountains, tributaries that came to mingle their waters with the river that separated them. Eventually, everything that the surface of the earth presents caused them not only infinite fatigues, but deprived them of the consolation they had in seeing one another, albeit from far away.

They followed the course of that prodigious river for more than three years. They finally arrived on the shore of the sea, in which it came to lose its pride and its name That immense expanse of water initially caused them the surprise that the first sight of that element imprints in all humans, but after a few reflections, they did not doubt that the discontented fay was presenting that object to them in order to terminate their destiny.

Unable to resist any further a separation to which they thought themselves eternally condemned, they gazed at one another, made one another gestures of farewell inspired by the most tender amour, and, with a common accord, they both hurled themselves into the sea.

The good Fay of the Meadows, who had always followed them, who had not been able to accustom herself to the solitude of the places that retraced for her continually the agreeable depictions of Tourlou and Rirette, and who had never had any other design than rendering them attentive, could not suffer that either one of them should fall into the sea. She therefore retained them in mid-air, and deposited them side by side on the same sand.

She left them for some time to the sensible pleasure of finding one another again. She did more; she waited until they had expressed regrets for their disobedience themselves, and did not have that delicacy inappropriately; she received for herself the chagrin of what their disobedience had caused that which they loved to suffer. When they had related their past pains and present pleasures abundantly, and had had the time to make a few reflections on the distance they were from their hamlet and the difficulty of their return, the good fay appeared to them.

They fell at her knees and begged her for so many pardons that the Fay of the Meadows, weeping, lifted them up, embraced both of them and assured them of the pardon she granted them. She promised them at the same time always to give them marks of her amity. With a thrust of her magic wand, she summoned her little carriage of green rushes, nailed and ornamented everywhere with the pearls of Aurora in the month of May, which she conserved with care as the rarest. She placed Rirette beside her, and Tourlou sat in front. She ordered her six short-tailed moles to take her home.

In a quarter of an hour, at the most, she found herself in the beautiful meadows of which she was the fay, and our lovers saw once again, with transport, the witnesses of their childhood and their amour. Mute as those witnesses were, they spoke to the lovers, knowing how to entertain them.

The fay had resolved to make their happiness; they did not desire any but that of an eternal union. She reestablished peace in the disunited families, and on the day that she had destined for their marriage she took Tourlou and Rirette to a little well-built single-story house; it was rustic, solid and clean.

The favorite, which had resumed its original form, had received an order, which it had obeyed, to enclose the house and the orchard; in sum, everything that one could desire for masters and flocks was found in that rural abode.

The fay sat them both down beside her, after they had carried out all the useful research of that agreeable dwelling with care, and as the good fay liked telling tales she said to them: "You cannot doubt, by virtue of the marks of my power and those of my generosity, that I am a fay. I have found a tale in our ancient annals that I am going to tell you."

The Yellow Bird

A fay whose conduct had not been perfectly regular was condemned by the Superior Council to suffer the penalty of sustaining for some years metamorphosis into an animal, the choice of which was left to her; but at the same time, she was ordered to make the fortune of two humans as soon as she resumed her ordinary form, in order to merit her clemency and satisfy her engagements. As she liked yellow very much she was transformed into a yellow bird, whose vivacity and color, and the beauty of its breast, could not be compared to any that humans have ever known.

When the when the time that her metamorphosis was due to end arrived, the beautiful bird was flying in the vicinity of Bagdad and was caught by a bird-catcher at the moment when Badi al Zaman[18] was walking outside his superb country house. Badi al Zaman was regarded in Bagdad as the most fortunate and most amiable of men, because he was the richest. In fact, his riches were innumerable; his commerce had always succeeded, and his fortunate ships never experienced any shipwreck or delay. His opulence was accompanied by the distastes that often accompany it: anxiety and ennui, as well as ill-humor, never abandoned that hero of Bagdad for an instant.

He was, therefore, at the country house that he had had built in order, he said, to withdraw from society there, and of which he had made with that design a palace that a hundred masters could inhabit, and which they did, indeed, inhabit. Bored with his gardens, in which Art constrained Nature at every moment, he was walking in the country in order to dissipate his ill humor. Instinct alone guided him to the places that a philosopher seeks for preference.

The bird-catcher who had just caught the yellow bird perceived him and thought the opportunity favorable to present a bird to him that he had destined for him since the moment when he had caught it. He had soon concluded the bargain, all the more so as Badi al Zaman, on considering the bird, perceived these words inscribed beneath its right wing: *The man who eats my head will be king*, while: *The man who eats my heart will have a hundred gold coin every morning when he wakes up*, were written in the same script under its left wing.

---

[18] Author's note: "This word means 'marvel of the age' in Arabic." Badi al-Zaman al Hamadani (969-1007) was the author of a notable collection of stories, of which Caylus would certainly have heard, although they had not yet been translated into French.

Delighted by that new favor of fortune, Badi al Zaman resolved to take advantage of it, Almost all rich men, however, have the misfortune of not knowing confidence. Among the prodigious number of his servants, he could not think of a single one that he could trust in an occasion of that importance. He therefore asked the bird-catcher if he was married, and he replied yes.

"Well," he said to him, "let's go to your home; if you wife cares to make me a simple stew with this bird, I'll give her a hundred pistoles; the bird might perhaps render me a appetite that I lost a long time ago."

The delighted bird-catcher consented to his proposition. They arrived shortly afterwards in the trapper's cottage; the bird was killed and plucked; the fricassee was made and served, but imagine Badi al Zaman's fury when he did not find the head on his plate and, on searching for the bird's heart in order at least to console himself for the loss of the head, he did not find that either.

The bird-catcher's wife threw herself at his knees and confessed to him that when he had left the house for a moment, her two children had tormented her so much that she had given one of them the head and the other a part of the giblets, two items that are ordinarily not eaten. Badi al Zaman left, full of fury, threatening them in general, and their children in particular, that they would not survive his fury.

Every rich man is to be feared, in every country, his injustices are ordinarily revered. The bird-catcher and his wife judged that they had no other recourse than to send their children away, but the wife, in order to console the husband, told him that he ought not to be anxious about it. Then she told him about the promises of the bird, which she had perceived while plucking it, and confessed to him that she had deprived Badi al Zaman with the design of making the fortune of their children.

They embraced them, gave them what they had in order to put them on the road, recommended them to go away and to separate, and made them promise to send them their news. For themselves, they remained in the city, hidden and disguised, and found the means to escape the anger of a rich and malevolent man who had always appeared to them to not to be maladroit.

Badi al Zaman, not content with the immense fortune that he enjoyed, died of the dolor and chagrin of having missed the one that had been presented to him, and the bird-catcher and his wife returned to their house to await news of their children.

The younger one, who had eaten the heart of the yellow bird, did not take long to perceive the treasure that he carried with him, for, indeed, every morning when he woke up, he found a purse with a hundred gold coins beneath his head. For the consolation of those who are not rich, nothing in the world requires as much care and precaution as wealth. The base accumulation of a treasure not only causes the person who hoards it to be scorned, but also puts the life of the man who possesses it at risk. The dissipation of the same wealth produces the same inconveniences and the same exposure to risk.

The younger son of the bird-catcher employed his income with profusion, and was suspected of having an inexhaustible treasure. At the sight of his riches, attempts were made on his life, so effectively that he succumbed.

His elder brother, the one who had eaten the head of the yellow bird, finally arrived, without any remarkable adventure happening to him, in one of the great cities of Asia. He fund everything in uproar; the election of an Emir was taking place, but the parties of those ambitious for authority being divided, it was agreed unanimously that the person to whom something singular happened would be declared Emir, without any appeal.

Our young man, rather poorly dressed and even more poorly mounted, ornamented simply by the rather agreeable face that he had, suddenly felt something alight on his head, and then saw that everyone had their eyes upon him; the astonishment that he perceived there was succeeded by acclamations. A white pigeon that had perched on his head was the occasion for the applause that he was given. He was taken to the palace and recognized as Emir—not, as one can imagine, without great astonishment on his part.

As there is nothing as pleasant as commanding others, there is nothing to which one becomes accustomed more easily, but the pleasure of something does not always counterbalance the difficulty. The young Emir commanded and governed, therefore; he made mistakes of every kind, and those whose party had been powerful before the election revolted and deprived him simultaneously of his life and his authority: a punishment that he merited all the more because he had not wanted to recognize the bird-catcher and his wife as his parents, and had allowed them to perish in poverty.

That rich man and that king might perhaps have been very good bird-catchers, perhaps even honest men, if their mother's ambition had not enabled them to change their estate.

"I have told you that story," the good Fay of the Meadows continued, "to tell you, my dear Tourlou and my dear Rirette, that the presents I have made you of this rustic house are preferable to all those that I might have made you. Promise me to work on the cultivation of your fields and the maintenance of your flocks, and keep your word better than you have done with regard to the care of the favorite. Don't allow yourselves to be overtaken either by neglect or idleness, and I promise you that abundance of the only wealth that is desirable will never be lacking. I can answer for it that you will combine the health of the body, the amusement of the mind and the constancy of the heart."

After that short speech, the good Fay of the Meadows assembled all the relatives and friends of Tourlou and Rirette, and gave them a wedding feast as in the good old days. The newlyweds were put to bed, to their great satisfaction. It was on that occasion that the couplets of the Tourlourirette were composed and sung,[19] the refrain of which has passed down to us, the only evidence that remains to us, after such a long time, of this true story.

Tourlou and Rirette loved one another well, followed the advice of the good fay exactly—which is very rare—and had many children, who completed the happiness of their life and the consolation of their old age.

---

[19] Like *trelintin, tourlourirette* could be found at the time when the story was written in the chorus of popular songs, especially some composed as parodies.

PRINCESS PIMPRENELLE AND PRINCE ROMARIN[20]

There was once a king and a queen who lived—although they have been dead for a very long time—almost as monarchs live today; which is to say, doing what they liked. The king, whose name was Giroflée,[21] liked hunting a great deal, although he was occupied with the affairs of his kingdom as much as he could be, and was incessantly arranging and disarranging his papers.

As for the queen, she had been very beautiful, but as she had enjoyed it so much, she was convinced that she still was, although she was more than fifty years old. It is true that the princesses and daughters of the theater also combine the privilege of being young and beautiful for a long time with that of being treated as such longer than any other women. The queen's name was Filigrane, a name that hazard had given her, and which subsequently thought to be a nickname, so thin and stiff was she.[22] She thought about nothing but imagining fêtes, balls and masquerades: in sum, all that luxury and gallantry combined have invented for the amusement of courts.

One can imagine how such a fine kingdom was governed; anyone who wanted to do so could take the provinces; provided the king's forests and the queens violins were left, all those events made no impression on their minds.

---

[20] The version of this story in *The Green Fairy Book* is entitled "Prince Narcisssus and the Princess Potentilla." The French *pimprenelle* does not correspond to the English pimpernel but to the herb known as salad burnet, while *romarin* is rosemary.

[21] Giroflée is the French name for a group of plants, of which the most familiar is usually known in English as the wallflower.

[22] Filigrane is the equivalent of the English filigree.

Queen Filigrane and King Giroflée had only had one daughter from their marriage; she promised from early childhood such a great beauty that at four years old Filigrane had become essentially jealous of her, and, foreseeing the injury that she would one day do to her charms, she resolved to hide her from the eyes of the entire court. In order to carry out that design, she invented some prediction, some poverty, such that it could not fail to be applauded by everyone surrounding her, and had an enclosure constructed on the bank of a stream that traversed the palace garden. She had a little house built there, in which she imprisoned the charming Pimprenelle—that was the name of the princess—in a tower. She was given all the things necessary to life, and a mute was give the responsibility of serving her. A corps of guards placed fifty paces from the tower had orders, under pain of death, not to allow anyone whatsoever to approach the house, and that order was carried out in its full extent.

As for the queen, she only ever spoke with a false dolor of the faults that she attributed liberally to poor Pimprenelle. She had repeated those evil remarks so often that she had convinced everyone of them, and no one formed any idea of her other than that of a monster hidden with reason from the eyes of the court.

That court was in the situation that I have just described, and the princess might have been fifteen, when Prince Romarin, aged eighteen, who was more beautiful than the light of day and somewhat less stupid than his age usually implied, appeared there, attracted by rumor of the fêtes and pleasures by which Filigrane was incessantly surrounded.

It is necessary to know who Romarin was. He was the son of a king and a queen, who might make the commencement of another tale. The good folk had died almost at the same time. They had left their kingdom to the older of their children, as is only right. As for Romarin, the younger, the one in question, they left him by testament to the fay Melinette, in order, I believe, not to have their conscience burdened by not having left anything to that amiable child. It remains that case that in doing that, they were making an intelligent move, for Melinette was as powerful as she was good.

The fay therefore raised the little prince with all imaginable care; she even taught him some of the secrets of Faerie, and neglected nothing of the knowledge with which the mind of a young prince always ought to be ornamented; but she had too much intelligence herself not to know that every man can employ his talents, as long as he is instructed in the usages of society. She also knew that the best princes are those that are confounded with their subjects.

All these considerations engaged Melinette to make Romarin travel and to leave him, in a sense, master of a conduct over which she still watched invisibly. With regard to invisibility, she gave the prince when she quit him a ring by means of which he could render himself invisible by putting it on his finger. Such rings are quite common; they are seen in many other tales.

Now that this explanation has been given, I think the reader knows almost all that is necessary about the people with whom the story is concerned.

So, Romarin arrived at Filigrane's court; he was the object of the attention and coquetry of all the ladies. He was presented to King Giroflée, who received him marvelously. He was even better received by Filigrane and her court, to which he delivered himself with the air of gallantry and intellectual coquetry that one can only have with the liberty of the heart.

After a time of sojourn when nothing happened that merits attention, Romarin heard mention of Pimprenelle, but as the stories were still excessive, she was described to him in a fashion so hideous, and at the same time so singular, that a curiosity was excited within him that he did not declare, but which he resolved to satisfy. He remembered the ring. The petty vanity of showing himself had prevented the prince from making use of it thus far. He remembered it. however, and resolved to make use of it, in order to judge for himself what he had been told and the effects that such a complete solitude might have produced.

He set forth invisibly, traversed the guards easily and crossed the wall that enclosed the most charming creature in the world. He saw her, and he was still searching for the monster that had been described to him, so much empire did prejudice have over his mind. He finally realized his error, and found her as beautiful as a morning rose, embellished by the simple ornaments that modesty and natural coquetry can indicate. Her attire did not depend on any fashion; it was simple and beautiful: Nature in its ensemble. Romarin was so impressed by everything he saw that the dart of amour was like a thunderbolt, and although, fundamentally, he was something of a fop and had the confidence of one, he dared not cease to be invisible, and contented himself with admiration.

Pimprenelle was sitting on the edge of the stream that traversed her retreat; she was occupied with the care of readjusting the most beautiful hair that can be imagined. After that personal attention she watered a few flowers. Compassion then led her to visit a bird's nest in order to relieve the mother in her needs, for in all the movements that our hearts deploy, and the most trivial bagatelles that its recesses reveal, the tenderness and benevolence of Pimprenelle had seduced everything comprising its Empire. By now, the birds had had the ability to admire her; she had domesticated them all, and had thus formed a petty court, which was not brilliant, in truth, but that court at least had the merit in her regard of sacrificing a familiar liberty to her. At the slightest sign or the briefest word they came to her in order to carry out all her orders. In sum, she was adored by them.

For some time, Romarin was the witness of those mild occupations; then he followed her into her small apartment; cleanliness reigned there; reading, one of the greatest relaxations she could have, had been a great help to her. Enchanted by everything that a mind can experience in response to the beauty by which it is enchanted, Romarin persisted in his invisibility. The timidity that was once born with amour is still one of its inseparable companions. It not only prevented him, therefore, from appearing to the eyes of the beautiful and simple Pimprenelle, but also constrained him to return to the palace, in the dread that his absence might give rise to suspicion.

That dread is a sentiment that I am very far from criticizing, but it has often had the effect of revealing what it is that one has the greatest desire to keep hidden. From then on he was no longer the Romarin who, having nothing in his heart, seized with intelligence everything agreeable that presented itself to say or to reply; he was a distracted and pensive man. As one can imagine, in a court as frivolous as Filigrane's, people did not take long to perceive that he had a passion in his heart. People made jokes about it, and his embarrassment confirmed those suspicions, without anyone being able to discover, no matter how much trouble they took, the fortunate objet that had made such a fine conquest.

The prince, preoccupied with the beautiful Pimprenelle, did not repent of his restraint; on the contrary, his heart and mind approved of the delicacy he had shown; they both applauded a timidity born as much from a kind heart as from veritable amour. He spent the first days satisfying the slightest desires of the beauty he adored; the innocence of her heart and the rectitude and justice of her mind completed charming him; her occupation with a flower, an assortment of silks, or the thread of a rush basket, far from revolting him, attached the strongest chains to him. In sum, the simpler Pimprenelle's desires were, the more Romarin's sentiments were increased.

After a few days of such an examination, he implored Melinette to entertain her with the most agreeable dreams. One can presume that he asked her, and obtained, that he might be the sole object of them, so that nothing would then engage him not to let her see his amiable face.

The agreeable ideas with which he filled the mind, and, gradually, the heart, of the beautiful Pimprenelle caused her, in a few days, to regard sleep as the sovereign of all goods. Insensibly accustomed by the dreams, Pimprenelle was more in a condition to receive Romarin's invisible declarations; he then satisfied her innocent desires more boldly. Sometimes he enabled a bagatelle that was distant and which she desired to arrive beside her. In the beginning, those actions caused her fearful reactions, at which the delicacy of her lover was in despair. He caused her to hear a few sighs, and then accustomed her to the sound of a voice, which his face would have embellished considerably.

Solitude enabled rapid progress. Pimprenelle came to be sensitive, although she did not yet know either the name of Amour or the face of her lover. Such revolutions, singular in themselves, would have embarrassed persons more experienced than our young beauty. Romarin read with transport in her heart and in her mind the effects of his own face, although she only knew it in dreams. He noticed in her, however, the troubles the desires and the agitations—in sum, the tender emotion—that only Amour can cause.

Pimprenelle desired to see the person whose conversation and obedient attention made an impression on her mind that was as agreeable as it was seductive, but she dared not confess to the one who maintained it the impression that the face she had seen in dreams had made on her heart. She dreaded incessantly that she might find them separate, and curiosity, the mother of so many disgraces, often tormented her.

"Romarin," she said to him one day, "I believe I love you. Your attentions charm me; they flatter my vanity, it is true, and your intelligence seduces me. You assure me that you are not deformed, and I want to believe it, but I sense that, if you are not made as I imagine, I would not be able to love you."

"There is a god," Romarin replied, "whom all men serve, in truth, but whom I serve more perfectly than anyone has ever served him. That god is named Amour. You know him; my sentiments have given you an idea of him. But that Amour has for a daughter another goddess, whose attributes and charms are infinite; her name is Delicacy, and it is her who prevents me from revealing myself to your eyes."

"But does that goddess love you?" added Pimprenelle "What will I become, if that is so? What advantages she has over me!"

114

"That evidence of your sentiments redoubles mine," said the charming Romarin, ardently, "but that goddess ought not to cause you any anxiety. She knows you; far from prevailing over you, she is submissive to you. She has ordered me to do everything I do for you; she even reproaches me for not yet doing enough."

"But she forbids you to appear to my eyes," Pimprenelle interjected, with vivacity, "and you obey her rather than me."

"Be satisfied for some time yet with my invisibility," the tender Romarin said to her. "Believe that it costs me infinitely, but let me please you with certainty; let me convince you, solely by the vivacity of my sentiments, of a passion that does not want to employ the effects if the face upon your heart."

All those reasons appeared feeble. Pimprenelle persisted, and the ring fell from his finger. What joy it was for the princess, to see that the mind and the character she loved were combined with the object of all her dreams!

The fay Melinette belonged to times past; she believed in the suitability of characters and the proofs of sentiment necessary to form the terrible knot of marriage. She therefore perceived with pleasure the keen and pure sentiments that were born in the hearts of those lovable children.

While our young lovers delivered themselves to all the vivacity of their hearts, only seeing themselves on earth, and they could not conceive the faintest idea of woe, they were at the moment of experiencing those troubles and chagrins that, in spite of the austerity and seriousness of philosophers, are the most sensible of life.

Pimprenelle was sitting on the bank of her little stream, in the place that her lover had occupied. The murmur of the water and the movement of its flow draws lovers involuntarily to reverie, so, needless to say, she was thinking about him with her entire soul, when, traversing the air in a gust of wind full of dust and straw, the genius Grumedan perceived her. The figure of a nymph, or, rather a goddess; admirable dark blue eyes, which perfectly dark eyelids rendered even more perfect; hair that descended below the waist; a charming complexion; a mouth accompanied by smiles and graces: all those beauties struck the genius. Well, who would not have been gripped by admiration?

He paused in his flight near Pimprenelle, and gazed at her for some time, his heart ablaze and desire augmenting. For a few moments he felt the shame of appearing in hunting costume; he had some desire to remain invisible, but such a resolution, for a being who feels amour, can only be sustained in a well-made heart; for, in sum, what chagrin there is in not daring to show one's own face when one experiences a passion founded almost entirely in self-love and the good opinion one has of oneself.

Grumedan's pride prevailed, therefore; he suddenly appeared to the eyes of Pimprenelle, who uttered a cry of fright and surprise. Both were well-founded, for he was not handsome, and his tall, boorish and obese figure was the image of his soul; furthermore, he was one-eyed. I am assured that he had lost his right eye more than nine hundred years before in a singular duel with one of his cousins over the matter of some territorial boundaries; the fays and the genii settled the affair, the combatants had remained friends but the eye had remained lost. He was, therefore, one-eyed and had a slight stammer; his hair was frizzy and his teeth rather fine, but long.

In spite of the princess's scream, which he only attributed to surprise, he paid her a compliment, long in itself and even longer because of the natural difficulty of his speech. Such as it was, he applauded himself for it.

"Ah, my dear Romarin!" cried Pimprenelle.

Grumedan replied to her with all the vivacity possible to him: "You shall have some, Madame; it isn't rare."

It is certain that she would then have revealed the secret of her heart if the good Melinette, ever attentive to what might interest her ward, had not come running. She rendered herself invisible and, taking on the sound of Romarin's voice, she said to her: "We are exposed to the greatest of all dangers; I am only alarmed for you, my dear Pimprenelle. Disguise your sentiments; let us hope in Amour; he will not abandon us."

Melinette had time to whisper those words, which left Pimprenelle in an extreme disturbance and agitation, while Grumedan, who was a great one for taking things literally, conjured all the rosemary in the region to come at his order. That little attention did not touch the beloved object; she asked him very coldly to be kind enough to send them back. He did so, with some difficulty, and as he was still content with everything that he did, he tried, insolently, to take Pimprenelle's hand, believing that he had merited that by the confession of amour he had just declared and the attention of which he had given evidence.

Then Melinette appeared, with all the splendor of Faerie. "Stop, Grumedan, stop; this beauty is under my protection; the slightest insolence will cost you a thousand years of captivity. If you can obtain the heart of the beautiful Pimprenelle by honest and decent ways, I won't oppose your actions, but you're mistaken if you flatter yourself that you can put into execution your abductions and ordinary procedures."

That declaration was a terrible blow for Grumedan, but he did not have any remedy to bring to it; it was therefore necessary to turn all his ideas in the direction of attentions, and although he was not in the habit of having any, the beauty that had impressed him was one of those for which one can make any sacrifice.

Melinette, quite certain of the safeguard that she had established, hastened to warn Romarin of what had happened. At the first mention of the words "rival" and "genius" his heart caught fire, and but for Melinette he would have yielded immediately to all the follies of a young head. Fortunately, she was able to contain him. She represented to him the authority of the genius and the danger to which his vivacity might even expose the object of all his desires; she promised him that Grumedan would not attempt anything that could displease him, provided that he was always invisible when he was with Pimprenelle.

When she had exacted his word, she told him that Grumedan was the most boorish and the most unjust genius that had ever been seen; she also told him that he had often been punished for his injustices by the Sovereign Council of Fays and Genii; that he had sometimes been imprisoned in a tree, only to emerge when the tree was felled or destroyed by the insults of time, and at other times he had been put under a large stone on a river bed without being able to escape except by virtue of the displacement of the stone; in sum, she listed a hundred punishments, the detail of which would take too long, but which had never been able to bring him to the mildness so commendable in a genius.

Grumedan, who feared Melinette's threats, was thus obliged to seek to please her and to imagine amusements in order to engage and seduce Pimprenelle; he had no doubt that he would succeed.

While the fay contained Grumedan, she had imposed on Prince Romarin the harsh necessity of invisibility; she had warned him that his conservation depended on that article, but she had assured him, in order to console him, that, given Grumedan's stupidity, he could have the consolation of seeing and conversing with Pimprenelle at any time. That was what both of them did not fail to do, but what is the effect of a prohibition in amour? It prevents the enjoyment of that which is accorded to us, and our cruel imagination is no longer occupied with anything but what is forbidden to us.

Grumedan and Romarin, the latter under the name of Melinette, in competition with one another, gave the object of their amour amusements continually, and sought to prove her all the sentiments by which they were animated.

To begin with, Romarin made use of the birds that I have mentioned; he had them all pronounce Pimprenelle's name; he made them sing it in the morning, and, carefully regulating the most fortunate sounds of their throats, the entire atmosphere resounded with the name of the rarest beauty, and all of them sang the praises of his discreet and constant amour.

Grumedan thought that idea had nothing new, that birds had always sung since the origin of the world and that lovers had always heard the guests of the woods talking about nothing but the objects of their amour. Unfortunately for Pimprenelle, he had read a few new operas, and the scant taste or presumption that he had, he had taken from those fine works; he therefore wanted to engender something absolutely new, for novelty in the genre of amusements has inconceivable charms. Whatever it is, when one can say that it has not yet appeared, everything is said, and the thing must be admirable.

He imagined, very agreeably, forming a concert that had never been heard, and which gave him an infinite pleasure. It was a gathering of a thousand frogs, which his great power assembled. He inspired them with the scant harmony that he imagined, and what he thought he knew about the art of singing. That frightful racket, that croaking repeated a thousand times, caused him a contentment that I cannot describe. He could not hide the satisfaction he experienced; he repeated his own eulogy a thousand times, sometimes with regard to the choice of performers, sometimes the novelty of the words, but always in an importunate tone. The words of which he was so proud caused him to sweat blood and water in order to complete their production; nevertheless, they were very trivial. Here they are, as they were repeated to me:

Adorable Pimprenelle
Always the belle,
What fires you start
In my amorous heart.

A gross genius like Grumedan is unable to set limits to his self-esteem, or put an end to its flattery. The concert was, therefore, as long as an Italian opera usually is—which is to say that it lasted nearly five full hours, without the slightest variety in the words. Pimprenelle, as one can imagine, would have died of the boredom during the concert and the lengthy repetitions if Romarin had not been present. He entertained

119

her ardently during the time when Grumedan was occupied in making the frogs exhale, to which he did not give the slightest rest. I am assured that he even caused a large number of the performers to perish.

In order to amuse the princess, Romarin made fortunate use of the stream I mentioned: he caused to appear—accurately, in miniature—the whole of Cleopatra's fleet, precisely and entirely as magnificent as history depicts it to us. All the vessels with crimson sails could be seen in the distance making all the maneuvers of ancient navigation. On the richest and most beautiful of the ships, Cleopatra was distinguishable by her beauty as well as her magnificence; when she reached the place where Pimprenelle was sitting, all the ships lined up, and the proud queen disembarked and came to present to the princess the superb pearl of which there is so much talk in history, saying: "You are more beautiful than I ever was; let my example serve to enable you to make better use of your beauty." Then she re-embarked, and the entire tiny fleet, the aspect of which was charming, continued on its way, and was perceived all the way to the extremity of the princess's little garden.

Grumedan was present at that little amusement. "I don't find anything pretty," he said, "in all those little people; they're marionettes. That's a fine way to give a pearl; why didn't you say, Madame, that you love them?" Immediately, he took a large whistle out of his pocket, and immediately, the water on the stream was seen to swell and become very muddy. In a moment, more than a hundred thousand oysters appeared, the shells of which opened in front of Pimprenelle and they all disgorged at her feet pearls of various sizes, but all admirable.

"That's how to produce pearls!" cried Grumedan. It is true that there were enough of them to sand the entire garden.

The following day, during the princess's walk, when she least expected it, Romarin suddenly constructed an arbor, mingled simply with flowers, which spelled out the monogram of the name Pimprenelle. Out of respect, more than fear of the genius, he dared not add his own to it. Seats of moss and grass, springs that ran in the corners and formed a natural ornament, without being subjugated to an exact symmetry, the murmur and freshness of which were charming, rendered the abode delightful. The repast was rural, but the rarest fruits, very agreeably arranged, formed its central ornament. A few invisible bagpipes played amorously, and only made themselves heard appropriately. Romarin read Pimprenelle's heart so well that at the slightest appearance of tedium, the music stopped. One of the princess's favorite nightingales, which really did have the most beautiful voice in the world, flew over the fruit singing brunettes and dance tunes.

"Oh! Who taught you so much, my dear Rigdi?" asked Pimprenelle.

The well-instructed bird simply replied; "Amour."

Grumedan was in an ill humor throughout that feast; he thought it insipid; he declared that the bagpipes did not make enough sound, and he criticized the birds. "What!" he said. "Will I always see birds? Furthermore, what is a picnic without crockery and a sideboard?"

In fact, he gave her one the following day in another corner of the garden. During the night he had built a cabinet of solid gold. The monograms of the princes and the genius were not forgotten, for they were distributed both inside and out. He had taken even greater care not to forget the sideboards; there were two of them, in fact, laden with riches and useless items, at which the eye could not gaze. The meal was composed of hot meats, heavily served; everything was cuisine of the old school. Grumedan ate like a demon, although Pimprenelle hardly tasted anything. At the fruit, about which there was nothing remarkable except the flying plates of glittering diamond, he said: "No singers or music, you've had enough of them; I only like noise when I make it, but your beauties won't be celebrated any less for that. Then, with a rustic smile, he sang the beautiful words he had written for the concert of frogs; at least he spared her the accompaniment this time.

In the desire to vary Pimprenelle's amusements—it is true that that was his first and only intention, but the second might well have had for his object the ridicule that Grumedan as always ready to pour when he was presented with a new idea—Romarin imagined giving her a nocturnal fête, and whatever Grumedan had said, he made use once again of the birds, but he employed all those in the region, as many great as small; he charged them with variously colored paper lanterns, and, following the orders he gave them, they set forth simultaneously and, when it was least expected, came together in the air, hovering and formed a temple in which all the orders could be distinguished perfectly; on the fronton, the words *To the divine Pimprenelle* were clearly visible.

When the temple had been remarked sufficiently, the birds scattered without order in the sky, which they filled with an infinite number of lights, very pleasant to the eye. Then they came back, following the orders they had received, to different meeting-points, and formed a bouquet in which all the flowers were easy to distinguish, either by the precision of the outline or the colors with which the lanterns were charged. While the bouquet appeared, other birds that could not be perceived, because they were not carrying any lights, spread in the air the distilled essences of the flowers designed for the eye, which produced a delightful rain, not only for Pimprenelle's abode but also for the entire town, attracted by a spectacle so novel in every respect.

Grumedan was a spectator at that fête; he was rather scornful of it. In an armchair, with one leg crossed over the other, his nose in the air, he could not help saying: "Oh, as for fireworks, if you like them, beautiful Pimprenelle, you only had to say so; you'll see some tomorrow in my fashion."

The next day produced an assembly of all the exhalations that are commonly called will-o'-the-wisps; he made them do exercises in a great plain that Pimprenelle could see from her windows. After Grumedan had said a hundred times over: "That's pretty, isn't it, my princess?" he suddenly caused a volcano to emerge from the ground, which threw off fire and flames, and spread torrents of fire all over the plain. He ornamented that agreeable and elegant spectacle with a few earthquakes. The loud laughter that gripped him at the fear of all the people cannot be expressed; nor is it possible to repeat all the stupid things he said on that subject.

"But after all," he continued, "Yesterday's fête had no conclusion. All firework displays at the town hall are crowned by a ball, aren't they? So Melinette didn't understand anything of the amusement she was giving you."

With those words he made the number of will-o'-the-wisps appear necessary to illuminate the princess's garden, and Grumedan, enchanted by his imagination, had a ball commence, composed of all the yew trees in the garden. It lasted a long time, for his own pleasure, even after the departure of Pimprenelle, who had retired, following the advice of Melinette, as soon as it was possible and decorous to do so.

Those were almost all the amusements that were provided for Pimprenelle. The poor princess was desolate as the importunity of Grumedan and the chagrin of not seeing the handsome Romarin, who, for his part, was itching under the constraint to which the most boorish of genni reduced him. In sum, no one was content, for Grumedan, stupid and coarse as he was, being in love, could see clearly that he was importunate and sensed that he was not making any progress in Pimprenelle's heart. That same amour did not allow him to be unaware that everything lively and attentive he had seen could not only be the marks of amity of a fay as sage as Melinette. He therefore became jealous—a trifle belatedly, in truth, but he nevertheless arrived.

Jealousy, that barbaric goddess, is only nourished by sentiments, intelligence is unnecessary to her, and she also resembles amour in finding means to arrive at her goal.

Those who have received the most intelligence at birth are often those who are the dupe of the crudest snares. In order to clarify the suspicions that had struck him, Grumedan apologized for having to leave on important business. He appeared afflicted to be obliged to separate himself from Pimprenelle; in sum, he made adieux that were very well received. When he was thought to be far away, Romarin was obliged to yield to the gentle violence that the princess exerted on him to cease being invisible.

Scarcely were they intoxicated by the pleasure of seeing one another again, and that of loving one another, than Grumedan suddenly emerged from a flower-bed in the garden, which opened up. The sight of Romarin authorized his jealousy and gave birth to his fury.

What satisfaction there is for a brutal man in seeing his hatred and ill humor well-founded. I have seen husbands outraged by their discoveries experience nevertheless a sort of pleasure in having been right.

Grumedan raised his club furiously, which could have fractured Romarin's skull. Pimprenelle did not doubting that his design had been executed, fell unconscious. As for the prince, he only escaped the bleak fate that threatened him thanks to the care of Melinette, who hid him cleverly from Grumedan's fury and transported him to her palace of clouds.

The cares of the genius recalled Pimprenelle to life, albeit with great difficulty, but how dolorous the consciousness she recovered was, for both of them. Pimprenelle, not seeing Romarin, after having accused herself of culminating the misfortunes she experienced, did not disguise from the genius any of the hatred that she had for him and the amour that she still had for her dear Romarin. She would have attempted to take her life a thousand times over, but the genius was too attentive to her movements for it to be possible for her to kill herself.

"My dear Romarin," cried Pimprenelle, dolorously, "you are no more, and my excess of amour has caused your misfortune. I wanted to see you; it has cost you your life; and to complete my woes, I am forced to survive you. Grumedan is glorying in your death, and I cannot doubt my misfortune; if you were alive, you would not leave me unaware of it; my despair would pierce your heart, you whom I have seen agonized by the slightest pain I felt. Your delicacy and perfect amour would not permit you to abandon me to the most horrible of genii. The absence of Melinette also proves my misfortune; she has abandoned someone she only loved because of you; I am odious to her. How I pardon you, divine fay, for detesting me! I detest myself, but in order to punish me for longer, you do not want to kill me."

Those words were the ones that Pimprenelle repeated incessantly, and the presence of Grumedan rendered their vivacity more eloquent.

It might have appeared thus far in this true story that Grumedan was as vulgar and as amorous as it as possible for him to be, in consequence of the fact that brutality held in his heart the place occupied by delicacy in Romarin's. At the commencement of these reproaches, the genius suffered them with a sort of impatience, but finally, he became accustomed to them, and formed the project most worthy of his character.

"You are making my unhappiness, little Pimprenelle, and I am determined to make yours; have no doubt about it. You might love or might not love your bauble Romarin, but you will be my wife, be even more certain of that than that you won't die."

The unfortunate Pimprenelle, having nothing but a faint to oppose to those words, lost consciousness.

The genius prolonged that faint until his return. He left Pimprenelle's retreat ad wanted to make an entrance into Giroflée's palace. Heavy as he was, he became heavier still, and mounted a chariot that was more like a cart; the wheels were full and massive and the shafts were as thick as two stout oak trees, but in fact, the whole machine was gold. He ordered forty-eight Auvergne oxen, the largest and strongest that the land had ever produced. They seemed scarcely sufficient to pull it, and the chariot, massive as it was, seemed liable to collapse under its own weight. He was leaning on a club, and held on his knees, with a sort of negligence, one of the largest lions in Africa, as many people in Paris have the habit of having lapdogs in their carriages to keep them company.

That equipage appeared at the gate of the city and took the road to the palace at about seven o'clock in the morning. Giroflée was already booted to go hunting; as for Filigrane, it would have been necessary for her to be woken up, she had only just gone to sleep, and no one in the court, least of all the king, would have dared to wake her. The king thought himself obliged to await the visit, and had his boots removed with extreme difficulty.

The city was large, so the journey was long, all the more so as the affluence of people slowed it down at every step. When the forty-eight oxen had turned around in the grand courtyard of the palace, Grumedan shouted in a voice that was naturally hoarse, whose loudness he increased further: "Where is he, then, this king? I want to talk to him—and summon his wife!"

Giroflée did not miss a single one of those words; they seemed to him to be slightly rude, but having consulted his favorite huntsman, who was fundamentally a rather good fellow, he made the decision to descend from his apartment and go to see for himself what was wanted of him.

When he was next to the vehicle, Grumedan said to him: "Put it there," holding out his hand. "Put it there, Giroflée, my friend, don't you know me?"

"No," said the king, in a rather embarrassed voice.

"I'm the genius Grumedan. I've come to make your fortune. Let's go upstairs; I want to talk to you."

For that he got down; he ordered the oxen to return to their affairs, and unhitched them himself. Nimbler than deer, they fled so promptly that they were lost to sight in an instant. Then he gave his chariot a tap with his club, which converted it into a heap of gold coins, which remained current in the realm for a long time, and a few of which can still be seen in cabinets of curiosities.

"I'm giving that to your servants as a tip," he said.

In sum, all he kept of his equipage was the lion I mentioned.

The cries of all those who were choking one another in order to get at the gold coins woke the queen. She rang in order to have those who were showing such scant respect hanged, but when she was told that there was a gentleman who wanted to talk to her, she thought that everyone had lost their minds, all the more so as there was also talk of oxen, gold, a club a big man and a lion. All her maidservants wanted to tell her about some particularity of what they had not seen, and what had been told to them confusedly.

In the meantime, the king was chatting to the genius, and found his conversation much to his taste. Giroflée had asked the genius in vain what could have attracted him to his court; the genius had always replied that he only wanted to tell him in the presence of the queen. She had therefore been asked several times to go to the king's apartment, but no one had been able persuade her to appear; she had not slept and she had a headache. How could she dare show herself; she would have looked like a mad dog.

All those affectations did not impress the giant; he till said that it was necessary for him to talk to her, but as he desired to please her, he asked a few courtiers who were standing in the room to take her his club, asking her to be kind enough to touch it—which was, he said, a proven and sovereign remedy to cure the worst headaches. Four of them were obliged to take it.

Extraordinary things sometimes find favor with ladies. Filigrane, with an attitude that was both scornful and complaisant, had the club brought to her; she felt it, and her headache disappeared instantly. It remains doubtful whether it was specifically the odor of the wood that operated the miracle, or whether it is necessary to attribute it to the large number of adornments that fell from the club at the moment when Filigrane touched it. Either way, such an agreeable prodigy made up the queen's mind; she promptly donned her royal mantle over a dressing gown, put on old diadem of diamonds on top of her night-cap, quickly applied a mass of rouge to each of her cheeks—which is to say, from the eyelid to the chin—and in that equipage, still hiding her nose with a large fan because of the broad daylight, she arrived in the throne room, muttering all sorts of complaints.

The genius came to meet her, more politely than was usual for him. He placed himself between the king and the queen. The entire court withdrew, out of respect, and the genius then said "My name is Grumedan and I am from the best and also the most ancient nation of genii. My power is a thousand times greater than my strength; however, all the many advantages that I unite within myself have succumbed, unable to resist the charms of your daughter Pimprenelle. I love her madly. I know full well that she does not love me, but I can't live without her. A certain coxcomb named Romarin, whom you knew, was able to please her, but I believe that he will no longer be an obstacle to my desires, in view of the fashion in which I treated him a few days ago. He was the young son of a king who doesn't have so much as a copper mine in his Estates. At any rate, I've purged the world of him. You can well believe that if I wanted to, I'd have no need of your consent to marry your daughter, but it's necessary that I obtain it because of a certain prude named Melinette, who protected little Romarin, and whom I have reason to handle carefully."

Filigrane and Giroflée were equally fearful of a son-in-law as terrible as the one who was proposing himself; however, with rather embarrassed expressions, they told the genius that his alliance would do them a great deal of honor, but that they would be glad to know a little more, in order that their subjects would not make them any reproaches for making the heir presumptive of the crown marry a genius that they did not know.

To that, Grumedan responded: "I'd gladly grant you a few days to get to know me, but I've detected in your minds that the dread of losing your kingdom worries you more that you've indicated to me. Don't worry, I'll give you sixty more, if you like them. In the meantime, I'll send for your daughter, in order for you to determine her yourselves to give me her hand."

With those words he took out of his pocket the large whistle that he had used to summon the oysters; it was his favorite instrument. At the noise it made, the lion, which was waiting tranquilly by the door to the street, arrived at his feet. He had no fear that anyone would steal it, because it had a collar with his coat of arms, on which his name was inscribed, which, combined with little bells, rendered its adornment complete.

"Mirtil," he said to it, "go fetch the princess. Bring her here very gently, right away."

At those words, Mirtil , running lightly, soon reached the extremity of the gardens. He made a gap in the troops guarding the princess's retreat. With a sweep of his tail he broke down the door, and loaded the princess, still unconscious, on his back, which he made into a sofa as best he could, and holding her clothes in his mouth, he returned in less than a quarter of an hour to the throne room, where Grumedan, Giroflée and Filigrane were having a conversation that was fundamentally quite trivial.

The arrival of the unfortunate princess, visiting her parents for the first time, was a rather singular spectacle. Grumedan then made her feel the tip of his club.

Scarcely had she opened her eyes than, on perceiving Grumedan, she uttered a dolorous scream, and would infallibly have fallen back into the state from which she had just emerged without the aid of Grumedan's smelling salts—which is to say, his club.

Pimprenelle's cries and tears continued, in spite of the strangers by whom she found herself surrounded, for great dolors are not retained, even when there are people present.

In spite of the dolor by which her daughter was overwhelmed, Filigrane, outraged by the excessive beauty she had by comparison with herself, approached her with a false expression of amity and interest that is all too common in the world. She proposed taking her to her apartment and having her put to bed, in order to let her rest, promising not to talk to her again about the matter that Grumedan had just raised with them, but that was more to render herself mistress of her person and to prevent her from being admitted by the entire court; she put a large handkerchief over her face, took her under the arm and guided her personally to her apartment, She had a camp bed set up in her wardrobe, and did not want anyone to serve her; under the pretext of letting her rest, she prevented anyone from seeing her.

As for the king, he addressed the genius and said to him: "We have nothing more to do here today; would you like to go hunting? My equipage is ready, and I know the whereabouts of one of the largest wild boars."

The genius accepted the proposal, the largest carriage horses in the small stables were equipped for his usage, and the two departed together. Let us leave them to hunt, to catch or not to catch, and return to the handsome Romarin.

The reader will remember the real obligation that he had to the good Melinette when the genius surprised him with Pimprenelle. She had no sooner saved him from the fury of the genius than, putting him in her chariot, she took him, as I have said, to her palace of clouds; but you do not know what that mansion was. It was a kind of retreat that she had had built, and which she often preferred to residing on the ground. She was not disturbed by any noise there; she worked there, she rested there, and in sum, did whatever she liked there. The palace was superb, and as it was situated in the highest clouds, the sun, whose rays were never obscured, shone there incessantly in all its purity.

So, it was there that Melinette took Romarin. He was not sensible, as one can imagine, to any of the beauties of the palace, nor to its singularities.

"What!" he said incessantly to Melinette. "You love me, but I shall never see Pimprenelle again! You've conserved my life, but you've abandoned such a rare beauty to the fury of Grumedan."

"Don't worry, my dear Romarin," said the good Melinette. "The full extent that the power of fays can have is,

130

as you know, limited by a few decrees of Destiny. Believe that everything I can do for you, I will certainly put into execution. I am leaving you the master here, you cannot lack anything; my butterflies and my favorite swallows are under orders to obey no one but you. Adieu, I am quitting you; let my amity give you hope."

Romarin did not think that Melinette had spoken in a sufficiently positive tone; he did not find in her words the consolation that she had mentioned, but everything necessary to afflict himself, for sadness and chagrin are artful in nourishing themselves. He therefore abandoned himself to the most baleful ideas.

As soon as the fay had quit him, he had no doubt that he would be separated forever from all that he adored, and, unable to survive his dolor, he precipitated himself a thousand times from the highest windows of the palace and launched himself from the top of all the terraces, but in vain. The clouds had orders to watch over his conservation; they were careful not to relax their attention.

Firmly convinced that it was not possible for him to take his life, Romarin addressed the cruelest and most barbaric epithets a hundred times over. Finding the light of the sun too bright for the sad situation of his heart, he abandoned the most agreeable and most magnificent apartments, ornamented and furnished with a taste that is rarely seen in great palaces; he disdained those superb surroundings and chose for his habitation one of the cellars of the palace—in which, in truth, obscurity was not spread, but it was assuredly not his fault if the daylight followed him. The light by which one saw there, and the air that one respired there, imitated the densest fogs of winter—I cannot give a more accurate idea of it than that— and it was there that he moaned as he wished, pronounced the name of Pimprenelle, and incessantly summoned death to his aid.

One day, when he was more afflicted than ever, he was thinking about his sad destiny, while recalling the beauty and the intelligence of Pimprenelle and retracing the memory of his past happiness, he heard a voice singing that was not unfamiliar to him. The sound of that voice struck him, even less than the words and the name of Pimprenelle. It was, in fact, one of the verses he had made for his adorable mistress. He emerged with ardor from his somber retreat. At the same instant, the faithful and charming Rigdi appeared to him.

Romarin's joy was unimaginable.

The faithful nightingale told him that a swallow from the palace where he was living had begged one of his cousins in his presence to carry out a commission for her, and that he had heard in their conservation that Melinette had doubled the service in her palace to guard Prince Romarin, and had in consequence learned the place of his residence. He had hoped to have information about Pimprenelle, and to bring relief to his pains, but that she had fainted at the same moment and had been unconscious for more than twenty-four hours.

Then he told the prince everything that had happened since his departure, and everything you have already read. Dissolving in tears at that point in the story, he told him that, unconscious as she was, a huge lion had me to take her away, that he had been unable to discover what had become of her, and that he had made the decision to come and weep, to share the affliction and to die with his dear master.

The arrival of Rigdi had at first been one of the greatest contentments that Romarin could have, but the news that he had brought put the cap on his misfortunes. His desire to die was redoubled, but the mild conversation of the amiable bird was, at least, a consolation for the unhappy lover. That is the condition that the inhabitant of the palace of clouds was in.

It seems to me that we left Grumedan and King Giroflée going hunting together. They did that in fact, and, with the king prettily mounted and the genius trotting on a great cart-horse, the hunt commenced.

Grumedan released his huge lion, Mirtil, and at the same instant, the boar was knocked over and torn to pieces. The king cried out in vain: "You're not hunting by the rules!"

"What does it matter," said Grumedan, "As long as I catch it?"

The huntsmen shrugged their shoulders at that manner of acting and speaking, and the king replied to them—when Grumedan was no longer looking—and made them a sign that it was necessary to pardon something in a man that was not yet *au fait*, and who was only on his first hunt.

They returned to the palace, and they had supper, as all hunters ordinarily do, without talking about anything other than large beasts, dogs, huntsmen, horses etc. The genius proposed an ogre hunt for the next day. It was easy for him to make the utility felt, and the novelty of the diversion piqued the appetite of all the huntsmen.

In spite of the exactitude of those who have given me memoirs and the care I have taken in assembling them, I am obliged to admit that the details of that jolly excursion have not reached me. I only know that a page of the company was eaten, and that the ogre, who was made to run, would not have stopped on such a fine route if Grumedan had not felled him with a blow of his club.

After a hunt as fine as that one, the genius, on returning to the palace, went to see the queen in order to beg her to make up her mind promptly and engage Pimprenelle to follow his will. He found Filigrane very obliging in his favor; the annoyance of seeing her daughter as beautiful as she was had advance the marriage considerably. They made their contract in that last interview, and the secret articles were that the kingdom would belong to Giroflée and to her throughout their lives and that Pimprenelle would never appear in any place where she was.

Grumedan consented to everything; in order to complete his contentment, the wedding day was fixed for the day after next, and in order to give some certainty to the engagement they were making, they found no gentler means than giving the poor princess the choice of the husband or a poisoned cup, which would be on the altar set up for the marriage. That news did not frighten Pimprenelle. A few people in the court who still imagined that one cannot decide in favor of death attributed the cheerfulness with which she received the news to the insipid joy of young women when they are to be married.

In order to give evidence of the contentment that he felt, knowing that Filigrane loved fêtes, Grumedan resolved to give one for her and the entire court. He chose the next day, the eve of the wedding; absolutely no one knew what the diversion would be, for the genius had not consulted anyone; he had not wanted his production to be suspected of being the effect of the slightest advice.

Everyone arrived in the hall of the spectacle at the moment when he gave them permission; when everyone was seated and the curtain was raised, they saw with a kind of surprise the stage enclosed by thick iron bars, which nevertheless left enough space for the performance of the actors to be perceived. How astonished the members of the audience were when they saw huge bears appear, walking on their hind feet, which came to recite a pastoral in garments such as one sees at the Opéra. As can be imagined, the top register of the singer who was playing the lead role—a shepherd—was a terrible bass-baritone. Everything was complete, with regard to numbers, and the choruses were certainly well-filled.

The first act was executed quite tranquilly on the part of the actors, but as for the spectators, it is true that they did not know where to put themselves. The ballet that followed the act was rather agreeable, in fact, for it was performed by very knowledgeable and very adroit great apes. The next act was not as well represented; there was a scene of rivalry in the script; the bears took it personally, and a duel to the death immediately began. It was all the more terrible because the chorus joined in, and almost all the musicians perished; then people were very glad of the bars, which had been mocked on arrival.

There is nothing so common in society as seeing people who not only do stupid things, but sustain them afterwards without wanting to let go. Grumedan was among that number; he always sustained that it was by virtue of a reflection as fine as it was judicious that he had chosen bears to represent his diversion. "If I had known," he said, "of an animal as appropriate to the theater as a bear, since it can walk on its hind legs, and more malevolent than a bear, I would certainly have preferred it. Well, they had a quarrel, that's natural, and it isn't my fault."

All these poverties and several others, which, out of pity for the reader, I shall pass over in silence, were heeded, and were even applauded, because the genius, instead of fruits and ice creams, had had the entire court served with immense bowls of gold coins and baskets filled with diamonds. I am assured that nothing was returned to the pantries.

The day after that fine fête, the day destined for the marriage, Pimprenelle was taken to the throne rom. She was walking between Giroflée and Filigrane, who was pinching her lips in vain in an attempt to redden them and grimacing as best she could, outraged by the applause that the princess was attracting. When they arrived in the middle of the hall, Grumedan appeared with a toupee, an enormous purse and a huge knot in his cravat, clad in a silver raincoat larded with pink—very similar, in fact, to the way we see foreigners dressed when they arrive in Paris, partly by virtue of their taste and partly on the perfidious advice of their tailors.

He was triumphant, and could not imagine that anyone might prefer death to him. That was, however, what happened to him; for, in accordance with the proposed alternative, Pimprenelle seized the cup avidly and, raising her beautiful eyes to the havens, cried in a voice that drew tears from the eyes of all the spectators: "Oh, my dear Romarin, how glad I am to lose a life that I cannot spend with you!"

At the moment when she was about to swallow the fatal cup, the windows of the palace opened, and Melinette appeared, splendidly glorious, mounted on the brightest cloud in the sky. Romarin, as beautiful as the daylight, was serving as her squire.

135

They entire court was surprised, and also somewhat dazzled. Pimprenelle perceived her lover, dropped the cup and ran to him.

Grumedan tried to put himself on the defensive as soon as he saw Melinette appear, but the fay, approaching on the side of his blind eye—for you will remember that he was one-eyed, although his favorite oath was that of saying: "By my eyes!"—seized him by one of his eyebrows, which were very well-furnished, lifted him up in the middle of the hall and caused him to dance about for a while in order to demonstrate her superiority; then she touched him with her wand and imprisoned him for a thousand years in the ball of a crystal chandelier.

"Receive the price," she said, "of your ferocity, and the scorn you had for me."

Then she married our lovers, to which she rightly gave the kingdom to govern, for Girofléee and Filigrane, to tell the truth, hardly governed it any longer.

The generosity of the newlyweds, who did not want to accept the kingdom, could not resist Melinette's orders. The king and queen were given, in their retreat, everything that could suit their tastes. Pimprenelle and Romarin appointed the faithful Rigdi as their prime minister. They were adored by their subjects, and they had charming children; it is said that they always loved one another, and were perfectly happy in the matter of sentiments. I would like to believe it.

THE GIFTS[23]

The Fay of the Flowers lived in a palace and held court in the midst of fountains and gardens. The Trianon and Marly were only deformed copies of that delightful abode. The places that we have chosen and ornamented ordinarily depict our character, so all the delights of Nature were assembled in that pleasant retreat. The charms of her society are inexpressible but the qualities of her heart were at least equal to them; not only did she help the unfortunate, but she took pleasure in going beyond their needs, while leaving them unaware that they were indebted to her. It was sufficient for her to oblige.

Her court was made up of young princes and princesses—for she loved children. She raised them from their earliest childhood or invited them to come to her, at thirteen for one sex and sixteen for the other. She usually endowed them with the gift that they desired to obtain. That was how the Fay of the Flowers composed her court and lived in the veritable delights of heart and mind, very different in that respect from other fays, who have not always known the pleasure of obliging, the only one that can make authority bearable when one is sage.

Without going into detail about the beautiful educations she had enabled, I shall only talk about Silvie, whom she loved as much as she merited being; her childhood was naïve, her character was lively but docile. Those presents of Nature gave birth to and nourished her amity for the lovable child.

When Silvie reached the age at which the fay distributed her gifts, she wanted to make her known to herself, and, without informing her of that design, to several princesses that she had endowed, in order that she could decide more sanely on the choice she had to make. "I want you, my dear Silvie," she

---

[23] The version in *The Green Fairy Book* is entitled "The Fairy Gifts."

said to her, "to go and spend some time with princesses I have endowed with different gifts. They will receive you well; have no anxiety; all that you have to do is render me an account, when you return, of the impression their character has made on you.

Silvie promised the good fay to carry out her orders and to obey the governess she gave her, and quit her with a great deal of regret. She was absent for two months. At the end of that time, the fay sent her the same equipage that had taken her away from her court, and Silvie returned to the good Fay of the Flowers with an infinite contentment. She answered all the questions that were put to her and thanked her for all the generosity that had been lavished upon her on her behalf.

The fay having asked for a more detailed account of her voyage, this is approximately what Silvie replied.

"You sent me, Madame, to the court to Iris, and I leaned from other women that it is you who have endowed her with beauty. She praised your generosity continually, but she never went into detail; it is necessary to pardon her; one does not like to owe one's beauty to someone else—at least, one doesn't like to admit it.

"I noticed that the beauty that you have given her, which appeared to me to be dazzling, took away from her absolutely the use of her intelligence; that in showing herself, and letting herself be seen, she believed that she had done everything. Sometime after my arrival in her court, she contracted a malady. The fear that her beauty might be depleted perhaps made her malady more considerable than it need have been; she resisted its most violent attacks, but her return to life appeared to me to be replete with woe, since, in fact, the beauty with which she was so content, had vanished to the point that she could no longer suffer herself. In the end, she was in such great despair that you see me greatly distressed by it, and I implore you to take pity on her.

"I promised to represent her misfortune to you," she added; "it is all the greater because I had time to converse with her, and I noticed that the words that the beauty she had had rendered supportable, and sometimes even agreeable, can no longer sustain her. They do not go, in sum, with ugliness; she feels that, and admits it herself; and her mind, which has never been occupied with it before, is continually agitated by dolor, without being able to do anything else.

"Judge, then, great fay," the amiable Silvie continued, "whether anyone in Nature has more need of experiencing your generosity than the unfortunate Iris."

"I am content with your reflections," the fay replied, "but I cannot help her; my power is limited, and I can only endow once."

After a sojourn in the delightful palace, the fay wanted young Silvie to quit it, for the same reasons. The same chagrins were testified and felt, but as soon as the butterflies were harnessed, young Silvie was transported, with her governess, to another realm: the one inhabited by Princess Daphne.

Silvie found the means to give a note to the first butterfly she encountered, to take to the fay, which it did. In that note she implored her not to let her absence last any longer long; it was, however, not yet a fortnight since she had departed from the palace of flowers. The fay granted her request and allowed her to return.

In order to satisfy her duty and to relieve her heart, Silvie cried: "Oh, Madame, where have you sent me this time?"

"To one of those who asked me for the gift of eloquence," the fay replied.

"How poorly eloquence suits a woman," said Silvie, with vivacity. "It's true that Princess Daphne speaks beautifully; her words are exact and well-chosen, but she never shuts up. She always begins by charming and ends up annoying. She loves more than anything the assembly of her Council, for it furnishes a thousand opportunities to talk, which no one can interrupt, so she prefers that duty of royalty to all the others. But what is more astonishing is that on emerging from the Council, she is only more enthusiastic for all the conversations that present themselves."

The Fay of the Flowers could see clearly that Silvie was sufficiently disgusted with eloquence. She gave her time to recover from the fatigue she had just experienced, and in spite of all the pleas she made not to travel any longer, young Silvie was obliged to obey her again The same carriage took her to the home of Silvanire, and she resided in that fay's court for more than three months.

When the fay thought her return necessary, she sent word to her, and Silvie came back to her with the contentment that brings us closer to those for whom we have a veritable and tender amity.

The curious fay, as usual, wanted to examine the impressions that Silvie had received from a prices as amiable as Silvanire, whom she had endowed with the gift of pleasing others. This was the young pupil's response:

"It appeared to me at the commencement of my absence that Silvanire was the most fortunate princess on earth, ornamented by your generosity with the fine gift of pleasing, combined with the splendor of youth. What mortal, I said to myself, can be happier on earth? A thousand lovers crowd around her, anticipating at every moment the slightest of her desires; fêtes, gallantry, sacrifices, the forgetfulness of the whole world—in sum, everything that can flatter self-esteem—is incessantly offered. I began by being persuaded that I would obtain a similar gift from your generosity."

"What? You don't intend to ask me for it?" said the fay.

"No, Madame, in truth," said Silvie, "And these are the reasons that prevent me from doing so. Seduced to begin with by the appearances of Silvanire's situation, I found all those lovers the most agreeable species of humankind; it appeared to me that the authority that Silvanire had over them was the acme of felicity; but after having made a closer acquaintance with the princess, I saw that her happiness was not real, that her heart was not satisfied and that the dissipations of self-esteem were not sufficient to occupy her heart. I understood that Silvanire abused the gift of pleasing, and that what she practiced was the coquetry for which you had inspired me with so much horror.

"Not content with the discoveries I had made by the examination of Silvanire, I followed the impressions that her procedures had made on those who were most strongly attached to her; I saw her flame gradually relenting, that the generosities, the attentions and the provocations that she was obliged to make in order to maintain their passion no longer made any impression on them, that they ceased to be flattered by them, and that in remarking that all those things were general, they were ashamed of having been duped by them, and that scorn was often their final sentiment."

"I'm content with your reflections," the Fay of the Flowers said to her. "Enjoy the repose of my gardens and the real charms of the life one leads here."

Silvie received those orders with satisfaction, but everything that she had seen and had not contented her embarrassed her extremely, for she could not decide on the request that she had to make.

At the end of a certain time, the fay wanted to send her away again, and Silvie's docility was obliged to subscribe to it; there was the same carriage, the same adieux, the same regrets, a similar return, similar pleasures on Silvie's part in finding the amiable fay again and similar questions on her part, to which this was Silvie's response:

"I was received, as you had been yourself, by Aglaia, to whose home you had sent me. She put to use the vivacity with which you have endowed her. Everything brilliant that intelligence and imagination can have of the seductive, Aglaia showed me almost momentarily. That desire to please me was founded on the obligation she conserves for you; my self-esteem, however, also played a part for her.

"I was dazzled, I admit, by the lively fashion with which she is able to occupy her court, and that gift of your generosity seemed to me to avoid all the inconveniences of the others that you wanted me to judge for myself. For a week I could not imagine that I could desire anything else, and that charm appeared to me to be one of the most essential for society. However, a longer examination of such a character has engaged me not to ask it of you."

"And what reasons have you for excluding that gift from those I can accord you?" the fay asked her.

"I noticed," Silvie replied, "that extreme vivacity has for society the same faults that coquetry has for sentiment—which is to say that neither one can give a full and entire satisfaction. Furthermore, I gradually became accustomed to that vivacity; it ceased to surprise me, and then it became distasteful to me, because I noticed that often, in order to maintain it, people said things too lightly, which became dangerous in consequence; and I finally perceived that the same vivacity often needed the help of intrigue to be sustained, and even more often that of trickery; and that in sum, vivacity employed everything without admitting any distinction."

The fay did not contradict Silvie's sage reflections; she praised them, and applauded herself for the good education that she had given her.

But when the time to endow her had come, and the fay summoned the entire youthful assembly to witness that solemnity, in the midst of which she loved to find herself, Silvie asked her for nonchalance,[24] and obtained it.

That character is divine; it usually leads to tenderness and all the charms of life at all ages.

Silvie did not, like a thousand others, ask for beauty for the sake of self-esteem and independently; the example of Iris had deterred her from that. She combined gentility with her

---

[24] The original has *un esprit paresseux*, which might be literally translated as "an indolent mind," (the Andrew Lang version renders it as "a quiet spirit") but in the next story Caylus uses the same phrase to characterize Nonchalante, so the substitution seems justified. The request seems odd however it is phrased, and the characterization of Nonchalante certainly does not make the gift seem as perfect as this story appears to want to assert.

beauty, she was made in such a fashion that if her attractions were disturbed by some inconvenience, or some chagrin, the strongest thing that could be said in talking about her change was: "Silvie is beautiful today, but I'm anxious about her"; and if, on the contrary, joy and good health reigned in her, grace and gentility produced the prettiest of all faces.

Silvie thus enjoyed fully the fay's gift, and the sagacity of the wish that formed it.

NONCHALANTE AND PAPILLON[25]

There was once a king and queen who lived in the great-est union, and that tender union succeeded the most ardent and the most thwarted passion of which mention was every heard, By virtue of the graces of her person, those of her mind and, above all, the tenderness of her heart, the queen, whose name was Santorée, merited all the sentiments that her husband, Gris-de-Lin, had for her.

The latter sovereign was all the more lovable because he had conserved on the throne all the virtues and charms of an ordinary individual, so no one doubted that a fay had presided over his birth. In fact, that fay, without having been contra-dicted by any of her companions, after giving evoked all the dead ancestors of Gris-de-Lin, had taken a virtue from each of them, as well as a charm, in order to form the character of a prince whom she wanted to oblige. Unfortunately, she gave him a dose of tenderness that was a little too strong; the mis-fortunes of honest people rarely have any other cause.

At any rate, no prince was ever happier than Gris-de-Lin. He loved as much as one can love an object worthy of his amour; that lovable object responded perfectly to his tender-ness, and what is more, he was the king of a very beautiful kingdom; but so many favors of fortune cannot be of long duration.

The beautiful Santorée fell gravely ill while bringing into the world a charming daughter who was named Nonchalante. The king, by virtue of respect for the mother, did not want that pledge of their union to be endowed. He did not doubt that, if she resembled Santorée a little, she would be preferable to all the princesses on earth. But the fays do not always render sen-timents the justice that is their due. It appeared to them that

---

[25] The version of this story in *The Green Fairy Book* is entitled "Prince Vivien and the Princess Placida."

that procedure infringed their rights, and to punish the king for that they made the queen's illness worse. They announced to the unfortunate Gris-de-Lin the deadly consequences of the malady, and that the queen had died.

It is certain that, but for little Nonchalante, nothing in the world would have been able to determine the king to survive a spouse so tenderly beloved. For that sole reason, however, he consented to live, but it was with such a great sadness that he became incapable of conducting any business.

In spite of what had happened, the fay Lolotte took charge of the education of the little princess and that of Prince Papillon, Gris-de-Lin's nephew, who had been sent to Gris-de-Lin's court while not long out of the cradle, because he had been orphaned. Although nothing was neglected for the education of the two children, they both proved that the cares that were taken could only reduce the faults of nature, without destroying them absolutely.

Nonchalante, both beautiful and pretty, perfectly well made, with a mind capable of anything, had a depth of indifference for all events that is difficult to express. Papillon, by contrast, charming of face, abused his vivacity; he seized even the greatest bagatelles with a surprising rapidity, and abandoned them with a similar promptitude.

As the two children were almost the same age, they reached at the same time that at which people could take an interest in them and form projects suitable to their character. Then sentiments were divided; tranquil people who loved peace saw in Nonchalante all the virtues they desired in their queen, while those animated by movement, partisans of the glory of the kingdom, hoped for everything from a prince like Papillon.

Those different fashions of thinking inevitably announced a civil war and division within the State; there was all the more reason to be apprehensive of that because the interior of the palace was not tranquil. The two amiable children, while rendering one another justice for their charms, nevertheless had an extreme mutual hostility caused by the opposition

145

of their characters, and that contradiction became an invincible obstacle to the marriage that everyone desired, and was the only thing capable of calming all minds.

Although he was very young, Papillon, who had a great deal of intelligence, sensed the advantages that he could obtain from a party that declared itself loudly in his favor. Either because he was determined by a sentiment of honor not to wrong his beautiful cousin, however, or because he wanted to satisfy his natural vivacity and levity, he formed the desire to seek adventures and travel incognito.

As soon as that idea presented itself to his mind, he put it into execution; fortunately, it came to him while he was mounted on a horse; if he had had his feet on the ground he might not have taken the time to ask his squire for one. He therefore departed, with no other project except to go away. At first, he was only occupied with leaving the realm. That unexpected departure threw the State into confusion, and a prince of whom such great hopes had been entertained, and whose fate was absolutely unknown, was generally regretted.

Utterly insensible as Gris-de-Lin was to all the events of life, he was touched by that loss, and although he could not see his daughter, the princess, without shedding torrents of tears, he wanted to judge her talents and her capacity for himself. Independently of the mental indolence with which she had been born, however, she had a fay with her who spoiled her as much as if she had been her grandmother. That fay had conceived for Nonchalante, since the moment of her birth, a misconceived amity, which is often more dangerous than hatred.

Gris-de-Lin perceived that, and could not help making reproaches to the good Lolotte. He made her admit her mistakes and she promised not to nourish the indifference of the princess any longer. In fact, she kept her word, and from that moment, poor Nonchalante had a great deal to suffer. She was obliged to occupy herself with the care of her adornment, the choice of her clothes and the variety of her pleasures. Rather than go into the slightest detail, however, she wore her old clothes, remained in great neglect, and never thought of appearing in public.

Things were not left there, however. Gris-de-Lin wanted people to talk to her about the affairs of her kingdom, and she appeared at the Council in order to give her opinion there, and to familiarize herself by that means with government. Then her palace and her Estates became importunate to her to such an extent that she implored Lolotte to take her away from a land where everything had become insupportable to her.

At first the fay refused very firmly to satisfy that whim, but what can the tears of the prettiest child in the world not accomplish, when she is beloved? Lolotte finally granted her request, and without making her quit a sofa that she preferred to all the other commodities of her apartment, she took her way to her grotto.

That second departure put all the subjects in despair, and Gris-de-Lin was as touched by it as he could be. But let us return to Papillon and see what his vivacity had enabled him to encounter.

Although Nonchalante's Estates were very extensive, the young prince's horse had sufficient strength to enable him to traverse them. That was all it could do, however, for scarcely had it crossed the frontier than it collapsed. Papillon was therefore obliged to go on foot, and although that fashion of traveling did not respond to his vivacity, it was nevertheless necessary for him to settle for it.

He found himself then in a forest whose respectable antiquity inspired a secret horror. He followed a path that seemed to him to be well beaten, but in spite of all the diligence of which he was capable he was overtaken by night. A little light that he perceived suspended his lassitude; he tired to approach it, but the more effort he made to reach it, the further it seemed to draw away. The unevenness of the terrain and the thickness of the wood often hid it from his eyes.

What a situation for an extremely lively prince who had never left a court and all of whose desires had, in consequence, been anticipated! Thus, one can say that he suffered that frustration with an extreme impatience.

Finally, unable to do any more by virtue of hunger and lassitude, he arrived in the vicinity of the light toward which he had been directing his steps for such a long time. It brought him to a wretched cottage. He knocked on the door rudely; an old woman answered it, but as she did not come quickly enough, he redoubled his blows and shouted in an authoritative tone—for it is with difficulty that one loses the habit of it.

The old woman, however, did not go any faster for that; she always responded simply and gently to whatever he said outside: "Patience." She seemed determined to open the door to him, but she took a long time before giving him that pleasure. He heard her chasing away her cat, for fear that it might go out when she opened the door. He distinguished clearly, by means of the conversation she had with herself, that she turned back in order to turn up her lamp, in order better to distinguish the person who was knocking on her door, and, perceiving that there was not enough oil in the lamp, she was obliged to fill it up. In brief, she did a thousand similar things while always responding: "Patience." Sometimes, she added: "My God, patience."

In sum, it was only after a long time that she finally opened the door.

The prince found nothing in that cabin but the image of poverty, and not the slightest appearance of nourishment. That sight almost put him in despair. He testified to the old woman his extreme fatigue and the excess of his appetite, but she made no other reply to him than the sad word: "Patience."

Coming to an examination of the help that she was able to give him, however, she said, in a mild tone: "You can have a bale of hay to sleep on. There it is, behind the door"—which she had taken great care to close again.

"And something to eat," Papillon added, brusquely.

"Wait," she replied. "Patience. I'll go pick some peas on the garden. We'll shell them placidly; then we'll light a fire, and then, when they're well-cooked, we can eat them without hurrying."

"And then I'll be dead," added the prince.

"Well, I don't go so quickly myself," replied the old woman, mildly, not without adding, still in accordance with her laudable custom: "Have patience," which was followed on this occasion, but the fine proverb: "Everything comes to he who can wait."

All these things were very hard to suffer, so Papillon was in a violent state, but what could he do? It was necessary to do things her way.

"Let's go pick the peas," said the good woman then. "Bring the lamp to light my way."

The prince obeyed her, but his promptitude extinguished the light several times; it was necessary to relight it with two little embers that were almost extinct and covered in ash, neatly piled up in the middle of the fireplace. Finally after much difficulty, the peas were picked; they returned to the house and succeeded in shelling them; and when the fire was lighted—which took a long time—it was necessary to count hem, for the old woman absolutely insisted on not cooking more than fifty-four of them. The prince represented the mediocrity of that number, and the scant importance that one pea more or less would have, but in vain. It was necessary again to do things her way.

The peas fell several times because of the prince's vivacity; in consequence, it was not only necessary to pick them up, but also to verify the count. Finally, they were put over the fire, and when they were almost cooked, the good woman took weighing scales from an old cupboard, took a small piece of bread, and set about dividing it up and weighing it. But Papillon did not give her the time; he threw himself upon it, ate it, and said to her in his turn: "Patience."

"You think you're joking," she said to him, still mildly, "but no; you've named me veritably, and you'll soon learn to know me."

They supped, however, and the twenty-seven peas that he had for his share, which she gave him very exactly, combined with a few glasses of very clear water, nourished him marvelously. He slept very tranquilly on the straw that she had promised him.

The following morning she gave him brown bread and milk for breakfast, which he ate wholeheartedly, delighted that there was nothing in that meal either to cook or to count. Then he asked her to tell him who she was.

"I consent to that," she said, "but it will take a long time."

"Well, in that case," said the prince, "I'll let you off."

"But it's necessary, at your age," the old woman said, "to listen to old people and accustom yourself to patience."

"But," he said, in a impatient tone, "it's also necessary for the old people not to wear us out." He continued: "Only tell me what the country is in which I find myself."

"Gladly," replied the old woman. "You're in the Forest of the Black Bird, and it's here that he renders his oracles."

"An oracle!" said the prince. "I'll go to consult it."

He tried to give the old woman some money, but she refused it. He threw it on the table and left like a streak of lightning, without having asked for the path he wanted to follow.

He took the first path that chanced to present itself in front of him and drew away, always running and often getting lost, without regret for a house that pleased him even less than the character of the woman who lived in it. He walked for some time, at random, but finally perceived in the distance a large building that towered over the entire forest, the color of which was black. That object, as lugubrious as it was singular, appeared to him to be the Temple in which the oracle was rendered that he was seeking.

He walked for a long time yet, however, and it was shortly before sunset that he arrived at the first gates of the Black Palace. It was surrounded by several enclosures of buildings and moats, the stones and water of which were the same color as the temple.

When he reached the first door he read, with difficulty, an inscription written in large letters of red-hot iron, which contained the words: *Mortal curious as to your destiny, strike the black bell, and be submissive to my worship.*

In order to carry out this instruction, the prince picked up a large stone and threw it at the bell, which rendered a terrible and cavernous sound. At that sound the door opened, and closed again with a prodigious rapidity as soon as he had entered. At the same instant, several million bats departed from the neighboring buildings, whose cries, and the obscurity they spread through the air, augmented the horror of the lace infinitely.

Anyone other than Papillon would have been frightened, but he walked with a firm and determined step as far as the second gate, which sixty black men clad in great black veils came to open for him. He tried to talk to them, but he recognized that his language was utterly foreign to them; the torment, which he did not yet know, of thinking ardently and not being able to make himself understood, reminded him sadly of the good woman Patience; but that was not all, for he was also obliged to submit to the sixty black men disarming him. After that afflicting ceremony, he was conducted vey civilly by the black ministers to a magnificent apartment, where ebony, jet and black curtains shone brightly.

Reduced to sign language, he expressed the need that he had to eat; and, also by signs, he was made to understand that in a few hours, he would be satisfied. In fact, they came to collect him—always with as much respect as slowness—in order to take him to a kind of refectory. He sat down there, along with all the black men, in the place designated for him; he saw several dishes placed before him; they were of various colors, but always including black.

He tried to take one of them in order to satisfy his hunger sooner, but he perceived that, like all the others, it was attached to the table, and he observed that his new but lugubrious company were only making use of drinking-straws, and that each one, as placidly as could be imagined, was sucking his portion. It was therefore necessary to make use of the drinking-straw that he found in front of him and eat in the same fashion, so little suited to his vivacity.

After the supper, they passed into a hall where the black men, two by two, began games of chess, which he was obliged to watch; when the last game—which was very competitive, and, in consequence, extremely long—had finished he was taken back to his apartment, still with the same slowness and still with the same respect.

The hope of consulting the oracle, and that of getting out of the sad abode, woke him up early in the morning. He testified the desire he had to go to the Temple, but without receiving any reply, he was taken to the baths, and made to understand that it was necessary to purify himself. He undressed swiftly and wanted to dive into the water, but the black men stopped him, and only permitted him to enter to the depth of an inch; and it was with great difficulty and great chagrin that he was made to understand that his bath would be augmented every day by a similar measure.

When he was convinced of that sad necessity, he lost patience completely; he implored, pressing by means of signs and even speech, although he was perfectly certain that no one understood anything he said, but it was all futile. It was necessary to submit, and sixty days passed in rendering his bath complete. Always eating with a drinking-straw, always observing silence, always guided and complimented slowly, and always watching games of chess—the game that was the most antipathetic of all to him—he finally succeeded in the good fortune of having water up to his chin.

The day after that fortunate day, the black men, clad in their black veils, each with a bat on his head, marching slowly, chanting nasally the most lugubrious of canticles, arrived with the prince at the gate that separated them from the interior of the Temple. In response to their chants, another troop of black men, who were marching much more slowly, came to receive

152

the unfortunate Papillon. The only difference he was able to remark between that cortege and the first was that the men who composed it each had a crow on his fist, the croaking of which became insupportable. The prince was then taken by the arms, not so much to do him honor as to contain him.

After a very long march they arrived at the first steps of the Temple. The prince thought he was at the end of his troubles, but they took more than two further hours to give him a black veil, after which he finally entered the Temple, where he spent at least as much time as a spectator of the various prayers that were offered there. The impatience of the prince was exhausted, and he had already been yawning continually, and probably scandalously, for some time, but nothing was capable of interrupting the order of ceremonies, and although he was their principal object, no one paid the slightest heed to the ennui that he displayed with such scant moderation.

The interior of the Temple, like the outside, was clad in the blackest marble; a great curtain, as black as everything else, separated it into two parts. After the thickest fumigations, that curtain was drawn, and the Black Bird appeared in all its majesty. It was a species of eagle, but much larger than a roc; it as perched on an iron bar, which traversed the Temple. At the sight of it, all the black men prostrated themselves, not daring to sustain its gaze.

When it had flapped its wings three times, and the air had been cleared three times, it pronounced these words distinctly, in Papillon's language:

"Prince, you will only be happy by means of what is opposite to you."

As soon as those words had been pronounced, the curtain closed again, and all the black men, as many from inside as outside the Temple, came very respectfully to kiss its two sides.

After that long ceremony, he was given a black crow for his fist, and taken back, just as slowly, to the gate, which opened as it had the first time. There he returned his crow, and was replaced in the hands of the first black men; a bat settled of its own accord on his head, and that escort took him back to his first abode, in order to take as many baths as he had already taken, in the reverse order. Then he was embraced by the last black men, who conducted him very civilly to the gate of the black bell, and returned his weapons to him with all possible signs and demonstrations of amity.

He responded very poorly to their politeness, for the door was no sooner opened than he started running with all his might, with no other design than getting away from a place in which he could not imagine that anyone could live. He repented a thousand times over of the curiosity that had engaged him to come and consult such a dismal oracle, which had not told him anything. He made a few reflections—very brief, in truth—on the futility and inconvenience of curiosity.

After several days of a very hard and very toilsome journey he emerged from the forest and found himself on the bank of a great river, the course of which he followed in the hope of finding some means of traversing it. He was in that embarrassment when one day, at sunrise, he perceived an object of dazing whiteness; his urgency was redoubled by that sight. He realized that it was a ship, the whitest, the best made and the prettiest in the world. It was moored in the great river, and its launch was at the bank.

The prince could not resist for long the desire to make use of it, nor that of visiting the ship. He shouted in vain for someone to come out of it, and, rendered impatient by the silence maintained thereon, he leapt lightly into the launch and conducted himself with an extreme facility, for the launch was made of white paper, as was the ship. The prince boarded it without any difficulty, and finding no one there, he examined without obstacles everything that he desired to see. Noticing that not only was there a good bed but also all the things necessary to life, he resolved to take advantage of them until further notice.

As he had been very well brought up at Gris-de-lin's court, he knew a little about everything, and necessity, in combination with the knowledge he had acquired, enabled him to find a fraction of the most necessary maneuvers. The ship, the river, and the surrounding countryside, everything that presented itself to his eyes, appeared to him to be uninhabited. The lightness with which the ship responded to his vivacity compensated him from the ennui that such a great solitude might have caused him.

Eventually, after a few days of navigation, the current of the river always carrying him toward its mouth, he found himself, almost without perceiving it, in the open sea. He had never seen it before; the sight of that immensity of water astonished him; courageous as he was, he was frightened, and wanted to get back into the river, but stronger currents carried him out to sea, and the wind, then blowing from the stern, caused him to lose sight of land in very little time. He remembered then that he had been forbidden in childhood to play with water, but it was too late. He sensed all the horror of his situation, and did not know how to preserve himself from the peril to which his lack of reflection had exposed him.

All that he could do was to get impatient and annoyed, two things that he did marvelously well; to complete his woes he was becalmed, and no one has ever been able to understand how he resisted a condition that displeases even the most patient people. He regretted the Temple of the Black Bird then, where at least he had seen human beings, he had been able to make signs to them, and the hope of getting out of it had sustained him in his chagrins; whereas, on the white paper ship, he had no society of any sort, and could not foresee how he might be delivered from that tedious prison.

His navigation was extremely long, and he did not discover any land. The first that he recognized, and which the ship approached, caused him such a great joy, and his haste to disembark was so strong, that he threw himself into the sea, resolved to reach the coast by swimming. But his project was futile, for his ship was always underfoot every time he returned to the surface after jumping into the sea. He was therefore obliged, reluctantly, to submit to the winds, to shut himself up in his cabin and dry his clothes by means of an alcohol heater that served him to cook the food that he found in abundance, and which he never lacked.

That final impatience was not of long duration. The ship arrived of its own accord in a port formed by nature and bordered by great trees. That sight delighted the prince, and when he came close to the shore he leapt on to it lightly. Contrary to his hope, he was finally liberated from the persecution of his vessel. He marched away in order not to see it any longer, and promptly found himself in the most beautiful forest in the world. He stopped on the edge of a spring, delectable by virtue of the purity of its water and the beauty of the cedars by which it was shaded. He had scarcely arrived there than he saw a gazelle, almost at bay, which came to fall at his feet, pronouncing the words: "Oh, Papillon, help me."

Astonished, and touched by the beauty and delicacy of the little animal, he drew his weapons and went to meet a green lion that was pursuing the gazelle ardently. The intrepid Papillon attacked it; the combat was fierce, but Papillon finally emerged victorious. As it fell the lion whistled three times, with so much force that the forest resounded, and the noise could be heard for more than two leagues around—after which the lion expired, apparently having nothing further to do in this world.

Papillon, slightly embarrassed as he was by the whistle, turned to the beautiful gazelle and said: "Well, are you content now? Since you're able to talk, tell me quickly what all this is, and how you know me."

"I need to rest for a long time," she replied, "and furthermore, you don't have the leisure to listen to me, for this affair isn't finished. You're in too much of a hurry," she continued, without becoming over-excited, "look behind you."

Papillon turned round and saw, in fact, a giant, who was marching straight toward him with great strides."

"Who the Devil," cried the giant, in a mighty voice, "made my lion whistle?"

"It was me," replied the prince, proudly. "But look: take my word for it, he won't whistle again."

"Oh, my poor Bibi!" sad the giant. "What a misfortune, my dear little friend! But at least, I can avenge your death."

With those words he presented to Papillon the huge snake that he was holding in his hand, and the only weapon that he had brought.

Without being astonished, the prince dealt the snake a mortal blow, and immediately, it became a giant and the giant became a snake. Papillon's thrusts caused a similar metamorphosis six times, but finally the prince delivered such a mighty blow with his saber that he cut the snake in two, picked up one fragment and threw it in the giant's face. The giant fell unconscious between the lion's paws. At that moment a thick cloud hid them from the prince's sight and carried them away with a extreme rapidity.

Without taking the time to sheathe his sword, the prince addressed the gazelle, saying to her: "You're recovered your senses now, you no longer have anything to fear; explain to me, then, what you are and the significance of that lion, the nasty giant and his comrade the snake. But above all, hurry."

"You'll be satisfied," she replied, "but there's no urgency. I'd like to take you to the Green Castle, and I'd also like not to go on foot; that's such a fatiguing business, and the castle is a long way away."

"Let's set forth for it immediately, then," said the prince, impatiently, "or I'll leave you and your story here. Isn't it a shameful thing that a young and pretty gazelle like you can't go on foot? Let's depart promptly, for the further away the castle is, the more diligent we need to be. Let's go, let's go," he continued. "We'll go gently; that's all that I can grant you. In any case, we can talk on the way."

"Let's do better," she said. "Carry me on your shoulders, but as I don't like other people to go to any trouble—you less than anyone else—you'll carry me, it's true, but you'll ride this snail."

In fact, by extending the prettiest paw in the world, she showed him what he took to be a huge boulder, so enormous was it.

"Me, ride a snail," said Papillon. "You're mocking me. Is that, then, in order to take a year to get there?"

"Well, don't do it, then," the gazelle replied. "We'll stay here. Personally, I'm quite comfortable here; the spring is fresh and the grass is tender. But believe me, follow the advice I'm giving you and mount up."

Entirely opposed as it was to Papillon's character, it appeared so ridiculous to him that he obeyed, and after having put the pretty gazelle on his shoulders, the snail, on his orders and at the thrusts of the heel that he gave it incessantly, slid along passably enough. The gazelle told him, futilely, that the vehicle was the gentlest that she had yet found; he only sensed its slowness.

Finally, after a very long journey, they arrived at the Green Castle. All its inhabitants were attracted by the singularity and progress of the vehicle. The gazelle having consented to be put down, resumed on the steps of the peristyle a form as tender as it was lovable, and revealed herself to Papillon as his beautiful cousin. The joy and gratitude that the princess expressed to him was tranquil and very mild; that of the prince, by contrast, was as keen as it was animated. All the maidservants with whom Nonchalante had been accustomed for some time to live learned by means of the few words that the transport of her joy caused her to pronounce of the defeat of the giant and the prodigies of her cousin's valor.

Nonchalante walked slowly in order to repose in the grand apartment of the castle. Papillon followed her in order to obtain promptly the story that he had already requested; the sight of his cousin caused him to desire it infinitely, but it was necessary before satisfying his curiosity for him to receive the compliments of the inhabitants of the Green Land, who, by virtue of the death of the giant, had just recognized him as their sovereign. He cut the speeches, which were always too long, short by half, and the complimenters were sent away as soon as it was possible. Finally, Papillon obtained from Nonchalante the story of her adventures, which she commenced as follows:

"After your departure, annoyed by the fatigues of the government in which people insisted on instructing me, I implored the good Lolotte, whom you knew, to take me to her home. It was with great difficulty that she granted me that favor, but she finally consented to it. She took me away on my sofa, and I spent a few delightful days in her grotto, where everything was as comfortable as it was tranquil.

"She was obliged to go to the Assembly of the Fays, and she told me on her return, dissolving in tears, that the favors she had done for me had cost her dear, that she had been scolded very vigorously, and that the Council had ordered her to put me in the hands of Mirlifiche, already charged with the care of your person, and whose conduct was very good in your regard."

"Oh yes, very good," Papillon interrupted, "if she was the cause of all the annoyances I've experienced. You can judge that in a little while; continue, continue, my beautiful cousin, for I know what has happened to me, but I don't know anything regarding you."

"At first I was very afflicted, "Nonchalante went on, "by the tears of the good Lolotte, but I consoled myself afterwards with the aid of the resources that tranquility furnishes. It wasn't long before I saw the fay Mirlifiche arrive, mounted on her great unicorn. She stopped in front of the grotto where we were living and asked the good Lolotte for me; her tears redoubled instantly, but she could not refuse me. She took me in her arms, gave me several nurse's kisses and put me on the rump of the fay's mount personally.

"'Hold on tight, little girl,' Mirlifiche said to me, 'if you don't want to break your neck.' I did, in fact, need all my strength not to fall, for the nasty beast went at a trot so fast that I was often out of breath. We trotted for a very long time, and when we arrived at a large farm, the farmer and his wife ran to meet the fay as soon as the saw her, and helped her to get down from the unicorn. I've found out since that they were a king and a queen whom the fay had reduced to that estate, as much to punish them for their ignorance and indolence as to try and correct it.

"When Mirlifiche had got down and I had been carried to the ground, almost dead of fatigue, she insisted that I give the necessary cares to the unicorn. To that effect she ordered me to go up to the hay-loft, which one reached by way of a ladder, and to bring down, one after another, twenty-four handfuls of hay for her mount's night. I had never felt such a great lassitude, and I still shiver when I think about it. I obeyed, however; I brought the twenty-four handfuls of hay to her, and then took them in the same fashion, on her orders, to the stables.

"That wasn't all; I was made to work on the supper. When it was finished, I thought I was quit of it, and could enjoy peacefully the little bed that the fay had brought next to her own. Not at all; I was not only obliged to prepare it, because it wasn't made, but also the one that had been brought for Mirlifiche. I would have preferred a hundred times to sleep in a chair than in a bed that cost me so much trouble, but it was necessary to obey, to close the fay's curtains and to render her a thousand services that never ended, and to which I was not at all accustomed.

"Finally, unable to do any more, and not knowing yet that I had to undress myself, I threw myself on to my bed just as I was. The fay, who perceived that, extracted me from the charms of first sleep in order to make me undress, but in spite of her threats, I kept some of my clothes; I was fortunate enough not to be perceived, and I'll tell you in confidence that I've always found disobedience very quite satisfying. It's true that one is often scolded, but one always gains something in regard to toil.

"At daybreak, Mirlifiche woke me up and obliged me to get up in order to go and see how her unicorn was and tell her how much hay remained for it to eat. She repeated her orders and oblige me to make several journeys, sometimes to see

160

what the weather was like and at others to tell her what time it was. I did it so poorly and carried out her orders so slowly that before she left she summoned the king and queen who had greeted her with the profoundest respect. 'Monarchs,' she said, mounting her unicorn, 'continue to make the most of our farm if you want to mount your throne again. I'm more content with you his year; but I'm leaving you this little princess'—she pointed at me—'make her work hard for me, so that I can mend her ways. Otherwise....'

"She didn't say any more, spurred her mount and disappeared from sight instantly. The king and queen turned to me then and asked me what I knew how to do. 'Nothing at all,' I replied, in a manner that must surely have persuaded them. In spite of that response, they went into the detail and choice of occupations in order to find out which as the most to my liking, but I still assured them that I had none except that of doing nothing, and I ended up imploring the to let me sleep.

"They not only had the kindness to consent to that, but also that of bringing me something to eat in my bed, from which I didn't want to emerge all day. The next day the good queen came to find me and said to me, with a embarrassed expression: 'My beautiful child, it's necessary for you to resolve to get up; I know full well that it's nice to do nothing; such as you see me, I know that from experience; for, in sum, when we were king and queen, my husband and I did nothing—nothing at all, I assure you—and I hope that a day will come when we can do as much, but we're not there yet, and nor are you. You heard what the fay said to us as she left, and you'll have us scolded, and perhaps expose us to worse, if we don't make you work. So get up, my child, for my husband has resolved to do that. We talked about you yesterday evening, and all night as well. Let's go, come to breakfast; I have good cream waiting for you.'

"It wasn't without difficulty that I followed her advice, and all went well until breakfast. When it was finished, they agitated again about what to give me to do, but I still said, believe me: 'Don't give me anything,' Finally, the queen gathered more than four pounds of hemp around a large distaff, which she accompanied by a spindle, and send me to guard the sheep, assuring me that that work would be all the more agreeable because I could rest as much as I wanted. Seductive as that promise was, I still made more protests, but they were futile, and I was obliged to depart.

"I didn't walk far without finding some charming shade; the place seemed delightful to me; I sat down on some tender grass and, making a pillow out of my distaff, I lay down as I would have done if there were no sheep in the world. As for them, they behaved as if they had no one to guard them and spread out as they liked through the fields, foraging all the crops. The local peasants were too interested in the damage to let it pass in silence. At the noise they made, the king and queen came out of their farm and, seeing what was happening, ran after their sheep, with all the more reason because people wanted them to pay for the disorder.

"Personally, I was tranquil. I watched them run, and I would have carried on doing it—for I was very comfortable—if the king and queen, out of breath, hadn't seen me in that situation. They obliged me to get up and ordered me to follow them, which didn't happen without a great many reproaches on their part. After, that, as you can imagine, I was charged with other things than guarding the sheep, but I always acquitted myself in the same fashion. Finally, I was able to reduce the most patient people in the world to such despair that, fearing one day that the queen might beat me, I left the farm in order to avoid her anger, and I found the boat that was used for fishing in the small river that traversed the farm.

"Scarcely had I sat down in the boat than the current carried me away gently. I didn't oppose that, and didn't pay any attention to the queen, who followed me screeching like an eagle: 'Oh, my boat, my boat! Come quickly, husband, the little girl's taking it away.'

"In the end she wearied of following it and screeching, and I let myself be carried away at the whim of the river's current, and found it so pleasant and jolly that I spent the night in that situation. I would have spent my life in it if my boat hadn't stopped at sunrise on the edge of a charming river; need, more than curiosity, made me approach a few houses of a very singular form.

"When I had walked a short distance I perceived in the air an infinite number of shiny things that weren't attached to anything but nevertheless remained fixed, and I walked in that direction. I found myself next to a silk cord that was hanging down to the ground, and I took hold of it because it came to hand, and in an instant, all the silver bells—those were the shiny things I had seen—formed the prettiest and most agreeable of all carillons. I sat down to listen to it, and when it stopped, as many birds as there were bells came to perch on each of them.

"They sang in a delightful fashion, and when that pleasant concert had finished, I saw a tall and majestic woman coming toward me, rather advanced in age, with a considerable bosom. She was followed by all the birds in the world; some of them swelled her court and others were occupied in her regard with all the functions by which vanity is usually served.

"As soon as she came close to me she said: 'What has given you the boldness, little girl as you are, to come here, where I don't suffer any inhabitant for more than a hundred leagues around, for fear of frightening my birds?' Looking at me, she went on: 'Still, if you're good for something, I'll see whether I can employ you.'

"'Madame, I said, you can leave me here in all security; I certainly won't disturb you birds; but for pity's sake, deign to give me something to eat.'

"'I consent to that,' she replied, 'before treating you as you merit.'

"Then half a dozen jays, that I judged to be pages, flew to the great aviary in which she lived, and came back charged with all sorts of biscuits, which I found perfectly good. In brief, I was served marvelously, but with too much promptitude and vivacity, for I don't like to be hurried. I found the fruits, above all, charming and delicious, for the birds knew them marvelously.

" I felt such a great desire to remain in that land that I could help expressing it once again to the lady who was treating me so well. 'You!' she replied, with a scornful and ironic expression. 'Remain in a land where everything is lively? Truly, no,' she continued, 'and it isn't here that I want to make use of you. I've fulfilled the duties of hospitality, and that's all that you'll have from me.'

"Then, very assertively, she tugged the cord that I've mentioned, and, far from producing the enchanting sounds that gave me such great pleasure, she started a bell ringing, the terrible sound of which frightened me. A moment later I saw a black bird of monstrous dimensions appear, which alighted at the feet of the fay, and said to her in a voice proportionate to its size: 'What do you want, my sister?'

"'I want you,' she said to it, "to take this beautiful Nonchalante immediately to my cousin, the giant of the Green Castle. Tell him to make her work night and day on the beautiful tapestries that he has made.

"At those words, in spite of my screams, the black bird lifted me up and departed in rapid flight."

"Good," said Papillon, "you're making fun of me, cousin. Say rather at the slowest speed. I know that wretched bird, and never has any slowness equaled that which surround it."

"It can do anything you wish," Nonchalante replied. "I don't like to argue, and perhaps it's not the same one you know, but in any case, that one carried me away prodigiously quickly, and set me down very gently in this castle, where you're presently the master. We entered through one of the windows, which it found open, and when it had presented me on the part of the Fay of the Birds to the giant of whom you had the kindness to rid me, it left, saying: 'Adieu, cousin, until we meet again.'

"I had scarcely had time to consider the place where I was when the giant said to me: 'You're an idler, then, since

you've been sent here. We've made others work. See,' he added, 'how all that is occupied.' I raised my eyes then and I saw
in an immense gallery, looms, winders, wools, designs, etc.
There were some looms at which more than a dozen young
women were working. That sight made me faint. When I recovered my senses, I was asked what I knew how to do. It was
in vain that, with extreme honesty and the greatest desire to
persuade, I replied, as I had at the farm: 'Nothing.' The giant
told me that I'd be taught, and that there was work for everyone.

"People were working in the castle making tapestry wall-
hangings of all the new tales of which the fays approved the
most. King Guillemot, Nabotine, Silentieux and Babillarde
and Violette appeared in all their splendor.[26] They tried to
make me work, but from the first classes into which I had been
put on arrival, I was always made to descend to the simplest
tasks. I was given in vain the prances that ordinarily succeeded
on the others, and it was also in vain that the giant showed me
his menagerie. It was prodigiously large and composed of all
the children who had not wanted to work. All that made no
impression on me, and I was finally reduced to drawing the
water for dyeing the wool.

"As I acquitted myself no better in that task than the others, the giant became angry with me this morning and made
me take the form of a gazelle. He took me to his menagerie

---

[26] These citations are problematic. Le Roi Guillemot appears
in a tale called "La Reine des fées" by Jean de Préchac, apparently first published in Estienne Roger's 1717 *Cabinet de fées*
and reprinted several times. The Mayer *Cabinet de fées* also
contains "Aglaé ou Nabotine," attributed to Charles-Antoine
Coypel, but that story does not appear to have been published
before 1779, and Caylus might have heard it read aloud in
Madame Le Marchand's salon, of which Coypel was a member. A character called Babillarde features in one of Mademoiselle L'Héritier's tales but she is not a fay; the origins of the
other two names are also difficult to trace.

immediately, and the natural timidity of the animal prevailed in me over the liking I had for repose. The sight of a dog made me take flight, and I ran out of the courtyard of the castle. For fear of losing me, the giant sent his green lion after me, with orders to bring me back at any price. However, I might perhaps have allowed myself to be caught or devoured rather than run any longer, if my good fortune had not caused me to encounter you at the spring."

The princess concluded the story of her adventures with a eulogy to repose and a mild and tranquil life, but Papillon assured her that he had remained in one place for too long, and that since he had seen her he had experienced situations that had not amused him at all. Immediately, and very rapidly, he told her the story of the good woman, that of the Black Bird and the story of his voyage in the white paper ship.

Then they returned the liberty of everything there was in the castle and the menagerie, the animals of which had resumed their original forms of princes and princesses at the moment of the giant's combat. They departed, giving them a thousand blessings. Nonchalante implored them not to work any longer and to burn all the looms. She accompanied the liberty that she gave them with magnificent presents, which one of her maidservants distributed to them.

However, Nonchalante and Papillon were not in accord regarding the execution of their projects, and although everyone was submissive to them in the Green Castle, they obeyed all the orders the Papillon gave slowly, and went very quickly to do what Nonchalante often did not desire. In the end, they became accustomed to confiding their difficulties to one another and condemning without perceiving it everything that displeased one or other of them. Afterwards, they came to console one another, and they did not take long to lend themselves reciprocally to one another's character reciprocally. They went on easily to applause, and from applause to sentiment there was only one step to make, for it is thus that the heart always seduces the mind; one believes that one loves, and one does indeed love, that which is naturally opposed to us. The progress of their sentiment was so prompt that Papillon only remained vibrant in order that Nonchalante should be indifferent to everything else in Nature, and Nonchalante no longer was to any object.

Papillon had an arbor constructed in one of the boscages of the park, and as he had traveled forests for a long time he had noticed the antipathy that all birds have for owls—for rapid people recover sooner or later ideas have struck them without them paying attention—he was the first to imagine the pleasure of a decoy, which, without giving any trouble, could please his lovely cousin and procure him at the same time the satisfaction of giving liberty to the unfortunate birds that came to doom themselves. For her part, Nonchalante proposed prizes for horse races, of which she varied the species infinitely.

Papillon, only thinking any longer about tranquil pleasures, had boscages planted, gave fêtes on the water that he caused to terminate in magnificent and elegant angling, and the princess imagined hunts, dances and everything agreeable that movement can inspire, not without finding infinite pleasure in them, or without sharing the difficulties and fatigues by which they are always accompanied.

One can easily imagine that their sentiments, combined with the solitude of the Green Castle and the authority that they enjoyed at a scantly advanced age, would perhaps have conducted their affairs with an undue diligence, if the fays, ever attentive to their particular interests, had not arrived in order to slow down the progress; they were piqued that amour had achieved in an instant what all their art and reflections had not been able to produce, and therefore resolved to put their sentiments to hard proofs and to torment the young lovers. It is thus that the fays, no longer able to experience the pleasure of amour, do their best to destroy it, in spite of the experience of contradiction always striving to animate it.

In order to succeed in their new project, they gave Nonchalante the appearance of the most ardent fever, and Papillon that of the most excessive languor; they easily persuaded them of the magnitude of the danger to which they were exposed, and caused them the sharpest of anxieties. Then Mirlifiche, attentive to the moment of finding them separated, appeared to them, and, addressing herself first to Nonchalante, said to her: "Papillon seems to me to be very ill."

"Alas, yes Madame," the princess replied, bursting into tears. "He's dying. Send me to the abode of the farmer king, resurrect the giant, and you'll see how I'll be able to obey them; I'll submit to anything, but cure him, I implore you."

"If you want to save Papillon's life," the fay replied, gravely, "it only depends on you. Depart instantly, and neglect nothing in order to find the mouse that trots and the finch that flies; bring them to me, and remember that time is pressing."

She had scarcely finished speaking when Nonchalante was already out of the Green Castle.

Shortly thereafter, the fay had a similar conversation with the prince, who implored her as tenderly as anything in the world to make him suffer anything, provided that she help his beautiful cousin; he assured her that black oracles and white paper ships would no longer be obstacles, if, by that means he could obtain from her the favor that he was asking with so much ardor.

Mirlifiche agreed regarding the dangerous condition to which the princess was reduced, but in the same terms, she assured him that if he could give her the pink mole, she believed that she could cure her.

Seeing nothing but the danger to Nonchalante, Papillon left the Green Castle and took, by chance, a route opposite to the one that his beautiful cousin was following.

Our lovers were thus differently occupied. The princess was only searching the woods, always running and always listening, devoting herself to continual movement in order to find, and furthermore to catch, two animals that seemed very difficult to surprise. She searched, however, with urgency, and relentlessly. The prince, by contrast, had his eyes continuously fixed on meadows, always attentive to the movements of all moles. He walked slowly on tiptoe, holding his breath, often motionless to the point that he might have been mistaken for a beautiful statue.

If the desire to succeed has not always produced talents, we can be sure that at least we owe their perfection to it. So, in a very short time, no mole escaped the prince, but what was his dolor, and how his anxiety was augmented, one seeing that these he caught with so much difficulty were as black as they usually are. Far from becoming impatient, he seemed at every moment to draw new strength to continue such a dismal hunt.

But the traits of patience and vivacity, which drove them both to excess, are the ordinary miracles of amour. The searches they made in a fashion so strongly opposed to their character were not interrupted by any event; they did not even recognize the country that they had reached. When one is occupied for the person one loves, especially to save them from a danger that one believes to be imminent, what does one see? What can happen that can cause the slightest distraction? So the prince and the princess did not experience any.

They both cried, at the same moment: "At last I have you, and everything that I love will no longer be in danger."

At the sound of their voices, by which they were struck, they turned their heads and recognized one another. Then, no longer thinking about anything but the pleasure of seeing one another again, they abandoned the ideas for which they had been searching with so many difficulties and cares, they forgot everything that they had to say to one another, and the surprise that they experienced prevented them from pronouncing a single word.

During the delightful silence they were observing, however, good King Gris-de-Lin, who was walking sadly on his own, as he usually did—for it was in his park that the lovers had arrived without perceiving it—recognized them and, running to them, he suspended for a few moments the charm that they were under in seeing one another. Great as their joy was in rediscovering such a good father—Papillon, in fact, had known no other—it did not prevent them from sensing at that moment the loss they had just suffered, for instead of finding next to them the finch, the mouse and the beautiful mole, they only perceived a beautiful woman they did not know, the black bird and the giant.

At the sight of that beauty, Gris-de-Lin fell in a faint in her arms; it was the beautiful Santorée, who had only been abducted, and whose abduction had perhaps been part of some other tale. In the end, unable to resist the joy she was experiencing, after such a long and cruel separation, she lost consciousness too.

While their children were giving them the cares worthy of the generosity of their hearts, the black bird and the giant resumed their original form of genii, and that same instant, marked by destinies for such great events, saw Mirlifiche and Lolotte arriving in their chariots. They enabled the monarchs to recover from their faint, and the company, content to find those they loved—for the genii were very attached to their natural forms—went to the palace, where they celebrated the wedding of Nonchalante and Papillon.

The fays and the genii spared no effort to render it magnificent and brilliant; in order to succeed in that they employed al their secrets and their intelligence. What was preferable to that prodigious splendor, however, by which the heart can only be feebly touched, is that amour rendered it charming by its pleasures.

After such a beautiful union, the beautiful Santorée and Gris-de-Lin did not want to mingle in any other affair, and retired to a tranquil place, sufficiently occupied during the rest of their lives with all the sentiments of the best-founded esteem and the most ardent tenderness. Their children imitated them in their fashion of loving—which is to say that they rendered their people happy, and were happy themselves, in consequence.

THE PALACE OF IDEAS

There as once a king and a queen, who left a son and a kingdom under the tutelage of the fay Minatine. She was good and benevolent; the realm was thus very well governed, and the prince, whose name was Constant, very well brought up.

When he had reached a certain age, the fay consented to the desire he had to travel. That school, in which the entire world is revealed in action, is perhaps the most useful of all; princes are those who have the most need of it, and make the least usage of it.

When the day fixed for the prince's departure arrived, Minatine separated from him with an infinite dolor. She did not recommend anything else to him except avoiding the charms of Rosanie. Constant promised his good friend to do that, and departed, convinced that nothing in the world could make him break his word.

The name of Constant, even more than the charms of his face, enabled him to experience the generosities of a large number of pretty women in the lands through which he traveled. He thought that he had experienced amour, but he was unaware of the abuse that is made of it and the vanity to which one is susceptible at a certain age. Content with the conquests he had made, inflated by his success, he gradually forgot the give to Minatine. Everything marvelous and charming he heard about Rosanie determined him to judge or himself the verity of the stories he had heard about her, and he believed himself to be above human nature.

He left the numerous retinue that accompanied him a few days away from the capital city in which Rosanie made her abode. He went there incognito. He arrived on the very day that the Festival of Flowers was being celebrated.

The custom of the land ordered the heiress of the Empire, or the first Princess of the Blood, to preside over the Fête of

Spring, and to appear at the head of all the pretty women in the realm, who were assembled with care; for in that country, with the sole exception of the royal family, skill and valor were the nobility of the men, while the grace and beauty of the women were their titles and their dowry. Those who made up the retinue of the princess could not be older than sixteen or younger than twelve.

A week was fixed for that festival, and during that week the most beautiful day was chosen for its celebration. At dawn, the serenity of the air was judged; oboes and bagpipes alerted the entire city by means of tender and cheerful songs that the ceremony was to take place. Constant thus arrived at the moment when the entire city came out to see a spectacle preferable to any other in the world, since that one had all the springtimes of Nature for its object.

The prince followed the crowds and stopped as everyone did, when he had arrived in a meadow that rose in a gentle slope. The highest part of the terrain was ornamented by a decoration of flowers, in the middle of which there was a throne of similar structure, on which Constant learned that Rosanie was seated.

In proportion to their beauty, the girls were seated in more or less close proximity to the princess; all the others making up the pleasant fête, numbering more than two thousand, formed an amphitheater on steps strewn with flowers, the middle of which was sufficiently spacious. All those beauties, ornamented by their hair, dressed in gauzes and everything simple that could render the agreeable, were coiffed with flowers, with the result that the odor of those natural perfumes and the sight of so many agreeable objects enchanted gazes simultaneously and spread through the heart the voluptuousness so well known under the name of the Daughter of Heaven, for which men must search with such great care.

Constant ran his eyes over an assembly more brilliant than Olympus had ever been. He made an interior tour of the enclosure, and when he was facing Rosanie he was dazzled by her. She combined with all the graces of her face the contentment given by the certainty of the impossibility of being eclipsed by any other beauty and the tranquility of soul that befits the visage so well.

She easily perceived the impression that she had made on the young foreigner. The least coquettish of women is never unaware of the effects of her beauty. The appeals of a herald drew the prince from the admiration into which the sight of so many charms held him, as if buried. The herald proclaimed the exercises of youth and cried that the beauty to which one was attached, or the one who appeared most agreeable, would be the prize of the strength or the skill that was about to be shown to the eyes of the assembly, while submitting to the usages of the country and the decision of the princess, who alone could order it.

By virtue of an impulse of which he did not give himself time to take account himself, Constant presented himself in the ranks first, with the vivacity that only amour and youth can inspire. He won all the prizes, but with a superiority and a distinction by which all the spectators were as surprised as the consternated losers.

He came to Rosanie's knees to receive the prizes that he had won in such a distinguished fashion. Then, seeing her at close range, his admiration only left him the usage of sight. When he was at the foot of the throne, Rosanie told him that he could choose any of the beauties that surrounded him. Constant replied, hastily: "I am only flattered by being victorious because I was to be crowned by your hand, and I am only sensible to the victory to the extent that the advantage I have just gained can place me within range of being your slave."

"You don't know the usages of the country," replied the charming Rosanie. "Princesses can no more choose in this land than any other; it is not appropriate for them to be preferred to their peers; you are forgetting your rank and mine." She pronounced the last words with as much pride as arrogance.

The bitterness that commenced their first conversation has often been the commencement of the greatest attachments.

The prince blushed at the state of simplicity in which he appeared to the eyes of the woman he already adored. Self-esteem almost engaged him to declare himself.

Surprised in her turn by the rapidity of his triumphs, while crowning him with her own floral crown—because the Master of Ceremonies had not found in the registers an example of a victor so disinterested, nor of all the victories being won by the same man, and half a dozen crowns would have overloaded the victor's head—Rosanie said to him: "Choose from all these beauties; there in not one that cannot be yours immediately."

"That offer is insulting!" exclaimed the prince. "How you are able to mingle bitterness with the generosity you have for me! I would not have disputed the prize if I had not believed that he prize as a means of acquiring you, and without the aid of that idea it is certain that I would not have triumphed." To the assembly, he said: "Dispute between yourselves the honor of possessing these beauties. I only competed for the honor." He said that as he withdrew, and pronounced the word with the acerbic tone of discontented and rebellious amour.

The exercises having recommenced by virtue of his withdrawal, he could not help mingling with the crowd, nor resist the desire to intoxicate himself again with the pleasure of gazing at Rosanie.

When the ceremony was finished and the marriages had been celebrated in accordance with the usual custom, the prince retired and went to seek a retreat in the least frequented outlying district of the city. He sent the squire who was the only person who had accompanied him to fetch his equipage and his men.

It is easy to believe that there was talk of the handsome foreigner throughout the city; hid skill and strength were the subject of conversations. The beauties he had scorned all found reasons to criticize the coldness of his procedure; they were annoyed with him. That was, it is true, to praise him more than anyone wanted; people said continually that they no longer wanted to talk about him, and yet the conversation always reverted to him. People asked incessantly: But where has he come from? When did he arrive? Don't you know him? Those questions or similar ones, were recommenced, although, for the moment, no one could respond. In sum, all the possible questions were asked and they were accompanied by all imaginable repetition, sometimes with bitterness and sometimes with admiration for a motive. All those words, as I have said, whatever they were, were genuine praise, but in the end, all the questions were futile.

In great cities, words are lively, but they have no duration; three days later, people were beginning not to talk about the prince any longer when he reappeared in the public promenade in an equipage worthy of him and of the fay who had ordered it. His amour has caused him to and everything that gallantry has of the most agreeable to everything that the fay Minatine had given him of the superb and the magnificent. He was recognized in the most elegant carriage as the vanquisher of all the youth and the object of the regrets of all the beauties in the land

Adornment adds to the most beautiful face; how, then, did he appear in the eyes of the entire court? He came to descend at Rosanie's palace, and named himself, requesting an audience with the king and the princess. It was accorded to him immediately, and it was there that, either because of the modesty with which he responded to the eulogies that his strength and skill merited, or because of the graces that the desire to please expanded in the conversation, he charmed the entire court. It was with a general pleasure that it was learned from him that he hoped to stay in the realm for a while.

He did in fact establish himself there, but if he sometimes touched Rosanie's mind, he did not make any progress in her heart.

Constant served Rosanie with all the skill possible in the foreign wars that were declared. His was not the least help in the troubles of her empire, since he calmed seditious and ill-intentioned minds, of which the capital was all too full, a thousand times.

Rosanie made him forget for several years that he had a kingdom, and more than anything else, his unfortunate passion always made him dread seeing Minatine again. The aberrations of amour have always feared the counsels of enlightened amity. What would he not have forgotten, since he had forgotten himself?

One day, distraught at his woes, when he was as sharply afflicted as one can be when amour is devoid of hope, he desired to see the fay, his true friend. To desire to see her and to see her were the same thing; she therefore appeared to his eyes.

"You have been punished enough for not following my advice, dear prince," she said to him softly, "without me heaping you with the reproaches that you merit. If Nature entire and my Art could render the indifferent Rosanie to you, it is certain that the upheaval of the one would be the effect of the other, but once a man loves a Rosanie, only death can deliver him from the attachment that he has for her. I predicted that you would suffer; only amour, as you know only too well, can recompense amour, and all the prodigies in the world cannot give any satisfaction to the sentiment. I can, therefore, only pity you; the only thing that it is possible for me to do, to prove my sincere amity to you, is to give you a consolation that your amour will not disavow."

Then she touched him with her wand and accorded him the faculty of entering into the Palace of Ideas. She combined with that the ability to construct it in all the places where he found himself and in all the instants that he might desire.

That palace maintains and nourishes constancy, but it is impossible to describe with precision. Sometimes it represents all that art and taste can compose of the most perfect; in the same instant it becomes a cabin as poor as it is solitary. It is equally situated, either in a delightful valley or on a sheer rock. The sea, rivers, forests and grasslands are found within its enclosure; solitude and the obscurity of caverns succeed in a moment the crowd and illumination of a ball. Funereal objects take the place in an instant of the most agreeable.

Prince Constant made continual usage of that palace, since he saw Rosanie there incessantly and she presented herself accompanied by all her charms. A thousand tableaux, all animated and all with a perfect resemblance retraced her incessantly in all possible forms. He conversed with her; then he said to her what he had always forgotten to say to her; but when, after seeing her gentle, tender and complaisant, he emerged from his palace, the cruel reality then became the torment of his heart.

Rosanie recognized, however, some difference in the general conduct of the prince. It often happens that a woman does not want to respond to the tenderness of a lover, but one is nevertheless determined not to lose him; either the princess was a victim of that petty vanity, or she was struck by another idea, for it is very difficult to know exactly what a young woman thinks. That reflection piqued curiosity, that author of so many inconveniences. She made Constant sense that she suspected him of having some dissipation, and of having less to lament than he boasted.

The mere appearance of suspicion, given the reaction that self-esteem can have to a reproach, alarmed the unfortunate Constant. There is never a secret for someone that one loves veritably, He made the confession of the fay's gift, but it was described to Rosanie with the vivacity of satisfied amour.

"I see you there incessantly," he told her, "when misfortune separates me from you. My vivid imagination depicts you there at every moment such as you are, and my heart dictates your responses. I give you fêtes, and everything that can serve my delicacy and you approve of my sentiments, are submissive to my orders. I give a tender interpretation to the most indifferent words that your coldness makes me receive in response to everything tender and passionate I can say to you. In sum, in that happy retreat, all of nature is submissive to my amour."

177

"You're in love," Rosanie said to him. "In consequence, your palace represents nothing but amour to you; but for me, who does not know tenderness, if I possessed one like it, it seems to me that I would make a charming use of it by means of the agreeable and seductive images that it would trace for me incessantly.

"I believe," Constant replied to her, "that these palaces not only owe their charms, but also their existence, to amour; but in any case, you desire one, and although everything alarms me on your part and I dread with reason that you would make use of such a present to do without me even more than you do now, everything that you desire is my unique joy. I will therefore implore the fay to satisfy you."

At those words, Minatine appeared between them; she touched Rosanie with her wand as she had touched the prince, and then she disappeared.

As soon as the princess had a moment of solitude at her disposal, she wanted to employ the new gift that had just been made to her. Although she had a great deal of intelligence, however, objects were scarcely retraced for her; nothing that she wanted to represent to herself had any consistency, and everything vanished, so true is it that the heart alone can fix ideas.

It is in my opinion an omen favorable for amour to see an indifferent person fall into reverie; a lover, if he is not jealous of it, ought to be charmed by it.

The objects that were depicted for Rosanie were cold; they were deprived of the grace and warmth so necessary to any depiction. After some time of a usage as unimportant as that for which the princess employed her palace, she perceived Constant one day, but to begin with she only glimpsed him, only at the extremity of an infinitely long gallery, and infinitely far away from her. His attention, his fidelity and his perfect devotion gradually gave more vivid colors to his portrait, and, in consequence to her palace.

All these reflections finally impressed Rosanie's heart, which was softened thereby. That tender pity ordinarily precedes the triumph of amour.

Virtue alone cannot prevent or banish the attention of a primary idea; it strikes with so much simplicity that it is not possible to reproach oneself for it nor to protect oneself against it; it usually insinuates itself by very gradual degrees, and when it has produced a strong enough impression, indifference is alarmed by it.

The detail of Rosanie's sentiments and their progress were, therefore, such as I have just described.

She was internally convinced of her defeat, but she still often asked Constant questions about the manner in which he saw her in his palace. The comparison that she made between his narration and that of her own sentiments sometimes gave her chagrin and often ill-humor. Although she blushed at the impressions that amour made in her heart when alone, the combats of her pride made Constant pay dearly for the commencements of his triumph.

If amour left a lover the liberty of his intelligence, he would be delighted to recognize an ill humor that always precedes the confession of sentiments and the submission of a young woman's heart. Often, after the questions I have just mentioned, Rosanie abruptly quit a prince who felt too much amour not to experience everything blindly, and with the stupidity with which the passion in question endows the greatest mind. He was therefore afflicted by what was conducting him to the goal of all his prayers.

Immediately after having quit Constant, Rosanie found him in her palace and saw him afflicted by her latest procedure; she sometimes wanted to applaud herself for that, but she always ended up reproaching herself for it, and even by being alarmed by it.

So many troubles ceased in the end; one day, each emerging from their palace, they encountered one another; their conversation began with the fortunate silence in which everything speaks within us except the voice. That pleasant situation in which the soul is attentive was finally interrupted; the narration of what occupied them, and the transport of their hearts, became a reciprocal declaration.

Nothing was ever opposed to Constant's happiness except Rosanie's indifference; the confession of the gift of her heart did not long precede that of her hand, and their marriage was soon concluded, to their great satisfaction.

Our lovers, although espoused, wanted to make use of their palaces as usual, but they no longer existed. Minatine was not a common fay; she had applied herself seriously to the study of the human heart; she had therefore withdrawn the gift that had been a great help to both of them. She had not taken that precaution lightly; she feared that the Ideas might be contrary to the happiness of their present situation, for, in sum, ideas can easily lead to jealousy. It is in vain that one gives that the fine name of delicacy; the delicacy of a husband is almost always a terrible jealousy, and it is certainly at least a lack of taste. Minatine therefore made the wise decision to remove the ideas from both of them, and my opinion is that she did well.

In exchange for what they had lost they received the gift of the palace of the most amiable reality. It is a palace full of delights, which, it is true, sometimes crumbles of its own accord, but misfortune never overtakes it by the fault of its foundations, and when the rapport of humor and tastes, and the charms of amity, combined with perfect amour, have built that charming edifice, it surpasses in solidity all those that we now in the world, all the more so because the breaches that time or various circumstances can cause are repaired every day by the infinite pleasures that the heart and the mind produce.

It was on principles as delightful as they were solid that Constant and Rosanie lived, a thousand times happier by virtue of their sentiments than the possession of two great kingdoms and everything that men regard as fortune. The veritable is, in every sense, in our hearts.

PRINCESS LUMINEUSE

There was once a king and a queen; the queen was named Marjolaine and the king Biribi; they lived together in great harmony, although they had married for love. The passion that dominated them both was that of gambling; it occupied their days and nights.

It is widely supposed that King Biribi was the inventor of a game that bears his name today.[27] The king spent his day in his cabinet imagining boards for his game and having the sections painted that were each more singular that the last. These paintings were all applauded, not only because they were the king's composition but also because he inhabitants of that great State had a natural love of playing games.

King Biribi employed the taste his subjects had for games very usefully; he set out to provide an example himself and it was followed in all the banks that he established in all the cities of his realm. He was careful of the comfort and amusement of the different estates, wanting to obtain it at any price.

---

[27] Biribi, otherwise known as cavagnole, was a game of chance akin to roulette (which largely replaced it), played with a board on which the numbers one to seventy are marked. The players put their stakes on the numbers, and a banker draws a "case" from a bag containing a ticket corresponding to one of the numbers of the board; the successful punters are paid sixty-four times their stake. Cheating was very common, and the game was eventually prohibited by law in 1837, but it was popular in the mid-eighteenth century, as were many forms of gambling; Casanova complimented himself on his skill in exploiting the game in his memoirs, and Voltaire founded his fortune with lottery wins in 1729-30, achieved by means that still remain unclear.

He made one very reasonable regulation to favor general bankers, which was an edict by which it was expressly ordered that one person from every family should draw a ball every day, without any reason being able to dispense with that obedience. Women were usually charged by the family with executing an ordinance so advantageous to the banks, because it is not that easy to hold on to a single ball.[28]

Fundamentally, King Biribi was not a gambler; no banker ever is; he only liked money and sensed all the advantage of his game. He relieved his people of all taxes and all entry fees, and did not want anything for the revenue of the crown but the profits of the banks. No duties were every paid by women with more good will and more exactitude, and no monarch ever found more considerable sums in his coffers.

That court, as usual, was governed by two fays of very different character. One was named Balsamine; she was naturally good, and the justice of her mind was infinite; she criticized heavily the declared taste of the king and queen for gambling and that fashion of extracting money from his subjects. She often tried to make the king ashamed, not only of what he obtained from the bank but also his collusion with the bankers, but her remonstrations were futile.

The other fay, who possessed the favor and confidence of Biribi to a much higher degree, because the conformity of tastes brought them closer to one another, was named Sansdent. She was a hardened player, who, in certain cases of loss would even have been capable of staking her wand. She was pale and thin; late nights and the deleterious effects of gaming had burned her blood, and the burned blood gave her a

---

[28] I have translated the terms in this paragraph literally; *boules* [balls] refers to a method of selecting the lottery numbers that is still in use today, but Caylus's fondness for *double entendres* is more evident in this *conte* than most of the others features in the present collection; the reader might detect other sly suggestions in the present story that are not employed—as the majority are—in the service of political satire.

frightful humor, very often causing her to make utterances that no one but a biribi banker would have tolerated. She combined with that deterioration the misfortune of not being able to please others very much and being a little bit envious; such was her character. As for her appearance, she never completed her coiffure, and one could not be any more badly-dressed, for everything she obtained from her income as a fay, instead of going toward her maintenance, melted away in the bank.

People perhaps do not know that, in spite of the great power of fays, they are submissive to a Council that demands an exact account from them of the employment thy make of the money of the treasury. Without that regulation, there is no doubt that Sansdent would have gambled, and, in consequence, lost, all the money the fays had, considerable as their wealth must have been.

The queen was a good, rather simple woman, who punted all day with an unparalleled zeal and patience. The king, who knew the strength of her game perfectly, gave immense sums to the queen for her small pleasures and her maintenance, knowing full well what would become of that money. In fact, she lost everything she was given, and was no better adorned than Sansdent. They both made use of excuses. Biribi, always attentive to setting good examples, had expressly forbidden anyone to target the queen herself, which says everything about the others.

When the king held the bank, the good Marjolaine served as croupier; she gave out the chips, in truth, in a golden ladle garnished with diamonds, and the gentleman of the chamber, who was aged, presented the bag; for it must be agreed that biribi could not be played with more dignity than when that great prince held the bank. He only quit the game in order to receive money from all the general bankers, verify their accounts, and send money back to those whose banks hazard had broken. In sum, he was occupied in keeping in order a large number of banks; nor did he neglect to punish the families that had not drawn balls in accordance with the ordinance. He published in the gazettes all the sums won during the weeks with, the names of the lucky winners, and he publicized in all fashions, with a little augmentation, the losses that the banks had made.

That was the exact state of the king's court when Queen Marjolaine found that she was pregnant. Neither late nights nor gambling prevented her from remaining healthy during the course of her pregnancy and giving birth very fortunately to a princess, who appeared in everyone's eyes to be as beautiful as the finest daylight.

Balsamine took charge of her education and named her Lumineuse. Sansdent, who perceived all the charms that already appeared in the admirable child, felt an envy that, as I have already said, was natural to her and which was redoubled because she foresaw that a little princess for whom she had take responsibility two years before, whom she loved as much as she was capable of loving, and whose name was Pivoine,[29] would have a face very different from that of Lumineuse, and that her intelligence would be far inferior. All these reasons engaged her to subject Lumineuse to all the inconveniences that are all too common in society, in a fashion that even the power of fays could not enable her to avoid them. Balsamine had only had the time to exempt smallpox from the misfortunes of Lumineuse's life, but there are, alas many others, and the Princess, in spite of the amity of the fay, was only too subject to them.

Balsamine perceived the malevolence of her colleague, but as it was not possible to remedy it, she made the wise decision to keep silent about the matter. The figure and face of Lumineuse, which could not have been more perfect, were surpassed by the vivacity and the justice of an intelligence equally borne to mildness and quietude. Balsamine did not give her the slightest advice regarding gambling, of the excess of which she disapproved; she knew full well that children, hardly ever have a taste for things that their parents have loved

---

[29] Pivoine is the French term for the kind of flower known in English as a peony.

excessively, so Lumineuse had an infinite antipathy to that passion all her life.

When Lumineuse reached the age of fifteen, she enchanted by her gaze and charmed by her intelligence; she would have eclipsed many beauties other than Princess Pivoine, whom Sansdent had with her at King Biribi's court. The latter's stature was short and stout, and no girl of her age had ever had such a prodigious cleavage. She had no other intelligence than that of gaming, and repeated from memory all the joke she had heard made about the cases of the board. Sansdent never scolded her because she did not spin out her money very well or because she did not stay on at the end of games in order to decorate the table and retain the layers for longer. She and Lumineuse did not like one another very much, although they had spent their childhood together.

The king and queen did not like their daughter very much either; the reason for that was quite simple: their tastes were different. Marjolaine had brought her daughter to her game several times in order to relax and amuse her, but she had always yawned excessively, for which she had been sent away, and called a little fool, etc. Those reprimands alas engaged Pivoine to swagger, because she regarded them as an indirect praise given to her own character.

Balsamine, being highly considered in all the corporations of the fays, was summoned to settle some important matters; it was the time of that absence that Sansdent chose to propose to the king and queen that Lumineuse be married. Sansdent proposed for their son-in-law the King of Fogs. She not only made much of the grandeur of that alliance, saying that he was a close relative of Night and much loved by physicians, but represented to them that Lumineuse's beauty would inevitably attract wars, during which it would be very difficult for them to be able to gamble, and the expenses of which would diminish the funds of the banks considerably.

"The King of Fogs is a good man who does not, in truth, have much commerce with society and is not received in many houses; but he will take your daughter away and you will be less certain of seeing her during the winter."

Such good reasons made up the minds of the king and the queen. The request for Lumineuse was made the same day, with all the usual ceremonies; the contract was signed immediately, and the marriage was celebrated the same evening. Lumineuse was docile, Balsamine was absent; what can a princess do who is only fifteen years old and dare not oppose the will of her parents? She submitted, and that was all that she could do.

The wedding was gloomy in spite of the quantity of candles that filled the apartments. The King of Fogs and his retinue, which he had reduced considerably out of consideration, blocked the light. The entire court caught a cold, because all fogs spread a great humidity. The excessively fortunate husband of the beautiful Lumineuse was a tall and stout man at least sixty years of age; he had a hoarse voice; he did not say much, and what he did say was infinitely diffuse. He appeared dressed as little children consecrated to swaddling clothes are; the entire court wore the same uniform, as well as that of limp hair, which did not heighten either their faces or their smiles.

The day after the wedding, the husband appeared, as usual, to be very amorous, while Lumineuse was as cold as she had been the day before her marriage, and not at all animated by all the dirty jokes that were made during the celebrations.

After having made his vulgar pleasantries, the king wanted to take his new queen to a part of his estates, which he established in a plain near his father-in-law's capital, and to give an idea of his magnificence he invited King Biribi's entire court to a big supper. Exhalations formed his palace, but the taste of the architecture was a trifle Gothic and the entrance door was so low that it was veritably necessary for everyone to duck their heads in order to enter the palace. When the whole company was assembled, a kind of trap-door was closed, in such a fashion that no one knew any longer either how they had come in or how they were going to get out.

The king, provincial by nature and by habitude, inferred from that circumstance that it was necessary to drink for a long time. The dish that was most dominant in the feast, of which the profusion was extreme, was woodcock.[30]

Although all of King Biribi's courtiers had come to the feast in frock coats and overcoats, and although the King of Fogs had had the attention to have them given caftans of waxed cloth, as at the audiences of the Great Sultan, the humidity of his palace inconvenienced everyone, and in spite of the desire he had to prolong the meal and the bad speeches he made in order to conclude it, the supper was brief, and when everyone had retired, Lumineuse was left alone in her husband's Estates, abandoned to her tears.

King Biribi and Queen Marjolaine having concluded the only affair that could distract them from gambling, returned home with their good friend Sansdent. She had always had the project of crowning the care she had taken of Princess Pivoine by an advantageous marriage; to that effect she had cast her eyes on Prince Grenadin, whose states neighbored those of King Biribi and whose face and merit made a lot of noise in society. The Prince was such a good catch that Balsamine, sage and enlightened as she was, had never desired any other for Princess Lumineuse.

When that good fay returned, what was her dolor at no longer finding her dear Lumineuse! The conversation was lively between the fays; the king and queen replied to the reproaches she made them that they had made a good alliance, and that they had deferred to the advice of their friend Sansdent. Balsamine was piqued by the scant consideration they had had for her; she departed and hastened to the abode

---

[30] I have translated *bécasse* [woodcock] literally but the word also has a familiar pejorative meaning in French analogous to the English usage of "goose" that implies stupidity. Any *double entendre* that might be attached to the English name of the bird presumably could not be applied to the King of Frogs, and should be ignored.

of the beautiful Lumineuse, whom she found alone in her boudoir. Their meeting would have softened even the hardest hearts of any witnesses.

Lumineuse embraced her a thousand times, saying: "Why did you leave me, my good friend? You know that I have no resources without you; never quit me again."

Balsamine responded, with tenderness: "Don't worry; sooner or later I'll avenge you on Sansdent."

"Alas," replied the princess, "I shall spend my entire life in an insupportable obscurity; I shall never accustom my temperament to the humidity that reigns in these somber places. I consent gladly to living without any society, provided that you don't abandon me, my dear Balsamine. To my misfortune, the king, my husband feels amour for me, and I only have for him an indifference well worthy of him and his dismal Estates."

"Hope for a happier situation," Balsamine said to her. "Don't yield to despair; count on me not to abandon you, and at least I shall keep you company faithfully, since Sansdent has made it impossible for me to give you other proofs of my amity."

Lumineuse felt the relief that the aid of amity can provide. The King of Fogs, who perceived the help that Balsamine's company gave to his queen, heaped her with all possible amities. Although his temperament was naturally cold, he felt the indifference that Lumineuse had for him keenly.

As soon as Lumineuse's marriage had been concluded and the new queen had been put into the hands of her husband, the old king, I said, if I remember correctly, that Sansdent, Marjolaine and King Biribi returned promptly to the gaming table; on the following days the same thing was repeated, and they resumed the same way of life that had preceded the wedding. Sansdent, who had not lost sight of her project for her fat favorite, Pivoine, occupied herself seriously with the marriage of her protégée to Prince Grenadin.

That charming prince had remained under the tutelage of his mother, Queen Brilliant, during his childhood. His father, the king, had contracted pleurisy during a butterfly hunt, of which he had died, greatly regretted by his subjects. Brilliante was therefore declared regent; she raised Grenadin with all imaginable cares. The prince had a marked aversion to marriage, but he had a real gallantry in his intelligence, with which he made the delights of his mother's court.

Such was the disposition of that court when Sansdent sent the same dream several times to Queen Brilliante, which concerned the aversion Grenadin had for marriage and assured her that it would only be overcome in the Estates of King Biribi, where he would find the fay Sansdent, to whom he could address himself in all security. That dream was sent to the queen so frequently, always so forcefully accompanied by the same circumstances that in the end, she decided to follow the advertisement that it gave her.

The prince departed, therefore, with an equipage worthy of his birth and his natural taste He was received by King Biribi with all the honors due to his rank, and as people usually assume that everyone has the same tastes as them, the gaming sessions were redoubled, in the design of honoring him further. Sansdent perceived with chagrin the distaste that Grenadin had for gambling. She did not want her project to be thwarted, however, so she decided to give the prince what is known, in all its forms, as a fête. In the gardens of the palace, which were not very well maintained, she used her wand to construct a hall of admirable architectural taste; she decided to give a ball there, to which the entire court was invited—but alas, no one in the country knew how to dance. Pivoine was the only one who knew a few of the steps of the minuet, but how did she do it? She had no ear for music, and without the attentions of the prince and his excessive politeness, he would have fallen backward ten times, she was so awkward. Her train was always getting between her legs, or catching on her slippers.

A ball in which there are so few dancers is necessarily very short. What could they do while awaiting supper? It was necessary, therefore to start gambling. The party sat down; Grenadin, beside the fat Pivoine, was obliged by politeness to gamble. Praise was immediately made of the nobility with which he lost his money. Pivoine said a thousand tender things to him that she had heard said while gambling; she advised him very seriously sometimes to take the Harlequin, sometimes another figure. "It's four days since it's come up," she told him, "I've marked it in my notebook." She asked him for the favor of taking the number 25, 7 or 52, and rendering him a very exact account of the Cabala, of which the prince could not understand a word, in spite of the princess's explanation.

As he made jokes, lightly, about those propositions, of which he could not be the dupe given his intelligence, Pivoine told him that there are things that it is necessary to know, not merely because they succeed in gambling, but also because they give the appearance of it.

"Would you believe," she added, "that I am obliged to it for having obtained preference for me over a princess with whom I was brought up in this court, and who was never able to retain a word of it, so closed was her mind."

The supper was served a long time before they went to table; the gamblers were piqued; it had been postponed several times, and when it was served it had long gone cold. During the supper, people tried to initiate a few agreeable topics of conversation, but they always fell back on gambling, on a piquant coup, on the nobility of some game or other, on one's exactitude in paying. In the end, those agreeable topics occupied the entire time of the supper. Scarcely had the fruit been served than everyone ran back to the gaming tables.

The politeness of the prince caused him a great deal of interior suffering, and engaged him to converse with the fat Pivoine sufficiently to give him an aversion for her forever and sufficiently for her to be gripped by a very strong penchant for him.

The conversation fell upon Lumineuse, and Pivoine said everything she could imagine of the most malevolent, which had an opposite effect on the mind of the prince. Pivoine wanted to turn to ridicule Lumineuse's aversion to gambling and the fashion she had of occupying herself in her apartment and remaining alone there. Those details, contrary to her intention, made a favorable impression on Grenadin's mind, and he was touched by the fashion in which such a beautiful princess had been sacrificed to a king such as Pivoine had depicted him.

The prince felt a kind of chagrin at the idea that Lumineuse had married such a husband; that chagrin was followed by a displeasure in imagining that she was married; afterwards, he formed regrets for the fact that he had not been informed instead of all the perfections of the princess; he was afflicted by the fact that he had not made his journey the year before, and repented of not having been proposed himself to marry her. A portrait of Lumineuse that the queen chanced to show him fortified all his ideas and gave him new ones.

Occupied with all these things, almost without thinking about it, as one is struck by singular events, as soon as he perceived a fog he left the palace, making use of the pretext of going hunting. He hoped by dint of searching that perhaps he would see her for himself one day. In order to satisfy his curiosity, he came to the point of running after fogs, as one searches for the first rays in sunshine in spring or the coolness of shade in summer. He spent some time in that rather sad occupation.

Finally, he perceived one day, in a very extensive plan, a huge fog of the greatest density, with the movement that one sometimes observes in exhalations of those sorts. The sun had just risen, and was gilding all the rest of the countryside. The prince ran to that fog. One could never render a precise account of the species of instinct that guides and strikes lovers.

In fact, his hopes were not disappointed. That fog was one of the petty palaces of the queen, and the lightest of those she inhabited. The King of Fogs made it march in the marshiest places, with the intention of gathering recruits for a project he was meditating toward the north. The queen was on a kind of terrace, or, to put it better, the extremity of the fog, in order to see the sun and respire a purer and calmer air. The prince recognized her easily, and could not help crying out: "Finally, then, beautiful Lumineuse, I've been able to see you!"

Struck by that compliment, the queen looked at him with the attention that his face could merit, and, without making any reply that might commit her to anything, expressed by means of her gaze that the compliment was agreeable to her.

How easily a lover understands that language! The palace went on its way, leaving the prince enchanted by what he had seen, and the queen ran promptly to inform Balsamine of that little adventure.

The fay consulted her Book of Hours and said to her, with a sigh: "Alas, my dear princess, you've seen Prince Grenadin, the man I hoped that you might marry."

When the queen learned that the man who had just seen was a prince, his face appeared even more agreeable to her, by virtue of the similarity of conditions. She made the comparison of Grenadin with the king, her husband. The mind covers all that ground in a moment, and the most austere virtue cannot prevent first impressions. In the end, solitude, amity and even more, the plenitude of her heart, engaged the princess to make the confession of all her sentiments to Balsamine. At first it was only to have the simple pleasure of talking about it. The fay, unable to refuse such a natural conversation, delivered herself to it with all the patience that it is necessary for a confidante to bring to the endurance of all the repetitions and restatements of a amorous heart.

She owed that complaisance to her all the more because, in accordance the law that Sansdent had imposed at the moment of Lumineuse's birth, Balsamine could not predict her future—which, fundamentally, was not such a bad thing, for the hope of amour predicts things to lovers sufficiently. It was therefore only possible for her to represent the past and the present. After having made a simple conjuration, she read aloud from her little Book of Hours, because everything one might desire to know about the past and the present was written therein.

She read, therefore, everything I have written about the indifference and gallantry of Grenadin while she was that the court of his mother, the queen. Then she read the dream that Sansdent had sent, the departure of the prince and his arrival at King Biribi's curt, his ennui for gambling, the detail of the dance and the vulgar flirtations of Pivoine. Balsamine went into the most exact detail of everything that had happened.

The princess read the fay's Book of Hours incessantly. It was ornamented by miniatures on vellum, and those charming paintings expressed in a natural manner all the events that could interest or amuse. Lumineuse saw with pleasure there the prince returning to King Biribi's abode after the encounter he had contrived with her. She perceived the redoubling of his ennui and the scrupulous search he made of all the thickest fogs; she feared for his lungs a thousand times. She witnessed all the trouble he took in order to obtain a copy of her portrait. It was with contentment that she remarked everything that Princess Pivoine suffered by virtue of his indifference for her.

Finally, she read that, as there were fogs in his own Estates, and that he had as much hope of finding her in that land as anywhere else, he made the decision to return there, after having constantly refused all the advantageous offers that Sansdent made him for Pivoine's marriage, and after having lost very considerable sums as nobly as possible to the king's bank.

Lumineuse perceived that Sansdent wanted to punish the prince and avenge Pivoine for the scant regard he had had for her person. She ran to Balsamine and said: "Save him, my dear friend; perhaps she's going to metamorphose him; at least don't let him lose his form."

"Don't worry," the good fay replied. "I've taken care of it."

In fact, he did not suffer the slightest accident, and the queen saw him depart without any obstacle.

Grenadin abandoned himself blindly to his passion; he sometimes declaimed against destiny, and above all against Queen Brilliante's dream. As for Queen Lumineuse, at least she had her little book, but she was no happier for that. When one is very much in love, one only thinks the help one has mediocre, and is only ever occupied with regret for the aid of which one is deprived.

The King of Fogs, agitated and tormented by the indifference of Lumineuse, and whose age was rather advanced, fell into a kind of languor. The physicians advised the king sometimes to take a cleaner air that that which he usually respired. He obeyed that prescription and, unfortunately—for him, that is—caught a sunstroke of which he died a few days later. The queen gave him all the cares imaginable; in brief, her conduct was admirable on that sad occasion, and all the fogs were enchanted by it.

When the last duties had been had been rendered to the king and he had been taken to the tomb of his predecessors in a great lake, Lumineuse formed the resolution to quit that sad abode and return to her father's Estates, and she wrote to him. King Biribi replied to his daughter that she had only rid herself boldly of all the authority that she had over her people and she would always find a refuge in his Estates.

After that response, Lumineuse packed all her bags with an incredible diligence. The fogs did not want to abandon their queen, for whom they had a veritable attachment, but all the efforts they made to engage her not to not to leave them were futile. She disengaged them from their oath of fidelity and quit them, and it is for that reason that they are wandering in different countries. Since that time, no one has taken the trouble to reunite them, nor that of governing them. All that I know about the particulars of the division of that great Estate is that most of them retired to England.

Lumineuse appeared at her father's court even more beautiful than when she left. The freshness and beauty of her complexion were further augmented; she was not at all pale by virtue of coming from such a country. The full mourning in which she arrived served as her pretext for not taking part in the king's game and gradually distancing herself from a life that did not suit her. Her mourning attire was all white, in accordance with the custom of the widows of Kings of Fogs, and might perhaps have depleted other beauties a great deal, but it only rendered her more beautiful.

Sometime after her arrival, on the advice of Balsamine she asked King Biribi for a terrain in which, with the help of the fay, she built a magnificent palace, simple in its exterior, whose interior combined taste and magnificence. It was there that she assembled a select court of individuals of both sexes.

The gardens responded to the magnificence of the palace, but the Arbor of Truth of which Balsamine made her a particular present was the most useful item to a person who only wanted to be surrounded by sincere people. That arbor contained the most admirable statues of white marble; naked Truth dominated all the others, and it was also on her, by virtue of the disposition of the design, that gazes initially fell. Candor was expressed throughout her face, and one also saw there the impressions that the vices had caused her to sense. The large arbor, in which Truth appeared in isolation, was divided into several spaces, which contained the various Virtues that humans ought to follow.

Those spaces formed Temples of Verdure each consecrated to one of those divinities. Amour could be seen in one, with Delicacy and Fidelity. Valor appeared in another, accompanied by Mildness and Composure. Gratitude for Benefits had for companion Memory and Sensibility. The Honor of Women was placed between Decorum and Modesty. The Temple of Religion was ornamented by Good Faith and Persuasion.

That superb arbor was open to everyone; an old man accompanied those whom curiosity brought there. How many people presented themselves at that arbor with the boldness and conceit that are only too common at court! How many courtiers saw Truth, who suddenly appeared to them to be covered in gilded rags, and hid from their eyes without allow-

195

ing them to see anything but the mask of deceit, and the horror of her face! How many lovers of both sexes obliged the figure of Amour to take on that of Falsity, and in the same way, Fidelity attested a thousand times instantly become light-footed Inconstancy, or perverse Coquetry! How many others, instead of Amour appearing to their eyes such as the had hoped to find him, were only struck by his deceitful expression! How many false Valors appeared, sometimes with the face of fear and the gestures of terror, and sometimes deprived of sang-froid, having need of action to sustain it, and yet others who could not perceived it without ferocity! Ingratitude appeared at every moment in the place of Gratitude, Forgetfulness took that of Memory, and Sensibility fainted with Memory. How many women, whose prudish manner expelled modesty in order to substitute debauchery for it, the sight of whom caused Decorum to faint! How many hypocrites and human projects did one not see in the Temple of the statue of Religion!

That arbor served Lumineuse abundantly, as well as her natural enlightenment, in order only to assemble sincere people around her. Her court was not numerous, but it was charming.

The princess was only occupied internally with Grenadin. She had seen in Balsamine's little book that the prince, bored by everything that was presented to him, had not been able to stay long at Queen Brilliante's court; that, always occupied by the desire to see her, he had departed in order to search for the thickest fogs; and that, to that effect, he had marched alone toward the most frightful countries of the North. It was no longer possible then to resist the pleasure of extracting him from anxiety by informing him of the death of the king, her husband, the state of liberty that she enjoyed, and the location of her abode, but she could not hope for any of the help that fays give to the young princesses they protect. It was up to Amour to facilitate what she desired.

She opened one of the windows of her palace and summoned a light mist that she perceived in her gardens. She recognized him as being full of vivacity and the desire to oblige, and as having served her with a great deal of attachment; he was a great traveler by nature. She told him where to find Prince Grenadin and gave him her orders.

As soon as Grenadin was informed of the whereabouts of Lumineuse, he avoided the fogs with as much care as he had sought them out and resumed the road to King Biribi's Estates urgently.

You will remember Sansdent's methods; they had displeased Balsamine for all sorts of reasons. The good fay, sage even in her anger, did not want it to burst forth until she had established Lumineuse in a fashion as agreeable as it was solid. Some time afterwards, the two fays had a very lively conversation. The dispute became so heated that it could no longer terminate in any other fashion than a single combat, the end of which might have been the overturning of the Estate, but the Council of Fays, having been alerted to it right away, summoned both of them.

Having arrived before that sage Tribunal, the two fays recounted what had happened to them.

Sansdent was convicted on all counts and sent to live among the Iroquois savages, under the pretext of civilizing them, but fundamentally to punish her by means of an honest exile, which was all the more sensible to her because there was not the faintest resource in that land with regard to gambling. Pivoine was summoned; Sansdent was not given permission to make her adieux to King Biribi and Queen Marjoline, but as she left she was given that of marrying Princes Pivoine to some King of Savages; then the Council dismissed both of them, without being moved by their tears.

On her return, Balsamine found King Biribi and Queen Marjolaine, who, saddened as they were by the absence of Sansdent and the anxiety of not seeing her again, were gambling while awaiting the decision of events. They came to meet the fay in the embarrassed manner that is given by wrongdoing. They were quite astonished when she begged them not to disturb themselves and to continue their game; but she wished to punish them in another fashion, which, without being explosive, was no less sensible to them. All the banks were broken by fortunate wagers, and that fortune was so sagely divided that all the gamblers in the realm regained precisely what they had lost, and found themselves in the same degree of opulence in which the rule of the game had found them. It was high time that the reparation was made, for almost all the families of the great State were absolutely ruined.

Balsamine wanted to console the king for the considerable loses he had just made, by enabling him envisage the inconveniences and the shame of the life had had been leading until then; she advised him, in the fashion in which one gives an order, to refer, for the government of his Estate, to the advice of Lumineuse; and his incapacity, combined with other reasons, determined him to follow the fay's orders, or advice.

In addition to the great intelligence that she had and the knowledge with which she was ornamented, aided by the wise counsel of Balsamine, Lumineuse reestablished police and order, and enabled commerce to flourish in a realm whose affairs had been deranged for a long time. Those changes were made in a very short time. The choice of men being the most essential part of a government, the Arbor of Truth served her usefully for discovering what was in the depths of hearts, and the degree of virtue of those she employed.

For the amusement of King Biribi and Queen Marjolaine, and that of their little court, all the games of commerce, like Oie, Trou-Madame and a thousand others, some of which have been passed down to us,[31] not to mention the game of Romance, and those that relate to Orthography and Geography,

---

[31] Oie—known in English as the Game of the Goose—and Trou-Madame are two of the oldest known games, both played in Medieval times; the former is a board game akin to snakes-and-ladders; the latter a game of skill in which disks are rolled toward wooden edifice with several doors, with the aim of introducing them into the chambers beyond the doors. Louis XIV is reported to have been extremely fond of playing Trou-Madame.

games that were then absolutely necessary because of the forgetfulness people had of those areas of knowledge.

Balsamine. in Lumineuse's name, expressly forbade, under rigorous penalties, all remainder games, above all Biribi. She had all the boards, bags and balls that she had collected from all over the kingdom burned, and I have no idea how, in spite of all those precautions, the game was able to be handed down to us, especially after such a long span of time

Alerted, as we have reported, by the mist, Grenadin departed as soon as he heard the good news, but he was so far away that Lumineuse and Balsamine had had time to do everything that has just been reported before he had had time to arrive. The prince, who thought he would find King Biribi's Estates in the situation in which he had left them, not only feared seeing Sansdent again—because he had left her furious against him and it was quite natural that he should fear her threats—but feared even more seeing Pivoine again, because she loved him, and nothing displeases a man in love as much as the amour of a disagreeable object. The prince therefore made the decision to arrive in the capital in disguise.

What joy it is for a lover to receive in response to every question he asks a eulogy to the woman he loves! The story of a virtue, an example of kindness, an instance of intelligence and sagacity: in sum, seeing the love of an entire people, who never weary of replying to the reiterated questions of the curiosity that amour inspires! Prince Grenadin, enchanted by so many flatting anecdotes, did not maintain his incognito, and, declaring his birth and his name, he had himself conducted to the fay, who was performing the functions of prime minister.

The interview was brief, because the fay took him to the princess immediately, who had witnessed via her book all the impressions that her lover had received and had observed continually the moments that had guided him to her. If Balsamine had not been present, fortunately, as a third party, the conversation would not have been elaborate in terms of words, by virtue of there being too much to say; by virtue of thinking too much, they could not speak. And who would not shut up, at that price, and make the proof of such a silence?

Grenadin asked for permission to be her principal courtier, assuring her that since she was free and her delicacy no longer had to suffer, he estimated himself only too happy to be able to see her and admire her. That permission was easily granted to him.

Grenadin confessed to Lumineuse and amour of which she had no doubt. She admitted herself to the liking she had for him. Grenadin threw himself at her knees, imploring her to crown his amour and permit him to aspire to the honor of her hand. The adorable princess yielded and consented to her lover's desires, but in order to have nothing for which to reproach herself and fully to satisfy her reason, she wanted to ask the prince to undergo the proof of the Arbor of Truth.

Grenadin was deeply offended by her proposal. "Anything that you order me to do," he said, "to prove the most tender and sincere attachment, it is certain that I will do. But can it be that you doubt the sincerity of my sentiments? Can it be that I owe you anything else, for your consent, than my amour?"

Grenadin pronounced those words with the vivacity of an offended delicacy, and in a fashion so touching, that Lumineuse, struck by his amour, begged his pardon for having made such a proposition to him, and disavowed it fully, making him master of her person and her Estates.

"Now the proof is acceptable to me," said the prince, kissing her hand delightedly. "Now I can run it without fear."

In fact, Grenadin drew away from the princess ardently and ran to the Arbor. Lumineuse followed him, agitated by all the troubles, all the anxieties and all the hopes of amour. But what was the joy of that tender princess when she saw Truth, who seemed to be embellished at the sight of her lover, Amour ran to him, followed by a host of attributes almost unknown in this world; Honor and Valor and, in sum, all the Virtues, set off after him and introduced him to Amour! What transport for Grenadin to see that he had been followed by Lumineuse, to whom Decorum and Modesty had run, and what satisfaction to distinguish the embarrassment of Amour and his amiable retinue, who did not know to which of the two, the princess or him, it was more just to defer!

In the end, Amour and Truth themselves formed in the Arbor the eternal union of the two most perfect lovers, and those two divinities never quit them in the course of a life as long as it was fortunate.

BLEUETTE AND COQUELICOT

There was once a fay named Bonnebonne who lost her appetite for the great employments of Faerie to which her character and her talents had elevated her; she chose for her retirement an island set in the middle of a beautiful lake, the shores of which were formed by the richest, most cheerful and most fertile country. That fortunate retreat was named the Isle of Wellbeing. People know that it existed, and are even convinced that it is still in the country of which they are a neighbor, but geographers have not yet place it on any map, and I have not read any voyager who has ever landed there; it is sufficient that the Annals of the Fays have given us knowledge of it.

Bonnebonne, having lost her appetite for society, not liking to pay court, asked the Queen of the Fays for permission to retire; she went to the Isle of Wellbeing, and it was there, with the finest library and all the knowledge that she had acquired in the world, that she became the cleverest of all the fays. She enabled the happiness of all her neighbors and gratitude was the foundation of her authority. In addition to the fact that her taste bore her to oblige others—and the remoteness of high society did not diminish that sentiment—it was a great satisfaction for her to see all those who surrounded her happy.

In order to satisfy that veritable pleasure, and not to be simultaneously heaped with all sorts of ridiculous requests, she had placed, at a short distance from one another, on the shores of the lake, white marble columns, to which those who had requests or complaints to address to her addressed themselves. Those columns were constructed in such a fashion that by speaking in a low voice, they relayed the sound of her voice very distinctly into a cabinet of the mansion. Bonnebonne ordinarily stationed a niece there, whom she was bringing up to be a fay, and who rendered her an account in the evening of everything that the columns had reported; the fay then decided what to do.

Bonnebonne's principal occupation was bringing up children and rendering them happy; at breakfast and at lunch she provided everything that could be desired of pastry and sugar, but when someone had lived in that happy abode for a fortnight, they no longer wanted candy; they spent the day walking on the grass, collecting nuts in the woods or flowers from the garden; they went out on the lake in pretty boats which they guided themselves; in sum, they did every day whatever they wanted, and wellbeing consists in large measure of liberty.

It is true that there were nursemaids and tutors, but they were invisible; they advised Bonnebonne of what had been done badly, and then she issued a reprimand, but always gently, because she was the nicest woman in the world. Sometimes the nursemaids and tutors ceased to be invisible, and then they were seen supping together on the grass, or dancing to music, or amusing themselves making toys and dolls; in sum, nothing had an air of severity in that happy habitation, so everyone wanted to live there, and no one ever left it without experiencing the greatest of afflictions; but as everything is submissive to destiny and the fays themselves have to obey it, when someone reached a certain age—which is to say, between twelve and fifteen years—when the fay's lessons had made a deep impression on the minds of her pupils and she found them sufficiently formed to enter into society, she was obliged to send them away, which she did by heaping them with caresses and presents, and assuring them of an amity of which she often gave them proofs in the course of their lives.

Among the number of children of whom she had obtained the confidence of their parents there was a little girl named Bleuette, who as so pretty and so well-behaved that Bonnebonne preferred her to all the others, and whom she loved madly. She was affectionate without being inconvenient and lively without being importunate. Her face announced the mildness of her character and her beauty increased with age.

Bleuette also possessed the splendor that dazzles, and it is to her rare beauty that we owe that fashion of speaking, still used in familiar language, where, in order to talk about something that has dazzled us, we say "I've seen bleuettes."[32]

A young child about two years older than her lived on the Isle of Wellbeing; his name was Coquelicot; his face was charming, as lively as his mind, and his natural gentility pleased Bonnebonne equally. What rendered them both as charming as one another is that from their infancy they had been inseparable, and the vivacity of the one was submissive to the mildness and tenderness of the other, made their charac-ters more moderate and more lovable.

Bonnebonne enjoyed incessantly the impression and the progress that veritable amour made on innocence and ingenu-ousness; she was continually occupied by it, and all the other kinds of wellbeing that she was able to procure so perfectly could not be compared to that one. In fact, what felicity can be put in balance with that produced by the union of two hearts that amour unites by virtue of the agreement and rapport of humors? Coquelicot, lively as he was, perhaps even a trifle excessive, was only moderate and mild with regard to Bleuette, who, for her part, only had vivacity with regard to Coquelicot. The birth and progress of their sentiments had made their delights; the mild flirtation they experienced made the charms of Bonnebonne's life, for she said a hundred times over: "My God, how pretty those poor children are, how much they love one another, and how happy they are; they don't give any thought to leaving my island, no happier subjects have ever inhabited my empire."

One day—it was the evening of one of the most beautiful days of the summer—all the lovable children were playing and

---

[32] This is not, in fact, a common expression in French, and I can find no evidence that anyone has ever made use of it ex-cept the Comte de Caylus. The masculine common noun *bleuet* refers to the flower known in English as a cornflower. A *coquelicot* is a poppy.

amusing themselves in the different parts of the enchanted abode. Suddenly, a chariot appeared in the air drawn by six flame-colored griffins. The chariot was the same color, heightened by black ornaments. It bore the fay Arganto, coiffed in brown with one or two red feet; her adornment matched her chariot. Her griffins alighted at the perron of the mansion where Bonnebonne and her niece were standing, in order greet the fay and lend her a hand to get down.

After the initial compliments, Arganto testified to Bonnebonne that, being unable to understand the pleasures of retirement, but disgusted by a few discontentments with the court, she had wanted to judge for herself the charms and difficulties of such a life; and, in order to be perfectly enlightened, she had made the resolution to come and spend a few days with her.

Bonnebonne responded politely that she would gladly satisfy her, and had nothing to hide from her. "The beauties of Nature," she added, "make the tableaux with which I am occupied; her fruits are my treasures, her secrets the object of my research, ad my dissipation attaches me to the wellbeing of others; childhood is the state of humanity that can render the most happiness, so you find me surrounded by the prettiest children that Nature has produced." As she said that she advanced into the island, finding troops of children of various ages and both sexes at every step, whose natural features inspired a veritable gaiety; some were dancing, others playing blind man's bluff; some were amusing themselves playing grown-ups; in sum, they passed suddenly from one whim to another; their characters were developing, and one could easily imagine what they would become at a more advanced age.

Arganto found that recreation of Bonnebonne rather mediocre; she judged it like a socialite—which is to say, with scorn. She said to her companion that she could only conceive those sorts of pleasures to the extent that one employed one's intelligence in order to make the most of them. It was in vain that Bonnebonne tried to praise them; she was not convinced. Finally, as they continued their walk, they perceived Bleuette and Coquelicot, who were talking to one another, who were only seeing themselves in Nature, who were only expecting their pleasures, their desires, their occupations and their will from themselves alone. Bonnebonne called to them; they ran to her with the confidence and amity that generosity and gratitude are able to inspire.

Arganto was struck by the charm of their faces; she told them that; they blushed and thanked the fay for one another.

"I understand," she said, "that nature cannot present a more agreeable image than that of these lovable children. However," she continued, "have they as much intelligence as their physiognomy promises?"

"Assuredly they have," replied Bonnebonne. "Perhaps it won't please you, for it's only natural; furthermore, they love one another too much to show it, especially to someone they don't know."

The fays gave them a thousand caresses, and left them together.

Bonnebonne agreed with Arganto that they would not constrain one another during her sojourn, and that she could devote herself to her ordinary studies, but as the other could not shut up about the impression that Bleuette and Coquelicot had made on her, she wanted them to keep her company.

Arganto was born malevolent, and malevolence can only suffer with impatience the happiness of others; it is only occupied with destroying it, with no other motive than doing harm. On those baleful principles, she employed the time of her sojourn depicting for the two children the coldness and insipidity of the place where they lived; and telling them that nature had formed them for the delights and ornament of the most brilliant courts. She made them an advantageous description of the abode of kings.

"You're enchanted," she said to them incessantly, "with the life you lead, but do you know any other? The brilliance of society, the fêtes that are given to beauty alone, the preferences that are accorded to you at every moment, are the veritable triumphs of a pretty individual." It was this that she spoke to Bleuette.

"And you," she said, addressing Coquelicot, "with the intelligence you have, what could you not do in a court? You must certainly have valor; of what would your merit not be capable?"

These perverse discourses gradually had the impression that Arganto desired on the minds of the lovable children. They sought one another out, as usual, but they surprised one another occupied with something other than themselves. They began by making one another a few reproaches; then they made reciprocal confessions, for they could hardly talk about anything other than the fay's ideas; amour and the hope of not being separated were, it is true, still the foundation of their projects, but in the end, curiosity, the novelty of everything that Arganto had said to them, and, more than anything else, self-regard, the poison of life, eventually seduced their innocence.

They abandoned themselves to the wicked fay, who, in order to make them fall more easily into the trap that she was extending for them, did not neglect to destroy the respect, the amity and the gratitude they had for Bonnebonne, saying to them: "She's a provincial fay whose tastes are not elevated; her character is unsuited to the court; she's only too glad to be able to keep you with her; she's sacrificing your fortune to her pleasure and the utility you have for her."

It was by means of similar discourse that she prepared the ingratitude of the children. She also promised them not to abandon them, and assured them that, being a more powerful fay than Bonnebonne, they had nothing to worry about. She did more; she prejudiced their minds against the things that the sage fay would say to them when she was informed of the resolution they had made. In the end, they promised to go with her after she had given them her word not to separate them.

When Arganto was assured of the decision they had made, she told Bonnebonne that it was time that she ceased to inconvenience her in her retreat, and asked her to the same time to approve of her taking Bleuette and Coquelicot with her.

The good fay, who had not perceived anything and had had no suspicion of her designs, because she had even ordered them herself to pay their court and to obey the fay while she retired to her cabinet, and above all because her good heart had not foreseen the ingratitude, consented to the request that she made, on the condition that they agreed to the proposition, firmly convinced that they would never want to leave her. They were informed immediately.

What was the astonishment of Bonnebonne when they accepted the proposal to go with the fay and abandon her! She said all the things to them most replete with amity and good advice, but in vain; they had been prejudiced. The Bonnebonne said to them gently: "It's persuasion that makes happiness, You'll cease to be happy in this abode, since you imagine a greater felicity elsewhere." With tears in her eyes, she said to them: "Go, let nothing retain you; may you be content."

Bleuette and Coquelicot were moved by that tender discourse to the point of falling at the knees of the adorable fay and imploring her to forget that they had had the idea of separating from her. The seizure that they experienced at that moment made both of them fall into a faint; thus, the mischief of Arganto became useless because of that return of their hearts; even she was touched by such a tender spectacle and found herself almost at the point of repenting of the chagrin that she was causing to three people who nothing to lament except having trusted her too much. Not knowing what decision to make, she was preparing to depart alone when Bonnebonne said to her:

"I could complain about the fashion in which you have abused the welcome that I have given you, but the greatest fruit of study and solitude is that of forgiveness. I am, therefore, not at all touched for myself, but I am for the misfortune of these young children. I loved them for themselves."

"I no longer want to take them away," said Arganto. "You can see that they've refused me, and you can't doubt the attachment they have for you."

"No," replied Bonnebonne, "I find myself forced to ask you to take away that which I loved best in my retreat; you have perverted them, their hearts are no longer what they were, they would only be staying with me out of complaisance. Even if they had art enough to disguise it from me, could I ignore their thoughts? Take them away then, I beg you, and at least look after them in the misfortunes to which you wanted to deliver them."

"Since you insist," said Arganto, "I'll satisfy you."

Then both of them were taken into her chariot, unconscious as they were. Arganto's griffins flew off rapidly and arrive promptly in the Kingdom of Errors.

The king who governed it then believed himself to be the greatest of all princes. Flattery had persuaded him that he was of the blood of the gods. In consequence of that idea, he had his subjects worship him. His throne of gold and precious stones, on which he only appeared once a month, was surrounded by tigers, lions and elephants held captive by chains of the same metal and covered in the most superb embroideries.

Without going into great detail regarding the etiquette of that court, the king practiced at every instant all that the pride of the diadem can inspire. Arganto was his good friend; she shared his pleasures; and it was into his superb palace, where his court was, that she took Bleuette and Coquelicot.

At the moment when they recovered consciousness, they had the pleasure of seeing one another again. The richness of the place in which they found themselves astonished them. Their uncertainty did not last long; Arganto came to extract them from it. They asked her right away for news of Bonnebonne. They fay told them that she had consented to their fortune and had implored her herself to take them away. Bleuette and Coquelicot were relieved by that story, for they had dreaded displeasing her.

Then Arganto said to them: "For you, beautiful Bleuette, this is the apartment that I destine for you; your household will be made this evening. In the meantime, here are your maidservants, whom I present to you."

At these words a dozen of them appeared, all well made and charged with the frivolous things that have become so necessary to luxury and adornment. They were followed by a similar number of valets, who were carrying coffers and caskets, and who equipped the most superb dressing table in a moment. The season's garments appeared next, in such great profusion that they occupied all the chairs and sofas of the large apartment.

When everything was arranged to the fay's liking, she said to Bleuette: "This belongs to you. You have no other study to make than that of learning to make use of it." Then she showed her a basket full of jewelry and a casket of precious stones as perfect in themselves as they were agreeably mounted. She said to her: "Beautiful Bleuette, this little jewel-case will amuse you. Let's pass on now to the apartment I have destined for Coquelicot."

Bleuette followed the fay, without being in a state to be capable of responding. Her surprise and her astonishment appeared to her to be a beautiful dream.

All three of them went into another apartment. It was simple but neat. Four valets who were in the second room came to present him with garments as elegant as they were superb, in order for him to choose the one with which he wanted to be ornamented that day. Then the door of a huge cabinet was opened, in which all sorts of musical instruments were seen. The same cabinet was equipped with bookshelves filed with books of history, and above all of novels and tales of faerie.

"There," said Arganto, "is what will help you relax when you desire to take a rest from your pleasures, or repose after your exercises." Then she ordered the person she had chosen to be his squire to appear. "You can take his advice," she said to Coquelicot. "He's a reliable man, and very good company."

She continued: "Show the things with which you are charged." Then men in livery appeared, who bore the most magnificent arms, the most perfect for war and for hunting.

"That's not all yet," said Arganto. "Let's put out heads out of the window."

They obeyed her, and they saw fifty horses, held by twenty-five grooms, superbly-dressed and well mounted.

"There," she said, "are your horses, for hunting and riding."

Then she ordered the carriages to appear: berlines, berlingots, vis-à-vis and caleches of every species files under the windows, harnessed to the prettiest and best braided horses in the world. Coquelicot experienced the same satisfaction as Bleuette, and observed the same silence.

"Learn, both of you, to make use of what I have just given you," Arganto said to them. "You are both charming, but believe me, adornment is necessary to beauty. Then she left them, each in their apartment, questioning their new domestics about the utility of everything by which they were surrounded, for they dared not give orders yet.

Finally, they got dressed, and, Coquelicot having gone into Bleuette's apartment, they were astonished by the agreeable effect of the adornment, and, proclaiming Arganto's good taste a hundred times over, they convinced themselves all the more easily of what she had said to them about Bonnebonne, whose simplicity was beginning to make them blush.

The entire court, informed of the arrival of Bleuette and Coquelicot, came to see them urgently, either out of curiosity or a desire to please the fay. The king himself did them that honor. The eulogies of the men for Bleuette and those of the women for Coquelicot satisfied them equally. They found that the language of which everyone made use in that land had an agreeable turn that was unfamiliar to them; they were impressed by it, and thought of nothing but imitating it. From the first day, Bleuette perceived that Coquelicot was not made for his clothes, and that he gave an impression of having borrowed them, which the other young men by which she was surrounded did not have.

In sum, both of them were occupied with a thousand new ideas. They saw one another every day, it is true, but they sought one another less, and the tender conversations, in which naivety, ingenuousness, candor and truth had once played so much part, were no longer in usage between them. Thy only sought to place the words and the turns of phrase that had impressed them in that new abode.

The adornment, the magnificence and the splendor with which they dazzled the entire court engaged everyone to give them the titles of Prince and Princess. They knew full well that they did not merit them, given the lowliness of their birth, but the error of others satisfied their vanity; they agreed between them to keep the circumstance secret, and each of them hoped privately that beauty and merit might enable them, in fact, to reach that estate.

Coquelicot was perfectly pretty, and his face was charming. He performed exercises with a marvelous success; almost all the ladies were taken with him. Bleuette was not jealous of his conquests in any fashion, and although one is not always equitable in situations of that sort, at least she had the justice not to make him the slightest reproach. She would, however, have merited some herself, for the court and its grand airs had deranged both their hearts and minds.

For her part, Bleuette, only seeking to please and to prevail over all the other beauties of the court, followed the flattering penchant of coquetry. One can imagine that, thinking in that fashion, she did not take long to make use of all the fay's presents. Soon, she invented fashions, which all the others, beautiful or ugly, were obliged to follow involuntarily.

For some time, that coquetry flattered her vanity, only presenting to her eyes jealous rivals and intoxicated, seduced men, who were flattered or rendered desperate by deceptive and perverse gazes and remarks. But Bleuette was beautiful; she had so much intelligence and grace that, while spreading woe, she was the object of all the eulogies and all the urgency of the handsomest men in the court. She even governed herself so well that it was impossible to make the slightest reproach to her virtue.

For his part, Coquelicot, the fickle adorer of a thousand various objects, flattered his vanity without ever satisfying his heart.

Such was the veritable and unfortunate situation that the two persons, once the most tender and the most lovable, experienced when that same vanity, the reef of so many fortunes, was itself sharply offended. Both dazzled by the splendor by which they were surrounded, they had received princely titles with pleasure. Nothing is unknown in society, and that vanity should in itself have inspired disgust for a lie, if virtue were insufficient.

A child brought up, as they had been, on the Isle of Wellbeing, having departed, as so many others had done, and traveled through various lands, was attracted to the court where Bleuette and Coquelicot lived. He was astonished to find the grand titles of Prince and Princess added to their names. He ran nevertheless to the fay's palace in order to embrace them; but, far from being well received, they did not even deign to recognize him. He made his complaints to anyone who cared to listen, and the entire court was promptly informed that Princess Bleuette and Prince Coquelicot were the children of honest folk, to be sure, but poor shepherds.

A court is a country where nothing is pardoned, and in which ridicule is sought out with extreme care, so everyone profited from that one. Songs and epigrams ran around in a moment; it was not possible even to ignore them, for, in accordance with the laudable custom of author of those sorts of works, the first copy is addressed to the interested individual. Coquelicot was chaffed by some of the wits of the court, but he extracted a prompt satisfaction, and the duel in which he killed his adversary did him honor in a land where truth is so rare, but in which a lie is nevertheless not pardoned. Justice was rendered to his valor, but he was no longer given the same welcome, for, after all, although riches enable anything to be

213

obtained, the ridicule of a humble birth that is displayed with vanity is rarely forgotten at a court.

As for Bleuette, whom wounded pride had rendered even prouder, and counted on repairing by her beauty and charms the disagreeable rumors that were spreading regarding her pastoral past, also had the dolor of seeing the sacrifice of a few letters that she had had the imprudence to write. Her attractions humiliated and her reputation compromised—albeit unjustly—she experienced a veritable chagrin, which engaged her to make reflections. Recalling then the memory of her past wellbeing, Bonnebonne's discourse came to mind.

Agitated, therefore, by all the ideas that led her to her original sentiments for Coquelicot, Bleuette no longer saw except with regret everything that she had done since she had been at the court. She was ashamed of it, but it was not possible to determine herself to talk to him with an open heart. She told herself that he would mistake for coquetry or chagrin the most sincere return, and that she could hardly complain about that. He would believe that, her birth being having become common knowledge, her projects of fortune had been disrupted, and had brought her back to him out of shame and necessity. *No*, she thought, *I shall not make him the witness of all the weakness of my heart and all the pains that the false generosity of Arganto has caused me to suffer.*

For his part, similar ideas were agitating Coquelicot. He believed that all those who were calling him Prince, as they had done before, were doing so derisively and to mock him. He had no doubt that those by whom the rumor had been spread had changed their conduct in his regard, only presenting a false front to him. That situation, afflicting as it might be, was not the only woe by which he was assailed. The memory of tender, faithful, simple and naïve Bleuette, the idea of Bonnebonne's abode and the graces and mildness of her company, spread such a great disgust over all the things that are called pleasures in society, and which he had mistaken for felicity itself, caused him to make the decision to flee the court.

They only had to talk to one another and they would have been persuaded and consoled, but, still young, they determined to do the one thing that ought to be avoided with the greatest care, in amour as in amity, and to maintain silence; for, in sum, it augments and poisons the injury one has, as well as that which one does to others.

Thus, not daring to look at one another—so much impression had the shame of their behavior made on their hearts—they made the decision separately, without communicating anything to one another, to retreat. Solitude appeared to them to be the situation most capable of consoling them. They departed on the same morning, as they would have been able to do if they had acted in concert. They close the simplest attire, not without regretting that the clothes they had worn when they came to the court, which would have brought them closer to their original innocence, by reminding them of all the ideas of their past felicity. They only took away their portraits, which Arganto had had painted in miniature, such as they were when they left the Isle of Wellbeing.

They set forth in opposite directions, but as they drew away from the court, nature spoke to their hearts. The song of the birds, the serenity of the air, the sight of the countryside and the sweet liberty that it inspires, all reminded them of their past happiness, softened their hearts and brought them back to one another.

But how shall we find one another? they said to themselves, incessantly. *I would have convinced him/her, he/she would have forgiven me. Let's return to the court. But how can I reappear there*—for each of them believed that the other had not abandoned the abode—*in a state as sad as the one I am experiencing?*

The memory of Bonnebonne presented itself to their minds; it is amity that one implores in adversity. They resolved, therefore, to have recourse to her generosity. Even if they had not known the delights of the Isle of Wellbeing for themselves; even if they had not been flattered by the idea of seeing again the places that had witnessed heir past happiness,

215

it is so natural to seek a similar habitation that one often sets forth for it on the word of others. They departed, therefore. It was very easy for them to find the road to it, having inhabited it so worthily.

Their design was to address one of the columns that I mentioned, and which relayed the requests that people made to the fay. What was their surprise—or, rather, what was their delight—to find one another again, to see one another in a place and in a costume that told them everything!

After the first transports, in which the eyes were scarcely sufficient to satisfy the soul, the first words they pronounced were: "Forgive me! I can't live without you." A thing that is asked and desired at the same time is ordinarily soon granted; it was not necessary for them any longer to implore the help of the fay. The union of their desires had already transported them to the most beautiful places on the island.

They wanted to justify themselves and beg Bonnebonne's pardon, but she stopped them.

"I know everything that has happened to you," she told them. "I shared your troubles, although they were merited. Enjoy the wellbeing of my empire; you are now more in a state to appreciate its delights."

They lived happily, since they never ceased to love one another, and they died at the same instant. Bonnebonne gave their name to flowers of the fields, with the intention of rendering their names immortal.

MIGNONNETTE

There was once a king and a queen who reigned well and simply over subjects as good as them, with the result that they were equally happy; but as there is no estate in the world that does not have its difficulties, the happiness of the king and the queen was troubled by the humor of a fay who had protected them since their childhood.

Madame Grognon, as she was named, was always muttering something between her teeth, and repeated the same thing a hundred times over, repeating it to everyone she knew, or, to put it better, to everyone she had ever known. It is true that she only had that one little fault, and that otherwise, she was the best woman in the world; for, to tell the truth, she was often obliging.

The king and the queen often asked her to grant them children, and Madame Grognon always replied: "Really? Children? And why? To hear them scream, to enrage you, and me too? What use are they, children? One doesn't know what to do with them. Girls are as difficult to keep as they are to marry, and boys become libertines."

That discourse, and a thousand similar ones, were the only responses she made to the insistent pleas of Their Majesties. The ill humored tone in which she made them, and her fashion of talking through her nose, rendered them insupportable. However, the king and the queen listened to them with an admirable patience.

In the end, either by an effect of chance or the permission of the fay—for she sometimes had good moments—the queen became pregnant; and, as is only right, she immediately informed Madame Grognon of a event so fortunate for the king and for the Estate. The latter arrived immediately, therefore, not to pay her compliments or to take part in the joy of the entire court, but to ask the queen why she was pregnant and reproach her simultaneously for not having been sooner.

In sum, she said so many disagreeable things to the queen that day that the poor princess could not hold back her tears; they flowed in such great abundance that the king, who loved her very much and whose tenderness was augmented by the situation in which she found herself, could not help getting angry and replying to her in terms that were a little too strong; and, unfortunately, he reproached her for her ill humor.

God knows how badly Madame Grognon took that conversation, and how, seeing the wrong that had been done to her—for, in fact, the king had said a little too much—she took advantage of it to recall all the wrongs that she claimed to have suffered in her life. She testified by means of a great abundance of words the joy of giving reason for the first time, and swore by her wand and her gamut to avenge herself for the scant deference that people had for her....

The king was so blinded by his wrath that he replied to her again, saying that he had no fear, and that kings were independent.

"Yes, you're a king," said Madame Grognon, "but truly, you're a fine great king, very docile, and you've profited well from the education I've given you. You're a king," she continued, "we can be very thankful to whoever made you one; you you're going to be a father, since you have so much desire to be; you're going to be, I swear, even more than you want to be. I'm very glad to see the fashion in which you respond to me, and we'll see how you like it."

Then she quit him abruptly in order to go and grumble at everyone she encountered.

The queen was alarmed by that adventure and the fay's threats; she made the king sense, when his anger had abated, the unfortunate consequences that it might have; but, not knowing what remedy to apply to it, they both remained in great anxiety.

Those who have fits of ill-humor are not always in the same state; often, they even repent of having made others suffer. Either because that was the case with Madame Grognon, or because she was more at ease in that court as regards grumbling, she reappeared there, without saying a word about what had happened, but in a worse mood than ever, not only because she had been wronged but because the king and the queen were more submissive than they had ever been.

Meanwhile, the queen, having become exceedingly pregnant, brought seven beautiful children into the world. When she said to the fay, with and extreme dolor: "Madame. That's a lot of children," Madame Grognon replied: "Well, you wanted them, children, here they are; to hear you, I thought you'd never have enough; it's your business, get used to it—but you're not done yet, I warn you, and you'll many other things. If you'd submitted to my prudence, and let me handle it, you'd have had children like everyone else, but you wanted them, and, oh, you'll have them, my word!"

"But Madame," the queen replied, "I already have a sufficient number, it seems to me."

"Good, good," said Madame Grognon, "seven, that's a bagatelle."

In fact, the queen, having recovered fully, became pregnant in very little time, and gave birth, as she had the first time, to seven princes or princesses, which it was necessary to receive without complaint, for fear of having even more."

After having scolded her for that excessive number of children, just as if the thing had depended on her, Madame Grognon, touched by her tears and her docility, promised her that she would not have any more. But fourteen princes of the blood are a great embarrassment to a State, and however rich one might be, such a large number of children is costly to nourish, to bring up and then to establish.

Like all ill-humored people, Madame Grognon forgot that it was her who had given herself the embarrassment of such a numerous family, and until the children were of an age to be weaned, she had great difficulty finding the large number of wet-nurses required to raise them. There was such a confusion in the children's room, the number being so great, that she did not know where to hide.

The simplicity of the courts of olden days was extreme, and the children of kings played with those of commoners every day, which is not astonishing, since they all went to the same school; politics then found reasons to authorize that custom, which are no longer found today.

Very near to the palace there was a good charcoal-burner, who lived tranquilly in a little house with the charcoal he sold; all his neighbors held him in consideration, because he was the most honest man in the world; even the king had great confidence in his capacity, and consulted him about affairs of state. He was known quite simply as the Charcoal Man, and for more than two leagues around no one wanted to have any charcoal but his. He took it to the houses of all the great lords and fays, and it was received marvelously everywhere, so that even the little children had no fear of him, and no one ever said to them: "Be good or the charcoal-burner will take you away."

When he had worked hard all day, he came back to his little house to enjoy repose and liberty, for he was the master in his own home. He had been a widower for a long time, and his wife, with whom he had lived, had left him a little girl named Mignonnette,[33] whom he loved madly. The regularity of her features was perceptible through the charcoal vapor with which her father's house was filled, and in spite of the poor clothing in which she was dressed, people were struck by all the graces that nature had lavished upon her.

---

[33] Mignonnette does not have the same meaning in French as the parallel term in English (which does not have a double n); it has several, but given Caylus' habits of nomenclature, the one he probably has in mind is a kind of flower, a variety of the one known in English as a pink.

Little Pinson,[34] the last of the king's children, was as lively as he was pretty, and by virtue of a natural sentiment, he always sought out Mignonnette, preferring her to all the other little children in order to play with her, to such an extent that one of them was almost never seen without the other.

The charcoal-burner, sensing that he was getting old, became anxious about the fate of Mignonnette when he was no longer there. The good will that the king had for him did not appear to him to be a resource for her.

"Well," he said, thinking aloud about the matter, "the king is overwhelmed by his family; he has so many things to ask of Madame Grognon for himself, and Madame Grognon is so difficult to get along with, that he'd never dare to put in a good word for my daughter, and even if he promised to do it, I have my pride." And his reflections always finished by finding the king more unfortunate than himself. In the end, however, after having thought about it hard, he did not know what to do, and nothing soothed his anxiety.

He went to all the houses in the neighborhood, but he was even better received in that of a benevolent fay who was known as the good Praline—and it was, in fact, her who gave her name to a kind of candy with which we are familiar, because she had invented it. One day, the good fay perceived the charcoal-burner in the courtyard of her mansion; she asked him a few questions, to which he replied in a manner that contented her. The anxiety that he expressed regarding the fate of Mignonnette softened her heart to the point that she resolved to take care of her. She therefore ordered him to bring her the following Sunday.

The worthy fellow, utterly charmed by the establishment of his daughter, but sorry to be separated from her, carried out the order he had received. He made her put on clean under-

---

[34] The original text renders this name Pinçon, which modern French dictionaries attribute to a mark left by a pinch, but Caylus uses it here and elsewhere to refer to a finch, and I have substituted the modern spelling of the name of the bird.

wear and new clogs, which he had bought the day before, with beautiful designs on top. Mignonnette leapt about, ran on ahead, came back to hold his hand, always saying: "We're going to the mansion"—which was, in fact, all that the charcoal-burner had told him about their journey.

Praline received them marvelously, but in spite of the beauties of the mansion and all the sugar and candy that she was given, Mignonnette did not want to quit her dear Papa. When she no longer saw him, she wept for the first time in her life. That good sentiment touched the fay, who only loved her all the more for it. All those who witnessed that separation said: "My little girl wouldn't do as much for me."

In the end, though, Mignonnette gradually cased to weep, and the fay, who did everything for her that she wanted, without giving her the trouble of either grumbling or having to tell her the her same thing twice, rendered her in very little time the prettiest child in the world, who always ran with open arms to embrace her Papa as soon as she saw him in the distance, even at the risk of blackening the fine clothes that the fay gave her incessantly.

After having kissed her father, she always asked him for news of Pinson, and gave him her finest toys and her best candy to take to him. The charcoal-burner carried out her commissions and the little prince, for his part, always asked for news of Mignonnette and said that he would like very much to see her again.

Ever more beloved by the fay, Mignonnette reached the age of twelve, and it was at that time that Praline asked the charcoal-burner to come up to her cabinet one day. She was so good that she never wanted to converse with him while he was standing up, but it was not without difficulty that she got him to sit down. It is true that it was rather singular to see a charcoal-burner in an embroidered white satin armchair, who did not know what countenance to adopt.

When he was seated, the fay said to him: "My good man, I love your daughter...."

"That's very kind of you, Madame," he replied, "but you're quite right; she's so lovely."

"And I want," the good Praline went on," to consult you about what I ought to do with her. You might or might not know that I shall soon be obliged to go to live in another country."

"Well, Madame," said the charcoal-burner, "you could take her with you, if you'd be so kind."

"That's what I can't do," the fay replied, "but I can establish her, if that's what you desire for her."

"Well, Madame," the charcoal-burner said, "make her the queen of as small a realm as you please."

The fay, surprised by that proposition, represented to him that the more elevated one is, the more difficulty one has.

The charcoal-burner assured her that he had heard it said that there are difficulties everywhere, and that those of royalty at least have more consolations. "It isn't," he added, "that I'm asking you to make me a king; no, I want to remain a charcoal-burner; it's a trade I know, and I don't know any other; but Mignonnette is young; it won't be difficult for her to learn the one I'm proposing to you. I know almost everything that it involves, for I see it every day."

"We'll see," said Praline, as she sent him away, "what it might be possible for me to do, but I warn you in advance that she'll have a great deal to suffer."

"Well, Madame," he replied, "I've suffered a great deal myself, without getting much for it. Only have the kindness to make her a queen, that's all I'm asking," he continued, as he went away.

In the meantime Madame Grognon had established almost all the children of the king and the queen. She had sent some to seek their fortune, and they had found kingdoms; the princesses had married well, without anyone ever having known the precise detail of their adventures. The youngest of the fourteen, little Pinson, was the only one for whom she had not done anything.

One day, she arrived at the court in her usual disposition, and, finding the little prince being caressed by his father and mother, she said to them: "That's certainly a spoiled child; that's truly the way to make something of him. I'll wager anything in the world that that one can't do anything at all." Addressing the prince, she went on: "let's see, tell me about the lessons you've just had and if you miss a word, I'll give you the whip."

Pinson recited his lessons marvelously, for he always had them at his fingertips. He even added many things that were quite surprising for his age.

The king and queen dared not testify their joy to him, for fear of redoubling Madame Grognon's ill humor. She always repeated that the lessons he was given were worthless, that they were too scholarly and too strong for a child. Turning to the king and the queen, she said: "But why haven't you asked me for anything for this one yet? That's what you've done for all the others; you've had me place all your simpletons, who will make the stupidest kings in the world, but because this one might be worth something, you want to spoil him at your ease, for I can see clearly that he's your favorite. Well, I declare to you that it won't be like that, and I want him to leave right away."

She went on: "It's a good bet that the child will commit murder if you leave him like that for much longer, and I don't want to have to reproach myself for that; it's too well-known in society that I'm your friend, and I won't suffer people throwing stones at me for a silly affectation like yours. Oh, not so many dirty looks—let's see together what we can do about it, for I take advice willingly."

The king and the queen responded to her mildly that it was for her to decide, and that they had no determination.

"Well," said Madame Grognon, "it's necessary to make him travel."

"That's well said, Madame," said the king and the queen, in unison. "But deign to consider," the latter continued, "that our other children have exhausted all our treasures, and, not being able to enable him to travel in a fashion appropriate to his rank, think what a disgrace it would be for us if he had to say, all along is route, while in a poor carriage: 'I'm the son of King   and Queen   .'"

"Oh, how vain you are!" cried Madame Grognon. "That's truly well-placed; vanity's a fine item of furniture when one has fourteen children—but after all, they've only cost you the trouble of making them. Oh, I'm glad to hear you talk as you are and learn to know you. You say that your children have ruined you; that's how you appreciate all that I've done for them. I've always said that you had a nasty heart."

"Madame," the queen replied, "we have all our expenses written in a book written in my husband's hand."

"That's a fine thing, that is" Madame Grognon interrupted. "No one's ever heard talk of a king who did such things. I've seen hundreds of kings, but I've never even imagined anything so miserable. Assuredly, I don't have to reproach myself for not having said anything to you and not having warned you about everything you do wrong, but since you never take any notice of my advice, I see that I'm too good, and I'll stop giving you any. Come on, let's settle this affair, for it's all beginning to warm up my bile. This little fellow is as lively as a butterfly, you've always applauded him for it, and certainly he's going to say all along the road: 'I'm the son of King   and Queen   .'" And, addressing him, she said to him: "Why are you going to say something like that?"

"Madame," Pinson replied, "I'll only say what you order me to say."

"That's not the point," replied Madame Grognon. "Answer the question I asked you: Why would you say something that you know isn't good? For you won't lack anything, since your father and mother, who know you well and excuse you even more, have made their complaints to me?"

"Madame," replied little Pinson, "They've told you what they feared, but I promise you not to do anything of the sort."

"Aha! How he argues already! But I'm not surprised; he has what it takes to answer back and be disobedient; one can see that a mile away, and a good dog follows his breed. But I swear to you that you won't say that along the road; I'll see to that."

At that moment she touched him with her wand and he became the little bird that still bears his name today.

The king and the queen, who wanted to embrace him, were no longer touching anything but a finch, for the change happened in the blink of an eye. They took him on their finger one after another, but they scarcely had time to kiss him, for he flew away, following the orders of the fay, who pronounced the terrible words: "Go where you like, do what you must."

The tears of the king and the queen softened Madame Grognon's heart slightly; however, she left them, saying: "Anyway, it's your fault; that's how you are, and you can see that you made me do it," and, muttering between her teeth, she mounted her Vinaigrette, pulled by six magpies and as many jays, which made a frightful racket as they pulled the vehicle.

Very annoyed by what had just happened to her, Madame Grognon went to the Council of Fays that was being held that day. She chanced to find herself sitting next to the good Praline, and as it is natural to talk about what is on one's mind, she told her about all the affairs of the king and the queen and the trouble she had had establishing fourteen children, all the while criticizing the king and the queen, whom she was scolding as if they were present. She ended up by asking Praline whether she did not have some kingdom at her disposal, or some princess, which might suit little Pinson,

Praline, who was the best woman in the world, and who privately condemned Madame Grognon's ill humor, assured her that she would gladly take charge of it, provided that it was left entirely to her and that she was permitted to act in accordance with her character and her sentiments.

"Do whatever you please," the other replied, speaking through her nose more than ever. "Do as you please, provided that I hear no more mention of it." And then she surrendered joyfully to Madame Praline all the rights of Faerie pertaining to little Pinson. They even made an authentic contract to that effect.

Struck by the rapports that nature had established between Mignonnette and Pinson, Praline resolved to examine them more attentively, with the design of making the fortune and the happiness of the little girl; but she was pressed for time, for the day of her departure was approaching. It was, however, necessary to find a means of allowing them, without inconvenience for their good faith, to work for their own establishment.

Her first concern was to run after Pinson, who, charmed with flying and naturally lively, seemed difficult to catch—but can a young bird rest the power of a fay? Praline caught him easily in a snare. Immediately, she put him into a beautiful cage and took him to her mansion.

As soon as the prince saw Mignonnette he resumed his original gaiety; he flapped his wings and flew at the bars of his cage, making every effort to break them and to get closer to her. What a pleasure it was to hear Mignonnette say: "Good day, my son; good day my little friend; my God how pretty he is," and what a chagrin not to be able to reply except by twittering. But he calmed down; he rendered himself charming, and gave her all the evidence of tenderness that a bird can give.

Mignonnette was touched by that, without having any idea of the truth, and said so naturally to Praline that she had always liked finches, and asked so insistently for that one, that the fay gave him to her, smiling. Touched by the impressions of Nature, she only recommended that she look after him very carefully. Mignonnette promised to do that without difficulty, and executed it with pleasure.

When the day of the fay's departure arrived she bid Mignonnette adieu. "Take care of the finch," she said to her, "and above all, don't let him out of his cage, because, if he flies away, I'll be annoyed with you and you'll be very unhappy."

227

Then Praline climbed into her gray paper chariot. Her mansion, her domestics, her horses and her gardens took to the air with her, and Mignonnette found herself alone and sad in a little porcelain house—which was charming, in truth, but when one is sad, what use is a beautiful habitation? The garden continually produced cherries, redcurrants and oranges—in sum, all the fruits imaginable always ripe and delicious to eat. The oven produced little cakes, biscuits and macaroons, and the larder was furnished with all the preserves we know.

So many good things were capable of consoling and amusing, but she perceived that the finch, who was so dear to her, was always asleep in its cage. She went to see him continually, without him giving the slightest sign of life. She addressed secret reproaches to the fay internally for depriving her of such a pleasant consolation. Finally, after attempting all means to wake him up, she made her decision and decided to look at the bird at close range, in order to see whether she could discover the mystery that the fay's conduct must contain.

It was not without difficulty that she made the resolution, nor without the remorse and dread that one always feels when one does something that we have been expressly forbidden to do. She opened the cage more than once and shut it again immediately; then she reproached herself for her timidity and, becoming bolder, she took the bird in her pretty little hand. Scarcely was it out of its cage, however, than it flew away and perched on the sill of a window, which, to complete her woe, she had left open, so far was she from foreseeing that accident.

Gripped by anxiety and dolor, she ran to recapture it, but the finch flew a few paces into the garden. She followed it, leaping through the window, which was only on the ground floor, but she was so troubled that she would have done the same if it had been on the fourth floor. The things she said to it then, in the attempt to recapture it, were as tender as they were naïve. However, the finch always flew off as soon as she thought she was about to catch it. Not only did it leave the enclosure of the house but, after traveling across country, it arrived on the edge of a great forest, which Mignonnette only perceived with an extreme dolor, convinced that it was impossible to find a finch in a forest.

That anxiety did not last long, for the bird, which she still had before her eyes, became in an instant the prince that she had known since infancy.

"What! It's you!" she cried. "And you're fleeing from me?"

"Yes, it's me, charming Mignonnette," he replied, "but a supernatural power obliged me to evade you; I want to approach you, but I sense that is preventing me from doing so."

In fact, they realized that they were obliged to be at least four paces apart.

Charmed, Mignonnette promptly forgot that she had disobeyed the fay, and her fears were calmed as amour took possession of her heart.

Neither one of them daring to return to the house they had just left, and, moreover, not knowing precisely where they were going, they went into the forest. There, while picking hazelnuts and asking one another a thousand questions about what had happened to them since they had last seen one another, about the joy of seeing one another again and the hope of not being separated again, the innocence of their hearts might have rendered the conversation dangerous but for the distance that was imposed on them.

They perceived a peasant's cottage and walked in that direction in order to ask for a refuge during the night, while awaiting a decision as to what they were going to do the following day. It did not take them long to arrive, but the prince, who did not want to expose Mignonnette to any risk, said to her: "Wait for me under this big tree; I'll go to examine the house and se who lives in it."

He left Mignonnette, therefore, in order to approach a good woman who was sweeping the area outside the door. He asked her if she would be willing to receive him and Mignonnette for the night.

The old woman replied: "You seem to me to be disobedient children who are running away from your parents, and who don't merit anyone taking pity on you."

Pinson blushed at first, but he then said the most seductive things in the world to her. He offered to work in order to relieve her, and finally talked like a man anxious for the person he loves, who feared that Mignonnette might spend the night in the woods, exposed to the wolves and the ogres of whom he had often heard mention.

While he was doing his best to persuade the old woman, the giant Chicottin, who was hunting bears in the forest, passed close to Mignonnette. He was the king—or, rather, the tyrant—of the region. Mignonnette appeared charming to him, but he was surprised not to find her charmed to see him, and, without saying anything else, he gave orders to his followers to capture the little girl and give her to him, placing her under his arm. He was obeyed, and, spurring his mount, he promptly took the route to his capital. Mignonnette's screams could not soften his heart, and it was then that she repented of having been disobedient, but it was too late.

Her screams interrupted the conversation of Pinson and the old woman. He quit her abruptly and ran to the place where he had left Mignonnette. What was his dolor when he saw her under the giant's arm! It is quite certain that if he had been with her at the moment of that violence he would have perished a thousand times over rather than suffer it, but he soon lost sight of Chicottin and his followers, and without looking at anything else except the tracks of the horses he followed in their footsteps.

The daylight, which was ending, did not permit him to go any further, and the obscurity of the night plunged him into a state of dolor that cannot be comprehended. It is even credible that he would not have had the strength to resist it, but, having sat down, he perceived a tiny light beside him, which he mistook at first for a glow-worm, to which he did not pay attention. The light was then augmented so considerable that it became large enough to contain a woman dressed in brown, who said to him:

"Console yourself, Pinson; don't abandon yourself to despair. Take this gourd and this basket; you will always find them full of whatever you desire to drink and eat. Also keep this little hazel wand, and put it under your left foot. Call me every time you need me, and I'll come to your aid. This dog that is accompanying me has orders not to quit you; you might need him. Adieu, Pinson," she continued, "I am the good Praline."

So much generosity and so many presents had not made much impression on the prince, but at that name, which Mignonnette had mentioned to him, he embraced the fay's knees, saying to her: "Oh, Madame, Mignonnette has been abducted; how can it be that you are occupied with anything other than the help she needs from you?"

"I know what has just happened to her," said the fay, "but she has disobeyed me. I don't want to hear any more mention of her; you alone can help her."

With those words he light was extinguished, and Pinson could no longer see anything. In the midst of his dolor, he was flattered to be the only one who could be useful to Mignonnette, but a thousand ideas of jealousy and anxiety were tormenting him, and the caresses of his new dog were incapable of dissipating his dolor for a single moment.

The daylight for which he waited with so much impatience arrived, and he continued on his way with such great ardor that he arrived in the giant's capital the same evening. There, everyone was talking about the beauty of Mignonnette and he love that Chicottin had for her. It was said that the king was going to marry her as soon as possible; it was added that a house for the new queen had already been built, for people accumulate facts and augment them with as much facility as an anxious lover is convinced of them.

Those items of news pierced Pinson's heart; and the people to whom he had been talking, seeing him with the basket that Praline had given him, all said: "That's a pretty shepherd.

Perhaps he's going to guard the king's sheep; he has need of one and he'd certainly be given that charge, if it were only known that he's praiseworthy."

Those remarks, combined with the desire he had to get closer to Mignonnette, engaged him to go to present himself to the king in order to look after his sheep

In fact, Chicottin, having examined him, found him very capable of it, and as there was no difficulty regarding what he was to be given for his trouble, he was received as the king's shepherd. However, that charge not bringing him close to the apartments, he was not much further forward. He only heard it said in the house that Chicottin was very sad because Mignonnette did not love him.

That news consoled him slightly, but a few days later, while conducting his flock, he saw a carriage coming out of the palace at a fast trot, in which he recognized Mignonnette, surrounded by a dozen black men on horseback, who all had large sabers in their hands.

"Where are you going?" Pinson shouted at them, with utter futility, presenting the iron tip of his crook to them.

Mignonnette, perceiving Pinson in such great peril, lost consciousness, and so did Pinson.

When he recovered his senses he had recourse to his wand, and Praline arrived immediately.

"Oh, Madame!" he said. "Mignonnette is doomed; perhaps she's no longer alive."

"No," the fay replied. "Chicottin, discontented by the fashion in which she has responded to him and the fidelity she maintains to you, has had her taken to the Somber Tower. It's up to you to find a means to enter it; imagine one, and I'll help you. Only remember that, having once been a bird, I can't give you that form. Moreover, I warn you that Mignonnette will have a great deal to suffer, for that tower is a terrible prison—but she's being treated as she deserves; why did she disobey me?" Having said that, she disappeared.

The prince—or rather, his dog—conducted the king's sheep sadly along the road that Mignonnette's carriage had taken. It was not long before he perceived the baleful tower. It was in the middle of a plain, and had no door or window. It could only be entered via an underground passage, the opening of which as hidden in a nearby mountain, and of which it was necessary to know the secret.

Pinson was very glad to have a dog as clever as the one the fay had give him, for it did all the work, while his eyes were continuously attached to the Somber Tower. The more he examined it, the more convinced he was of the impossibility of being able to get into it, but amour, which comes to the end of everything, finally furnished him with a means. After having regretted his former state of a finch a thousand times, of which he had never made any other use than that of flying indifferently, he implored the good fay Praline to change him into a kite. She consented to that, and gave his dog the power to do it.

After barking three times, it took the hazel wand in its mouth and, touching the prince, he became a kite, or ceased to be, in accordance with the occasion. Afterwards, with the help of the dog, the fidelity of which was extreme, he had himself lifted up, and easily reached the top of the tower. What a joy it was for him to find himself beside Mignonnette and to hear the assurances of her love, and what a pleasure he felt in testifying to her—for he had retained the use of speech—his gratitude for the sentiments that she had for him, and the crown that she had refused for love of him. He might easily have forgotten that he could not stay on the tower forever, and that he was obliged to lead his flock, if the dog, more attentive to his duty than he was himself, had not taken care to reel in the string when it was time to go.

Having returned to the ground, Pinson resumed his pretty form and took his sheep to the king's palace, only thinking about the happy moment that he had spent with Mignonnette.

On the days when there was no wind to lift him, therefore, his dolor was extreme, but at least he had the consolation of thinking that Mignonnette shared his chagrin. They saw and spoke to one another in that fashion for some time, but finally, as there are always people who meddle in things that do not concern them, and others who want to be informed, and they are in the greatest number among those who wish to pay court, the kite was noticed, it was seen to alight on the Somber Tower, and a account of it was given to Chicottin, who soon came to the plain, resolved to punish the temeritous individuals who dared to use that means of taking letters to Mignonnette—for he could not imagine that the kite might be useful for anything else.

Mignonnette and Pinson were then engaged in the most tender conversation in the world, but the sweet conversation was interrupted by the vivacity with which the faithful dog promptly took the prince away. He had acted thus because Chicottin was running toward him after having shouted several times: "Where's the shepherd? Where's the shepherd? I have to kill him, since he hasn't alerted me to what's happening here."

The dog, fearing with good reason that the giant might snatch the string that he was holding in his mouth and easily dispose of the prince, to whom he was very attached, made the decision to let go and abandon the kite to the effort of the wind, which was blowing with great force that day.

The kite went to fall more than a league away on the mountain, and the dog had had time to pick up his master's gourd, basket and wand before Chicottin had arrived. It was easy for him to evade the pursuit, and, taking note of the place where the prince had fallen, he joined him in an instant and immediately enabled him to resume his original form.

They both hid without difficulty on the mountain thanks to nightfall, while Chicottin, fuming with anger, was obliged to take his sheep back to his palace himself. In order to prevent anyone approaching Mignonnette he had all his men-at-arms come into the lain, ordering them to stand sentinel day and night and to prevent anyone from getting near the Somber Tower.

Pinson saw all that from the mountain, where he had remained, only thinking about means to liberate Mignonnette. He invoked the aid of Praline again, but when the prince had asked for men-at-arms to combat King Chicottin's, she disappeared without saying anything, only leaving him a handful of sticks and a large bag of candy.

It is very difficult to hear mockery when only believes that pleasantries are being made about the thing most dear to one's heart, but the prince did not testify any ill humor at the ridiculous nature of that present. With the confidence that one ought to have in the fays, and filled with that which amour can give, he took the bag under his left arm, but the handful of sticks in his right hand, and, followed by his dog, he marched proudly toward his enemies.

As he approached them, he saw that their stature diminished and that their ranks broke up. Surprised by that event, when he was within earshot and recognized clearly that all those big soldiers and grenadiers with moustaches had become four-year-old children, he shouted at them, making his voice harsh: "Surrender right away, or it's the whip. Immediately, almost all of the army folded up before him and fled, weeping. The dog, which ran after them, completed putting them in disorder and frightening them.

He gave candy to all those whom he could each, and by that means they became submissive to his orders and determined to follow him everywhere. The example of those brought back several of the ones who had run away, with the result that not only did Chicottin no longer have an army to defend him, but Pinson commanded a formidable one—for all those who had pledged themselves to him resumed their statue and strength.

Chicottin arrived at the end of the affair to witness the loss of his army, and in spite of his strength and great stature, at the sight of Pinson, he not only became a child like the others, but a very small dwarf with crooked legs. The prince made him a dragoon's helmet and livery with dangling sleeves, in order to put him in a state to carry Mignonnette's train in the apartments.

Pinson's first concern after that great victory was that of running swiftly to the entrance of the Somber Tower and freeing Mignonnette. Then, the distance to which they had been condemned no longer subsisted; the anxieties that she had had latterly for the kite had depressed her so profoundly that she was not recognizable, but the pleasure of finding herself free and that of owing it to a beloved lover, rendered her instantly prettier than she had ever been.

Mignonnette and Pinson were beginning to converse, and they had arrived in the city with the joy that one experiences after great events, when Praline and Madame Grognon arrived from different directions, each in her carriage. The fortunate lovers expressed their gratitude to the fays, and asked them to decide their fate.

Madame Grognon replied: "For myself, I declare that I shall have no truck with you; one would have to be mad to charge oneself with such merchandise, so I shan't take the slightest care of it. Don't I have enough to do with your family? Who has ever had parents like yours?" she added, taking Pinson to one side. "What parents!"

"My sister," Praline said to her, gently "You know our conventions. Only have the goodness to send for the king and the queen, and tell them to bring the charcoal-burner. I'll take care of the rest."

"Which is to say," Madame Grognon replied, "that I'm the wedding-carriage here."

"No, my sister," Praline replied, "but if you don't want to take on that responsibility, simply have the goodness to say so, and I'll go if I must."

Madame Grognon, always muttering: "There's a fine mission! There's a bitch of a commission!" ordered the Vinaigrette—which was enlarged in accordance with need—to go and fetch the king, the queen and the charcoal-burner, and while Praline embraced and caressed the lovable children, she encountered Chicottin, now a little lackey. So far as grumbling was concerned, anyone was good enough for her, and God knows all that she said to him, how she reproached him for having a bad temper and vanity. "You're punished for it now," she told him, "and that's good, for no one will feel sorry for you, and all your subjects are making fun of you now; they've always made fun of you, but in whispers, now you only have to listen to them."

She took advantage of the dissipation that hazard had given her until the arrival of the king and queen, to whom she said on disembarking: "It isn't me who's made you come here, and I'm very sorry to see you here, for you're going to become more difficult to live with than you've ever been; it won't be possible to talk to you any longer. Oh well, it won't be me who'll give you advice; it'd fall on deaf ears; you can get it from whoever you like, it doesn't matter to me; that's what I find to be the best. Go on, get in, you're dying of envy and I can see clearly that I'm insupportable to you, but all that will change on my say so." She looked at the charcoal-burner: "That won't do," she said. "A fine object to be at a prince's wedding!"

He was not a man to remain without response, nor to constrain himself with regard to the truth, but fortunately, the worthy Praline interrupted the conversation, by asking the company to enter the palace. She could never obtain from Madame Grognon to remain in a place where joy was bursting forth on all sides; in fact, snorting and muttering several things at the same time, she climbed back into her carriage and quit the company.

Mignonnette embraced her dear Papa a thousand times, to whom nothing was lacking, for Praline had given him the little porcelain house, in which he had often received and re-galed the king and the queen. They embraced their dear little Pinson, and consented to his marriage with Mignonnette, whom Praline proposed to them. After having dispensed Chicottin's subjects from the oath they had made to him, she had Pinson recognized, who found himself by that means the king of a fine and large country and the husband of the pretty

Mignonnette, with whom he had fine and very sage children, who were also kings and queens, so true is it that a sage and pretty young woman makes her own fortune and that of her relatives.

THE IMPOSSIBLE ENCHANTMENT[35]

There was once a king much loved by his subjects, and who loved them very much for his own part. That prince had an infinite repugnance for marriage, and what is even more astonishing, amour had never made the slightest impression on his heart. His subjects represented to him with so much insistence the necessity of giving himself a successor that the good king consented to their demand. But as all the women he had seen until then had not inspired the feeblest desire, he resolved to go and seek in other lands what his own had not been able to present to him; and, in spite of the bitter and piquant pleasantries of the beautiful and ugly women of his homeland, he undertook voyages, after having given a form as tranquil as it was solid to the government of his Estates. He only wanted to be accompanied by a single squire, a man of abundant common sense, but who did not have much brilliance in his intelligence. That sort of companion is not the worst on journeys.

The king traveled several countries in vain, despite making every effort to fall in love, but his time had not yet come. After two years of absence and fatigue he resumed the road to his Estates, and came back with the same indifference that he had taken away. At any rate, while traversing a forest he heard a frightful mewling of cats. The good squire did not know what to think about the commencement of such an adventure. All the stories of witches that he had heard told returned to his mind. As for the king, he was quite firm; courage and curiosity engaged him to wait and see what was making a noise as strange as it was disagreeable.

Eventually, when the racket drew closer to the place where they were, they saw a hundred Spanish cats going by,

---

[35] A previous English version of this story appeared in Andrew Lang's *Grey Fairy Book* (1900) as "An Impossible Enchantment."

which traversed the forest before their eyes. Someone had covered them with a cloak, so that they were very excited, and they were getting carried away. They were supported by two of the largest monkeys that have ever been seen. They were wearing long coats, amaranth in color; their boots were the prettiest in the world and the best made. They were mounted on two superb English bulldogs, and spurring them on while blowing into little fairground trumpets.

The king, surprised by such a spectacle, was looking at them attentively when he saw twenty little dwarfs appear, some mounted on lynxes and leading relays, others on foot, leading unmatched couples of cats. They were dressed in amaranth like the huntsmen; that color was the livery of the equipage.

A moment later he perceived a young woman, charming for her beauty and the proud air with which she was mounted on a huge tiger, whose gait was admirable. She passed in front of the king, going at full tilt, without stopping and without even saluting him, but although she had scarcely darted a glance at him, he was enchanted by her, and his liberty disappeared in a flash.

In the disturbance that seized him then, he saw a dwarf separate from the equipage and remain behind the others. It was to him that he addressed himself, with the warmth that he curiosity of amour gives to the questions of whoever is touched by it. The dwarf told him that the person he had just seen was Princess Mutine, the daughter of King Prudent, in whose Estates he found himself. He also told him that the princess was very fond of hunting and that he had just seen her rabbit equipage pass by.

The king only sought further information as to the road he ought to take in order to render to the court. The dwarf indicated it to him, and spurred his mount in order to rejoin the hunt. The king, by virtue of an impatience that always accompanies a nascent amour, spurred his own, and found himself within two hours in the capital of King Prudent's Estates. He had himself presented to the king and queen, who received him with open arms, all the better when he declared his name and that of his Estates.

The beautiful Mutine returned from hunting some time after that presentation. Having learned that she had forced two rabbits that day, he tried to compliment her on such a fortunate hunt, but the princess did not reply to him with a single word. He was a little surprised by that silence, but he was even more so when he saw that during supper she did not say any more. He only perceived that there were moments when it seemed that she wanted to say something; but he noticed that King Prudent, or the queen, his wife—who were never drinking at the same time—immediately started speaking. That silence did not prevent his amour for Mutine augmenting.

The king retired to the beautiful apartment that had been destined for him, and it was there that the worthy squire did not seemed unenthusiastic regarding the joy of seeing his master in love. He did not hide from the king that he was annoyed by it.

"Why that chagrin?" the king replied. "The princess is beautiful she's assuredly all that I could desire."

"She's beautiful," said the god squire, "but in order to be happy, something more than beauty is required in amour. Look at her, Sire," he added, "she has something harsh in her physiognomy."

"It's pride," exclaimed the king, "and nothing suits a beautiful young woman more."

"Pride, harshness," the squire went on, "call it what you like; but the choice she's made for her pleasures of so many maleficent animals is, in my opinion, a convincing proof of her natural ferocity. Furthermore, the attention with which they prevent her from speaking seems very suspect to me. Her father the king isn't named Prudent for nothing; I even suspect that name Mutine; it can only be a blunting or a diminutive of impressions that she has given; for, you know as well as I do that it's all too customary to flatter the faults of persons of her rank."[36]

The reflections of the worthy squire were sensate, but, as all difficulties only augment amour in the hearts of all men, especially those of kings, who do not like to be contradicted, the latter asked for the hand of the princess in marriage the next day. As everyone had been informed of the king's indifference, the triumph of Mutine's charms was complete. The princess was granted to him on two conditions; the first was that the marriage should take place the following day, the second that he should not speak to the princess until she was his wife. The pretext given for the condition of silence was a vow, the first excuse that came to mind, and that vow was assumed by the king to be proof of a truly religious heart.

Those great precautions were a further occasion for long speeches made by the squire, but they made no greater impression than those which had preceded them. The king ended up, after having listened to them, saying to him: "I've had so much trouble falling in love; now I have; what the devil do you want? I'm sticking to it."

The rest of the day was spent, like the following one, in balls and feasts. The princess was in attendance at them all, without saying a word, and the first word that she was heard to pronounce was the fatal "yes" that attached her to him for life.

As soon as she was married, she no longer constrained herself, and the first day did not pass without her making a distribution of loud insults and offensive remarks to her maids of honor. In sum, the mildest words with which she accompanied the most difficult service in the world had no other character than ill humor and abruptness. Her husband the king was no more exempt from those fashions of speaking than anyone else, but as he was in love, and a good man besides, he suffered everything patiently.

A few days after their marriage, the newlyweds took the road to their realm, and Mutine was not regretted in her fa-

---

[36] *Mutine* means refractory or insubordinate.

ther's Estates. The welcome that Prudent had always given to strangers had had no other motive than the hope of an amour similar to the one his daughter had just inspired and that of a passion forceful enough to pass over the knowledge of mind and character.

The good squire had been all too reasonable in his remonstrations, but the king perceived that too late. All the time that the new queen was on the road, she made her entire retinue experience despair, dolor and impatience, but once she had arrived in his kingdom, her ill humor and malevolence redoubled.

After a month of residence in his Estates, her reputation was perfect; there was no longer any but a single voice to regard her as the nastiest queen in the world.

One day, when she mounted a horse and went for a ride in a wood near her palace, she perceived an old woman on foot, who was following the highway. She was simply dressed. The good woman, after having curtseyed as best she could, continued on her way, but the queen, who was only looking for an opportunity to exhale her ill humor, sent one of her pages running after her in order to bring her back.

When she was in her presence she said to her: "I find you very impertinent not to have made me a more profound reverence. Don't you know that I'm the queen? It wouldn't take much for me to have you given a hundred lashes with a stirrup-leather."

"Madame," said the old lady, "I have never known very well the measure of reverences; it's apparent that I didn't want to offend you."

"What!" said the queen. "She dares to respond!! Attach her right away to the tail of my horse; I'll take her at a rapid pace to the best dancing-master in the city, to show her how to make me a reverence"

The queen's order was carried out. The old woman cried for mercy when she was attached, but it was in vain that she boasted of the protection of the fays; the queen took no more account of those last words than the others.

"I'm no more afraid of them than of you," she said, "And even if you were a fay, I'd act as I am doing."

The old woman allowed herself to be attached, patiently, to the tail of the horse, but when the queen wanted to give it a thrust of the spur, it remained motionless. She redoubled the thrust of her heel in vain; it had become a horse of bronze. The cords attaching the old woman changed in an instant into garlands of flowers, and the old woman herself suddenly appeared eight feet tall. Then looking at Mutine with proud and disdainful eyes, she said to her: "Wicked woman, unworthy of the name of queen that you bear, I wanted to judge for myself whether you merited the bad reputation that you are given in the world. I'm convinced of it; you shall judge whether the fays are as scantly redoubtable as you have just said."

Immediately, the fay Paisible—for it was her—whistled between the two fingers of her hand, and a chariot was seen to appear drawn by six ostriches, and on the chariot the fay Grave was recognized, even graver than her name. She was then the doyenne of the fays, and presided over affairs regarding the Corporations of Faerie. Her escort was composed of a dozen other fays mounted on short-tailed dragons.

In spite of the astonishment caused to her by the arrival of the fays, Queen Mutine lost nothing of the proud and malevolent air that was natural to her. When that brilliant company had dismounted, the fay Paisible recounted her entire adventure. The fay Grave, who carried out her responsibilities with a great deal of severity, approved the conduct of Paisible. Then she opined that the queen should be transformed into the same metal as her horse; but the fay Paisible was not of that opinion, by virtue of a unparalleled kindness. She softened all the rigorous voices that tended to the punishment of the queen.

Finally, Mutine was only condemned to become Paisible's slave until she had given birth—for I've forgotten to tell you that she was at the beginning of a pregnancy. The same sentence, which was rendered in the middle of a field, ordered that the child she brought into the world would be the slave of the fay in her place, who would be free after her childbirth to return to her husband, the king. The fays had the politeness to notify the king of the sentence that had just been passed. He was obliged to consent to it, but even if he had opposed it, what could the good prince have done?

After that justice, the fays all returned to their affairs, and Paisible waited momentarily for her chariot, for which she had sent. It was a small jet chariot in several colors drawn by six hinds as white as snow, ornamented with green satin cloths embroidered with gold. With a tap of her wand, the queen's garments were turned into those of a slave. In that attire she was made to mount a coughing mule, and it was at a rapid trot that she followed the fay's chariot.

After an hour of trotting, the queen arrived at Paisible's house. She was, as one might imagine, in a great affliction, but her pride prevented her from shedding a single tear. The fay sent her to the kitchen to work there, after having given her the name of Furieuse, that of Mutine being too delicate for the wickedness to which she was borne.

"Furieuse," the fay Paisible said to her, "I've saved your life, and perhaps my conscience will be burdened by that. I don't want to overwhelm you with toil because of the child with which you're pregnant, and who, as you know, is to be my slave. I'm taking you out of the kitchen and putting you in charge of sweeping my apartment and that of not leaving a single flea on my little dog, Christine."

Furieuse understood easily that there was no point in appealing such a ordinance. Se therefore made the wise decision to carry out exactly what she had been charged with doing during the time of her pregnancy. When that time was over, she gave birth very fortunately to a princess as beautiful as the daylight, and when she had recovered her health, the fay gave her a long sermon on her past life, made her promise to behave better in the future, and sent her back to her husband, the king.

One can judge by the generosity that the fay Paisible had shown to such a wicked queen all the attentions she had for the young princess who was to remain in her hands. She came to the point of loving her madly; that was what engaged her to have her endowed by two other fays. She took a long time over the choice of those two godmothers, as to whom she could have confidence, for she feared that the resentment they had always had against her mother might extend as far as the daughter. Finally, she thought that the fays Divertissante and Eveillée did not have as much ill humor in their nature as the others.

As soon as she had alerted them, they arrived in a berline of Italian flowers drawn by six gray hacks, hose manes were the most beautiful flame-color. Eveillée was clad in parrot feathers and coiffed like a mad dog. As for the fay Divertissante, she had a chameleon-skin dress that made her appear all the colors imaginable. Paisible received them both marvelously, and in order to engage them to do, I am assured that she put into the good soup that she gave them a little wine flavoring.

After such sage precautions she had the beautiful child brought to them. She was in a rock crystal crib; her swaddling clothes were scarlet embroidered with gold, but her beauty was a hundred times more brilliant than her attire. The little princess smiled at the fays and made them little caresses, which rendered her so agreeable that they resolved to shield her, as best they could, against the anger of their Elders.

They began by giving her the name Galantine. The fay Paisible said to them then: "You know that the punishments that we ordinarily employ among ourselves and are most in usage consist of changing beauty into ugliness, intelligence into imbecility, an most often of all having recourse to metamorphosis. As it is not possible for each of us to endow with more than one gift the person that we want to oblige, my opinion is that one of us should give the child beauty, another intelligence and that I endow her with the inability ever to change form."

That opinion was agreed and executed immediately. When Galantine had been endowed the other two fays returned home and Paisible employed all her cares henceforth in the education of the little princess. No cares had ever been employed more successfully, for at four years old her grace and beauty were already causing abundant rumor in the world.

There was too much of it; for, the affair having been reported to the Council of Fays, one day Paisible saw the fay Grave arriving in the courtyard of her palace mounted on a lion. She was wearing a long and very ample dress, with a great many pleats, sky blue in color. She was coiffed in a square bonnet of gold brocade. Paisible recognized her with as much anxiety as chagrin, for her costume and mount were those she employed when she wanted to render some sentence. When she perceived that the fay Reveuse was following her, mounted on a unicorn, that she was dressed in black leather lined with varying taffeta and similarly coiffed in a square bonnet, she could no longer doubt that the visit had a very serious motive.

In fact, the fay Grave made a speech, and said to her: "I am very surprised by the conduct you adopted with regard to Mutine; it is in the name of the entire Corps of Fays that she offended, and I've come to make reproaches to you. You can pardon your particular offenses, but you don't have the same right over those that regard the entire Corps. However, you treated her mildly and with generosity throughout the time she was in your house; thus, I have come to execute an equitable order and to punish an innocent girl for the wrongdoing of her culpable mother.

"You have wanted her to be beautiful and intelligent, and on the other hand, you have put an obstacle to metamorphoses. I can still prevent her from enjoying throughout her life the advantages with which you have ornamented, and which I cannot take away. She will only be able to emerge from an enchanted prison that I will construct for her when she has rendered to the desires of a beloved lover. It is my concern to prevent that from ever being possible."

The place of enchantment consisted of a very high and broad tower constructed of seashells of all colors, in the middle of the sea. On the ground floor there was a large room for bathing, into which water could be made to enter at will. That room was surrounded by steps and platforms on which one could walk with dry feet. The first floor composed the princess's apartment, and was veritably magnificent. The second was divided into several rooms. In one of them there was a beautiful library, in another a wardrobe full of superb garments and underwear, for all ages, all as magnificent as one another. Another room was destined for music; another was filled with the most agreeable wines and liqueurs. Finally, the largest of them all only presented to the eye all kinds of dry and liquid preserves, candy, and all the pastries imaginable, which by the force of enchantment, would always remain as hot as they had emerged from the oven.

The extremity of the tower was terminated by a platform on which there was a flower-bed in which the most agreeable flowers were renewed and succeeded one another incessantly. In the same garden there was a fruit tree of every species, on which, every time a fruit was picked, another immediately came to take its place. That beautiful place was ornamented with arbors, which the shade and odorous bushes rendered delightful; and those charms were further increased by the songs of a thousand enchanted birds.

When the fays had taken Galantine into the tower, with a governess named Bonnette, they climbed back in to their whale and, drawing away from the great edifice to a certain distance, the fay Grave summoned two thousand of the most malevolent sharks in the sea with a flick of her wand, and ordered them to mount a most exact guard—in sum, not to allow any man to approach the tower and to tear to pieces all those bold enough to make the attempt. As ships do not fear sharks very much, however, she summoned a sufficient number of remoras,[37] which she ordered to station themselves in advance

---

[37] The literal referent of the word remora, which exists in both English and French, is a kind of sucking-fish that attaches itself to others—including sharks—but the word is also used

and stop all the vessels that hazard or will guided toward the tower.

The fay Grave was so fatigued by having to do so many things in such a short space of time that she asked Reveuse to fly up to the height of the tower and to enchant it in the direction of the air with so much exactitude that even a bird could not approach it. The fay obeyed, but as she was infinitely distracted, she bungled her ceremonies slightly, and could not help making a few mistakes. If the enchantment of the sea had been no more flawless than that, Galantine's honor, with which they were so preoccupied, would have been poorly assured by the sea.

The worthy governess was only occupied with the care of bring Galantine up well, and although she regarded all the talents that the princess might have as always bound to be unknown, she neglected nothing to give her a good education and to ornament all the imaginable talents.

When the princess had attained the age of twelve, it appeared to the governess that she was a prodigy. All the beautiful qualities that she discovered in the princess afflicted her by virtue of the reflections she made on the sad destiny of such a lovable person. Galantine did not know anything regarding herself until one day, seeing her governess sadder than usual, she asked her the reason with so much urgency that Bonnette told her the full story, and that of her mother.

Galantine was struck by that story as if by a thunderbolt. "I had not yet made reflections on my estate," she said, "and I believed that when I was grown up I would no longer inhabit the solitude in which I find myself, but since I'm condemned to spend my entire life in this desert, might I not as well be dead?"

The princess fell silent for a few moments after that sad lament, but then she added: "You say, my dear Bonnette, that

figuratively in French to refer to an impediment or obstacle of any sort.

the enchantment to which I am submissive can only end when I love, and I have given proof of it. Are those two things so difficult, then? I do not know what is involved, but I see no reason why I cannot resolve to get out of here."

Bonnette could not help laughing at Galantine's simplicity; then she replied: "In order to love and to give proof of it, it would be necessary for some young prince to enter here, that he love you, and that you love him, in the design of making him your husband; otherwise, the things about which you're talking cannot happen to you. Furthermore, you can see for yourself that no man cam enter here; have I not told you about all the precautions that have been taken, either on the side of the sea or that of the air. It is therefore necessary, my dear Galantine, for you to resolve to spend your entire life here."

That conversation wrought a great change in the mind of the princess. All the things that had amused her previously no longer had charms for her; her ennui became excessive; she spent her days weeping and thinking of means to get out of the tower.

One day, when the princess was on her balcony, she saw an extraordinary form emerge from the water. She summoned Bonnette promptly in order to draw it to her attention. It was a kind of man whose face was blue-tinted and whose unkempt hair was sea-green. He advanced toward the tower, and the sharks raised no obstacle to his design.

"I believe," said the governess, "that it's a merman."

"A man, you say?" cried Galantine. "Let's go down to the door of the tower; we'll see him at close range."

As soon as they had arrived there, the man stopped in order to gaze at the princess, and on seeing her, made several signs of admiration. He said several things in a hoarse voice, but as he saw that she did not understand his language, he had recourse to signs. He was holding a small rush basket in his hand full of the rarest seashells, which he presented to the princess. She took it, making signs of gratitude for her part; but when night approached, she withdrew and the merman plunged into the sea.

As soon as Galantine had arrived in her apartment, she said to the governess with chagrin: "I find that man frightful; why have these wretched sharks that guard us let such an ugly man approach by preference—for apparently, they don't all resemble that one?"

"It's certainly necessary that they resemble him," Bonnette replied. "With regard to the fashion in which the sharks have let that one approach, as they're inhabitants of the same element, apparently they don't do any harm to one another; they might even be relatives, or friends."

A few days after that first adventure, Bonnette and Galantine were drawn to one of the windows of the tower by a kind of harmony, which appeared to them to be extraordinary—and, in fact, was. It was the same merman that they had already seen, who still in the water up to his waist, with his head covered in reeds, blowing with all his might into a kind of marine conch, the sound of which was similar to our ancient ram's-horns. The princess went to the door of the tower then, and received politely the coral and other marine curiosities that were presented to her.

After that second visit he came every day under the princess's windows, to make dives or grimaces, or to play the beautiful instrument. Galantine contented herself with making a few reverences on her balcony, but she no longer went down, in spite of the pleas that the merman made to her by means of signs.

A few days later, the princess saw him arrive with another person of his species, but of a different sex; she was coiffed with a great deal of taste, and made a charming voice heard. That augmentation of the company engaged Galantine and Bonnette to go down to the door of the tower. They were very surprised to see that the lady, whom they were seeing for the first time, after having tried several languages, spoke the one that was natural to them, and paid Galantine a compliment on her beauty.

She perceived that the ground floor, or bathroom, which I have mentioned, was open and that it was filled with water.

"There," she said to her, "is a place expressly made to receive us, for it is not possible for us to live absolutely outside our element."

She placed herself as one places oneself in a bath, and her brother took his place beside her n the same attitude—for she was the sister of the man about whom we have already spoken. The princess and the governess sat down on the steps that surrounded the room.

"I believe, Madame," said the mermaid, "that you have abandoned the abode of the land because you ware obsessed by too large a crowd of lovers. If that is the reason for your retreat, your intentions will not be fulfilled, for my brother is already dying of amour for you, and when the inhabitants of our great city have perceived you, it is quite certain that he will have them all for rivals."

At that moment he brother suspected that she was talking about him; he therefore approved with hand gestures; she stopped talking about him, of which he also approved. The siren explained the chagrin that her brother had in not being able to make himself understood. "I serve as his interpreter by means of the languages I learned from a fay."

"You have fays among you too?" said Galantine. She accompanied that question with a great sigh.

"Yes, Madame, we have them," the mermaid replied. "But if I'm not mistaken, you've received a few chagrins from those that inhabit the land? At least, the sigh that has just escaped you leads me to believe so."

The princess to whom no one had recommended making any secret of her adventures, did not miss out on the pleasure of indiscretion on this occasion. She recounted everything that Bonnette had told her about herself.

"You're to be pitied," the mermaid said to her, when she had finished informing her. "Your woes are perhaps not without remedy, but it is time to finish a first visit."

Charmed by the hope with which she was flattering her, the princess made her a thousand amities, and they separated, promising to see one another often.

"We are going," she said to her governess, "to make the acquaintance of several of these mermen; perhaps there are some who are not as ugly as the first we have seen. In any case, we shall not be eternally in the most profound solitude."

"My God," said Bonnette, "how easily young women flatter themselves. I'm afraid of these people, myself. But what will you say," she added, "to the handsome lover whose conquest you have made?"

"That I shall never love him," replied the princess, "and that he displeases me infinitely. But in sum," she went on, "I want to see whether, by means of his relative, the marine fay,[38] he might be able to render me some service."

"I repeat to you," said Bonnette, "that those faces, of which the colors are bizarre, and those long tails, ought to make you afraid."

But Galantine, being younger, was, in consequence bolder and less sage.

The mermaid came to see her again several times, and always spoke to her about her brother's amour; and the princess, always occupied with her prison, always talked about that to the mermaid, who promised in the end to bring her the marine fay at the earliest opportunity, and assured her that she would instruct her as to what needed to be done.

---

[38] Thus far I have translated the term *marine homme* as merman, that being the usual English equivalent, and have rendered *sirène* as mermaid in order to preserve symmetry, although I have often preferred the direct transcription siren in other translations, especially where the term *triton* [triton] is employed as a male equivalent, tacitly accommodating the terms to a different legendary context. The term *marine fée*, however, is more problematic, and I have used a direct transcription rather than the improvisation "merfay," although the individual in question is clearly formed anatomically in the same fashion as the mermaid.

That fay came with the mermaid the next day, and the princess received her as a liberator. Shortly after her arrival she proposed to Galantine that she show her the interior of the tower and that they take a turn around the flower bed together, for she was able to walk with the aid of two crutches. It was easy for her, given her status as a fay, to remain out of the water for as long as she desired, although she was obliged to moisten her forehead from time to time. In order to satisfy that necessity, she always carried a little silver fountain suspended from her belt.

Galantine accepted the fay's proposition, and Bonnette remained in the room to entertain the rest of the company.

When they had arrived in the garden, the fay said to the princes: "Let's not waste time; let's see whether I might be able to do something for your servitude."

Galantine told her story in full, and the fay then said to her: "I can do nothing for you, my dear princess, with regard to the land, and my power does not go beyond my element, but you have a resource for which I can offer you all the help that depends on me. If you care to do Gluantin the honor of marrying him—an honor that he desires with an infinite ardor—you can live with us. I can teach you in a moment to dive and swim as well as we can; I can harden your skin without altering its whiteness, and I can prepare it in such a fashion that the coldness of the water, far from inconveniencing you, will even give you a great pleasure. My cousin," she added, "is naturally one of the best catches that there are in the sea, and I will give him such great advantages in favor of your alliance that nothing will equal your good fortune."

The fay spoke so forcefully that the princess was hesitant, and asked for a few days to make her reflections.

As they were preparing to return to join the company, they perceived a ship. The princess had never seen one as distinctly, because none had ever dared approach so close to the tower. It was easily possible to make out a young man on the deck of the ship, reclining under a magnificent awning, who appeared to be peering very attentively in the direction of the tower with his binoculars,[39] but the distance prevented her from distinguishing any more. The ship began to draw away.

Galantine and the fay returned to join the company, the latter very content with her negotiation. She assured the princes as they separated that she would come back son in order to know what she wanted to do.

As soon as the fay had left, Galantine told her governess everything that had happened; the latter was very afflicted to learn about the decision that her ward as on the brink of making; she dreaded infinitely being obliged to become an old mermaid in her old age. In order to remedy all the inconveniences she foresaw, this is what he decided to do. As she painted very well in miniature she spent the following morning making a portrait that represented a young man whose hair was blond and waved by long curls. He had the most beautiful complexion in the world, blue eyes, and a slightly turned-up nose; in sum, she assembled all the features of a charming face, and we shall see in due course that a supernatural power must have aided her in a work that she had only undertaken in order to show Galantine the difference there was between a human and a marine lover, with the design of turning her away from a marriage that was not at all to her taste.

When she presented her work, the princess was struck with admiration, and asked her whether it was really possible that there as a man in the world who resembled that portrait. Bonnette assured her that nothing was more ordinary, and that there were many who were even more handsome.

---

[39] The French *lunettes* usually refers to spectacles, but the reference in this story is clearly to a binocular telescope; the first such instrument was allegedly constructed in the early seventeenth century, as soon as telescopes became widespread, but even the limited number that are known to have been constructed on the first half of the eighteenth century were very clumsy and ineffective. This is not the only detail in the story suggesting that it is set in a world at least as technologically advanced as that in which it was written.

"I can scarcely believe it," Galantine replied. "But alas, neither he nor his peers can ever be for me; they will never see me and I shall not see them for as long as I live. How unfortunate I am!" she cried.

However, Galantine spent the day considering that painting; it had the effect that Bonnette had expected; it ruined Gluantin's affairs, which had been making good progress—but the governess repented of having made a portrait that was so handsome, for in contemplating it at length, the princess lost her appetite for food and drink. If ever the amour that a portrait might inspire were accompanied by some plausibility, it is assuredly in the case and the circumstances of this story.

The marine fay came back a few days after the visit I have described, in order to discover what Galantine's intentions were, but that young person, entirely occupied by her new passion—for it was veritable amour that she had conceived—was unable to conduct herself with prudence. She therefore broke abruptly with the fay, but did not do it very well, because she gave evidence of so much scorn and aversion for Gluantin that the marine fay, outraged by that refusal, quit the princess firmly resolved to avenge herself.

Meanwhile, the princess had made a conquest of which she was unaware. The ship that she had seen so close to her habitation was carrying the most beautiful prince in the world. He had heard mention of the enchantment of the tower, and had wanted to get closer to it than anyone else. He had excellent binoculars on his ship, so good that while examining the tower with the sole design of satisfying his curiosity he perceived the princess, and the proof that he had very good eyesight, and the quality of his binoculars, is that he fell madly in love with her.

Like any young man and new lover, who will always take any risk, he wanted two things: to moor next to the tower and have the launch put into the sea; and to confront all the dangers that the enchantment might make him run. His entire crew prevented him from doing so, however, prostrating themselves at his feet. His squire, whom fear had gripped most forcefully, or whose knowledge rendered him more enlightened, was also the most eloquent.

"You're leading us all to an inevitable death," he told him. "Deign, Sire, to come and moor on the shore, and I promise you to go and find the fay Commode; she's my relative, and has always been very fond of me. I can answer for her zeal and talent, and I'm quite certain that she'll help you."

The prince yielded, albeit with difficulty, to so many good arguments. He therefore disembarked on the nearest coast and sent his squire to go and find his relative, to implore protection and ask for her aid. As for himself, he pitched a tent on the shore, and, his binoculars always in his hand, he gazed either at the princess or her prison, and his heated imagination often retraced for him things that, in reality, he only had in his head.

After a few days, the squire returned with the fay Commode; the prince made her extraordinary caresses. The squire had told her on the way what it was about.

"In order not to lose any time," she said to the prince, "I want to send a white pigeon, in which I have infinite confidence, to sound the enchantment; if it finds some weak spot, it will go into the flower bed and garden that crowns the tower. I'll order it to bring back a few flowers to us, as proof that it is possible to reach it. If that happens, I'll find a means to introduce you to it."

"But can I not, by mans of our pigeon," said the prince, "write a note to the princess to inform her of the passion that she has inspired in me?"

"You can," Commode told him, "and I'll even give you the advice to do so."

Immediately, the prince wrote this letter:

Letter from Prince Blondin to Galantine.
I adore you, and I am informed of your destiny. If you care, beautiful princess, to receive the homage of my heart,

there is nothing I will not attempt in order to render myself the
most fortunate of all men by ending your woes.

Blondin

When that note was written, it was attached to the neck of the pigeon, which was only waiting for its dispatch, for it had already received its orders. It flew off with good grace, at top speed, but when it approached the tower and impetuous wind emerged therefrom, which repelled it violently. It was not deterred by such an obstacle; in the end, it circled the tower so many times that it found a place that the fay Reveuse had enchanted poorly. Immediately, it slipped through and flew into the flower bed in order to rest and wait for the princess.

The princess ordinarily walked alone, by taste, because she had a passion in her heart, or by necessity, because the governess could no longer climb the steps, except with great difficulty. As soon as the pigeon saw her appear, it went to her in the most flattering fashion in the world. Galantine caressed it, and, seeing a pink ribbon around its neck, wanted to see what purpose it served; what was her surprise on seeing the note!

She read it, and this is the response with which she charged the pigeon:

Letter from Princess Galantine to Prince Blondin
You have seen me and you love me, you say. I cannot love you, nor promise to love you, without having seen you. Send me your portrait by the same courier. If I send it back to you, have no hope, but if I keep it, in laboring for me you will be laboring for yourself.

Galantine

She attached that letter in the same fashion as the one she had just received and sent back the pigeon, which did not forget that it had been ordered to take a flower from the flower-bed. As it was unaware of the vivid ideas that lovers often attach to bagatelles, however, it stole one that it perceived on the princess's bosom, and flew away.

The return of the bird caused the prince such great joy that, but for the anxiety he still had, he might perhaps have gone mad. He wanted to send the pigeon back again immediately, charged with a portrait of himself, which, by the greatest hazard in the world, he had in his luggage, but the fay asked him for an hour's rest for her courier, which the prince employed in making these lines of verse, by which he accompanied her portrait:

How you have touched my heart!
How you have rendered it sensible!
Alas, why is it not possible
For me to express its ardor?
Yes, my happiness would be extreme
If the charming object that I love
Felt in the end a little
Tiny spark of this fire.
I will never lose the hope
Of undoing the enchantment;
Armed with love and constancy
Nothing deters a tender lover.

The pigeon set forth on campaign, therefore, charged with those lines and the portrait. Although the princess was not certain that it would arrive, she was nevertheless expectant; she was in the garden, and had not told the governess anything about that latest adventure, for she was beginning to sense the mystery and the reserve that the first sentiments inspire in a young woman.

She hastened to take the portrait with which the pigeon was charged and her surprise was infinite when, on opening the locket, she found that the portrait of Prince Blondin resembled perfectly the one that Bonnette had painted, by one of those fortunate hazards for which one cannot account.

259

Galantine's joy was extreme in making that agreeable discovery. In order to express in a gallant manner all that she felt herself, she took the portrait of the prince out of the locket that contained it, put in its place the one that she loved most of all those that Bonnette had painted, and immediately sent back the pigeon, which was beginning to get a little fatigued and would not have been able to serve the lovers, whose commerce was so lively, for much longer.

Prince Blondin had his eyes turned toward the tower, waiting for his courier. He finally saw the blessed pigeon arrive, but what became of him when he recognized around its neck the same locket with which he had charged it!

He nearly died of dolor. The fay, who had not quit him, did her best to console him. She took the locket herself, which he had not even deigned to look at; she opened it and made him see how wrong he was to be afflicted. In a moment, he passed into an extremity of joy that can only be compared to that of his chagrin.

"Let's not lose any time," Commode said to him then. "I can only render you happy by changing you into a bird. I'll return your original form to you when the time comes."

The prince submitted without hesitation to the disguise, and to anything that might allow him to approach the object of his adoration. Then the good Commode touched him with her wand, and he became in an instant the prettiest hummingbird in the world, which combined the charms that Nature has imparted to the bird in question with that of talking very agreeably. The pigeon was charged once again with guiding him.

Galantine was astonished to see a bird that she did not know, but, seeing it arrive with the pigeon, her heart was stirred, and the hummingbird, flying to her, said to her: "Good day, beautiful princess."

She had never heard a bird speak; that novelty redoubled the pleasure with which she received this one. She took it on her finger and immediately, it said to her: "Kiss, kiss Hummingbird."

She consented to that joyfully, and made it a thousand caresses. I leave it to you to imagine how content the prince was, and whether he was not sorry, at the same time, only to be a hummingbird, for lovers are the only people in the world who experience opposites simultaneously.

When the princess, enchanted by her new bird, had walked with it for some time, she came to rest in one of the arbor of her garden, and lay down on a bed of thornless roses. She was then wearing the most delightful negligee; everything that had happened to her, everything that her heart had experienced during the day, had not given her time even to think that her dressing table existed. The warm weather had engaged her not to wrap up the beauties that she alone could show. She placed the hummingbird in her bosom, and was beginning to yield to the charms of a light sleep when Commode found the means of waking her by returning the prince to his original form, which was executed so promptly that when she opened her eyes, she found herself in the arms of a lover that she loved.

Astonishment, agitation of the heart, the very ignorance in which she had lived, and the first embarrassment of that species, were not capable of defending her against the most tender lover, so the enchantment was destroyed.

Immediately, the tower was agitated; it trembled, and even began to split. The alarmed Bonnette, who was in the apartment below, ran up to the terrace, in order at least to perish with the princess. The violent shocks by which the tower was agitated were increasing at every moment, but when she arrived at the top of the tower and saw it leaning over, ready to collapse into the sea, she fainted, at the very moment when the fays Paisible and Commode arrived in a chariot of Venetian glass drawn by six of the largest eagles.

"Save yourselves promptly," they said to the two lovers. "The tower is about to fall, and you'll perish with it."

They climbed into the fays' chariot without having the time to make them the slightest compliment. The princess, however, had enough to throw the governess, unconscious as she was, into the bottom of the vehicle.

Scarcely had they begun to rise into the air than the tower collapsed, with a frightful noise, for the marine fay, Gluantin and his friends, in order to avenge themselves on the princess, had undermined the foundations of the tower.

Seeing that the fays' rescue was opposed to her designs, the marine fay wanted to see whether she might be able to take possession of Galantine by means of open warfare. She suddenly formed a huge vehicle of exhalations, in which she placed herself with her entire family, and filled it with oysters in their shells, rocks, stones and other trifles of that sort. With that carriage and its munitions, she had it conducted by a great wind toward the coast, and cut off the route of the glass vehicle.

The marine fay did more; she ordered all the wild ducks, scoters and other birds dependent on the sea for two leagues around to come and obscure the air in order to oppose the disembarkation of the fays, which was executed with an insupportable squawking.

Our two lovers thought they were doomed. As they had acquired a taste for destroying enchantments, they would gladly have taken measures against that one, but the fays did not judge it appropriate. Commode took from the trunk of the carriage a large quantity of petards and rockets, which she had brought, apparently with the design of putting on a firework display. At any rate, they came in handy, for she threw such a large number at the importunate poultry that they were obliged to get out of the way.

Then the enemy chariot put its last resource to work. The mermen had no doubt at all that with the stones and oysters they could soon shatter and bring down the glass chariot. The project was not bad; it can even be resumed that it would have had all the effect that they expected; but the fay Paisible took from her pocket an ardent mirror, which she always carried with her.[40] To tell the truth, I have never known exactly why she charged herself with that utensil. She placed her mirror in such a manner that it heated up her enemies in fashion that was as importunate to them as it was unfamiliar. They uttered frightful screams, and, the exhalations having dissolved instantly, the entire marine family, including the fay, were precipitated pell-mell into the sea.

Our victorious fays continued on their way with the design of arriving in the Estates of Queen Mutine. They found that she was no longer alive; she had died, partly by virtue of the dread of a further punishment and partly by reason of containing the harshness of her character; to that effect she had swallowed so many malevolent and insulting remarks and had constrained herself so prodigiously that after several serious illnesses she had finally succumbed a few years before.

The good king who had married her adapted very easily to the mildness of widowhood, and although he had no children other than his daughter, whose he did not hope to see again, nothing in the world would have persuaded him to marry a second time. He was governing his Estates very peacefully, and good King Prudent, Galantine's grandfather, had come to stay with him, in spite of his advanced age, in order to spend his vacation with him.

What joy those good princes experienced, on seeing the fays arrive, bringing back the princess! They communicated it to their entire court, charmed by the daughter of their king. The order was given for the marriage of the lovers to be celebrated the next day. Couriers were immediately dispatched in all directions to beg the fays to be so kind as to honor the oc-

---

[40] The idea of using a concave mirror as a weapon originated from a tall story invented by the Roman humorist Lucian, which alleged that Archimedes had use one to destroy a Roman fleet. The story was taken seriously by many later readers, even though all attempts to do something similar, even on a small scale, failed dismally.

casion with their presence. As you can imagine, they did not forget to invite the fay Grave.

The fêtes, balls, tourneys and great feasts went on for a long time. Criticisms were made, at the same time as many thanks were offered, to the fay Reveuse for the mistakes she had made in her enchantment. She got away with it by saying that, lovers always being adroit, and enchantments inexact, it was not possible to find any way to stop them.

I forgot to say that the governess recovered from her faint when she arrived at the palace. In sum, everyone was content, and the fays, having taking part for several days in the public joy, returned to their affairs, or to other pleasures. Our lovers always loved one another, and were the happiest prince and princess in the world.

PRINCESS MINUTIE AND KING FLORIDOR[41]

There was once a king and a queen who died rather young, and left a very beautiful realm to the princess, their daughter, who was then thirteen years old at the most. She imagined that she knew how to reign, and all her good subjects were convinced of it too, without really knowing why. It is, however, a profession that inevitably has its difficulty.

When they died, the king and the queen at least had the consolation of knowing that their daughter was under the protection of a fay, one of their friends. Her name was Mirdandenne; she was a good woman, but she combined that with the fault of allowing herself to be prejudiced, which she could never get over. As for the young queen, she was so petty that she had been called Minutie.

That beautiful kingdom was, therefore, governed by prejudice and pettiness. The princess had never been able to correct the liking she showed for bagatelles; it was for her that all those little presents and knick-knacks that have overwhelmed us since were invented. That princess signaled the grandeur of her ideas by one instance that I am choosing among a thousand. She did not want to retain for the general of her armies, and even exiled from court, an old man commendable for the services he had rendered to the Estate. Why? Because he had come to see her in a hat bordered with silver at the same time as a coat braided with gold. She thought that a man capable of such negligence at court was perfectly capable, for the same reason, of allowing himself to be surprised by the enemy. The discernment that she flattered herself with

---

[41] A previous English version of this story appeared as "Princess Minute and King Floridor" in *Beauties, Beasts and Enchantments: Classic French Fairy Tales* (1991) ed. Jack Zipes.

having shown on that occasion and the solidity that the fay found in her petty ideas, would have unhinged a much stronger head.

Nor far from that great country there was a small kingdom, so small that I don't know what to compare it to. A queen mother had governed it for a long time in the name of Prince Floridor, but that good queen died. Floridor, the most affectionate of sons, felt that loss keenly, and always conserved the recognition of the obligations he had to her. One of the greatest was a perfect education, the hardest in regard to the body, which had rendered him as robust as he was healthy, and the mildest in regard of the mind, which had given it charm and solidity.

The young prince was handsome and well built. He governed sagely, without abusing a despotic authority. His desires were regulated. In a word, he was an amiable individual. His subjects adored him, and foreigners who passed through his court agreed that he would have made the happiness of the greatest of empires. What was not known, however, was that he owed a great number of advantages to a charming ant.

She had been attached to him since childhood. On the death of the queen, the worthy ant was the sole consolation to which he could have recourse. He did not take any action without first consulting the ant, in a wood in the palace gardens, which she had chosen for her residence. He often abandoned his court and its pleasures in order to seek out her conversation. No season prevented her from appearing to his eyes, and however rigorous the winter might be, she always came out of the best-regulated anthill that there was for a hundred leagues around. She gave him advice as full of prudence as it was of sagacity.

It will easily be conceived that the pretty ant of which we speak was a fay; her history went back seven thousand years, and continued to the twenty-second thousandth year of the world, page four hundred and sixty of that year. I would therefore have been easy for the ant to give the king she loved a few kingdoms; fays disposed of them at their whim; but the ant was prudent, and prudence always leads to justice. It was not that she did not wish ardently for Floridor's advancement, but in order to obtain it she only wanted to employ the means that could flatter the veritable glory that she had imprinted in his heart. The ant was naturally patient; she therefore waited for opportunities to bring to light the virtue of her pupil.

The conduct of Minutie and the prejudice of Mirdandenne soon furnished her with the means It was learned that the fires of revolt had been lit in Minutie's great kingdom. When that news had been confirmed by all the gazettes, the good fay ant wanted King Floridor to depart with a single squire to go and help the queen, his neighbor. She reassured him regarding the government of his Estates during his absence, promising him not to abandon them.

When he departed she only gave him a little sparrow, a little knife, commonly known as a jambette, and a nutshell. "The presents that I'm giving you," she told him, "might seem mediocre, but be tranquil with them; they will serve you when the need arises, and I hope you will find them good." He promised her without difficulty a confidence that she had merited well in his mind, and when he had bid her a tender adieu, he set forth, regretted by all his people as if he had been the brother, son or friend of each of his subjects.

He arrived in the capital of Minutie's Estates, and found it in uproar, because it had just been learned that a neighboring king was advancing in rapid stages, followed by one of the most terrible armies. He had come with the design of taking possession of the kingdom. Floridor learned that he queen had withdrawn to a delightful house she had near the capital, where all the trinkets shone extravagantly. That retreat had a motive, however; she wanted to meditate very seriously and make a decision, without being interrupted, as to whether the troops that the fay had raised to oppose the usurper should wear blue cockades or red cockades. However, the queen was then twenty years old.

Having been informed of the road that led to the country house in question, King Floridor hastened there urgently. His handsome face prejudiced Mirdandenne in his favor. The compliment he made to the queen and to her only augmented the good opinion that he had inspired initially, and the offer of his services was all the better received because the State was in an embarrassing situation.

Minutie seemed charmed by Floridor, while the king fell madly in love with her; then the zeal and vivacity always inseparable from amour burst forth in his speech and in his actions, as it shone in his eyes, and it was with extreme care that he made himself aware of the present situation. He wanted to have recourse to the power of Faerie, but the blind prejudice on Mirdandenne had engaged her a long time ago to give her wand to Minutie with the aim of amusing her, and the princess had made such prodigious use of it that it was worn out and no longer had any force or virtue, especially for serious things. Floridor went into the capital, but he found no fortifications or munitions.

Meanwhile, the usurper was getting ever closer. Floridor only saw a rival in the person of the enemy king, and, not finding any resource, he was obliged to propose to the queen that she flee, proudly offering her a refuge in his Estates. Prudence counseled him a course of action that belied his courage, but it was a matter of saving an unfortunate princes. He only made the proposition, however, on the condition of returning personally in order to expose himself to all dangers and make every effort to render the queen a throne that belonged to her legitimately, as soon as he had put her person in security in his little realm.

Mirdandenne, convinced by everything the king represented to her, accepted his proposition, but the queen only consented to depart when she was promised that the horse of which she as to make use would have pink harness and that Floridor would make her a present of the sparrow that the fay had given him on his departure. The bird was soon given, but, although the departure was urgent, it was necessary to wait until a harness of the sort the queen desired had been brought from the city. It finally came, and Floridor and Minutie, with no other retinue than Mirdandenne, took the road to the king's Estates.

Floridor was delighted to be taking Minutie to his homeland, and to imagine that he was useful to the woman he adored. Being in love and traveling are things that lend themselves to saying a great deal. Floridor, in announcing the smallness of his Estate, which sometimes made him blush, could not shut up about the obligations he had to the good ant; however, in coming to the detail of his departure, the nut, the little knife and the sparrow appeared to the queen to be very singular presents. She wanted to see the nut; the king gave it to her without difficulty.

As soon as she had it in her hands she cried: "Good gods, what do I hear?" She lent an ear more attentively, and then said, with a surprise mingled with curiosity: "I can hear, quite distinctly, little human voices, the whinnying of horses, and trumpets, in sum, a very singular murmur. That's the prettiest thing in the world," she added.

While the king was occupied himself in what was making the amusement of the woman he loved, he perceived the couriers of the army of rebels, about to overtake them, and in consequence about to stop them. Then, in that peril, by virtue of a mechanical movement, he broke the nut, and saw thirty thousand soldiers emerge from it, including cavalry, infantry and dragoons, with artillery and the necessary munitions.

He set himself at their head, and, confronting the enemy, without permitting any inroads into his own troops, he occasioned the finest retreat in the world. By that mans he took possession of the mountains that were in his path and saved the queen from falling into the hands off her rebel subjects.

After that fine military maneuver, which was nevertheless fatiguing, and the alarm of the danger the queen had run, they rested for a few days in the mountains, but as the entire country was under arms, as they advanced to continue their route they perceived another army much more numerous than the one they had evaded, and which they could not attack without temerity.

In that cruel situation, the queen asked for the little knife that the ant had given him, in order to make use of it on some bagatelle with which she was amusing herself, but, finding that it did not cut as she wished, she threw it away, saying: "That's a funny knife."

As soon as it touched the ground, it made a very large hole; the king was struck by the talent of the jambette, and immediately traced profound retrenchments around the mountain, which rendered it impregnable.

When that operation was finished, which only took the time necessary to go around it, the sparrow of which he had made a present to Minutie took flight, seized the summit of the mountain and, flapping its wings, cried in a terrible voice: "Let me be; you're going to see a fine game. Everyone get off the mountain, march on the enemy and don't worry about anything."

It was obeyed immediately, and the sparrow lifted up the mountain as easily as if it were a wisp of straw, and, flying through the air. It dropped it on the enemy army, of which it doubtless crushed a great fraction. The rest took flight and left the passage free.

The prince, who was only occupied with the desire to see the queen safe, wanted to be able to use his horses' speed, but as the march of an army is necessarily conducted slowly, he would have liked to put it back in the nutshell. Scarcely had he formed his wish than it was, indeed, enclosed the again. He put it back in his pocket.

They arrived in the little kingdom, where the good ant received them with all the marks of pure amity. When Floridor had given all his instructions in order for Minutie to be at her ease on his palace, and to make sure that she would lack nothing, he no longer thought about anything but his departure, all the more easily as the amity of the good ant reassured him about everything that might concern the queen.

During the journey he had just made, and the short time he had spent in his Estates, he had had the liberty to make Minutie the confession of an amour by which she had the kindness to allow herself to be persuaded. In the end, it was necessary for them to separate; their adieu was tender and Floridor departed without any help except that of a letter from Minutie addressed to all her good subjects, in which she requested them to obey King Floridor in whatever he ordered them to do.

The good ant did not give him the nut, not the little knife, which he had given back to her on his return; the queen only wanted him to receive from her hands the sparrow that he had given her, begging him always to carry it with him, as well as a minuscule scarf that she had made herself.

The king followed exactly the same route that he had taken to bring the queen, not only because lovers are touched to see again the places embellished by those they love, but also because it was the shortest route.

When he came to the transplanted mountain, the sparrow rose up into the air and departed in order to pick it up with the same facility as it had employed a few days before, and take it back to the same place that it had occupied previously. The sparrow, making use of the terrible voice that it was able to employ when it wished, said to all those who had been imprisoned under the mountain: "Be faithful to Minutie, do what King Floridor commands you to do on her behalf." Then the singular sparrow disappeared. The mountain was hollow, so all those who had been trapped, as if under a bell, had lost nothing except the time during which they had been imprisoned.

All the soldiers and officers who saw the light of day again with such great pleasure, struck by what they had just heard, ran in a host to Floridor, whose handsome face was interesting, and, gazing at him as if at a god, wanted to worship him. Touched by their obedience and the new oath of fidelity that they swore in his hands to their legitimate queen, the king received their respects but not their adoration.

After showing them the letter with which he was charged, he made a review of the army; he chose fifty thousand of the finest and those whose determination always enables the projects of generals to succeed.

He established a very exact discipline in the new army, of which he was the author and the example, and it was with those troops, which he rendered invincible, that he defeated the innumerable troops of the usurper, whom he killed personally in one of the final battles. His death rendered to Minutie a kingdom that had been utterly lost.

Floridor traveled all the provinces of that great Estate, and reestablished the authority of Minutie, whom he went to bring back. But what a change her found in the character and the mind of that lovely queen! The counsels of the good ant, and, more than anything else, amour and the desire to please and to be worthy of Floridor, had corrected her. She was ashamed of having always done petty things with great help, while her lover had done such great things with very little. They were married and lived happily.

THE PRINCE OF HEARTS AND PRINCESS GRENADINE

There was once a king who governed his Estates well enough for a man of his age, for he was only twenty years old. He was one of those kings whom destiny put on the throne, who would never have mounted it of their own accord; his face was rather commonplace and his character passable enough, but as there are sympathies of which one cannot take account, he charmed the fay Furette, who had raised him.

The injustice of amour consists mainly in the scant justice that one renders to oneself, Furette was an example of that; she promptly forgot the disproportion between her age and that of the prince, and, in sum, everything that ought naturally to separate them. I do not know whether fays have an age, given that their power gives them the facility of appearing, when they wish, beautiful, pretty, tall or short, but the prince, having been brought up by the fay, had been witness to her veritable face for too long to be seduced by the false beauties that she could borrow. When one is bringing up a child, does one take the precautions that amour and desire might suggest? The most enlightened divinities cannot foresee the amour that they will feel. Thus, Rubi—that was the king's name—only knowing the fay in terms of a severe face, which had always alarmed him, and an authority that had displeased him, found a hundred defects in her character that perhaps she did not even have, for dependence always renders people unjust.

The king, therefore, received the fay's proposal of marriage rather poorly, and was especially alarmed by the protestations of constancy with which she accompanied her declaration. He pointed out, with an embarrassed expression, the reasons that engaged him to make an alliance by means of which he might have children. That was tantamount to reproaching her for her age; he perceived that, and wanting to repair his gaffe, listed a hundred others at least as considerable.

Without wanting to excuse the king—I am not a good enough courtier to be suspected of that—even those who are known for having more intelligence would have been just as embarrassed in trying to get out of such a situation honestly. He was therefore only doing on that occasion what the majority of men would have done, and that is sufficient for a king. Furette, however, felt the affront she had just received very keenly, and was all the more piqued by it because she did not know the prince to have any attachment.

On that point, she was mistaken; a rival would have afflicted her more, but the chagrin one feels always seems more complete. By what misfortune can one not say as much for pleasures?

Piqued or afflicted however—it hardly matters—Furette quite naturally formed the resolution to avenge herself. Worldly usage caused her to dissimulate her project, and reflection confirmed her in the design of punishing the king by means of amour; her own experience informed her that the pains and woes of that passion are the most sensible of all. It is true that Rubi was not yet amorous, but men are rarely exempt from foibles or flaws, of which vengeance can take advantage. The desire to have a wife, the project of seeing a queen at court, occupied the prince; for the petty ideas of marriage and children still find a place on the throne.

Furette took advantage of those dispositions, and had the first princess who came to mind proposed to him. The marriage was moderately suitable; it was, at any rate, the work of the fay. She, therefore did not have to be begged to consent to it when Rubi asked for her approval, with the deference due to her rank.

After having done his duty, the prince did not have the slightest suspicion of the discontentment or chagrin that she might have; he even convinced himself that his conduct had been good, and that the fay could not possibly conserve any memory of what had happened. It was not that Furette disguised it completely; omnipotent as she was over nature entire, she was weak in regard to sentiments, and the revolt of the heart can never be hidden perfectly, but Rubi was born devoid of finesse and the world was unknown to him.

In order to arrive at her goal, the fay appeared to applaud and interest herself in the choice that he had made of Princess Emeraude, and even said as many and more stupid things as the courtiers did about the advantages of the alliance, the graces of the princess's figure, and her intellectual charms, although, in truth, none of that existed—but courtiers are adroit in finding reasons for criticism or praise, in accordance with circumstances. The court was no longer occupied with anything but fêtes, and the appearances and intelligence that ought to accompany the presents; reawakened gallantry no longer presented any but agreeable things to the eyes and minds of those who composed it.

Furette, whose vengeance was imminent, also wanted to appear to contribute to the public joy and thus conform to the tone of the occasion. To that effect, she built a superb castle in a single night by means of her wand; its architecture was austere and its location magnificent, close enough to the capital for its magnificence to be discerned from the windows of the king's palace, the view from which it embellished.

When the wand had responded perfectly to the fay's desires, she appeared at Rubi's morning audience and, before the whole court, whose members could see the castle and were asking what it could be, what it meant and why it was there— and a thousand other things that only idle and futile people have the talent to produce—she begged Rubi to be kind enough to accept the present.

"You have no county house," she added, "and this castle has a hundred properties that its habitation will reveal to you. Nothing can destroy it; time and human effort will only serve to increase its solidity. When one is familiar with its habitation, one can never resolve to abandon it. The surroundings, as you can see, Sire, are delightful; everything there respires elegance; it is only right, since it is to be your abode, that the delicacy and vivacity of amour seem to have no other dwelling. Finally, it is in this beautiful place that I ask you, in recognition of the cares that I have taken in your education, to celebrate your wedding and spend at least the first few days of your marriage there."

"But," said the king, charmed by the magnificence of the present, "although it might not be honest to criticize a gift, do the keep and the obscure towers that I perceive from a distance depend on the castle? It seems to me that they scarcely suit it."

"Yes, Sire," replied the fay, "they depend on it; you shall see them, in time, and I hope that you shall know their usage."

Rubi did not push his curiosity and his vague criticism any further. Princes, in any case, have a habit of only being polite in asking questions, so the response is often indifferent to them. In any case, Rubi was too occupied with the pleasure of soon having a wife of his own—it is taking propriety a bit far to be sensible to that—and therefore contented himself with telling Furette that the superb house would be called the Palace of Delicate Amour. He no longer thought of anything but proving that delicate amour to Princess Emeraude by means of all the attentions of which he was capable, especially informing her by means of the couriers that she would find on her route, and who were departing at all hours of the day, how fortunate he deemed himself to be marrying her. The beauty of that extreme joy is that he did not know her, and had not even seen the portrait that served as a pretext for his enthusiasm. How many other people resemble that good king when the malady of marriage grips them!

Rubi finally reached the desired moment; the wedding was celebrated in the Palace of Delicate Amour, to the great applause of the court and the great contentment of the king. He believed himself to be the only happy man in his realm, and soon, like all husbands, he was convinced that there had never been a wife comparable with his, and that nature had surpassed herself in the present she had made him.

Content with the success of her project and sufficiently avenged by leaving the king in a palace such as husbands, even less than lovers, never experience, the fay left the court on the wedding night. It is even said that she spent it in the keep and the towers by which the king had been struck; what is certain is that she was not seen thereafter, and it was a long time before she reappeared. Rubi did not spare her a thought, for princes forget easily, and from then on, the members of the court only preserved the memory of her in order to make criticisms. I have no idea what became of her, but I cannot believe, wherever she was, that her commerce and society were very agreeable, especially at the beginning of her absence.

Gallantry shone in the first days of the marriage of Emeraude and Rubi, but those happy days did not last long; alarms soon succeeded veritable tenderness; their anxiety necessarily produced difficulties in commerce; reproaches came afterwards, and the shame of a sentiment that they did not dare to express inspired remorse. One does like to admit to one's wrongful actions, one holds them against those whom one accuses of having given birth to them. Bitterness and mistrust took possession of their hearts, and filled them with all the dismal passions. But these confessions, which were never made by the interested persons, are much too historic. This is how I am assured that it happened.

"Don't you think," said King Rubi to Queen Emeraude, a few days after the marriage, "that these gardens, these windows and these open doors let in too much air, and that they even furnish too much facility to importunity?"

The queen, whose jealousy wanted to be enlightened, did not want to agree. That refusal augmented the king's suspicions and caused him to employ his authority to withdraw into a darker apartment, which brought them closer to the keep.

A few days later, Emeraude found that the circle of ladies was inconvenient, for they were still receiving members of her court and sometimes had sad apartments.

277

"The host of men seems more importunate to me," replied the king, "So we can't do better than ask the courtiers to stay at home and leave us in peace more."

Orders were given in consequence.

With such dispositions they began to show themselves in public less frequently, and soon they avoided entirely, not only the eyes of the court but also those of their staff.

The jealous couple enjoyed their retreat; they were comfortable; but the difficulty or facility they had in obtaining it similarly left traces of care and anxiety in their minds, for they always wanted to take account, to examine, to calculate and to mistrust motives. In sum, two jealous people are sad when they are together and, in order to be occupied personally, they no longer have anyone but each other.

The unfortunate couple thus abandoned the mild and pleasant buildings of the palace, the gracious avenues and cheerful gardens, in order to retire gradually into the funereal keep. One arrived there through a hundred doors, which, in spite of the thickness of the wood, were armed with bolts and ingenious locks; the daylight scarcely penetrated, the brightest sunlight only spread a sad gloom therein; and every living creature was banished from that frightful abode, which the silence and the sight of crumbling walls rendered even more terrible to the imagination.

It was in that sad dwelling that, after nine months of the common captivity of the husband and wife, the queen brought a daughter into the world. She died a few days afterwards, delivered from a torment a thousand times more frightful than death, no matter by what horrors it might be accompanied.

The king was sensible to the loss he had just suffered, but he had been so prodigiously jealous that perhaps he found some relief in his affliction, great as it might be.

As is customary with dominant passions, however, jealousy still reigned in his heart. It is the culmination of wisdom to admit and be convinced of one's wrongdoing, but the king was far from that; he wanted, on the contrary, to have been right, and in order to authorize his past conduct, not only did he order all the members of his court to relate to him a story of the deceits of women, and especially queens, but listened to them with so much pleasure that he made an ample collection of them, and he was seen to be writing in his own hand, at the foot of each incident: *My wife might have done that, so I've done well; I believe that she's done it*, he continued; *I want therefore to write and place myself in the ranks of the jealous deceived*....which he did, carefully.

It was in vain that his courtiers represented to him the scant correspondence there was between those stories and his own, the precautions he had taken and the character of Queen Emeraude, assuring him that even if he had been less clairvoyant, the honors that one renders to a queen were the guardians of her virtue.

"Kings interested in princesses," he replied, "of which this is the collection, have flattered themselves with what you want to persuade me; people have been able to calm their suspicions in the fashion in which you are calming mine; I have therefore done well to write," he cried, joyfully—for it is a relief for a jealous person to have evidence, true or pretended, of the only thing that seems reasonable to him.

In the end he did it so well that he convinced everyone of the certainty of the most ill-founded dreads of society.

The little princess, his daughter, ended up making him forget the unfortunate Emeraude entirely. She was named Grenadine, and her beauty appeared splendidly in her most tender childhood. Either by a refinement of conduct or the principle of jealousy distributed in his blood, the king resolved to bring her up in the greatest retreat, and to neglect nothing to make her a princess faithful to her husband.

That project was a satisfactory reason to engage him not to abandon the castle—or, rather, the prison—that Furette had given him. The most intelligent and knowledgeable women were chosen to form Grenadine's mind and to give her talents; but a lover, and the sole desire to please, without even having a determined object, forms, instruct and nourish the mind of a woman more surely and more easily that all the sciences can do.

What was the result of Rubi's cares and scholarly method? Not being distracted by any object, Grenadine became knowledgeable, it is true, but her knowledge was dry; she had intelligence, but she allowed herself to overindulge the pleasure of having it. Metaphysics was the only thing that touched her, and by that means, became precious to her. Unable to know amour save by way of the intellect, she talked about it incessantly with the scholarly mannerisms and affected terminology unknown to veritable sentiment. She had read novels, but her great mind scorned them. Twelve volumes filled with a chaste and purified passion appeared to her to be a monster of libertinage; the heroine had always loved too much at her whim and had declared it much too soon.

When she reached the age of fifteen, she formed the project of a book on which she worked with great attention; it was a treatise on the difference of esteems, those of inclination, preoccupation, interest, recognition, amity, alliance, complaisance and jealousy: in effect, what the truth was of the marvel with which that century was occupied.

In another country, the name of which I have never known, there was a very young prince, who had neither a father nor a mother, and who had been brought up under the supervision of the fay Tranquille. He was known as the Prince of Hearts. That name, which seems an insipidity invented by a silly mistress or a base courtier, was genuinely merited by the fashion in which he seduced the most opposed characters. He was able to please; the portrait is complete.

Tranquille had employed all her intelligence and all her sang-froid in order to endow him at birth; what is more, she had cultivated the gifts she had given him sagely. We are, therefore, only occupied with the Prince of Hearts in terms of the society in which he lived. The happiness of the subjects of that amiable prince was complete, and, in consequence, the envy of all his neighbors. Foreign sages attracted to his court by curiosity almost all ended up taking up residence there permanently, or at least testifying the deepest regret when they were obliged to leave it; as for light-headed travelers, fops of a sort—for the fashion is not new—they did not like it and did not stay long; the one is the consequence of the other.

Eulogies and criticism are, in general, not very detailed in society; thus, the knowledge and marvels of Grenadine were published far and wide, and it was repeated from mouth to mouth that she had a great intelligence—which produced an astonishment all the greater because women had not yet pretended to that kind of glory. At any rate, those rumors caused the Prince of Hearts a curiosity that he wanted absolutely to satisfy. Tranquille consented to his departure with difficulty, but everything she said to him about the impossibility of seeing Grenadine, far from diminishing his enthusiasm, only excited it.

He departed, therefore, with a modest retinue, not wanting to be accompanied by any of his guards or courtiers; the former embarrassed him and the latter are a burden when one has intelligence. That was not all; he constantly refused all the assistance of faerie, which Tranquille would gladly have lavished on him. That sentiment, which might have been called delicacy, if he had been in love, was probably only inspired in this stance by a species of generosity that did not want any foreign aid—or, to put it better, by self-esteem. So he set forth, and, completely disguised as he was, he pleased people in all the places that he simply passed through, and when he stayed for a time he was sure of being eternally regretted, for he was mild without being insipid, polite without distinction, and when he argued, it was always without displeasing and often ended up convincing.

The Prince of Hearts arrived without any incident worthy of being reported in the court of King Rubi. He did not want to make himself known, in order to be able to examine at leisure the people with whom he was dealing.

Several princes arrived every day from all parts of the world, some to satisfy their curiosity, others in the hope of

281

contenting their ambition and obtaining Princess Grenadine—whose Estates were considerable and whose intelligence and beauty were renowned—by their merits. But, you might ask me, how were those princes so constant to a princess they did not see and had never seen? For it is true the King Rubi's jealousy no longer permitted the princess to emerge from his palace or the princes to enter it.

This is how: Portraits of Grenadine were posted all over the city; they shone on walls and in all the squares, in marble, in metal, in wax, in oils, in distemper and in miniature; they were seen in pastels, in busts or in full-length, and in lockets, with all the attributes that fable history and allegory can invent. In sum, the city was virtually covered with them; one could scarcely make out the walls, especially in the main square, where princes incessantly broke lances in order to satisfy their vanity and prove their skill. It was also in the same place that they were obliged to present verses, tales and works of intellect, which, more often than not, were written for them by poets and scholars, of which there was an abundance in the city.

Intelligence was regarded as a means of succeeding in that court; authors, therefore, arrived in a host, at first out of vanity, and then having obtained a magnificent advantage by means of their wit; it is not without reason that they regret those happy times every day, for the princes paid almost as much as they believed the works to be worth. The success of works was absolutely confounded, without anyone being able to allege the cruel proof that retail sales provide. The printers were paid beyond their hopes; works were given to the whole court and spread throughout the city; by that means, successes were equal, everyone could attribute them to themselves, so everybody was content.

Questions to be resolved were also brought to the square on the part of the court, following the fashion of the Orientals; for the princess admitted all intelligences and did not know any dissipation. In truth, anyone else, who had not received such an education, would have been very unhappy, but woes are only relative; she only knew the rewards of what is known as intelligence—or, rather, its errors—and she enjoyed them. The greatest genius in the capital, or the man whom Grenadine regarded as such reported the names of the authors faithfully, and gave an exact description of the circumstances of all their productions, natural or borrowed. In accordance with that account, Grenadine had questions asked in her turn, in order to judge, by the response, their merit and intellect. That was the condition of the court in question, which had intelligence for all nourishment—that being the way people talked in those days.

The Prince of Hearts, initially charmed by the portraits of the princess, witnessed several responses made by rival princes to the following question and the fashions of enunciating them:

"How would you say that gold and silver are necessary to commerce?"

"I would say that commerce has two divinities, the second suns of cities and the Gemini that preside over navigation...."

That response had been so successful that the city drummers had be sent to the home of the prince who had made it, as well as to the door of another, who had been asked how he would define discourse.

"I would call it very simply," he had replied, "the face of the soul...."

Applause given to things of that sort surprised the Prince of Hearts infinitely. He understood the words, but he was not at all accustomed to seeing them assembled in that fashion. He began by reproaching himself for his lack of intelligence and accusing himself of vulgarity, for well-born people have no presumptions and are the first to criticize themselves; however, after mature reflection, he found that he was not so unreasonable. Even so, the fashions of speaking that he saw applauded would indubitably have put him off his own project if the beauty of the portraits and the physiognomy they indicated had not prevented him from adding credence to those accounts. He imagined them to be invented, and only had a greater desire to judge for himself whether the painters and sculptors had not flattered the princess. Thus, increasingly animated by the desire to judge a intelligence whose marvels were sung continually, he only occupied himself with means of introducing himself into the palace.

It is notable that he had never dared to have his name inscribed by the secretary of the court, who seemed to possess a vapidity to which he had not paid the slightest attention until now. He therefore made the decision to remain silent; he only confided in himself and only invested his hopes in hazard. However, he attached himself increasingly to simple acquaintances that he had made in the city; he appeared to them in a very short time, in spite of the taste of the time and the reigning ambience, to be the most amiable man on the world.

Only following a course of action that might bring him closer to his design, the prince, known under an imagined name by which he had wanted to disguise his own, attached himself most particularly to a lady of the palace; she was old, and her intelligence was mediocre, but she liked those who had the reputation of having some a great deal; incapable of judging for herself, she found—apparently by instinct—that she was bored, without knowing why, by that which reigned over the court. The reputation that the prince had acquired among those who had announced him, reassured her with regard to the doubts that his first visits had given her; she had understood everything the prince had said to her, and in good faith she would have sworn that intelligence was what one did not understand; until then she had not had any other idea, but once she was convinced that there was a man of intelligence that one could understand, she became more sensible to his charms.

I shall not go deeply into the impressions that the prince made on her heart; he was amiable, she had been assured that he had intelligence, everything he said was within her range: those are good reasons for establishing a scandalous chronicle, but history passes over the matter in silence; it is not for me the deprive anyone of reputation, nor attribute to him an affair that he might not have had. At any rate, the prince only made use of the credit that he acquired with her to make her consent, at the risk of whatever might happen, to take him with her into the palace, by promising to keep her company and entertain her—for it has to be admitted that everyone in the princess's household was dying of boredom.

It is necessary to say everything; I cannot hide that the lady had admitted all her difficulties to him, confided to him what she had been indicated to read to the princess, and told him that, in spite of the obligation she had to her, since the princess would never read anything without her, she was aware of her own ingratitude. In brief, she had added, while bursting into tears, that she was disgraced by not having been able to lend herself to a infinite number of words and speeches that were in fashion, and which she did not believe to be good because they had not shown that to her. The prince assured her that her way of thinking was the better one and heaped her with praise; he would have admired it if it had been necessary. What would he not have done in order to see the princess?

One can see by the liaison that he had with that species of schoolmistress that the prince had not sought to make very elevated acquaintances, but for important affairs, petty friends are not the least useful, and one often finds more honesty, common sense, and sound reasoning in them than in courtiers; the latter do not have the time to be sincere, their ideas are not fixed, and they are excessively dominated by other people's prejudices.

The prince was, therefore, disguised as a female slave, his age and his face necessitating such a precaution against the severity of King Rubi; he was even engaged to maintain a profound silence, in order not to run any risk and not to expose his protectress to any. But when one sees a beautiful person whom one wants to please, it is very difficult to refrain from speaking; in fact, the prince had scarcely arrived in the palace before he no longer wanted to remain silent, nor to remain with the lady who had brought him, and who was swollen with pride at having him by her side and at her disposal. He did not disguise his charms, and all the ladies were soon disputing his conversation. One is precious by art and natural by sentiment; thus, the natural pleases no matter what.

The prince easily obtained several opportunities to see the princess; that sight gradually banished from his mind all the defects—or, rather, all the ridiculous things—against which he believed himself to be armed; for, to tell the truth, she was much more beautiful than her portraits. He felt, nevertheless, that he could never speak to her in the tone that reigned at the court. Without having sorted out all his ideas very well, however, he soon reproached himself and convinced himself that he was wrong. He hoped to correct himself; the example had been sufficient to change his sentiments. What can an example not achieve, when it is set by the person one loves!

Meanwhile, Amine—that was the name the prince had adopted along with his disguise—pleased everyone, but in the fashion of a country girl who amuses ladies encountered in a manor house by her naivety.

It did not take Grenadine long to hear advantageous mention of the young slave-girl; she wanted to judge for herself the charms that people praised without being able to define them; she had her come to the foot of her throne and asked her a few questions on various subjects. Amine responded to them with grace, but with so much simplicity that the court and the princess could not imagine why they were sometimes contented and touched by them.

By virtue of an involuntary sentiment, Grenadine ended up asking her what amour was. The false Amine replied: "It is you, Princess...."

Then they all shrugged there shoulder and said to themselves: *In truth, it's a pity that, having such a good mind, she's been so badly brought up.*

"That isn't what it's necessary to respond," said the princess, with an air of instruction and mental superiority. "It's

286

necessary to say that amour is the partisan of desires. Don't you see," she continued, "that you've paid me a vulgar compliment, which doesn't define anything in general and doesn't give any idea in particular? Everyone, in sum, could say what you've just said, and everyone could understand it immediately. Employ your intelligence, then, and don't limit it to the range of ordinary and common people."

Amine received that correction mildly, and expressed the gratitude that her generosity merited with so much grace that Grenadine was touched by it, and resolved to form and cultivate her mind. Soon, it was no longer possible to separate them, and it was not long before she wanted Amine to be her slave

But while Grenadine was only thinking of forming the language and manners of her dear Amine, the amorous prince was only occupied by the ardent desire to give birth to sentiments in her heart. In order to succeed in that, it was necessary to banish the intelligence therefrom, and that was not the work of intelligence. Too many details of Grenadine's preciosity would be boring, so I shall pass over them in silence in order to arrive at more interesting things.

There is more than one kind of shepherd's hour; the heart, it seems to me, has its own; amour brings those instants without one thinking about it. This is how it brought this one about.

One day, the princess was glorifying herself for having asked all her lovers which was the more ancient of amour or beauty. Some had replied that Amour was a god, that he had created beauty in order to eternalize his empire, and that the princess was evidence of that. Other sustained that amour and beauty, being inseparable, had been born at the same instant. Those different sentiments, accompanied by insipid comments and over-refined words, divided the court, and the two parties awaited the judgment of Grenadine with equal impatience. Before pronouncing it, however, she wanted to know Amine's sentiment on that important question.

The false slave replied to her with the tender vivacity that will always be elegant: "I have seen, I have loved...."

Those words were accompanied by a gaze so persuasive, so tender and so sincere that when the princes wanted to reply by natural habitude, her seized heart could not find any reply. The blush redoubled her beauty and her submissive mind was extinguished to the extent that, for the first time, she spoke without reflection, and said: "Amine, do you think so?"

The prince regarded that response as a reproach to his temerity and withdrew, while the timid Grenadine, disconcerted by the first impressions of amour that Amine's response had borne into her heart, feared discovering that she was what she suspected her of being. She trembled for her days, fearful of the severity of King Rubi, which appeared to her from that moment on as a tyranny. In a word, she feared everything that amour makes one fear. However, by virtue of a justice that was only a delicacy and an applause of the liking that she felt, she gave the prize to the one who had given the advantage to beauty.

That was the final verdict that the great princess rendered. It occasioned several complaints. The author of the response had not been declared; all the formalities and customary practices had been neglected; but the princess took no account of that and did not say any more.

Meanwhile, in scant accord with herself, she made herself a few reproaches; but intelligence is always perfectly submissive to passion; one finds that one has too little of it for the beloved object, and from then on it is a matter of indifference to have enough for that which is foreign to it. Thus, the questions of the main square languished; the princes, and even the authors, dared in their turn to propose a few doubts, and the princess was content to blush at having made her delights of those sorts of amusements.

The rivals sensed the amour before it was declared to the one who inspired it, so the suitors all withdrew under various pretexts and left the capital, while the poets and the authors stayed, declaiming against the inconstancy of the court, having nothing else to do but prepare sad epithalamia for Grenadine's marriage, when it pleased Heaven to order it.

The word love, when one feels it, has more variety in its pronunciation, and perhaps gives evidence of more intelligence than all books contain. The Prince of Hearts was convinced if it, and took pleasure in repeating it a thousand times; soon, Grenadine acquired the pleasant habit. However, the prince was not yet known as such, and the princess was content merely to know that he was her lover; he pleased her, therefore, in himself, and for that reason he found himself at the peak of happiness. Finally—for amour goes rapidly when it reaches a certain point; the heroines of all the novels once scorned and considered vulgar are thus excused and justified—the good lady of the palace, who had come to read, was recompensed for having introduced Amine into the palace; she resumed her former favor, she was found to be a good woman, her society was preferred to all the others, she was welcomed and even loved. Not only are tender hearts indulgent, but the gratitude of lovers is as keen as it is elegant.

However, it is natural to want to know the person one loves; I have even been surprised that Grenadine could have remained ignorant of her lover's name for such a long time; it is true that one cannot think of everything, and that great revolutions had occurred within her. Finally, one day, she asked the prince the question. He replied, lowering his eyes: "I'm known as the Prince of Hearts." It is true that that name, charming when others pronounced it, had an air of fatuity when repeated by himself, but, being unknown to everyone, it was necessary to obey, he ought not to impose.

Scarcely had he finished pronouncing his name than Grenadine cried, with vivacity: "You're a prince! So much the better for my father…."

That response, being far from preciosity, charmed the prince, and it proved to him how much he was loved.

All these particular details, however, and that last event, had happened unknown to King Rubi; was it not right that he should have been deceived, as the jealous eternally are?

Furette, still animated against him because she still loved him, was only occupied with causing him chagrin; there are even historians who claim that she gave facilities to the Prince of Hearts in order for him to introduce himself into Grenadine's palace. What is certain is that Furette came running with extreme diligence, and that she arrived at the moment when the prince made the confession of his passion. It is also certain that her first concern was to inform the king of everything that had happened.

At first, he did not want to believe what the fay said; certainty caused fury to follow that doubt, for offended self-esteem does not pardon those whose dupe it has been. Thus, the king, tormented by all those ideas, implored the fay to make a severe example and to punish both the temerity of the prince and the disobedience of his daughter. What will a jealous man not do in order to be avenged?

It is said that the pleas were tender, and that he even assured her that the procedure would touch his heart. So Furette, who would have overturned the universe for much less, granted his wish. With a thrust of her wand, the prince became the most beautiful blue snail that has ever been seen, and the princess the prettiest parrot that America has ever produced.

They were together at the moment of that cruel metamorphosis, and if they saw their lovable forms vanish, they at least had the consolation of not being separated. Although they had conserved intelligence and memory, however, what conversation can a parrot and a snail have? They could have been more unfortunate, though; to think that one is loved, the memory of its pleasures, is at least a consolation.

The prince could not say anything; he could not even be reproached for his silence without injustice. It was not the same for the process, who conserved a proud attitude in her form as a parrot appropriate to a princess of her rank. She carried her had marvelously and did not lose a feather of her beautiful black collar or the long and beautiful tail that flattered her incessantly. It is since that time that, having conserved the impression, all ladies have added them to their finest garments. The misfortune of her situation was that, not being able to hear herself speak, she thought that she was saying the prettiest things in the world, and even the most tender, while she was pronouncing no other words than: *Hello, pretty Polly! Who's there? In the cellar*.... and, most of all, uttered such stupid burst of laughter that everyone was exasperated by them. It was necessary to be as amorous as the prince for him not to retreat into his shell at such moments much more rapidly that he had emerged from it.

Furette also consented to punish the lady of the palace, for she had related the detail of the adventure and the jealous demand many details; they always want to know how, how many times and when; the simple fact is never sufficient for them. In order to satisfy King Rubi's anger, therefore, she metamorphosed the lady in waiting into a doctor of law, without teaching her any more than what she knew, only giving her a desire to speak and profess, which she did to the great pleasure of the students, who turned her to ridicule.

She occupied her chair for quite a long time, for the punishments of princes tend to be quite long-lasting, but Tranquille finally put things in order. She went to report Furette's irregular conduct to the Council of Fays, adding that she was a bad example and would prevent kings from ever confiding the education of their children to fays. The council approved her reflections and gave her the power to conclude the affair as she saw fit.

As soon as she departed, the canaries that were conducting her carriage took her to Furette and King Rubi, who were not expecting their intimacy to be interrupted.

"What!" the king was saying. "One can never keep a woman safe?"

"One can," Furette replied, "but you're too good; you let too many women into the palace; they're a thousand times more dangerous than men, and more adroit for intrigues."

"But it was necessary to give her an education," said the king.

"Veritable jealousy doesn't care about intelligence and talents!" Furette replied.

It was at that moment that Tranquille appeared. That visit surprised them equally; they were even more touched by the mild but well-founded reproaches that she made of the injustice of their actions.

"You have only one thing to do," she added, "and that's to get married. Furette, who no longer has any power of faerie, has sacrificed everything to her frenzied amour, and you" she said to the king, "would be an ingrate if you didn't recognize by the gift of your hand the unfortunate attachment that she has had for you until now."

A tranquil tone is often more persuasive than any other, so they gave their consent to that union. Immediately afterwards, Tranquille went into the apartment that contained the parrot and the snail, and returned them to their original forms, as she did with the doctor in law.

While all the preparations were made for the superb wedding of Grenadine and the Prince of Hearts, Furette and Rubi tried to infect them with the sad poison of jealousy, but their efforts were futile; candor and probity were always the foundation of their union, whereas Furette and Rubi, enclosed in their cruel keep, lived in rage, despair and the torments they incessantly caused themselves by their insupportable jealousy.

Grenadine and Rubi thus provide evidence that women, being more tender and more sensitive than men, are more easily corrected by amour.

PRINCESS AZEROLLE; OR, EXCESSIVE CONSTANCY

In one of the great lotteries in which the fays in which the fays draw lots for the realms they are to protect, that of Aglantiers fell to the fay Babonette. She was a good creature, too simple to know evil and too timid to disapprove of it, credulous by virtue of good will and virtuous by virtues of weakness, with no sort of intelligence, no memory, and a negligence for her person that greatly augmented the unpleasantness of her old age,

The Council of Fays applauded the luck of the draw; the realm of Aglantiers was governed by a king so sage that the title of protectress was only an honorary one; but in those days, as today, prudence was almost always the victim of events. Babonette had scarcely taken possession of her charge than the good king died of apoplexy, recommending to the fay a unique son whom he left in the cradle.

Babonette, delighted to be able to make use of her authority, had no sooner been declared regent than she quarreled with the little prince's maidservants; she dismissed the nurse because she did not know a single ghost story, and took her back after having made her swear to learn by heart all those that she told her. The king's name was changed to Doudou,[42] which was, she said, more expressive and more appropriate to win the hearts of the people.

As soon as the young king was old enough to receive ideas, Babonette thought of nothing but inspiring him with a mortal aversion for women. Otherwise, the care of his health

---

[42] Doudou is French baby-talk for what is nowadays known in English as a "security blanket," or a "cuddly toy." It is derived by phonetically doubling the word *doux* [soft].

occupied her uniquely; the fear of its deterioration made her dismiss his masters at the first sign of distaste for lessons, so the prince, at fifteen was still on his ABC; the rest of the realm was brought almost to the same condition.

The ministers easily perceived Babonette's incapacity, but, far from bringing to the young king's education the cares that might have substituted for it, they secretly applauded his ignorance. That false politics has only been abolished after long experience of its lack of success.

The prejudice that the fay had inspired in Doudou was soon manifest. As soon as he could be obeyed, he forbade women entry to his court. The annoyance resulting from the execution of that order gave birth to the phrase that old people abuse: "it wasn't like that in our day...," which was established then as a maxim.

The young men became vulgar, dirty drunkards and hunters. The ministers yawned in the council, supped sadly and went to bed quarreling with their valets. The courtiers went to sleep in every corner of the antechamber; ambition scarcely had the force to wake them up.

Things were in that state when the fay Canadine arrived in the court. Curiosity, and a few duties of decorum had engaged for to visit Babonette; she was received as a fay of importance. The king, as absolute as a spoiled child, dared not refuse to see her, but the audience he gave her was brief, serious and embarrassed, and ended with two or three bows that he made as he withdrew, without looking at her.

However, Canadine was made to attract the attention of those who saw her. Her stature and her beauty were equally majestic. It is true that her features were a trifle pronounced; she could have passed for a Roman beauty; but she had so much splendor that, at thirty, she scarcely seemed to be older than twenty. Decided in her sentiments, firm in her resolutions, violent when her desires were opposed, disarmed by submission, good in principle, attentive by virtue of self-esteem, her commerce would have been charming if an unfortunate passion had not partly obscured her good qualities.

Proud of the victories she had won over her heart in scorning the amour of the greatest kings, she had not protected herself against the challenge of a child, handsome, in truth, but so sullen that a less difficult woman would scarcely have looked at him. However, the first glance decided Canadine's passion. If there are unlucky stars, there are glances that are no less cruel.

Astonished by the impression that the young king made on her, Canadine only attributed it, at first, to the kind of compassion that affects us when we see precious things profaned; she made reproaches to Babonette for the lack of care she had taken in forming a prince who, in spite of his boorishness, showed so much natural grace, and who could have been made into a prodigy with a little art.

"One can see that you're speaking as a fay of the world," Babonette replied. "I don't regret what I've done; women are the ruination of youth. In my time, a young fay wouldn't have dared to say what you say; everything's going the wrong way at present; I don't say a word, but if women were wiser, men would only be better for it. Anyway, what I say isn't to annoy you; I'd be very sorry to do that. Wouldn't you also like it if I had killed the poor child making him learn this that and the other? It's all very well to be scholarly, but all those geometries only put stupidities in a young man's head; my Doudou is healthy, that's the main thing. When I marry him off, we'll see...."

Canadine, having no doubt that it was futile to combat such well-established prejudices, only thought about repairing the damage that they had done to the young king by proposing to improve him. Her heart, virtuous of its own accord, deceived her; an interest dearer than that of generosity was making her act.

In order to succeed in her enterprise, she set aside as far as she could the method ordinarily followed in the education of youth; her power responding to the fecundity of her imagination, there was nothing of all that furnishes objects of study or amusement to the entire world that she did not present to young Doudou in agreeable forms. Curious, like all children, his questions would have exhausted any other complaisance than that of amour, but, far from responding, as is commonly done, by evasion or by substituting one error for another, Canadine did not let any opportunity escape to explain the king the causes and effects of everything that struck his senses.

Amusements, whatever they might be, are an immediate liaison with the arts of the sciences; the prince, having the necessary dispositions was soon beyond all the educations given and received with so much fatigue. Doudou's joy at each discovery was communicated to the fay; she obtained sensual pleasure from perfecting the object of her tenderness. Only the good fortune of being loved surpasses that of being necessary to the person one loves.

The king, fully occupied by curiosity and the pleasure of satisfying it, no longer gave the fay any evidence of his general hatred of women; it was even necessary that, as his intelligence developed, confidence being established in his heart, he gradually came to the point of no longer being able to do without Canadine. However, a cold respect, and a marked inattention to her face, made it evident that he considered her to be old because she was fifteen years older than him. The chagrin that the fay felt at that profound indifference opened her eyes to the state of her heart. At first she revolted against a penchant so humiliating for her, but there was no longer time to fight it; the intelligence, graces and sentiments that she had given the prince—all her benefits, in sum—had become weapons against her.

In vain, Canadine had recourse to the pride that had enabled her to triumph so many times; her combats had the usual result. As weak as a mere mortal, she loved no less, and no longer thought of anything but rendering herself lovable, redoubling her attention, care and complaisance for the king.

Perceiving from day to day that she was not making any progress, amour suggested to her a means of winning his heart that seemed to do honor to her reason. To the same extent that the young prince showed a taste for the arts and things of pure amusement, he showed repugnance for business and politics. Canadine could not imagine a sacrifice more delicate and more useful to his interests than giving him her hand, since, by taking sole charge of affairs, nothing would prevent the king from devoting himself to his pleasures.

She went to find Babonette; after having exaggerated the necessity of marrying off her ward, she made her see all sorts of inconveniences in giving him a young woman, and told her that the realm of Aglantiers had become so dear to her since she had been resident there that she was ready to sacrifice for the good of the state the repugnance she had for marriage.

"What!" cried Babonette, transported by joy. "You'd really like to marry my dear Doudou? How good you are! Oh, virtuous people always do the right thing! The poor child will be delighted to caress you; I've told him so much about his mother, whom he has never seen, and whom he'll think he's rediscovering."

Although Canadine was hardly content with the representation, the foundation of the speech was so much to her liking that she did not doubt the success of her project any more than Babonette did.

They were both mistaken. The fay protectress ran to see the prince in the same transport of joy that had gripped her at Canadine's proposal, but no matter how she represented the advantages of such an alliance and the dangers of a refusal, the king remained unshakable in his resolution not to love any woman. He assured the fay that the good will he had shown to Canadine was of no consequence, that he had profited from the instruction she had given him, but that, fundamentally, his gratitude was quite independent of amour, that she annoyed him too frequently with a detail of sentiment that he did not understand at all, and that, in sum, if she demanded that he pay for her benefits with his person, she could withdraw whenever she liked.

Babonette, slightly disconcerted to hear her Doudou talk like a king, had to take that response to Canadine. Seeing that

297

she maintained a profound silence, and that dolor was painted on her face, she suspected that the prince's refusal did not please her.

"You're very good," she said, "to be chagrined. If I were you I'd leave it there and wouldn't give it any further thought. That's what comes of having put foolish notions in his head; I'll wager that if you'd left him to me, he'd have married you gladly, but good minds think they know better than others; I've always heard it said that they only do stupid things."

Canadine shut herself away within herself, devouring her shame and her dolor, formed a thousand plans destroyed as soon as they were projected. Retreat appeared to her to be the most decent course of action and she was trying to affirm herself in the resolution to follow it when Babonette, which had carried on talking, said to her: "You've had a fine dream, you couldn't find a nicer husband. You're much older than he is, you'd put him to rights; he loves you, I know, what more does he want?"

"He loves me?" exclaimed Canadine, waking up as if from a profound sleep. "He loves me! Oh, I'm only too sure of his hatred."

"Oh, as for hatred, you're mistaken," said Babonette. "I know full well how I've brought him up; if it weren't for me, I'm sure he'd love you forever."

Hope is as inseparable from amour as from life; the idea of being loved, wherever it comes from, and however ill-founded it might be, bears a seductive charm into the soul, against which an unfortunate amour cannot defend itself. Canadine could not resist it; her generosity, equal to her tenderness, completed her determination not to quit the king.

He hasn't yet attained the degree of perfection to which I want to bring him, she said to herself. *He needs my care, for himself and his kingdom; would I not be guilty of all the faults he might have if I abandoned him because of an unjust impulse of my self-esteem? Since I love him, it's up to me to please him. Oh, what would be my advantages over him if my generosity did not surpass my ingratitude?*

How uplifted a decent woman is when she can find in amour the semblance of virtue!

Doudou and Canadine saw one another without explaining themselves; once the embarrassment of the first meeting was past, the king resumed his ordinary progress; he even believed that the fay had no part in Babonette's proposition, since she never mentioned it.

Canadine had too much knowledge of the heart to compromise herself by making the king the reproaches he merited; she even felt that, in order not to make him draw away from her further, it was necessary to measure prudently the hours hat she spent with him. She often sacrificed the pleasure of seeing him to the fear of being importunate; but, always present by virtue of the benefits and pleasures she procured the prince, she found a more delicate sensual pleasure in multiplying them infinitely, although she did not enjoy them herself.

Following the plan of that new conduct, Canadine, who had previously accompanied the prince when he went hunting, only went with him rarely; she contented herself during his absence with preparing fêtes for his return.

One day, when the king, left to his own devices, had been separated from the rest of the hunting party while pursuing a hind too ardently, he was extremely surprised, after having penetrated a fort with a great deal of difficulty, to find himself in a kind of hall of vast extent, and to see in one of its corners a young woman under an awning of silver gauze, sitting next to an old woman who seemed to be asleep.

Doudou stopped a few paces way in order to consider that prodigy. The young woman was holding a book, but as she raised her distracted eyes from time to time, which she returned to her reading with as little application, she perceived the prince, almost at the same time as he stopped to gaze at her. Their disturbance was equal.

After a moment of attention, the young woman put her book down on her knees and began tidying her coiffure, which the wind had deranged slightly; a few flowers placed artlessly in the most beautiful hair in the world were its only ornament; a large curl was readjusted and brought back over her cleavage with a care suggestive of a desire to please rather than modesty.

For his part, the prince, after having arranged himself on his horse and giving himself as much grace as he could, took out his handkerchief, wiped his face, put on his gloves in haste, and advanced as close to the awning as possible. He dismounted and approached the young woman with a trouble and an embarrassment that were unknown to him.

"How beautiful you are!" he said, putting one knee on the ground. "How much adoration you would merit, if you weren't a woman!"

"I'm not a woman," she replied. "My name is Azerolle.[43] The fay Severe, whom you see here, has made my castle inaccessible. But is your name not Turlupin?"

"No, Madame," replied the king, slightly disconcerted. "Princes of my blood have never borne ignoble names."

"I'm very sorry about that," replied Azerolle, lowering her eyes.

"Why?" said the prince. "My name is Doudou."

"That's of no consequence," she replied. "I see that I've been deceived."

"How?" said the prince. "Has someone talked to you about me?"

"I thought so," she replied, "and I don't understand this at all."

"Me neither," he said. "Explain yourself more clearly, I implore you."

"I'll tell you everything," the young woman continued. "Perhaps you can clear up my doubts. I've never seen anyone except the fay; she tells me that I once had a father and a mother. Do you have those, yourself?"

---

[43] Azerolle, more usually rendered Azerole, is a species of hawthorn sometimes known as the Mediterranean medlar

"Of course," the prince replied. "They were a king and a queen."

"Mine too," said Azerolle. "But tell me, since you have a father, are there many men in the world?"

"A great many," replied the king, "And almost as many women."

"Oh, that's good," said the princess. "I'm beginning to see the light."

"And I," said the prince, "understand you even less."

"It's no longer necessary, now, for you to understand me," replied Azerolle, sadly.

"What are you saying?" cried Doudou. "Every moment augments my curiosity; I feel that it isn't possible to live without being enlightened as to your fate."

"Well," said the princess, "since you want to know everything, I want to tell you everything, but on condition that you also tell me whether you're a man."

"Oh, nothing is more true," replied the prince, hotly, "but charming Azerolle, why did you doubt it?"

"Since you're a man," she interjected, "your name is Turlupin?"

"Oh, let go of your Turlupin," said the prince, impatiently. "Never mention him to me again."

"I won't talk about him anymore," said the princess, "since it distresses you; however, I would have liked to tell you that Severe is bringing me to him in order that he will marry me and make me his queen."

"What! You're going to be married!" cried Doudou.

"Yes," said Azerolle. "I've been told that he was the only man in the world; I was very glad about that, but now...."

"Go on, beautiful Azerolle, go on," said the prince, with a vivacity whose cause he could not determine. "Do you desire that the fay should change that resolution? How happy I would be..."

"Oh, no," replied the princess "Apparently, all men resemble one another, and it's all the same to me."

"Oh, that's women!" cried the prince. "I haven't been deceived; they're perfidious even before knowing perfidy."

"I believe you're quarreling with me," said Azerolle. "What have I done to you?"

"Nothing, Madame," replied the prince. "Your beauty made me forget that I ought to flee you. Your speech has returned me to myself. Adieu, Princess."

"Wait," said the princess. "I have something else to say to you."

"Oh, cruel woman!" said the prince. "You'll see whether I flee."

"Won't you come to see me when I'm a queen," she went on.

"Doubtless you'd like that," said the prince. "My unhappiness would be one more triumph for your charms."

"I don't understand what that means," replied Azerolle, mildly, "but in truth, I'd be very sorry if you were unhappy."

The princess pronounced those words in such a naïve and tender tone that they completed the destruction of the residue of prejudice that was still combating in the prince's heart.

"You don't want me to be unhappy?" he said to her. "Well, love me, then. I adore you, Azerolle; you've triumphed over the most insensible of hearts; you've made it experience the delightful sentiment that is called amour; I can't be mistaken about that. But I shall lament if you don't feel it for me! If it's in your heart, as I see it in your eyes, it will unite our souls, and my happiness…."

"Get up," said Azerolle blushing. "If the fay wakes up and hears you, I believe we'd be doomed. Flee," she added, pushing him away with one of the hands that the prince had seized and was kissing passionately. "Go away, since it's necessary for us to part."

Doudou, alarmed by the princess's first words but reassured by the tone of the last ones, knelt down, as if there were no Severe in the world.

Their sentiments were to naïve and too tender for dissimulation to have any place therein. They made mutual confessions as ingenuous as the hearts from which they departed.

Neither of them would have thought of separating had it not been for a movement on the part of the fay, which persuaded them, this time, that she was about to wake up. Hastily, they imagined a thousand means of seeing one another again, which appeared to them to be very easy to execute.

The prince mounted his horse and drew away, not without looking back for as long as he was able to see Azerolle. When he had lost sight of her, he remained so preoccupied that he did not emerge from his reveries until he reached the entrance to the peristyle of his palace, without knowing how he had arrived there.

It is not necessary to be a fay to perceive the slightest change in the heart of the person one loves; a more touching languor, a tender gaiety, a tranquil reverie and a softer speech all reveal a veritable amour. Canadine perceived her new misfortune a moment after the king's arrival; does not jealousy give rise to simple suspicions and cruel doubts that one wants to dispel, from which one only emerges into an even crueler certainty?

Doudou was too amorous not to respond ingenuously to the fay's first question, although it had no connection with his adventure; he blushed and immediately recounted his encounter with Azerolle. He painted her beauty, graces and naivety delightedly, but he only said what was necessary to express the sentiments that she had inspired in him; in order to doubt that, Canadine did not even have the resource of exaggeration.

That confession had a very different effect on the two fays. Babonette wept with joy: "What a stroke of luck!" she said. "The poor child, how well he said all that! It reminds me of myself. But where is this little Azerolle, so that I can go in search of her for you?" Addressing Canadine, she continued: "How happy they will be! We'll marry them. I'm sure that they'll never cease caressing one another; we'll rejoice in that." She turned to the prince and added: "Are you very much in love, then? Come here, my little sparrow, so that I can embrace you."

When the impatience of the mind is combined with that of the heart, it is very difficult to impede their effects. Carried away by jealousy, chagrin and indignation, Canadine touched the king with her wand and said, with a bitter smile: "There, Madame, put that cherished sparrow in a cage."

"Oh, you're right!" said Babonette, running to the prince, who was now a sparrow. "It's necessary to lock him up. You're a little quick, but that's not to make you any reproach; he's very pretty like this."

Noble souls do not commit any sin with impunity. Shame followed immediately after Canadine's impulse. She got up precipitately in order to go in search of the unfortunate bird and return him to his original form, but he had already escaped through an open window. Instinct combining with amour guided him at top speed into the forest where he had left Azerolle.

When he arrived there she was still arguing with the fay, in order not to quit a place where she hoped to see her lover again. The prince found so much pleasure in attributing to himself the resistance that she was opposing to Severe's orders that he did not think of being afflicted by the tears that she was shedding in abundance. He perched on her shoulder, and by means of chirping he tried to express his tender gratitude to her, but the princess was too occupied with him to perceive him.

The fay, surprised and impatient at Azerolle's resistance, pulling her rudely by the arm, forced her to climb into her chariot. The king, unsteady on his feet, lost his balance because of the involuntary movement that the princess made, and was obliged to use his wings to follow her. What efforts it cost him in order to match in his flight that of the crows that bore the chariot away with an extreme rapidity! But no matter how long they last, the fatigues of amour are never felt.

After having traversed immense spaces, Severe, Azerolle and the sparrow, in convoy, finally arrived in the avenue of a castle situated on a mountain much higher than those that surrounded it, which were nevertheless the highest in the world. That place, sad in itself, had been chosen by Turlupin's father for his son's habitation in preference to many others that he might have built with the magical art in which he was very knowledgeable. In spite of his art, however, and in spite of the consideration he had acquired among the fays and the genii, his son had remained so prodigiously stupid that he had not found any place more appropriate to hide him than the inaccessible castle.

Turlupin, who was stout and restless, might have had a passable appearance without a dirtiness that neither shame not the desire to please could correct.[44] Familiar without respect, importunate without self-esteem, curious by virtue of vanity, proud by virtue of baseness, he was fond of gaiety and tenderness above all. The former was expressed by laughter as continual as it was misplaced, the latter by a gesticulation as tiresome as it was impertinent.

He was very young when his father died; his aunt, the fay Severe, had taken responsibility for his education. She soon sensed that nothing could be done with such a good-for-nothing prince, but ambition is not limited by the measure of talents. Severe, who took it for a virtue—because she knew no passion more blameworthy than amour—thought that it could not be taken too far; she therefore determined to give her nephew a kingdom. It was in consequence of that resolution

---

[44] This description suggests that Caylus might have had in mind when attributing this name to his character the members of a fourteenth-century religious sect who were called "turlupins" derisively; orthodox Churchmen who condemned them as heretics condemned them as dirty, indecent and promiscuous, apparently because they wore scanty clothing in order to emphasize their vow of poverty. The verb *turlupiner*, however, means to bother or pester someone.

that she had brought up Princess Azerolle, the heiress of a great State, in complete solitude and ignorance; because she knew that the secrets of her art were insufficient to veil Turlupin's faults, and in order to engage the princess to marry him, it had been necessary to deprive her of means of comparison, the sole arbiter of the value of things.

In addition, Severe had no knowledge of the heart; she was mistaken, as many people still are today, about the power of the sacred knot of marriage, and had no doubt that the princess would love her husband as soon as it was tied.

She had noticed Azerolle's resistance that day, and the tears she had shed had caused her some anxiety, but she reassured herself as to the authority of which she had always made an infallible usage. She contented herself with ordering the princess to be cheerful, in a tone apt to fortify the least well-founded sadness.

As they approached the castle, they saw Turlupin, who was amusing himself by sweeping his courtyard. He was clad in black culottes, the lining of which could be seen through a few rips, an old dead-leaf damask indoor jacket, retained for the third time, a calico kerchief knotted around his neck, and a night-cap, the short head-piece of which left a fleece as yellow as it was dirty visible at the top. Although he was expecting the ladies he was very surprised to see them; surprise is always the first reaction of simpletons.

Turlupin's astonishment did not end this time; as soon as his eyes were assured that his aunt was arriving, he fled, crying with all his might: "Fire! Fire!" At the same time, he unleashed a salvo of canisters so prodigiously laden that the majority burst and wounded with their shards the crows that were drawing the fay's chariot. The frightened birds scattered in panic and, applying her effort unequally, fractured the chariot, which was only made of lightly woven canes. Fortunately for Azerolle, the chariot touched down at that moment. The fay, however, was unable to avoid a slight wound in the arm. Azerolle, who was lighter, did not come to any harm; she only showed the tender sparrow a leg that caused him to remember his metamorphosis with more regrets than the fatigue of the voyage had caused.

Severe and Azerolle picked themselves up as best they could, for Turlupin, who had promptly put on a coat and donned a wig powdered with the best flour in the house, in order not to lack dignity, was waiting for them on the perron shouting: "O joy! O joy! Don't be afraid…"

"That's a fine amusement!" the fay said to him, as she approached.

"Ha ha, Aunt!" he interjected, bursting into laughter. "You're not a good trumpet horse, since you're scared by noise. It doesn't matter; let's have fun."

The fear of the reply prevented Severe from responding; she contented herself with making a sign to him to give his hand to the princess. He obeyed, but going in first, he pulled her after him, pointing out the beauty of the apartments. When they had arrived in a magnificent drawing room that terminated them, he stopped, and turned to Azerolle.

"Let's go, Mademoiselle," he said, bluntly, "You know why you're here; we'll soon be familiar together; let's begin to banish ceremonies." At the same time he grabbed Azerolle's head, and would have kissed her in spite of her resistance but for the tender sparrow, which had come in at the same time as the company, and which, flying into Turlupin's face, pecked him on the cheek with all his might, while Severe, already in a bad mood because of her fall, losing all patience, slapped him on the other.

"Oh! It's you, then, Aunt, who wants to be kissed?" he said, embracing her before she had thought of defending herself. "I know how one avenges oneself for slaps given by ladies." Perceiving then that blood was running down his cheek, he looked around. "Oho!" he said, angrily, but with an affected laugh. "It's a bird that's allowed itself to be shut in. "That's funny! Someone fetch my cat; you'll see a fine game; you'll see how he swallows them. That'll amuse you, won't it, Mademoiselle!"

307

At that cruel threat, the sparrow flew into Azerolle's arms, hoping to find a refuge there.

Every unfortunate creature is protected by tender souls, but that protection is even surer when one requests it of those who are feeling the pains of amour; moved by an impulse more forceful that ordinary compassion, the princess asked for mercy for the bird.

Turlupin replied to her in a self-contented fashion: "Mademoiselle, you have only to pronounce it." Then he asked the fay to heal his cheek, which was done instantly. She seized that pretext to take him to one side, and make him reproaches regarding all the stupid things he had done since their arrival.

"Good, good," replied Turlupin, still laughing. "You have your reasons." Drawing closer to the princess and giving her a knowing wink, he said: "It's because she's jealous, but I'm not fooled. She wants me to bore you with compliments; in truth, they give me a headache. Here, Mademoiselle, I'm a cheerful fellow who doesn't engender melancholy. Oh, you'll love me, once we've…." He interrupted himself. "But reply to me, then!"

"No, Monsieur," replied Azerolle, without having heard what he had said.

"Ah!" he cried, laughing more forcefully. "She's playing the little sweetie! But we'll see, when I'm your husband…"

At the word *husband*, the princess, who was dreaming with all her heart about the one she would have liked to have, looked up at Turlupin, and could not hold back tears that flowed in abundance,

"Uh oh!" he said. "That's even worse. Come here, Madame Severe; I don't know what to say to people who weep."

The fay approached; but, struck by the sight of the sparrow sitting on the princess's shoulder, to which she had not previously paid any attention, she stopped, seeking to disentangle the truth of the suspicions to which the power of her art had just given birth regarding the metamorphosis of the prince.

She considered him attentively, unembarrassed by Azerolle's tears. Azerolle continued to weep, without perceiving the fay's stare. The tender bird, uniquely occupied with the dolor of his princess, was fluttering around her throat and passing his beak over her chin, without worrying about the astonishment of Turlupin, who never ceased crying: "That's admirable! One might think there was finesse in it," when Canadine and Babonette came in, making a racket that extracted all four of them from their occupations.

Canadine, who had immediately repented of having metamorphosed the prince in the first place because of the sole regret of having offended him, had no sooner perceived his flight than, reflecting on the facility that he had of rejoicing Azerolle in the form of a bird, she sensed jealousy gripping her heart again with more vivacity than repentance had made had caused her to lose it.

Her dolor, in changing its motive, only became more violent. *How blind anger is!* she thought. *My vengeance has given him the means to flee me and return to my rival. Doubtless he's already with her, softening her with his innocent caresses; in spite of his metamorphosis they'll see one another, understand one another; amour will lend them an intelligence superior to any other power. Doubtless they're complaining about me...perhaps they hate me...me, I'm creating hatred! Oh, if I merit that frightful sentiment, constancy, virtue and delicacy, are you nothing, then, but fruitless chimeras of a tender and generous heart?*

In the midst of the saddest reflections, the dangers that the prince was running presented themselves to Canadine's imagination; all other interests yielded to that of preserving him. "Come on, sister," she said to Babonette, "Let's run to his aid."

"It's always well done to help the unfortunate," replied the old fay, "but where are they...? What does it matter? Let's go anyway, perhaps we'll encounter them...I love you for being so good...."

Canadine consulted her books and soon discovered the prince's movements. She also discovered Severe's designs, which reassured her a little; but Doudou was enjoying the sight of her rival; it as necessary to separate them.

She sensed the need she had of Babonette, as much to carry out decently the project she had formed of abducting the young king as to balance out the power of Severe by the authority that her great age gave her.

They both mounted into the first chariot that came to hand and five minutes later they arrived at the inaccessible castle. Canadine was so impatient to see what was happening there that, not finding the door open, she went in through the window. This time, Turlupin's stupidity had no part in his astonishment; and entire equipage passing through a window would have astonished many others.

Severe went to meet her sisters, whom she recognized immediately, but Canadine, without responding to her compliments, advanced precipitately toward the sparrow king. The caresses he was making to her rival had not escaped her first glance.

"Oh, cruel man," she cried, "the surest means to extract you from the pleasure you're taking is to render you your original form!" At the same time, she touched him with her wand, and he tender sparrow became the tender Doudou.

Azerolle's confusion suspended the pleasure she had in rediscovering her lover; she blushed and lowered her eyes with as much embarrassment as if she had been aware of the indecency of the liberties that the prince had taken.

Indignant to the last excess, Severe would have punished him for his temerity immediately if Canadine had not shoved Babonette, whispering to her: "If you don't make use of the superiority of your power, your child will perish."

That was the only fashion of loving her. "Gently!" she said to Severe. "Although it's not honest to contradict people in their home, I won't permit you to do anything against King Doudou. But to show you that it isn't by virtue of ill will that I'm opposing my power to yours, I consent that he be judged and punished, if he merits it, by the council that we'll hold, and that, submissive to our united will, we can dispose of him one after another. You have virtue, Canadine has intelligence and I have experience; we're worth our price. Let's go, my sisters, let's assemble and judge."

Although Canadine was very annoyed that Babonette had taken away the absolute power that she had over the prince, it was necessary to subscribe to it. Severe, no less mortified to find a power above her own, dissimulated, resolved to profit from the mistake that the fay protectress had just made or to try to bring the council to her will. She contented herself for the present with remonstrating to the two fays that it would be indecent to leave the prince and the princess while they were occupied in determining their destinies.

"You're right," said Babonette. "What shall we do with them?"

"If you'll permit," said Severe, "I'll prevent them from talking to one another."

"Willingly," said the fay protectress, "provided that you don't do them any harm."

"Have no fear," replied Severe. At the same time, she touched the prince and the princess with her wand; they became the most beautiful white marble statues that had ever appeared. At that moment, the prince was looking at Azerolle in a fashion so tender, and seemed so penetrated by amour, that Canadine could not see him without an emotion in which unhappy tenderness and timid jealousy were mingled. Azerolle, who had finally dared to raise her eyes, still humid with the tears she had shed, toward the prince, was expressing the pleasure of seeing him again with so much naivety that the two statues gazing at one another, and the fay, almost as motionless, formed an interesting group.

Severe and Babonette extracted Canadine from her sad reverie; all three went into a neighboring from to hold council there, and Turlupin remained alone with the prince and the princess. Since his initial astonishment, so many others had succeeded it that his eyes were still staring and his mouth open. In that attitude, he did not weary of circling around the statues, without having understood anything of what had happened. On their return, the fays found him still in the most stupid admiration.

At first, the council had been very agitated. Babonette, stimulated by Canadine, wanted absolutely to take her prince back to his Estates. Severe claimed arrogantly that the insult rendered to her nephew, whose wife the princess was to be, demanded an exemplary punishment. Canadine represented, with all the moderation that her prudence could suggest to her, that the law only ordered the punishment of infidel women; that, unjust as it might be, it was necessary to follow it and punish Azerolle, by making her suffer a few light penalties. Severe, in refuting that proposition, commenced to mingle so much bitterness in the dispute that Canadine, fearing Babonette's weakness, proposed a compromise.

"Your principal interest," she said to Severe, "Is the marriage of your nephew with the princess. You could oblige her to marry him, but since you don't find her worthy of him so long as she has a penchant for the prince, it's necessary to try by all sorts of means to detach them from one another. Let's put them to all the proofs that might render them inconstant; they'll doubtless succumb, and in completing your project you'll satisfy your revenge. Let's commence by rendering the princess ugly, in such a fashion that Doudou will by the first to become disgusted with her."

Severe made a few difficulties, but she yielded, because she was fundamentally convinced that it was not every day that she would find queens and realms to give her nephew.

Babonette delighted to hear that no harm would be done to her prince, consented willingly to his heart being broken by the contradictions that his amour was about to make him experience. Petty souls are only aware of bodily pains and reverses of fortune.

They went back into the drawing room to carry out their project. Either out of malice or awkwardness, as she pronounced the fatal words, Severe touched both statues instead of one; as they were reanimated they both became frightfully ugly; their eyes encountered one another without recognition, but, their stature and their clothing leaving them in no further doubt of their misfortune, they both uttered a cry as they said; "Is that you I see?"

Each of them, to begin with, only suffered on the part of the object of their tenderness; their self-esteem was not involved. Severe did not leave them in that consoling error for long. She led them to a mirror and forced them to look at themselves. The two unfortunates were no sooner convinced that they were experiencing the same deformity than, putting their hands over their faces, they uttered another cry more dolorous than the first, and each fled through a different door.

Turlupin was beginning to accustom himself to prodigies; the last one only provoked a loud burst of laughter, and he said to Severe: "Oh, that's a good trick, that one! But it's nothing to laugh at, is it? For, frankly, if the princes I'll have from that ugly mug resemble her, I won't have any great pleasure in caressing them. Come on, they've gone; let's amuse ourselves; I want all my servants to get drunk this evening, in order to welcome you."

"Shut up, fool," Severe said to him.

"Thank you, Aunt," he said, putting one foot behind the other. "Mesdames," he added, "I beg your pardon for my aunt. She's always in…in…arguments. That's what makes…but what does it matter? As for me, I like to laugh. Come on, to joy, to joy!"

At the same time, a very loud band of musicians entered, playing *Le Descente de Mars*.[45] Turlupin hastened to offer his hand to Canadine, asking her to dance the courante with him, "which I find," he said, "very gay and in good taste."

The fay declined.

---

[45] "La Descente de Mars" from the opera *Thésée* (1632) by Jean-Baptiste Lully, features a striking trumpet fanfare.

"My word, Mesdames," he said, in a mocking tone, "you're difficult; for myself, I can't do any more; it's necessary to excuse a poor country boy."

Severe was suffering too much from the impertinence of her nephew to give him time to make any more gaffes; she proposed to the two fays that they go to the apartments that were destined for them, under the pretext that she needed to rest before supper. She conducted her nephew to his, where she was tempted to lock him in.

The prince and the princess had both fled in different directions, finding a great many open doors; the last one led them into a garden of prodigious extent. They kept walking, without knowing where they were, each so occupied with their sad adventure that they would not have stopped if hazard had not led them into a hornbeam arbor, to which the two long pathways that they had followed led. Although the night was already sufficiently dark to hide their features, there was still enough daylight to make out their faces.

"Is that you, my princess?" said the sad Doudou, turning his face away.

"Yes," replied Azerolle, hiding hers with a handkerchief.

"How unfortunate we are!" they cried.

"You are less so than me," said Azerolle, "It would take a lot for Severe to have disfigured you as much as me."

"Oh," said the prince, "what would it matter to me to be even more horrible," said the prince, "if I didn't fear appearing odious to you?"

"If you only have that anxiety," said the princess, "you have nothing to lament. Just now, while walking, I recalled your features; I still find them less disagreeable than those of the vile Turlupin."

"What!" cried the prince, falling to his knees. "You don't hate me? Perhaps you haven't looked at me properly. When you've seen me, I'll horrify you."

"Why do you have that dread?" said Azerolle. "I don't have it, myself. Although I'm much more frightful than you, I imagine that you'll still love me, because it isn't my fault."

"What charms that confidence has for my heart!" the prince said to her, transported. "Yes, my dear Azerolle, yes, I shall adore you as long as you live; but alas, you'll be obliged to marry Turlupin; I won't survive that frightful misfortune."

"Well," said Azerolle, "Marry me quickly. Since you're a king, you can make me a queen just as well as him."

In spite of his chagrin, the prince could not help smiling at Azerolle's ingenuousness. "The proposition you're making me, Princess," he said, "is the unique object of my desires, but Severe will always oppose my happiness, as long as she hopes to oblige you to be her nephew's wife."

"Oh, I assure you that I never shall be," replied the princess, "unless I'm married without my perceiving it. I don't know how that's done, but I'll keep myself on my guard."

"They can't marry you without you knowing," said the prince. "Your consent will be the knot that binds you."

"Well, if that's the case," she replied, "I'm your wife, for I consent with all my heart to be."

"That confession delights my heart and my senses," replied the prince. "What would my happiness be, my dear Azerolle, if I were free to take advantage of it!"

"What!" said the princess, nonplussed. "You don't want to be my husband?"

"Pardon me…," said the prince, swiftly.

"No, no," she interrupted. "I can see that you fear loving me too much. Severe has told me that one loves madly, as soon as one is married. I already love you a great deal, but I'd only want to be our wife in order to love you more."

"Your words penetrate my soul with tenderness," replied the prince, squeezing one of Azerolle's hands in his. "My heart can't suffice for all the love you're giving it. Yes, my dear princess, I experience what happiness and extreme misfortune can be, united in a tender heart at the same time."

"I believe it's necessary for you not to hold my hand," said Azerolle, taking it away.

"Why?" said the prince.

"I don't know," she replied, slightly nonplused, "but it seems to me that it's not good."

"Eh! What do you fear, my princess?" he added, moving even closer to her.

"Nothing," she replied. "Let's go. It's dark; they're doubtless looking for us. I'll be scolded."

The young king, as respectful as he was tender, dared not resist Azerolle's will. On the way, the lovable children made new vows to love one another forever. As they approached the castle, sadness spread through their hearts; it increased as the light came closer. In communicating to one another the dread they had of seeing one another again, with how many tender protestations was it not accompanied!

The three fays had been so occupied, Severe with scolding Turlupin, Canadine with her dolor and Babonette with visiting every corner of the house, that no one had perceived the absence of the lovers. They did not appear until it was time to sit down at table. Prepared as they were to see them, their first glance made them shiver; for the rest of the evening they did not raise their eyes again.

The supper was sad, in spite of the long bursts of laughter that Turlupin uttered every time he looked at the prince. For a few moments, scorn aided the young king to moderate himself, but in the end he became so impatient that he would have made Turlupin pay dearly for the distress that his joy was causing him if Severe had not imposed silence on her nephew. The entire company had so little pleasure in seeing one another that they separated early.

Gradually, the fays found themselves established in the inaccessible castle, without knowing when they would leave it, since only the inconstancy of the prince or the princess could divide the interests that bound them together.

In fact, whatever was added to the ugliness of the prince and princess, all that the necessity of always being together could produce of quarrels, ennui and distaste, and although the young levers were forbidden any other dissipation and any other pleasure save that of talking to one another, which was made into an obligation, they seemed no less fond of one another and no less eager to be together.

The knowledge with which Canadine had ornamented the mind of the young king was an infinite resource for him to sustain long conversations; in clarifying Azerolle's mind and developing her heart he rendered her a thousand times more lovable. She thought in a more refined way, without having lost her ingenuousness and without her candor diminishing; she expressed herself more gracefully. Those amiable children, entirely occupied with their sentiments, grew accustomed to their ugliness, to the point of no longer regretting their former beauty.

Only Canadine was unhappy, not because she had hoped that the prince's deformity might weaken the tenderness she had for him—in the heart of a reasonable woman, amour is independent of looks—but because her pains were much increased by the resentment that Doudou showed her whenever they met. Since the day of the first metamorphosis she had not found a moment to justify herself. The prince avoided her with as much care as she took to seek him out.

Finally hazard contrived what vigilance had not been able to achieve. One morning, when Severe had prolonged the reprimands that she made to the princess regularly every day, Canadine, on going into the assembly hall, found the prince alone there, waiting impatiently for Azerolle to emerge. She approached him with the timidity that virtue humiliated by amour inspires.

"You're avoiding me," she said, "If you'd care to listen to me...."

Scarcely had she pronounced those few words than the prince interrupted her, saying: "I know, Madame, everything that you want to say to me; this is my response. You caused my misfortunes; there is only one way to make me forget them and to regain over my amity the rights that your former generosity had acquired. I love Azerolle; you cannot doubt that; if you were as attached to me as you say, would you not have

317

found a means to free us from the unjust power that retains us here? Render me happy with the one I love and I will forget the offense that you have done me."

"Oh, cruel man!" cried the fay. "Can I not give you my life; it would cost me far less than what you are asking? You only read your own heart; if you knew mine, far from complaining, you would take account of all that it has not done to avenge me for your outrages. But you owe me nothing," she added, with more composure. "It's me who owes you sacrifices; name any that are in my power and you will be obeyed. Only know that nothing can remove you from this place except yourself; cease to love Azerolle and you will be free."

"I would prefer the most horrible slavery to the liberty that would cost me my amour," replied the young prince. "I ask you nothing for myself; render the princess the beauty that Severe has stolen from her, and I will be satisfied."

After a moment of reflection, Canadine replied to him: "You shall see your princess again with more charms than she has ever had, Prince." Adopting a sadly ironic expression, she added: "You will see how unnecessary beauty is to please you; you will stay as you are until you have learned what it costs to love without return."

The young king did not hear the fay's last words; content with what he had obtained, he quit her abruptly and ran to discover whether his dear Azerolle had come out of Severe's room, in order to tell her the good news.

Amour outraged and fortunate amour are both reefs for virtue. Canadine, in despair, lost much of her generosity; she could not refuse a vengeance that the prince had just indicated to her himself. After having assembled Severe and Babonette, she represented to them the mistake the three of them had made in wasting time for which they were accountable to the universe; that it was futile to hope to see distaste born between two lovers who, only seeing one another, naturally would not quit one another, however horrible their faces were.

"I don't understand that at all," said Babonette. "I would have bet my key, my wand and even my hood that those two young people would have quit one another by now. But since it's still the same, my opinion is that we should marry them, as we couldn't, with all our art, match them better. That Azerolle is the best child in the world; she suits my Doudou perfectly; what prevents us from rendering them happy? For myself, I consent to it."

"What!" retired Severe, red with chagrin. "Have you forgotten the outrages that your Doudou has committed against me? Have you forgotten that I've only taken care to raise Azerolle in favor of my nephew and that I don't want to lose the fruit of so much trouble?"

"Oh, you're right," said Babonette. "Yes, yes; what should we do?"

"If you would let me dispose of the fate of the princess," replied Canadine, "I'd commence by restoring her original beauty."

"That's well imagined!" Severe put in, sarcastically.

"My God, let's do that," said Babonette. "She has more intelligence than us. Come on, I give you back my power; you're good, you love my prince, all will be well."

Severe contested as best she could the futility of the project. Canadine, after having assured her that she would not stop there, reminded her of their convention, and made her understand that her power was nothing without Babonette's and that she ought to yield gracefully to their combined wills. Severe, confounded, withdrew without replying.

Canadine did not waste a moment in taking advantage of the authority that she had just acquired. She rendered the process not only her original splendor, but added graces, charms and I know not what, rarely united in extreme beauty, in profusion. She went to present the king to his beautiful princess herself, attentive to the impression that the change would make on him. She enjoyed her vengeance as soon as the first glance.

The admiration that Azerolle's beauty caused Doudou was not so pure that a mixture of sadness could not be discovered therein, which revealed the return of self-esteem. His transports were timid, his joy was embarrassed, and the thanks he gave Canadine included a slight reproach for having done too much. For her part, the princess, whom Canadine had placed in front of a mirror, content with her beauty, which a little jealousy caused her to compare with that of the fay, also wanted to surpass her in the majesty of her stature. She stood up straighter; her bearing became nobler; she mingled a modest pride with the tenderness of her eyes, the comparison of which also satisfied her. But while she was enjoying her triumph, she bore into the heart of her lover, without being aware of it, a first affliction of chagrin, which was followed by many others.

The prince had too little knowledge of women to think that a simple emulation of beauty might steal moments from amour. Azerolle appeared to him to be too occupied with herself, and attributed the new augmentations that she added to her charms to the scorn that his ugliness inspired in her, To hide the disturbance that his reflections spread over his face, he went out abruptly, without listening to Canadine, who tried to prevent him from doing so.

Azerolle, whom vanity could not distract for long, tried to follow him, but she was stopped by Turlupin, who ran to present her with a cat, which, he said, had just fallen from the clouds. Accustomed to his platitudes, no one paid any attention to what he said. The princess liked cats, she could not forbid herself to accept that one with eagerness; it was worth a graceful bow to Turlupin and thanks by which his stupidity was disconcerted.

"Fie, Mademoiselle," he said to her. "You take things to seriously; anyway, it's yours, you can make cabbages or beets of it, it didn't cost me anything."

While Turlupin was confounded in compliments, the princess praised the beauty of her cat. It was not that there was anything singular about the color of its fur—it was black marked with white, like many others delivered to the gutters—but two large black prominent eyes, a high forehead, and ears placed by the hand of the Graces, formed a tender physiognomy, a thousand times more deductive than beauty; its mouth, small and agreeable, did not belie the mildness of its gaze; it only opened to give expression to her caresses by a delicate, fluty and methodical mewl; never teeth, nor claws. In sum, the qualities of its heart seemed to compete with the charms of its face.

Although Azerolle was enchanted to possess that marvelous animal, she did not forget that the prince had quit her in chagrin; she departed like lightning, holding the cat in her arms, caressing it on the way; she ran everywhere that she thought she might find the afflicted Doudou.

That cat entered considerably into the designs of Canadine; she remained very surprised by the little distraction that it had caused the princess.

Turlupin, without knowing why, was even more astonished by it. "But...but...but, Madame," he exclaimed, "she's taking the cat away." That sentence is conserved so exactly in the archives of the house of Turlupin that its descendants still make use of it today in cases of unexpected flight.

Meanwhile, Azerolle, after having run in vain to all the places in the garden where her lover was accustomed to walk, finally perceived him on the edge of a freshwater canal that limited one of the sides of the vast enclosure. He had his face propped up by his hands, in the attitude of a man dreaming sadly.

Azerolle slowed down as she drew closer to him; her step was so light that she arrived next to him before he perceived her. She extracted him from his reverie by giving him two or three taps with her cat's paw on his hand.

Young Doudou's mind had so little disposition to gaiety at that moment that that innocent teasing made him resentful of the cat; he pushed it away rudely, and reproached the princess for that pleasantry with so much bitterness that, astonished by such a new fashion of speaking, she thought that the animal's claws had scratched him. She made him tender apologies, but the prince, without replying to them, explained himself immediately with regard to the scorn that he thought he had remarked in her eyes.

The ingenuous Azerolle justified herself with so much candor that the reconciliation followed immediately after the explanation.

That first quarrel, however, was soon followed by a second. The king, having become anxious, could not abide the caresses that Azerolle gave the cat during a conversation whose pleasure he did not want to be shared. The princess replied to his reproaches again in a fashion to disarm him, but still without quitting the cat.

"Isn't it cruel," the prince continued, "that you prefer to me the most malevolent of animals? Azerolle, Azerolle," he added, "You would not have treated me with this repugnance when our misfortunes were common; I'm beginning to displease you; soon you'll find my frightful. I am, it's true, but is it for you to reproach me?"

While the prince was speaking, the cat—which, in addition to the annoying humor typical of its species, seemed to be impelled by a particular interest—put to use everything it could to attract the attention of young Azerolle: caresses, attitudes, gestures, everything was employed with the most seductive grace.

Unless one has a natural aversion to those animals, can one resist their provocations? The process yielded to admiration, picked up the cat, and kissed it enthusiastically, saying: "Come, pretty puss, you're too lovable."

At those words, the young king, carried away by an unprecedented impulse, snatched it abruptly from Azerolle's hands. He was about to throw it in the canal when it escaped, and became a young man, with a face such as one would take if one could choose, of a beauty equal to Azerolle's.

"Stop, Prince!" he cried to the king, who was advancing toward him with fury painted in his eyes. "When you have heard me out, you can do what prudence suggests to you." At the same time, he drew nearer, in a manner as noble as it was respectful.

He told the king that his name was Zumio,[46] and that for a long time, Canadine had rendered him the unhappiest of genii, by the scorn with which she repaid the insurmountable amour that he had for her; that his woes made him sympathetic to those of others; and that he only occupied himself with helping unfortunate lovers. Having discovered by the enlightenments of his art, not only what the prince and the princess were being made to suffer, but also the traps that were being prepared for them, he had come to offer his services, without demanding any gratitude from them, because he admitted candidly that the desire to avenge himself on Canadine had some part in his design.

The tone of honesty that the genius displayed in his speech, and the interest that he seemed to express in exaggerating the dangers that threatened the tender lovers, penetrated them with fear and confidence. They employed all the expressions that the generosity of their souls could furnish them to persuade Zumio of their gratitude and to obtain a positive promise from him not to abandon them.

The genius assured them modesty that, his art being inferior to Severe's, he could only help them with his cares and his advice. It was therefore necessary to imagine means that might lead them to the end of their troubles. The adroit genius, while destroying all those that Doudou proposed, did not fail to praise their invention, and only received the small suggestions that Azerolle mingled with theirs from time to time with the benevolent smile that is accorded to children who say pretty but futile things.

So much deference on the part of Zumio, and so little reason for jealousy, completed gaining the confidence of the

---

[46] Caylus's genius was co-opted from the present story into one of the moralistic tales penned at the end of the eighteenth century by the Comtesse de Genlis, translated into English in *Tales of the Castle* (1785). It seems unlikely that the character assisted the modern adoption of the term for a kind of vibrator, in spite of his seductive conduct in feline form.

prince, to the point of making him agree that is was first necessary for the genius to pretend to be in love with Azerolle, and that if the king took no umbrage at that, he would be thought to be inconstant, which was the only way to procure their liberty.

Zumio added that his interest ought to be their guarantee of good faith, since by means of that arrangement he was working for his own happiness, because Canadine might become sensible by virtue of jealousy, not having been by virtue of amour.

He spoke of his passion in such a penetrating tone, and affected so much indifference for Azerolle, taking the precaution of warning her, in such a cold manner, that she would only be the pretext, and not at all the object, of his gallantries, that she blushed, and Doudou could not help smiling.

They separated from him in order better to conceal their intelligence. The genius went to prepare himself in order to arrive at the castle in pomp; the prince and the princess hastened to return there, in order subtly to enjoy the surprise that his arrival would cause Canadine, without forgetting to applaud themselves on the way on such a fortunate encounter.

They found Severe, Babonette and Canadine at the windows overlooking the avenue, watching Zumio's carriages, which were already beginning to file along it. They were as elegant as they were magnificent, brilliant and numerous, traveling in the most beautiful order.

The two old fays were asking questions reciprocally about the unexpected visit. Canadine, unaccustomed to pretence, carefully avoided those addressed to her; a violent passion can inspire ingenious deception, but an elevated soul sustains it poorly.

As for Turlupin, in the disturbance in which so much unfamiliar society had put him, he had run to his grain-loft, from which he cried out with all his might: "Close the gates, they'll make my courtyard dirty!"

Finally, after a prodigious number of pages, liveried servants, carts and horses, the handsome genius was seen to arrive in a varnished pink cameo caleche with harness and ornaments decorated with emeralds. Seeing the ladies at the window, he descended at the gate and came toward them with a noble, easy-going and respectful air, making graceful reverences from time to time. He was followed by brilliant young people as gallantly clad as he was.

Severe waited for him gravely in the fine drawing room, and Zumio, after having bowed to her three times, addressed a compliment to her on her nephew's impending marriage, on the part of the sovereign genius, who had charged him, he said, with the title of ambassador to her, in order to be a witness to that great alliance. Severe was so flattered by such a distinction that her face became almost cheerful. She replied to the genius with dignity; then they went into another apartment, where the conversation became general.

Zumio had so much grace, he was so handsome, and his adornment had a festival air that rendered him so brilliant, that Doudou, prepared as he was to see him, could not look at him without a certain interior tremor. More familiar to jealous hearts than easy to describe; his face became a burden to him. He dared not speak for fear of being noticed; his embarrassed gaze wandered from the genius to Azerolle, whom he found to be much too occupied with that new company.

In a few days, Zumio became necessary to everyone. He amused Babonette with tales, Severe with moral treatises, Doudou with the hope of his happiness, Azerolle with praises of her lover and Turlupin with puns. He gave fêtes; every day brought a new one. The pleasures succeeded one another so rapidly that had they left people with the liberty of thought, they would not have found time to communicate their reflections.

However, the gaiety spread over faces only consisted of demonstrations; no one was content. Canadine was suffering even more from the pretence that she had imposed on herself than her unfortunate passion.

325

Azerolle delivered herself to the diversions like a young person savoring them for the first time, but that was not without regretting the days when she had had no other pleasure than that of conversing with Doudou. She lent herself in good faith to Zumio's cajoleries, with no other design than advancing her lover's happiness, but the inevitable dissipation in the tumult gave her, without her being aware of it, an appearance of coquetry that tore the heart of the tender prince.

The difficulty the latter had in talking to her, the impossibility of putting a stop to the fêtes that were insupportable to him: everything drove him to despair, including the chagrin of not daring to hate his rival. As soon as Zumio perceived any discontentment on his part, he hastened to heap him with amities and protestations; then he deployed threats of abandonment so cleverly that he reduced him to begging him insistently to continue playing the same role.

It is sufficient to be unhappy, or to be honest, to be duped. Doudou was both; the artifices of the genius would have deceived the most suspicious.

For her part, Severe, in spite of the honors that flattered her ambition, was no more content than the others. Apart from the chagrin that pleasures in general caused her, she feared that Zumio's gallantries might indeed render Azerolle infidel, but in his own favor, which would produce nothing for her nephew. She took Canadine to task one day.

"There was no point," she said, in giving you our power, "if you didn't want to make any other usage of it except rendering Azerolle more beautiful. Instead of the efficacious help you promised me, I see nothing but gallantries that wound me and fêtes that irritate me. If you had less empire over Babonette I would soon have determined her to let my power act, and we would see as many useful punishments as we are seeing frivolous amusements.

In order to calm her, Canadine was obliged to make her party to her designs. "You have seen," she told her, "that ugliness has not altered the amour that we wanted to destroy. The distaste that the young people were supposed to acquire for

326

one another when you obliged them to be together relentlessly had no more success; nothing remains to you to test their constancy but jealousy and infidelity. Jealousy was born in the heart of the prince the moment I embellished Azerolle, and you shall judge how right I was to summon Zumio here to serve your vengeance....

"He is," she continued, "one of the genii who resemble men most closely; he has limited his powers to deceiving women. After having deceived a large number, he found that Souveraine was lacking to his triumph; why not employ them to seduce her? He succeeded in that, but almost as soon disillusioned as she was vanquished, the firmness of her soul led her courageously to sacrifice her reputation to an exemplary vengeance.

"She convened a numerous assembly; after having had the perfidious genius dragged before it, she invited all the fays who had reproached him to add their voices to hers, in order to confound and condemn him. But she offered herself as an example in vain; she made them sense the price of the sacrifice she was making for the common, and not one of them spoke. The blushes on the faces of some, the embarrassment of others and the consternation on all the faces did not even leave the old beyond suspicion of having a good deal to say.

"'Well, my sisters,' said Souveraine, 'since a false shame, or perhaps a residue of seduction, prevents you from confounding the traitor, I'll take charge of the vengeance myself. You'll be a cat,' she told him, 'until in that form you've inspired the jealousy of a perfect lover. But your punishment would be too mild, if I limited it to so little; I want,' she added, 'that the knavery that is so natural to you, to be the instrument of your mercy or your torture. Until the end of the centuries you shall have the most decrepit face with the most violent desires, unless within six months from today you triumph over a constancy proof against anything, without pleasing, without loving and without the object that you want to seduce discovering the falsity of your character....'

327

"See," added Canadine, "whether I could have put the infidelity of the princess in better hands. Since the wellbeing or misfortune of Zumio is dependent on it, what success should we not expect of his skill?"

"That's all very well for Zumio," replied Severe, "but what will my nephew get out of it?"

"The conditions that Souveraine has attached to the success of his enterprise are so difficult to fulfill," replied Canadine, "that there is every appearance that before their accomplishment, the prince will have rejected a futile constancy, and you'll be left the mistress of disposing of Azerolle."

Severe contented herself with those arguments, being unable to find any better; she even forbade the princess to speak to Doudou, in order to contribute in some way to the advancement of the project; but that new contradiction only augmented the pains of the lovers without decreasing their constancy.

Azerolle incessantly made reproaches to Zumio for having engaged her in a deception that, far from being useful to them, rendered them more unfortunate. For his part, the genius reproached her so often that her pretence was to poor too deceive the fays that in the end, the credulous princess went to so much trouble to appear infidel, that her lover soon had no doubt that she was. That was not enough for Zumio to bring his enterprise to a conclusion, however; it was necessary that Azerolle betray him.

A pure and confident soul does not easily acquire ideas disadvantageous to the person she loves. Perhaps the artful genius would not have succeeded in convincing Azerolle of the infidelity of Doudou if the unfortunate prince had not seemed to accord with him to contribute to his misfortune. His jealousy had increased considerably since Severe had forbidden Azerolle to speak to him. Deprived of the relief that the jealous often find in making reproaches, and unable to suffer the dolor that was devouring him, he saw no one but Canadine who could soothe his heart by sympathizing with his pains.

If dread has made gods, needs have made amity; they are treated similarly. So long as Canadine's instruction had been necessary to the young king, he had had a sort of amity for her; fortunate amour had entirely stifled it; afflicted amour caused it to be reborn.

The silence that the fay had long imposed on her passion, and the scant interest that Doudou had taken in it, had easily made him forget that she loved him. It was, therefore to her that he addressed his plaints, with no anxiety as to the fashion in which they might be received.

The tender fay immediately felt pleasure in the prince's confidence. She flattered herself momentarily that she might find enough satisfaction in the amity that he showed her to compensate her for her amour. She even had the generosity not to augment the young king's pains be seconding, by means of a falsity of which she was capable, his suspicions of Azerolle's infidelity. The situation was too delicate to be sustained for long, however, so Canadine became even more unhappy than the lovers themselves. Her long and frequent conversations, always in private, only served to second Zumio's designs.

The genius, whom time was pressing, and who knew the hearts of the lovers too well not to dread a return if he let things drag on, imagined a deceit that succeeded. He had noticed a cabinet fitted into the wall that was adjacent to the bed where Azerolle slept. Although the door was exactly sealed, the force of his art caused it to open. He had one of the young men of his following hide there, who took an oracular tone while the process was asleep and repeated to her several times the words: "Princes Azerolle will only recover her faithful lover by uniting herself with Zumio in the knot of marriage….."

That oracle had all the effect that the genius had promised himself.

The dread of engaging herself to Zumio, and the hope of recovering her dear Doudou, as tender as her, agitated her all night long, without her being able to decide what she ought to do. It was reserved to the genius to determine it.

It was not difficult for him to extract from the princess the confidence of her embarrassment. It was then that, affecting considerable disinterest, he feigned more dread of uniting himself with her than she had of making indissoluble engagements with him. In skillfully persuading her to give him her hand, he appeared to be making a greater sacrifice than her. The artifice was pushed so far as to demanding from her a promise confirmed by oaths that if the prince did not intervene at the first words of the ceremony, she would not take it amiss if he abandoned his design.

With precautions so specious, was Azerolle able to doubt his good faith? She swore more oaths than he wanted never to be his; and, their arrangements made, the genius quit her, in order to dispose Severe not to trouble the fête.

The most difficult part was done, since Severe had permitted a tone of gallantry to be established in her house more revolting for women of her sort than amour itself. It did not require much artistry on Zumio's part to make her consent that he should marry the princess in his quality as an ambassador in order to put her at that very moment into the hands of her nephew. He did not fail to let her understand that she would be immortalized in the realm of the genii by rescuing him from the vengeance of Souveraine.

It is necessary to know how ambition works is a false mind to understand the satisfaction with which Severe pressed Zumio to bring his enterprise to a conclusion.

During that conversation, Azerolle, delivered to herself, could not resist the penchant that drew her toward her lover. Seeing that she was not observed, she ran to him, but he was so irritated by the long conservation that she had just had with Zumio, to which he had been a witness, and the keen interest that she had seemed to be taking in it, that, far from receiving her with tenderness or even with reproaches, he drew away from her in order to go and join Canadine, saying to the unfortunate Azerolle: "It's too late, Madame, my decision is made; I'm quitting you forever."

A more skillful woman would easily have detected the violence of the amour in the tone of those terrible words, but the tender princess only heard the sentence of death. Convinced that she had reached the culmination of misfortune, she went out to look for the genius, and pressed him to bring forward the sole means that remained to her to attempt to bring the infidel Doudou back under her dominion.

Delighted, Zumio assured her that everything was ready for that same evening; that, in order to avoid spectators, he would give a masked ball what would occupy the youth of his retinue, always importunate in such situations.

As the hour approached, Azerolle's dread and hope took on new force. She believed, however that she could not take too many precautions to assure her liberty; she went to throw herself at Severe's feet, and only quit her after having demanded the fay's word that the ceremony that was about to take place would not engage her to Zumio. Severe gave it to her, with all the less scruple because she was deceived herself.

Reassured regarding the danger of her engagements, Azerolle was not sure of the promises of the oracle; her mortal anxieties were redoubled at every instant.

The prince, who knew nothing of what was happening, devoured by his despair, sought to soften it by imparting it to Canadine.

It would have required a great deal for the tender fay to savor tranquilly the hope that she could not forbid herself; she reproached herself bitterly for leaving Doudou in an error that rendered him so unhappy. A hundred times she was ready to reveal Zumio's artifices, but amour prevailed and she remained silent.

As for Babonette, she applauded everything, as usual.

Turlupin, leaving the care of his interests to his aunt, only thought of amusing himself. While everyone was occupied with such important matters, he had slipped, without being perceived, into the cabinet that the pretended oracle had left open; it was the place where Severe enclosed under thirty keys the magical compounds and implements necessary to great enchantments. Turlupin, delighted to be rummaging in a place that he had never had permission to enter, amused himself by composing, with everything he found there, a gallant masquerade in order to surprise the company agreeably.

Scarcely had the ball begun when the woeful Doudou went into the next room, as usual, with his friend the fay. As soon as Zumio perceived that, he made a sign to Severe and the witnesses designated for the ceremony, and presented his hand to the princess to conduct her to it. The tremulous Azerolle allowed herself to be drawn, without having the strength either to oppose it or to consent to it; a mortal pallor expressed the state of her soul better than she felt it herself.

While the apparatus for the ceremony was being arranged and the genius beside her was able to sustain her, her eyes were avidly attached to those of the prince, seeking to detect there a return of tenderness, which cost her a great sacrifice. The prince, who had obliged Canadine to reply to his questions, informed of the cause of the preparations he could see, was gazing at Azerolle, but with a fury whose effects only seemed to be suspended by the choice of victims.

Zumio, hastening the ceremony, was already mocking Souveraine in the depths of his heart. The excessively credulous Azerolle was about to renounce forever the man she loved, believing that she was drawing closer to him, when Turlupin suddenly emerged from the cabinet, ridiculously clad, with a great torch in his hand, shouting with all his might: "I am Amour! I am Amour…."

Scarcely had the light of the magic torch struck the eyes of the tender lovers than they ran into one another's arms, crying simultaneously: "You love me! I can see it!"

Zumio, less surprised than in despair at the sudden effect of the torch, of which his art permitted him to know the virtue, tried to retain the princess, but she turned toward him indignantly. "Stop, wretch!" she said to him. "I know you: you're an evil genius."

Those words—which still find accurate applications to-day—were no sooner pronounced than the castle was shaken to its foundation. The air became as brilliant as the brightest daylight, and Souveraine appeared in all her majesty.

A mortal tremor seized the perfidious Zumio; Souveraine touched him with her wand.

"Go, traitor," she said, "wander from country to country until the end of time, inspiring everywhere the scorn that you merit."

At the same time, his seductive face, which had contributed more than a little to his perfidies, was changed into a humiliating decrepitude, passions took possession of his heart, and he disappeared.

Souveraine then addressed Severe. "You have spent centuries," she said to her, "composing that torch in order to know and punish tender hearts; spend as many composing another that discovers false virtues. You will discover what there is in veritable ones more essential than the consequences of amour."

To Babonette, she said: "As for you, I limit your empire henceforth to taking care of my menagerie."

Looking at Canadine, she said: "For you, Madame, I can only have pity. If you want to come with me, I offer you my amity. I would be glad if it can soften the pain caused to you by a constancy so poorly rewarded."

Canadine threw herself at Souveraine's feet, after having thanked her with as much nobility as sensibility. She implored her, by all the generosity that she was testifying to her, to take away from her the privilege of immortality.

Souveraine did not refuse that entirely, but she postponed it until a time so distant that it as easily visible that she was counting on the fay discovering a cure for her heart in the meantime. But Canadine, after having lived in an obscure retreat for centuries, finally achieved the only happiness to which she aspired; she obtained permission to die, and did not take long to profit from it.

All her orders having been given, Souveraine returned King Doudou to his original beauty, and invited him to mount her chariot with Princess Azerolle, leaving Turlupin in his castle, his mind so charged with astonishments that he amused himself all his life recounting them to his valets. She took the happy lovers to the realm of Aglantiers, where she left them, after having honored with her presence the brilliant spectacle of their union.

They lived for many years, without anything diminishing their happiness or their constancy.

FLEURETTE AND ABRICOT
A FRAME STORY

There was once a prince and a princess whom the fays had resolved to render happy even under the yoke of marriage, a happiness that is incontrovertibly the most perfect, but also the rarest. They had endowed Fleurette and Abricot—those were the names of the royal couple—with all the talents necessary to inspire a general admiration. The two children were brought up in the same court, and everything proceeded as the fays wished; the habitude of seeing one another, which ordinarily impedes the birth of amour and often destroys it, only served to render them more passionate for one another. While loving one another uniquely, they had reached the delightful age when the first desires accompany all the graces to which youth gives birth successively. One was fifteen and the other seventeen, happy times in which the soul has the faculty of enjoying happiness without foreseeing its end.

One day, they were in one of the most agreeable arbors of their garden, uniquely occupied with their desires and their charms—in short, they were enjoying the pleasure of complete intimacy—when Morgantine, who was flying overhead, perceived them. She was a wicked fay, who took pleasure in upsetting everything, in general and particular, and tormenting those who were happy. The sight of the two young lovers, which would have interested, and perhaps softened, anyone else, immediately revolted her, and without yet having determined the kind of pain that she wanted to cause them, she stopped the bats that were conducting her chariot and rendered herself invisible. Then she approached Fleurette and Abricot in order to listen to their conversation. But the charm of their faces soon made her forget the project that she had formed, and their discourse succeeded in changing her heart in spite of herself.

The young couple had reached the point at which one was expressing his eagerness and the other was gently alleging honor and virtue in order to defend herself, without annoying her lover, or at least without displeasing him.

"Why, Prince, ask me for what I cannot grant you?" Fleurette said to him. "If you were in my place, you would have the same rigor."

"Me!" cried Abricot. "Could I, who would give my life a thousand times for the slightest of your desires, resist you? Make no mistake, Princess, you would be satisfied; the more it would cost me, the more prejudice I would have to overcome, the further I would go to meet your wishes."

Fleurette responded again; the prince replied. Their tender dispute, always interrupted by slight favors, became heated, they said and repeated the same things to one another a hundred times over; in brief, in spite of their different fashion of enunciating it, they were perhaps experiencing the greatest charm of amour, the keenest attraction of which is founded on the pleasure one savors in always talking about oneself; self-esteem tries hard, but that sweet illusion can only exist and find itself complete in amour.

Morgantine, who was still listening, became bored, in accordance with the custom constantly reserved for the third party; but, unable to resolve to leave anything in its natural order, finding herself softened, and her heart even stirred by the tender scene that she had before her eyes, said to herself, after having reflected for some time:

Let's get something out of this. I've heard what they've just pronounced a thousand times; I remember very well having once had similar conversations myself, and I foresee that others will make use of the same expressions in their turn. Let's see what it's about, let's discover clearly for once the veritable source of all prejudice, and judge whether they really hold to what I imagine.

336

Then, after having waved her wand, she said: *I want Abricot to become a princess and Fleurette to become a prince, only for a year.*

But the tenderness and the desires of the young lovers were so sharp and so pure that they did not perceive their metamorphoses, which were sudden, so absolute was the authority that Morgantine had over nature. She alone was able to enjoy the revolutions that she caused, and she saw with great pleasure that at the same moment, Abricot became more reserved and Fleurette more eager. It is true, however, that they did not partake of the ides of their present situation to the same degree that they had both experienced in their original condition; they had fewer prejudices to overcome, and that is not a petty matter for the common run of humans. So, by virtue of a necessary consequence, in a matter of moments, Fleurette triumphed over Abricot, and the weak Abricot expressed the most tender gratitude to her lover

Amour had scarcely succeeded in completing his victory, and was perhaps even seeking further conquests, when the protective fays, whose great knowledge left nothing unknown to them, arrived from the various corners of the world to which their affairs had taken them, indignant at the conduct of their pupils. Their first impulse was to scold and punish them, but Morgantine, who appeared, declared the truth to them, and confessed that she alone was culpable of the young lovers' sin—a sin all the greater because, at that time, it was considered to be unprecedented.

"You want to marry them to one another?" the fay said to them. "What can prevent you?" Smiling she added: "Can it be what has just happened? I'll gladly take charge of the wedding."

"Truly," responded the others, "that's not the problem; of course it's necessary to marry them, but think about what you've done. Are you forgetting that you've only ordered this metamorphosis for a time, and that, when that time has elapsed, they'll resume their true sex. See to what inconveniences you've exposed them; by this means, they'll be neither prince not princess."

"I sustain that my conduct isn't unreasonable," replied Morgantine, "and if intelligence can't prevent them from committing stupidities, it's necessary that it serves to repair them, or at least to obtain something from them. I want, therefore, the subjects of Fleurette and Abricot to change sex every year, on their birthday. You'll be astonished by what such an exchange will produce. By that means, the education of men and women being similar, they'll no longer have any reproaches to make one another and, the two sexes having equal courage, these people will be invincible. Furthermore, they'll unite the graces and the enjoyment of strength of mind and the extent of ideas, and this nation, more amiable and more united, will also enjoy variety, even in savoring the greatest pleasures." She finished by saying to them: "I have even more things to add to my project, but I want to leave you the pleasure of examining it."

The two protective fays would have had me response to make, but circumstances obliged them to consent to Morgantine's will.

Fleurette and Abricot married, lived happily, and loved one another uniquely, under either sex.

As for Morgantine, she ceased to be wicked, and by virtue of a natural sentiment, she attached herself to her work, that exchange of sexes being the most flattering production of her mind. She did not lose sight of the fortunate subjects of the royal couple; she gave them laws and followed for her amusement all the adventures that such a change inevitably produced, and of which one still finds a few impressions today in all the peoples of the world.

Moreover, it is from the great portfolio of Morgantine that all the stories that follow are taken, which she had collected with care; it is a pity that some of them have been lost, because they were doubtless the best. Such as they are, they are offered to the public.

THE MANGY WOLF

There was once a king and a queen who loved one another very much and who desired ardently to have children, although they did not have much to leave them. They often went to the door of several fays in order to present their petitions and ask them for children, but those who consented to give them an audience always repeated to them: "You have come a long way to search for what you have close at hand."

They did not understand that mysterious pronouncement, and always went away embracing one another and saying: "What do we have close at hand?"

"We'll find it someday, let's be tranquil," said the queen.

"That's well said, if we can," replied the king. That response was only a manner of speaking, for he was the most tranquil and patient man that Heaven had ever formed.

One day, when the queen was spinning, sitting in the corner of one of the most beautiful hedges of their estates, and the king was hunting skylarks in a neighboring field of stubble, he had the good fortune to catch one; it is even said he was neither very skillful nor very lucky, and such a notion in not devoid of plausibility, for in the fifteen years that he had been hunting every day, he had never caught one before.

How did he catch that one? It is very important to know. It had thrown itself into his arms in order to avoid a hawk that was pursuing it and was on the point of seizing it.

The hawk said to the king more than once, in a menacing voice: "Give me my skylark, King, or you'll regret it."

The prince, keen to conserve his catch, as is only natural, and finding himself, fortunately, in a disposition of pride that was not usual to him, replied: "It's in my field, it's asking me for shelter; I don't want to give you the skylark.

As he said that, he looked at the bird; its keen and piercing eyes redoubled his courage, and its little heart, which he

339

could feel palpitating in his hand, maintained his compassion. Animated by those sentiments, he pulled down his hat, looked proudly at the hawk, and said, showing it the skylark: "Look at it well. You can wipe your beak, as people say in my realm; you shan't have it, I swear. It's not in my estates that someone can ask impolitely for an injustice."

Then, without worrying about what the hawk might do, he turned his back on it in order to carry his catch to the queen and ask whether the proud and generous action that he had just performed might cause him to run any risk.

The queen was still too far away to hear him when he shouted "Good hunting!" and showed her the little skylark at a distance. The good queen dropped her distaff in order to go to meet him and see what he was showing her.

The king presented it to her, with the joy and pleasure of a huntsman presenting hr with a trophy. "Receive, Madame, a homage that is due to you."

The queen accepted the little skylark, kissed it a thousand times, and said: "the next time you go to town, buy a cage; we'll hear it singing, we'll domesticate it, and it will play with the little child that we'll have one day."

She made a hundred plans in a moment, all of which the king approved. She might perhaps have made more, but in the midst of all those Castles in Spain, the little skylark, which had had time to recover its wits, said: "What time is it?"

The joy of hearing it speak was so great that the king and queen did not respond at first, but at the second question they both said, for it was something within their range, as it is of many people: "It's about half past four."

"You'll soon see," the skylark added.

That apt and consequent response struck the king and the queen, and caused them to remain motionless, eyes staring and mouths open, in order to see what they had been promised they would be shown.

Indeed, a few moments later, the skylark took the form of a tall and beautiful middle-aged woman, whom they recognized by her embroidered hood, her wand and her fine key, to be a fay.

At that sight the royal couple shivered, and the king, prostrating himself, said to her: "My God, Madame I hope I didn't squeeze you too tightly when I held you in my hand."

"As for me," said the queen, who was in the same posture, "remember, if you please, that I found you very pretty, and that I caressed you, and if I talked about putting you in a cage, it was to protect you from the cat."

"Get up," the fay said to them, kindly. "I owe to you the life that a wicked fay, who will pay me back sooner or later, would have taken from me without the courage and firmness of the king. "Speak," she continued. "Is there anything that you desire? My power is not one of the most extensive, but you will have evidence as long as you live of the gratitude owed to you by the fay Mimi."[47]

"We ask you," said the royal couple, with a common accord, after having thanked her abundantly, "for a little child, to be the consolation of our old age."

"A child" said the fay. "That isn't difficult to have; it's true that they often give trouble, and that one doesn't get the one that one wants; but you want one, and it's necessary to get you one; it's the least I can do for the obligation that I owe you. Let's see, first, for what reason you don't have one; you're both healthy enough, there must be something underneath this."

---

[47] In 1741 "Mimi" had acquired none of the rich literary connotations that it acquired in the nineteenth century. Caylus would have been aware of the Latin term, a plural of *mimus* [actor, the feminine being *mima*] but is far more likely to be adapting an item of baby-talk, as in Doudou, especially as he uses the term *mie*, which would nowadays refers to white bread or is used as a term of endearment, to mean "nurse-maid."

341

"I assure you, Madame," the queen interjected, making a slight curtsey, with an expression that was half-piqued and half-polite, "that there's nothing underneath."

"Let's see anyway," said the good Mimi touching her book with her wand; it opened immediately at the place where she wanted to read. "This is what I've found. The Fay of Brambles doesn't want the king and the queen to have children."

"Will we never have any, then, great Mimi," asked the king and the queen, "since a fay doesn't want it?"

"The matter becomes difficult," replied their protectress. "We're dealing with a wicked fay, black-hearted and obstinate. Can you imagine that it's her who afflicts wheat with smut and sheep with scab-rot, that she commands caterpillars, of which she always has a quantity in her pocket, and engages them to eat all the produce of the earth?"

"What a woman!" cried the king and queen. "That makes one shiver."

"That's not all," the fay went on. "It's her who's annoyed with me, and who made herself into a hawk in a fit of temper, and it's her who, but for you, would have eaten me as the skylark I was. I can and ought to help you; you shall have a child, or I'll burn my books. Without the obligation I have to you, I would have responded as my companions have, for one doesn't like to have dealings or to commit oneself with women of such character, and I read in my book that all those who have seen you have said to you: 'You have come a long way to search for what you have close at hand.'"

"That's true, Madame, they said exactly what you've read."

"They were right," said the fay. "Do you see those brambles a hundred paces from here, near that heap of stones?"

"Yes, Madame."

"Well," Mimi went on, that's where the person lives who doesn't want you to have children. Wait for me here; I'll make every effort to make her come out, for it isn't possible for me to enter her abode without her consent, although I don't fear her in any fashion at present. Even so, I can't give you better evidence of my gratitude than taking such a step."

"The royal couple obeyed her and stayed where they were. During the time that Mimi took to go to the heap of stones, and to make a few conjurations with her wand, the king and queen rubbed their hands and embraced joyfully, and the king said: "Finally, we'll have a child; as soon as a fay gets mixed up in it, it's not permissible to doubt it."

"No," said the queen, "it's as if I could see him. Oh, how content I'll be," she went on. I'll feed him."

"You won't feed him," said the king. "We'll get a nurse."

"I'll feed him, I tell you…"

"You won't feed him, I assure you. Do you want to exhaust yourself, doom yourself?"

The queen wept; the king became annoyed; in sum, the first quarrel there was between the couple, which was quite sharp, arrived because of a child who hadn't even been conceived.

The dispute about nursing would not have finished yet, if the king and the queen had not lent their attention to loud bursts of laughter that they heard; they recognized that it was a group of children who were playing with the security and carelessness that only that fortunate age knows.

That laughter, so close to the door of the Fay of the Brambles, being an insult to a character like hers, she emerged from the heap of stones with a whip in her hand in order to convert the laughter that revolted her into tears, and Mimi, whose means of bringing her out had succeeded, made the children disappear and approached her.

Seeing them coming toward them, the king and the queen went, as is reasonable, to met them half way, but cap in hand, in a respectful and suppliant attitude. They perceived that Mimi and the Fay of the Brambles were speaking with a great deal of vivacity.

"I consent to forget the insult you've done me and the evil designs that animated you against me," said Mimi. "I promise not to make any complaint about them if you have some complaisance for these good people, and above all, if you accord them a child."

"Their realm suits me, small as it is, for one of my friends," replied the Fay of the Brambles. "I'm waiting patiently for them to die. Can I do better? It's true that I'm opposed to their posterity. Anyway, how can I grant a child to people who don't have the wherewithal to nourish it? It's a service that I'm rendering them by refusing, and for which you ought to be grateful to me if you have some interest in their regard."

The king and the queen tugged Mimi's sleeve the, and said to her: "I assure you that people far less rich than us nourish their children every day, and that we're in a state to have one; we're not asking for more of them; judge for yourself whether we could ask for less."

Mimi then made further pleas, to which the fay ended up responding, with an extreme anger: "They'll have a child; I consent to that, but it'll cost them dear."

The king and the queen, without being embarrassed by the price and the threat, started jumping for joy and repeating: "We're going to have a child."

"I hope, at least," said the Fay of the Brambles, looking at the benevolent Mimi, "That you'll be grateful for my kindness." And without waiting for a response, she turned her back arrogantly, returned to her heap of stones, and disappeared.

Meanwhile, the king and queen, who could not see any further than the tips of their noses, were only occupied with their joy and their satisfaction, so they scarcely listened to Mimi when she wanted to share in the chagrins they were about to experience.

Seeing that she could not make them listen to reason, she gave them a whistle, and said to them: "Every time you need me, blow into that and I'll appear, but make use of it in moderation. Adieu; always be sage and reasonable, and count on me," she said to them, causing her chariot to appear, drawn by two small white sheep, into which she climbed.

Sometime later, the queen perceived that she was pregnant. That event gave as much pleasure to the father and the mother as if the occurrence would have been impossible in itself and the fays had not merely given their consent. Perhaps the king was even more flattered than the queen; one might have imagined, on seeing him, that he alone had the secret of making children.

However, the slightest nausea, distaste or discomfort, which were only necessary consequences of pregnancy, caused the queen to run to her whistle and the good fay arrived immediately. She told them several times, mildly, that it was necessary only to summon her appropriately, but the king and queen had no more idea of what was appropriate than a thousand people one sees every day. In any case, although the benevolent Mimi thought that there are cases in which gratitude is extremely fatiguing, the goodness of her heart always prevent her from giving the slightest evidence of it.

The queen's pregnancy went very well, but as soon as the first labor pains made themselves felt, she turned to the king; he whistled for more than a quarter of an hour and he was still whistling after the fay had arrived. This time, she did not make him any reproach, her presence being necessary to endow the child that the queen brought into the world a few moments after its arrival. It was a charming little princess. Mimi took her on her knees, and, wanting to endow her with her a calm mind, in general as well as in detail, she started with the hands and said: "She will have beautiful white hands."

At that moment, the Fay of Brambles appeared in the room. "She'll have anything you wish, but no one will see anything unless I consent to it. Endow, Mimi, endow at your ease: I won't belie any of it," she went on, furiously, climbing into her chariot drawn by frightful bats.

That compliment threw the company into confusion; the fay did her best to reassure the good folk, who were as astonished as bell-founders. She promised not to abandon them and to soothe them in their troubles.

She endowed the beautiful child in a low voice, and for a day to come. She wanted to take away the whistle that had caused her to make so many unnecessary journeys, assuring them that it was no longer necessary to them and that she would watch over their interests sufficiently.

The little princess, in accordance with Mimi's first gift, had hands so white and so beautiful that she was named the Princess with the White Hands; when people had seen her they could not name her otherwise. It is not even certain that she was ever given another name; at least, it is certain that she was not known in society by any other.

Her childhood was unremarkable; the king and the queen brought her up in accordance with their ability and capacity; that is not saying very much, but their natural goodness substituted for the shortfall.

When the Fay of Brambles went past the door of the king and queen—which happened quite often because of their neighborhood, she made the little princess afraid of ghosts, or snatched away her doll, and all those nasty procedures were accompanied by a brace of slaps that she gave her, crying: "Oh, how ugly she is!" which the little princess could not hear without weeping—but she was consoled by the king and queen, who loved her madly and who always told her the truth, but very quietly, while slapping her back: "The fay is lying, don't cry, my child, you're very pretty."

However, the good father and mother, who had not forgotten the threats of the Fay of Brambles, repeated to themselves incessantly: *Doubtless she permits us to see her as she is; the enchantment isn't made for us.*

"Don't you find her charming, wife?" said the king.

"Yes, husband," said the queen.

To tell the truth, though, she could have appeared to them as ugly as to everyone else who saw her; the blindness of mothers and father will last as long as there are children. It is true, however, that the Fay of Brambles, by virtue of a refined malevolence, permitted all hunchbacks and all deformed individuals to see her as nature had produced her—which is to say, charming—so that all the people of that species who saw her became passionately amorous of her, and whenever a hunchback passed through the village all the little girls said: "He's come for the king's daughter."

She might have been feted and caressed by all those bandy-legged individuals, but, far from becoming accustomed to their forms, she played tricks on them incessantly; the worst was to talk incessantly about their humps, without ever letting them believe for a moment that it was possible to efface it or hide it from her eyes. She also questioned them about the accident that had deformed them, and incessantly compared their effects with one another, always in the presence of interesting humps. It was thus that she sank all the princes and other deformed gentlemen who gave themselves the epithet, in those remote days of "inconvenienced," and came in the end to get rid of them completely.

All the hunchbacks, therefore, had departed, when a prince, the son of a neighboring king, whose parents had sent him traveling, perceived the princess one day, without paying any more attention to her, in truth, than her scant beauty merited; but, pressed by an ardent thirst, he said to her: "My good child, might I have some water?"

White-Hands, who was not accustomed to greater respects, and who thought the prince very pretty, offered to take him to the fountain with so much politeness and grace that he was enchanted by her. Her conversation did not diminish the favorable impression that her mildness and politeness had already made; he was astonished and delighted to learn that she was the king's daughter. The simplicity of her apparel had not given him the idea of such a elevated rank; it also served him as a excuse for the liberty he had taken.

The Princess with the White Hands replied to him with a marvelous sagacity that fortune gives opulence, and good nature sentiments. That common saw, so well placed, inspired more respect for her in the prince than if she had appeared to his eyes seated on a golden throne covered in diamonds and surrounded by the most brilliant court.

When they had arrived at the fountain, however, and she took her cup from her pocket in order to give him something to drink, causing her beautiful hands to appear—for she always kept them hidden beneath her apron, out of modesty, and perhaps a desire to protect and preserve them from sunburn—the prince was dazzled and confounded; his exclamations and admirations of their beauty were never-ending.

She told him that her hands were her best feature, but the praise that the heart and mind avow does not leave room to think about the rest, and what pleases always commences by sufficing. In sum, in a moment, amour was so well-established in the heart of the prince that he resolved to love her all his life, so he made her the confession of his most tender sentiments. White-Hands, who found him all the more to her taste because no well-made person had ever even looked at her, did not know how to respond; but silence is almost always a favor for lovers.

They were in that tender embarrassment when the Fay of Brambles, whose malevolence prevented her from remaining in the same place for long, surprised them.

"What! You love her!" she said to the prince. "And you're not hunchbacked!" You example will alarm and correct all well-made people."

As she spoke she touched him with her wand, and he became the prettiest white goat that had ever been seen; he had no horns and no beard.

Far from changing sentiments in taking on a new form, the prince only became more attached to the princess; for he saw her from the first instant of his metamorphosis with all the beauties that she had received from nature; thus, far from quitting her and far from reproaching her for his misfortune, he bounded, gazed at her, played with the dogs, and animated the flocks, which, whatever anyone might say, always appear more attached to their needs than their pleasures. In sum, he did not neglect anything to please her and to maintain his idea in her heart; for after all, the less one has, the more one gives.

The impression he had made was too well engraved in White-Hands' heart to fear seeing it effaced, but the dread of losing it—or, rather, the avarice of amour—always ensured the conservation of its existence.

Mimi, continually attentive, was not unaware of these events; she hastened to console the princess, exhorted her to constancy, and quit her raising her shoulders at the unjust procedures that she blushed to see in one of her companions.

Meanwhile, the king and the queen, to whom the princess presented the white goat without telling them what he was, received him marvelously; soon they were charmed by him, and they would have spent all day playing with him if the princess, who wanted to keep him for herself, had not told them often, even being ready to weep, that she wanted to be the only person in the world who made him play. The king and the queen had that complaisance for her, which seemed reasonable to them.

Wicked people of the most redoubtable species ordinarily have intelligence, and know how to make use of it in order to know situations, to destroy those that are happy and agreeable and to give birth, as well as to maintain, to ones that are annoying and unpleasant. So the Fay of Brambles soon found that Princess White-Hands and the goat prince were a thousand times too happy. Seeing one another and loving one another without obstacles and without rivals was too much for the appetite for persecution that dominated her and the chagrins that the pleasure of others caused her. Furthermore, she was inconsolable at being unable to prevent the charms of the princess from shining in the eyes of the prince, but that was a necessity of enchantment.

In order not to leave them such a sweet consolation, she resolved to separate them; they loved one another, so absence was already a certain torment. She began by abducting the princess, and left the goat with the king and queen, who, without knowing him, loved him like their own child, taking much better care of him than the fay would have desired. Those attentions were necessary to him, for as soon as he no longer saw the princess, he no longer wanted to eat, he no longer capered, and he went everywhere bleating, unable to ask for her or to express the woe he experienced in being separated from her in any other fashion.

Meanwhile, as soon as the fay had abducted the Princess with the White Hands, she stuck a pair of gloves over her beautiful arms, and stuck them so well that nothing could remove them. Then she took her to her Palace of Fleas.

Complete and well-conditioned malevolence ought to have the appearance of generosity. All the pleasures and sumptuousness of courts filled that palace; however, it was a real torment that the fay had imagined, for decorum dictated that, in spite of the stings and the cruel itching that one experienced incessantly, people were constrained to ignore them. The number of insects was so great that the palace was black with them, and seeking to kill the fleas would have been a futile occupation. The magnificent palace was filled with a numerous court, but although the lords and ladies who composed it were accustomed to the fleas, the unfortunate princess suffered inconceivable torments there.

Not content with bodily pains and the chagrins of absence, the wicked fay also wanted to make her sense mental torments; thus. by a cruel irony, she had not only transported her to that court as the daughter of a king, but had ordered that she hold the first rank there; in a word, she was regarded there as the queen.

White-Hands had never seen so many people assembled, she had never had any knowledge of society; it was, therefore to make fun of her, without any circumspection, that the fay had transported her to the milieu of that court. Her timidity and her country manners were the subject of a thousand immoderate bursts of laughter, and the ridicule with which she was covered soon became the consequence of the inappropriate statements she made on the throne as she acquired the pleasant habit of authority.

The Fay of Brambles often came to savor the malign joy of seeing her suffer so many torments that she applauded herself for having invented. When she arrived she had all the inapposite things that the princess had said or done related to her, and mocked her in her presence; afterwards, she said to her: "Go on, play the queen."

Immediately, she was obliged to mount her throne, and for that the wicked fay released a few thousand extra fleas, whose rage she redoubled by means of her power. It was a pleasure for her to see the various contortions that the unfortunate princess was obliged to make, and the less the attitudes suited the majesty of the throne, the more the fay enjoyed herself and was amused.

However, dolors apart, the Princess with the White Hands obtained an advantage, for the rest of her life, from the evil that the fay intended to inflict upon her. Because, after all, it was a court to which she had taken her, and the most ill-composed court is still capable of forming someone. Thus, the princess, who had intelligence, was able to repair, by virtue of the sojourn that she made there, the defects of an education that the scant genius and opulence of her father and mother had prevented them from giving her simply and suitably.

The good Mimi, informed of everything that her enemy was doing against those she was protecting no longer believed herself, with reason, obliged to any consideration; she revived the insult that she had received while she was a sparrow. She had only promised secrecy on conditions that had not been fulfilled; her word being thus disengaged, she lodged a complaint with the Council of Fays.

The frankness and goodness of her character were so well-known that her story as believed without difficulty; not only was it found that she merited justice, but she was given all the powers necessary for the punishment of the Fay of Brambles, and anything that it pleased her to do was approved, for no example of such an attempted murder committed by a fay against one of her companions had yet been seen.

Satisfied and content with the procedures that had been enacted for her, she gave a sign to her little sheep to go as fast as they could, and she soon arrived in the dismal habitation of the wicked fay, for, by virtue of her powers it was permitted for her to enter it. She said to her: "I want to pardon you again; I consent to forget everything that has happened, but promise me no longer to torment the prince and White-Hands."

Mildness and honesty always render the truly wicked more insolent, so the Fay of Brambles replied to her with disdain; "What! It's for that, my colleague, that you've come here? You displace yourself or a bagatelle of that species? Oh, truly, you're not there; I haven't even begun to torment them yet, your foolish children; you'll see, you'll see later."

"I shall only see your punishment," Mimi relied. "Learn, then, that I have the power, and that your fate is in my hands."

"You can't take my life," she said. What are you going to do to me? Neither you nor your fine authority can oblige me to consent to the marriage of your wretched protégés."

"That remains to be seen," replied Mimi. "I shall punish you, I swear, until you have satisfied me, and to begin with," she said, touching her with her wand, "become a wolf."

Then she left the new wolf and sent it with diligence to the palace to fatten the fleas. Then she went in search of the goat, who no longer knew what to do, because the Fay of Brambles, a few moments before, had metamorphosed the king and queen into turkeys. The malevolence was not great; it made little difference to their character, but it was one more, which increased Mimi's pain. The good fay, unable for the moment to render them any other service, had them given some good mash to console them and at least satisfy the appetite of their estate. After that mark of attention she took the pretty little goat in her arms and took him to Princess White-Hands.

When the little animal perceived her he gave her so many caresses, and made so many leaps and bounds to mark his joy that one cannot begin to describe them. The fay left them content to see one another and quit them, saying: "Beware of the wolf."

Meanwhile, the Fay of Brambles did not find her new estate as a wolf too bad. *I can bite*, she said to herself, *I can do harm. Mimi is an imbecile; she ought, in order to avenge herself, to have made me a chicken or some other placid animal; I would have suffered more, I would have been more embarrassed by my person. Feeble characters like hers don't know how to inflict pain. Meanwhile*, she continued, *I have more intelligence than the other wolves; I have seen them become the favorites of kings; why shouldn't I play the same role.*

Immediately, she set forth, and had no difficulty in finding a king, for there were a lot of them in those days. She encountered one who was hunting; immediately she gave herself to him, glad to escape by means of his protection everyone calling after her: "Wolf! Wolf!" as people were already doing, which is really very inconvenient for someone who is traveling.

The king having welcomed her, she was very well-received at his court; she lived there flattered by the king, but biting and doing all the harm that she could, especially to the petty people.

Mimi, who was able to follow her and who observed her conduct, in the fear that she might eat the little goat, thought she was obliged to prevent the disorder she was causing; she found no better expedient to make her lose the king's protection than to render the wretched wolf mangy, by which everyone would be repelled.

The means succeeded, as soon as the mange appeared, everyone drew away, and even resolved to kill her; the wolf, having heard that, understood that she was obliged to quit the court, which she did as soon as possible. Her rage and natural malevolence was redoubled by the fashion in which everyone, on seeing her, not only cried "Wolf!" but added the epithet *mangy*, something for which it very disagreeable to hear oneself reproached.

The fay had no other alternative, therefore, than to roam the countryside attacking people and animals, but especially little children, which she ate raw. In a word, she became the "evil beast" that makes the whole world tremble.

Informed of all the harm that she was doing, and seeing her take the road to the Palace of Fleas, Mimi had her stopped and put in an iron cage, which was placed in the middle of the public square, where all the little boys came incessantly to insult her, throw stones at her, and do her all the harm that their strength permitted.

Finally, the Fay of Brambles, exceeded by all the evils that she had attracted, consented to everything that Mimi desired of her, promised to be good, asked that the mange be taken away and her liberty returned, promising to go and spent all the time that she had to be a wolf in the forests of Muscovy. Those mercies were accorded to her.

Then Mimi returned his true form to the prince, and enabled the Princess with the White Hands to be as beautiful as nature had formed her to everyone; it was possible for her to take off her old gloves, and the marriage of the young couple was celebrated with splendor, after the good fay had returned the king and the queen to their original form.

It was appropriate that they always retained a little of their metamorphosis, and that all courts retain an impression of fleas, which can evidently be recognized by virtue of the continual agitation that everyone there experiences.

BELLINETTE; OR, THE YOUNG OLD WOMAN

There was once a fay, worthy by virtue of her intelligence of the nickname that had been given to her in the College of Fays; she was known there under the title of Sublime. In spite of all the worldly affairs with which she was continually occupied, she was also charged with the education of little Princess Bellinette and the conduct of the beautiful realms that had belonged to her since the death of the king and queen who had given her the light of day.

The first years of the childhood of the little queen were employed with the greatest success in her instruction. The fay almost never quit her, affecting all the external appearances of service and submission, but really conserving all the authority; she asked the queen for orders while she gave ones that were entirely opposite. Bellinette, too young as yet to think of governing, contented herself with acquitting new charms every day; she responded so perfectly to the fay's cares that her subjects already loved their little queen, and the entire court, which saw her at closer range, lost their heads over her,

Sublime was delighted with the progress of her pupil, and especially with the attachment she had been able to inspire in her. However, she foresaw that there were still reefs ahead for the princess; she feared the impression that the continual applause and incessantly repeated praise might produce on the mind of a young person born on the throne—which is to say, far from all truth. She began to perceive that the certainty of success, the habitude of never being contradicted and the approval that she could not help giving Bellinette herself might inspire in her a self-esteem so violent that it might be dangerous. The sentiment to which one seeks to give birth, extend and fortify in children, which it is good to confound with emulation becomes, at a more advanced age, the cause of all errors. It is not necessary to be a fay to judge thus.

That was not, however, the only defect with which the little queen could be reproached; a natural desire to please, which thus far had added to her charms, was beginning gradually to degenerate into coquetry, a fault all the more dangerous because its nuances are imperceptible. Sublime, therefore, who wanted to render her education perfect, and who feared that her excessive tenderness for Bellinette might be capable of blinding her, determined—not without difficulty, in truth— to make a violent but necessary decision.

Bellinette had reached her fifteenth year when, one morning while she was dressing, and even prettier than usual, ran in haste to Sublime's apartment; she went in with the confidence and gaiety of a young person accustomed to being caressed. Occupied with a new fashion that she had imagined that day, she took no account of the fay's seriousness and even asked her, with vivacity, how she was; but Sublime contented herself coldly with showing her a mirror that was beside her and telling her to look at herself in it.

The young queen, convinced that it was a roundabout fashion of saying: "My God, how pretty you are today; how well that adornment suits you; how well imagined it is!"—in brief, all the things that her self-esteem had represented to her—was quite content with that response, and accepted the proposition joyfully.

The ridiculous face of an old woman, which she perceived in the mirror as soon as she had looked into it, at first caused immoderate laughter; afterwards, she turned round precipitately in order to consider the old woman, ridiculous by virtue of her adornment, at closer range. Seeing no one behind her, though, she moved closer to the mirror with vivacity. What was her astonishment on perceiving that the old woman she had mocked so wholeheartedly was none other than herself!

She uttered a piercing scream, dropped the mirror and fainted.

The fay had taken her precautions to have no witnesses to that scene; she felt sorry for her to begin with, but, determined to follow her project, she only thought about bringing her round.

When the princess had made a new confirmation of her misfortune with her senses, the fay tried in vain to calm her down, but all her knowledge and great intelligence proved to be unable to console her for the sudden loss of her charms.

"No, no one must see me," cried Bellinette, penetrated by the most bitter dolor. "I shall never show myself; only the most frightful desert and the most profound obscurity are appropriate to the woeful state that I'm in."

This despair was followed by the most tender tears and the most touching discourse.

"What, Madame!" she said, again, "I shall be nothing for you, then, but an object of horror! Is it possible that you can resolve to see me in the cruel situation to which I'm reduced? I must now inspire the most frightful disgust in you, and give you the most horrible difficulty in looking at me. What! It's you, who would render me young and pretty if I had the misfortune to be old, it's Sublime herself, who has let me fall, or has precipitated me, into the ultimate misfortune! What an example for your justice and the kindness of your heart! What will people say when they see the woe that I'm experiencing, me, who was loved so much? Will they not have the right to suspect me of the greatest crimes? Is there anyone, in fact, who could merit such a punishment?"

The hope of obtaining mercy made her add a thousand other things.

Sublime, touched by compassion, had difficulty vanquishing herself; however, without wanting to tell the princess whether that cruel metamorphosis was her work, she contented herself with saying to her, firmly that it was necessary to submit to the order of destiny.

"Take away my life, then," cried Bellinette, in a fashion so determined that the fay was alarmed by her despair.

Then, in order to soften the pain, she said, tenderly: "All that I can do for you is to render you alternately young and old."

That had always been Sublime's project, but with the idea of enabling her to find her misfortune more supportable it had been easy for her to make her fear a greater one. The princess, fully persuaded that she could not obtain anything, wanted nevertheless to have nothing for which to reproach herself in such a cruel extremity; she therefore made all the objections to the fay that self-esteem could contrive, with the aid of intelligence.

"How do you expect me," she said to her, "to appear old before my time in the eyes of a people and an entire could with which I am surrounded. Will not such a change make you as ridiculous as me?"

But Sublime, who had anticipate everything, replied: "I also consent that you spare yourself to this extent: I shall enable you to pass for your great-aunt, who was once abducted by Grondine the Wicked, and of whom no mention has been heard since. I shall say that, touched by the story that I have told you of her misfortunes, the goodness of your heart has made you desire to cede your throne to her every other day, in order to give her at least a few happy moments before the death that her great age will not permit the belief that it might be distant. I will add that you have even engaged me to obtain that mercy from Grondine, on condition nevertheless of your going to occupy her place. That evidence of generosity cannot fail to do you honor.

"That will not," she added, "be the sole advantage that you will obtain from your disgrace; you are going to see uncovered all the people who surround you; you will be alarmed by the lack of sincerity that you will find among that crowd of courtiers whom you have seen until now uniquely occupied with pleasing you and admiring you. The natural fashion in which they talk to you about yourself, in favor of your disguise, while unmasking their character to your eyes, will also serve to enlighten you about your faults, and, in consequence, give you the means to correct them."

"Well, Madame," said Bellinette, with vivacity, "a friend like you leaves something to be desired; would not the desire to be worthy of you have sufficed to render me perfect?"

"The voice of one sincere friend has little power against a multitude that flatter," the fay replied. "In any case, that's enough. I don't want to hear any more. I won't recommend the secret to you; you have too much interest in keeping it. I'll think about establishing and preparing the court for the return of your great aunt. During the time I need, I consent to return your youth and your charms to you, but when I've arranged everything, you'll submit to taking the face that you've seen."

Then she touched her with her wand and left the apartment. Bellinette seized a mirror; she looked at herself a thousand times, always fearing that old age might have left some impression on her face. When she was fully reassured, she reappeared to the court.

Sublime left her for some days in that pretended repose, if one can call thus the state she was experiencing, for if, on the one hand, she was enjoying the pleasure of finding herself young and pretty again, she trembled at the thought that it would be necessary to cease to be. One of the things that served to torment her most was the satisfaction that she was obliged to show at the return of her great-aunt. The fay talked about her continually, and never ceased to heap her with eulogies; and those eulogies, repeated by a crowd of courtiers, pieced her heart.

When Sublime had sufficiently established the return of the old woman, whose age was indeed so considerable that no one remembered having seen her, she announced her arrival for the following day. Everyone took their leave of the young queen with the appearance of the most intense dolor, for it was supposed that she would spend her time very badly in Grondine's abode; no one knew her, but her reputation for malevolence was well-established.

It was then that the princess sensed, with the most violent despair, the approach of old age. In fact, all the old women that one has seen, or will see, have had time to prepare for that misfortune; they have first noticed a wrinkle or a gray hair, in a word, the smallest alteration; in seeking to repair it, they have flattered themselves with the idea that they have not perceived it; they have seen that they still please people; they have gradually grown accustomed to the defect; often it has vanished from their sight, by virtue of the discovery of another, to which it is necessary to give the same cares.

That succession of time brings consolation to the mind more easily; the habitude of the eyes and the quantity of examples engage one to play one's part. Self-esteem comes to the rescue and incessantly persuades one that the cruel age that one disguises from oneself does not show; that one is well-preserved and surely does not look as bad as so-and-so, the veritable or false example of whom is easily presented to the eyes.

The entire court was occupied by the scene that was about to take place; several councils were held on the manner of receiving the queen. In the end, it was agreed that everyone would put on the most serious clothes they had in their wardrobes. Those who only had clothes that were too young made the decision not to show themselves on the first day; in the hope of success, bonnets, scarves and mantlets were imagined immediately; nothing as serious could be invented. Even in the old age, adornment is always the occupation of courts.

Sublime did not forget that old women ordinarily get up very early, and as she did not want to neglect anything for the success of her deception, she made Bellinette climb into her chariot at first light, in order to bring her back a few moments later under the name and face of Belline.

"Remember," she said to her on the way, "that you are now a person of a very advanced age; don't forget that your speech and your deportment must now respond to the opinion people have formed of you."

The sadness of Belline played the role in her of wisdom and reserve. On her arrival at the court everyone hastened around her; she had not yet spoken when everyone was already praising her wisdom and intelligence, and the excess of her great prudence. In sum, all the stupid courtiers, departed from the most brilliant as well as the humblest of estates, could not shut up about the advantages of being governed by a queen of consummate experience; for in a court, the exterior alone decides, and the person who judges most promptly is the one whose opinion necessarily prevails.

The old woman was only fifteen years old, and her speech, regarded the day before as light and frivolous, had not acquired any solidity, but prejudice suffices; that is what decided, and the court, similar to the people, always allows itself to go with the flow. Belline, therefore, succeeded perfectly at the whim of her subjects; her prudence was lauded, her wisdom celebrated, and her misfortunes excited sympathy. A few inconsiderate words and a few youthful vivacities that escaped her were regarded as precious residues of the charms he had once had and echoes of the old court, always commendable in a woman of a certain age.

People eventually reached the point of criticizing Bellinette, even with bitterness. In spite of her indignation, Belline appeared to applaud that; then people no longer retained any circumspection.

"It's spending life playing with dolls," said one, "being governed by a queen of that age; the naivety that is praised in her is in truth only stupidity, the pleasures that she procures are only an utter fatigue, which the body can't resist without the mind ever finding any satisfaction therein. In sum, that eternal infancy to which it's necessary to submit must be regarded as the ultimate in humiliation for an enlightened court; so, from this moment on, we're commencing to live and breathe...."

Belline could not get over her surprise.

The next day's scene, however, added to her astonishment, for she was received with all the marks of the most veritable attachment; it seemed that the hope of her return had been the unique occupation during the day of her absence. No one had yet recovered from the ennui they had experienced the day before. No one could understand how anyone could have the courage to show herself in such an excess of decrepitude; it was even easy to perceive that the old queen had never been pretty and her mind was even poorer than her age comported—in a word it was a perfect dotage....

If, on the one hand, it was cruel for Bellinette to spend her life being torn apart in both her forms, the situation also had its embarrassments for the courtiers, for it was necessary to pass overnight from black to white, to contradict what one had admired the day before, to applaud what one had criticized—in sum, to act in a completely opposite fashion. That continual metamorphosis soon became an excellent lesson for a young princess born with a superior intelligence; she discovered clearly the scant weight that it was necessary to give to the eulogies that were lavished on her incessantly. The bitter criticisms that she endured were all the more piquant because they were accompanied by all the malignity that the desire to seduce inspires alternately for the young and for the old. So the princess, after having experienced the most frightful torment, learned to know the court in particular and human beings in general.

Such, then, was now the situation in Bellinette's court. The curiosity of seeing something so singular had attracted several foreign princes there, for in the times of faerie, even kings sought to learn, but the ridiculousness of a court where one passed alternately from blind man's bluff to the embarrassment of daring to show oneself without a crutch could not engage anyone to stay for long.

Prince Brillant, guided by the good fay Cotteblanche, who had presided over his education, and who loved him so much that she could not separate herself from him, appeared at the court with a equipage befitting his rank. He was well made, his manner was agreeable, and his lively and cheerful conversation responded perfectly to the name he bore. If

Bellinette appeared charming to him, it did not take him long to make an equal impression on her mind.

That impression is one of the surest routes of which Amour makes use in order to exert his empire; ideas are communicated, the heart opens, the head fills, and that tender habitude eventually becomes the most solid occupation. Brillant was not without faults, but are there any—or, at least can any be perceived—when the graces of youth, intellect and the face are combined? Furthermore, it is youth itself that judges and decides; it does what suits it.

Bellinette, however, had lost a part of her gaiety and cheerfulness since her misfortunes. The old age that awaited her every day afflicted her more sensibly than the return of youth gave her satisfaction. Those mortifying ideas, without damaging her charms, merely spread an air of languor and restraint throughout her person. Sublime took account of that; she regarded her diminished vivacity as a commencement of wisdom.

The amour that Brillant inspired in her altered her character, but the change was advantageous, in spite of the violent anxieties that it caused her to experience. Only seeing one's lover one day in two is certainly not enough when one is very much in love, although there are those unfortunate in amour who might find their happiness in such a regime.

Bellinette had strictly forbidden the prince ever to appear in Belline's court; she only wanted to see him when she was sure of pleasing him; independently of all coquetry, one does not like to appear old in the eyes of one's lover. She had been obeyed in the beginning, but the prohibition soon became a powerful attraction for him, and Brillant was not yet sufficiently amorous to know the price of a sacrifice or the charms of a veritable submission; he had the errors of his estate and those of his age—that says it all. He therefore made it a delightful idea to please Belline and only to love Bellinette. In the eyes of the same court, that was to unite all that a man of good fortune could desire, as long as he believed himself sheltered from any clarification.

The first time that the princess perceived him under the appearance of the old woman she received him with the coldest expression in the world, firmly resolved not to speak to him. The prince, convinced that he only owed that reception to the lack of urgency of which he had given her evidence, only thought of repairing it; he put everything to work in order to seduce her. The princess was piqued by that; only homages rendered to her beauty could touch her; she was unaware that there are other means of pleasing, but coquetry soon served her as a lesson. Intelligence was her unique response; she employed it, and the prince was enchanted by it.

The next day he had a few reproaches to endure, but, the passion of the princess always acquiring new force, she gradually accustomed herself to appearing old in her lover's eyes. Ceasing to see him and ceasing to please him appeared to her more to be feared than the pains she had envisaged at first.

For his part, the prince, becoming more amorous every day, spent life agreeably enough, or at least fully occupied; he could not quit Belline without difficulty, and always found Bellinette again with more pleasure. He finally reached the point of no longer hiding his sentiments from either of them.

"I've never loved you so much," he sometimes said to Bellinette, "and yet, I feel that I would give me life to prolong Belline's days. I'm sure," he continued, "that at your age she had your charms, and if it were permissible for me to believe that time could exercise its power over you, I'd believe that you'd have her features and figure one day; could I never savor at the same time, then, the transports of amour and amity?"

"I'm not jealous," the princess told him. "I wouldn't be happy if amour were the sole passion that could occupy your soul. Love Belline; that's the greatest evidence of passion that you could give Bellinette." For, by virtue of coquetry, she was flattered to be loved in her days of old age, during which Brillant surely had no rivals.

Meanwhile, the good fay Cotteblanche had not abandoned the prince since his arrival; like mothers who believe that they have done everything when they have not lost sight of their daughters, she had never given him the slightest advice regarding his conduct, but, charmed by the amour that he had inspired in the princess—or, rather, the preferences he seemed to be obtaining—she came to see Sublime one day and said to her: "Our children love one another; why defer uniting them? Amour will be more useful to them than all our lessons."

"It's not yet time," said Sublime. "It requires a great deal for them to know and feel amour, in the elevated idea that I have always formed of it. I agree that the passion in question, even experienced in a mediocre fashion, reliably corrects any defect in the beloved object, but reflections and examples are nevertheless necessary to conduct oneself with regard to the world in general, especially for sovereigns who must govern others.

"Bellinette is not perfect, I know," she continued, "but your prince still has many errors; his heart is often blinded by his mind; the habitude of the throne makes him think that all people are born for him; he regards the attachment that they testify to him and the services they render him as a debt that they are acquitting. I agree that gratitude is not a virtue of princes in general, but it ought to be a virtue of our pupils; in brief, it's necessary that Brillant be perfect, or that he renounce the princess."

Cotteblanche, whom reflection had never taken very far, was quite astonished by Sublime's discourse. At first she wanted to be annoyed, but the fay represented to her gently that the wisest are subject to making mistakes, like everyone else; that reason serves not only to admit its errors but also to repair them; and that her conduct with regard to Bellinette was a confession of those she recognized having made. Finally, she led Cotteblanche to agree that there had been a good deal of negligence in the education that she had given to Brillant; that, for lack of having accustomed him to reflect, he had gradually become habituated to regarding people from the height of his throne as being a species different from him; that he had sometimes sacrificed the riches and the lives of his subjects to his whim and his ambition, as property belonging to him.

The good fay believed that she had made those discoveries by herself, although she had been added prodigiously by Sublime. So she added several other things, all with the same idea, for she was so astonished to be reasoning—perhaps it was the first time in her life—that she could not resolve to stop. Meanwhile, Sublime hazarded a few more criticisms of the abuse of intelligence and false brilliance; but, those reflections being much too delicate for Cotteblanche, she did not want to abuse her superiority, and contented herself with seeking with her means to enlighten the prince's mind and enable him to renounce his errors.

The fays believed that they were sovereign mistresses of their pupils but, omnipotent as they were, they experienced obstacles themselves, so true is it that everything that breathes is frustrated.

Grondine had once tormented Belline, as was mentioned at the beginning of this story, but that fay had not become any milder or more reasonable for having been punished for her bad conduct. When the time of her punishment had elapsed, her humor being, on the contrary, only more embittered, she could not console herself for no longer having Belline in her power. Always occupied with anything relating to that princess, she imagined that Sublime had only made her reappear in society in order to remind her of her punishment.

Her humor soon made her regard as certainty what she had initially only conceived as suspicion, and, no longer consulting anything but her fury, she resolved, whatever might happen, to disrupt the project of her colleagues and to bring down her wrath on Prince Brillant and Princess Bellinette.

To that effect, one day when the prince was hunting, she enveloped him in a thick cloud, in the midst of which she suddenly appeared. She made him mount her chariot, which harnessed dogs and cats were drawing as best they could; for what ill-humor ranges and discord draws does not usually progress very smoothly.

The surprise and astonishment of the prince caused him to remain silent, and Grondine took advantage of that to vituperate against the animals drawing her vehicle, which were veritably at odds with one another. When they had arrived in the obscure cavern where she lived, which as always filled with all the animals that nature has rendered antipathetic, Brillant asked her proudly what she had resolved to do with him.

"What do I want to do with you?" she said, in the hoarse tone of voice that bitterness and ill-humor usually produce. "Truly, truly, there are many fays that one could interrogate in that that fashion! But see, I beg you! I'm going to tell him what I want to do with him; I shall instruct monsieur; I'll see whether my conduct has the good fortune to be approved; I'll reform it if it doesn't please him…!"

That fine tirade, which went on much longer, was interrupted a thousand times by the threats she made to the dogs, which were fighting, as well as to the cats, which were swearing. When Brillant had found a more favorable moment, he said to her, mildly: "Hey, Madame, what have I done to you?"

"What! You're always going to be asking me questions?" she replied, furiously. "I'm well made to respond to that! Sublime and Cotteblanche will repent of what they've done to me, I swear."

"But what do I have in common with those respectable ladies?" the prince continued.

"They love you," replied Grondine. "It's only by tormenting you that I can make them feel that my power equals their authority, and Bellinette herself…"

"What, Madame!" Brillant interrupted. "You can threaten that lovable princess, whom nature entire ought to adore?"

Sentiments of amour always revolt hearts given to hatred; thus, that tender interest and those mild words dictated by amour caused Grondine a redoubling of bitterness so considerable that, while babbling. and setting aside all sugar coating,

367

she cried, as if she had been seized by the throat: "Bellinette...! You love her, I swear...you love her, I swear...well, you won't see her again...."

Before she had finished—for if she had she would have pronounced the terrible word "ever"—Sublime, who had not lost sight of the prince, was behind her, and whispered to her: "Until you're worthy of her...."

Many people, without being blinded by anger, or finding themselves in a state as violent as Grondine, routinely take the words that are presented to them, so the evil fay repeated that without even thinking about it.

After that important service Sublime withdrew and let Grondine speak, whose words could no longer be anything but noise.

Brillant was entirely unaware of the risk he had run, but, seeing that he could not gain any purchase on the mind of the fay, silence appeared to him to be the wisest course to follow. Ill-humored people interpret it badly, and ordinarily regard it as a mark of scorn; that was not, however, the prince's intention; separated from Bellinette, his ideas only presented memories to him, and his pleasures were only regrets.

Grondine wanted nevertheless to make him welcome, and to bring him back to politeness, but her nature and her manners rendered her mildness so incongruous that when she was polite people regretted her wrath.

In sum, in the sad sojourn that the prince spent with her, he observed not only the inconvenience but also the futility of bile, bitterness, irrationality, injustice and prejudice. That terrible and so oft-repeated example served to render the rest of his life even and moderate.

In the beginning he flattered himself vainly that he might be able to soften the mind and character of Grondine, but all his efforts only served to irritate her more. Not being able to see Bellinette, therefore, nor to console himself with Belline, he spent the cruelest moments one can imagine.

After such a sad sojourn, the fay, exceeded by the prince—for ill-humor gnaws itself—transported him while he was asleep to a country that was unknown to him.

It was certainly not the noise that interrupted his slumber, for none could be heard of any kind in that realm; on awakening, however, he found himself surrounded by many people who looked at him in astonishment. He tried to talk to them but that proved futile; in order to enlighten himself he had recourse to gestures, and was immediately understood. Before the day was out he recognized clearly that all the inhabitants of that land were deaf and mute.

The desire to shine and the liking for showing intelligence, which had not yet abandoned him, were then no resource for him; his natural eloquence, his vivid imagination, the enthusiasm by which he was piqued—in sum, all his talents, so marvelous during the error of youth—became completely useless to him.

Brillant soon perceived that it was necessary for him to be very different from what he had always been, in the midst of a people composed of sage, serene individuals whom a gesture governed. The usages to which he was constrained to submit and the reflections that he was obliged to make eventually became an excellent lesson for him; in a short time he acquired judgment, common sense and a reasonable deportment.

It is true that the chagrins of absence contributed a great deal to putting him in tune with that sad land. People had all possible regard for him, he was allowed all sorts of liberty, people hastened to oblige him, but no one could give him news of Bellinette. Even if he had not been in love, the pleasures that deaf mutes can obtain and procure would have seemed quite insipid to a man endowed with all his senses, but that situation is frightful for an unfortunate lover who can only find consolation in the recitation of is misfortunes.

After having traveled that sad realm, the prince realized that the people had received an order not to let him leave it, for he only experienced hindrance or constraint when he approached certain places that he judged without difficulty to be the frontiers of their estate. Seeing that he could not hope for liberty overland, he turned his attention to the coast. The sea bordered a part of that vast country, the people even had a considerable navy, but the prince found to more facility there; the sailors and pilots were all inexorable, all incorruptible.

Finally, after a long time, when he could not imagine any resource to get out of the sad land, he was taken to the edge of the sea, where he found a ship fully equipped, in which it was permissible for him to embark. It has always seemed highly likely that the liberty that was granted to him was the work of Cotteblanche, or, rather, of Sublime.

After a month of navigation, the mutes who had served him at sea as well as on land made him understand that they were obliged to separate from him, but that he would not lack anything necessary. Thus, after the most tender adieux on either side, they disembarked him on his own on a small island, and set out to sea.

An arid and dry mountain that rose up as far as the eye could see occupied the greater part of the island. The prince was frightened by it at first, but having taken a few steps he perceived a narrow plain between the mountain and the shore whose aspect have nothing savage about it; everything there depicted a simple and cheerful nature. Between the trunks of the most beautiful trees a fertile terrain appeared, delightful in spite of the dense shadow of the magnificent forest. All the large trees, commendable by virtue of their antiquity, were ornamented by small tables on which were placed thousands of bouquets of various sizes, but all formed by the fortunate assemblage of the most superb flowers. The air there was embalmed, and the eyes were charmed by it.

Geographers and voyagers have only ever mentioned that land under the name of the Isle of Bouquets. The prince saw new ones arriving continually, some of them showing themselves with as much sumptuousness and ostentation as urgency, and taking their places in the most apparent locations; others more modest, without being any more sincere, bloomed immediately, content to have arrived. They were all in carafes, and on the carafes the names of the people who had sent them were engraved, the motives of their presents, and the monograms of those to whom they were offered. On examining them, the prince saw with pleasure the names of several individuals of Bellinette's court and his own.

The most inanimate things that speak to us of those we love, however indirectly, are always heard and have a powerful attraction for us. They are a consolation or the woes of absence, and their presence alone can distract and console troubles, for they recall and enable us to hope for happier times. Those flowers and carafes, however—in sum, everything that was presented to Brillant's eyes—were as many enigmas for him.

At the moment when he was most occupied with these reflections, he saw with surprise that some of the bouquets faded at the very moment of their arrival, that the water in almost all the carafes blackened and became muddy and corrupt. He also noticed that, sometimes, a few flowers and sometimes entire bouquets disappeared without anyone appearing to approach them. Surprised by those prodigies, he advanced into the plain in order to satisfy his curiosity.

He had scarcely taken a few steps than he found himself in the center, facing a statue of the most beautiful white marble. It represented a woman of agreeable proportions, charming in her modesty, her candor and the simplicity of her coiffure and garments. She formed a group with lions, tigers, panthers and snakes, which appeared to be caressing her and to be gentle for her. The group was facing all the parts of the little plain, and the pedestal, circular in form, had a ledge half way up that formed an altar, on which three or four wild flowers were seen, alive and in all their splendor; chipped carafes carried them, but the water therein was as pure as the most beautiful spring.

The names of several people of simple estate were legible thereon. One carafe was distinguished from the others by virtue of its position on the altar and by the words: *Only one flower is wanted, but my life is always ready....*

The mind of the prince was finally enlightened, on reading the inscription on the statue, written in capital letters, which was conceived in these terms:

Blush, mortals, on seeing those that I have subjugated.

Brillant, gripped and touched, as well-born people always are at the sight of virtuous objects, could not tear himself away from that place and wanted to discover all its particularities. The fays, content with his sentiments and the respect with which they saw that he was penetrated, permitted the statue to be animated, to abandon the pedestal that bore it, and to accompany Brillant during the sojourn that they had resolved that he would spend on the island. Their cares were not limited to that moral support; they also enabled him to encounter, at the foot of the most beautiful tree in the forest, a small habitation in which all the necessary things were found, without any superfluity.

Animated Gratitude never quit him, and spoke to him in these terms: "Born with the world, few princes before you, Sire, have known me, even fewer have visited me; however, if one relied on the discourse of all men, my empire would be of vast extent. There is no one who does not boast of rendering me a perfect and continuous worship; you see, nevertheless, Sire, the narrow extent of the terrain that gratitude occupies on the entire surface of the earth. I have made a scruple for a long time of demanding even a flower from those who have received a few services, but in sum, I wanted a few witnesses to the benefit to exist; complete forgetfulness gives too much facility to ingrates.

"You have been able to remark the ostentation with which I am sent this accumulation of flowers, which often only conserve their splendor and their odor for a few minutes; Ingratitude, my enemy, desiccates them and fades them incessantly. She has a hundred means to succeed in that. Sometimes she makes use of intelligence to destroy me; she develops and supposes motives for the obligation received, she alleges procedures or recalls negligences in society. What can I do? She puts everything to use and succeeds only too well in banishing me from hearts, even those which I believed myself to be the most solidly established.

"She does not have far to go to exercise her perfidies," she continued. "That terrible, arid and steep mountain you see there was once only a molehill, in which ingratitude was imprisoned. It has increased gradually and has finally become that enormous mass, which contains immense caverns, still too narrow for the host of courtiers that surround her and to contain all the faded and desiccated bouquets that fly continuously into her sad dwelling, where they serve her as trophies. By virtue of a law of destiny, however, the name of the person who has given it to her remains attached to the bouquet, and when hazard permits the benefit and the name of the person to whom it was addressed to be read, it is then that Ingratitude alleges all that intelligence or the frustrations of society are so perfectly able to suggest to her, and that she always finds excuses applauded by the crowd of those by whom she is surrounded.

"Thus, my empire is shrinking every day, the mountain gains ground on me incessantly. It's true that this little corner of the world is still too extensive to receive and contain the sincere offerings that are sent to me. Experience ought to have rendered me sage, but nothing corrects me; too sure of working for the false triumph of my rival, I still expose myself joyfully every day to running the risks, and my efforts are not wasted, in my opinion, when I find one grateful heart in a thousand.

"I can talk to you," she continued, "all the more freely because your name can be found here. Perhaps it ought to be found more frequently," she added, lowering her voice, "but follow me."

The prince obeyed her. After having waked a few paces, he perceived a bouquet that he offered to Cotteblanche in recognition of the care she had taken of him. Bellinette's carafe addressed to Sublime was beside his own; the flowers were fresh in all their beauty.

"I don't see here," exclaimed the prince, "the proof of my sentiments and my gratitude for the generosity of Bellinette!"

"The gratitude one owes to Amour doesn't concern me," the goddess replied, blushing.

Brillant wanted to examine the sentiments that a few people he had treated with the greatest distinction might have preserved, but he did not perceive any of their carafes.

"It's not here," said the goddess, "that it's necessary to look for them. You'll find them in my enemy's abode."

During the conversations that he had with Gratitude, the prince experienced the expansion of the heart and the charm of virtue that speak incessantly within honest people and are the torment of corrupt hearts.

"I have been able to know you," he said. "I have been able to feel you. I have been able to admire you. Can I forget you as long as I live? A secret charm, stronger than me, obliges me to go away. The misfortunes of my situation are such that I am going, reluctantly, where I have a horror of finding myself. Grondine, the cruel Grondine, not content with snatching me for such a long time from the person I love, is forcing me once again to quit you, mild and delightful goddess, in order to go to see her friend and our common enemy, Ingratitude."

With those words, penetrated by affection and tenderness, he embraced Gratitude and took the path to the mountain.

The two divinities were such close neighbors that the prince did not have far to go to find himself in Ingratitude's lands—or, rather, at the entrance of her cavern. The goddess appeared there, followed by a brilliant court, of which she maintained the false joy with her hundred faces. Excuses, dressed in all colors, and frivolous pretexts accompanied her incessantly. In spite of the splendor of her numerous cortege, and in spite of the gilded decorations with which her cavern appeared to be paneled, the prince could only look at her with horror. Can a man filled with gratitude envisage ingratitude in any other way?

The scorn that he showed immediately diminished the obliging welcome of the pernicious goddess. Afterwards, anger took possession of her mind and her pretended mildness was converted into fury, exhaled in scornful words.

"Go," she said, "your pretended generosity, your great over-refined sentiments are only encountered in company with stupidity; if your intelligence develops one day, you'll be able to find me again; society and its examples will bring you back to me. Get out, if I can't please you yet; your presence will cause woe and pain to those who are attached to me."

Without being piqued, the prince contented himself with looking at her with the indignation that virtue inspires against vices. Content to draw away, he left, with no other design than to avoid such an object.

He had only taken a few steps when a chariot drawn by doves appeared before him. As soon as he had climbed aboard it, the doves took flight and traversed several expanses of land and sea.

Finally, he felt a gentle and charming expression in the air. The doves stopped and alighted in a country so fertile and delightful that the prince was struck by it, in spite of the sadness and chagrin that had tormented him since he had been separated from Bellinette. After having refreshed his eyes for some time with all the natural beauties that were presented to him on all sides, he got down impatiently from the chariot that had brought him.

So many charms spread over that land enabled him to hope that he might encounter Bellinette there. *What other object*, he said to himself, *could animate this prodigious quantity of beautiful flowers?* Tender hearts are always sensible to the attractions of mild nature, for it only depicts and draws amour.

Prince Brillant walked for some time, more dissipated than he had been since the torments that Grondine had exercised upon him. He was surprised, however, not to perceive any inhabitant in such an agreeable country. He finally saw, not far away from him, a little old woman, simply dressed, who was running to help a bird that had trapped its foot between two branches and was giving evidence of its pain in the fashion in which it was struggling. What were the astonishment and joy of the prince on recognizing Belline, the Belline whose intelligence had charmed him!

He ran to her with more vivacity than she ran herself, and said to her: "Oh, my dear Belline, what good fortune for me to encounter you!"

Fidele, for his part, who was not far away, having seen Belline running, had quit everything to join his beloved eagerly, in such a fashion that he arrived in time to hear the affectionate words that the prince pronounced. Those words, emerging from the mouth of a amiable and well made young man, made him shiver and chilled him with fear; it was the first surge of jealousy that he had ever experienced. The misfortune of that sentiment is to reason very poorly, so Fidele was afflicted and his heart was torn.

Belline, meanwhile, seemed surprised by the familiar welcome that she had received, and did not reply to the prince.

Fidele might have been reassured by this evidence, and by the age of Brillant, who could not have known Belline, who, for at least thirty years, had neither seen nor even imagined anyone but him; in any case, the sentiments of the princess and all past events ought to have tranquilized him. But jealousy is deaf and blind; the judgments and impressions of others count for nothing, and are impotent to calm it. One is jealous of the object one loves, to the extent that one is excusable, because one wants all of it.

Belline, who perceived the pain that Fidele was suffering, became even more embarrassed, and wanted to retire.

"What! You're making a semblance of not recognizing me, my dear Belline!" the prince said to her. "You, to whom I have such great obligations, whose intelligence I love and whose heart I revere?" He went on, with more vivacity: "But speak to me naturally? Shall I not see Bellinette tomorrow?"

"What! You already have pet names!" cried Prince Fidele, dolorously.

That confusion only lasted a few moments. The old couple finally disentangled the truth by means of the clarifications they gave one another. Then they took Brillant into their dwelling. A few palm trees formed it; beds of moss and assorted furniture, charming in their neatness, sufficed in a temperate land where no dangerous animals were found.

It was there that Brillant had the necessary time to admire the tender cares of those good and veritable lovers. His heart was penetrated on seeing their amour: it was vivid and it was pure, without jealousy and without sacrifice. In sum, it was amicable amour, which combines all desires and completes all necessities. Fruits alone nourished them; they were produced without culture by soil already ornamented by flowers, irrigated by little streams of clear fresh water, which, never swelling, did not bring any obstacle to traversing them.

The sight of so many beauties produced cheerful comparisons in their conversations; it embellished the expression and depiction of their sentiments; that beautiful country provided, in sum, all their ideas and needs. Only the birds troubled—or, rather, amused and decorated—their solitude; those happy lovers had no fear of distaste, they loved one another as on the first day. The memory of what they had suffered, always present in their minds, augmented their enjoyments; their hearts and their tastes were entirely in accord. That tender union never having given them children, nothing made them envisage the future, and everything attached them to the present.

It was there that Brillant learned to love, or, rather, to know veritable amour. However, Belline and Fidele, instructed by all that had happened to them, did not content themselves with the good examples that they set him incessantly. Belline also wanted to tell him her own story. Could she give him a stronger idea of constancy, nor retrace anything more useful to him?

She therefore spoke to him in approximately these terms:

"Grondine was once charged, in her quality as a fay, with governing the realm that the succession of time was later to cause to fall on my head and that of the prince, my brother. That fay, naturally ill-humored, became even more insupportable when she was obliged to combine with the conduct of her affairs with the education of two children that my father, the king, and my mother put into the world. The little prince is known in history under the name of Millefleurs, and you know that my name is Belline.

"Everyone is pretty in childhood, if one believes the stories; it even seems that self-esteem is not involved in that avowal; however, people spoke to me so many times about the charms of Millefleurs and my own during our childhood that I believe I can agree with them. People were astonished that Grondine, far from being touched by them, seemed, in the contrary, to be revolted by them. I have even been assured that ill-humor carried her away to such an extent that one day, she gave the little prince a slap.

"The queen, who loved her son madly, had a scene with Grondine on that subject, so heated that they were on the point of separating and creating a scandal that could only be dangerous, but an accommodation was reached in which it was agreed that Grondine would no longer be involved with the prince and I would be abandoned to the fay absolutely. It is not only today, as you can see, that girls are sacrificed within all families to what is thought to be advantageous for boys.

"I was, therefore, the victim of that accord, and I became a victim in every possible fashion. Not only was I scolded for two, but I did not have the consolation of recounting my pain. The impressions of childhood make such profound traces that, in spite of the number of years that have gone by since then, I still remember that I was obliged to hide in the corners of my room in order to weep in liberty; I shall not forget that I was in the cruel necessity of running after Grondine when she called me, and it was never for anything but to be scolded more quickly, for she did not like to wait, even to get annoyed.

"I was incessantly obliged to hide my tears; if the fay had seen them, her ill-humor would have been redoubled by them. In brief, in order to have some repose, I had to appear as content as if I had been continually caressed. People took note of my pain, but it was in such a disguised fashion. They felt sorry for me, but so quietly, that I had difficulty perceiving it. No one, in sum, not even the king and the queen, dared to say what they thought; that would have been a means of rendering me more unfortunate.

"Those torments and difficulties did not prevent me from growing up, and becoming beautiful enough to engage several princes to declare themselves for me. The dread that Grondine inspired in them drove them all away sooner or later. Prince Fidele, whom you see, was the only one who, having nothing to fear, in the shelter of his frankness, abandoned himself to the chains of a passion that was soon repaid by the most tender return.

"Grondine, who scented amour as ogres scent fresh flesh, did not take long to discover our sentiments; fury transported her, and, always grumbling without listening to the slightest reflection, she abducted us both in her black chariot and took us to the shore of the glacial sea. She took me to the foot of a very high mountain and placed the prince on the summit, saying to us 'Seek one another now, talk to one another, deceive me, if you can; I consent to it; you're not, however, far away from one another.'

"In fact, when one went up, the other descended, and when Fidele stopped, so did I such was the enchantment of the fay, whom to complete our woes, made us climb and descend by different paths, in order to take away from us the pleasure of encountering one another momentarily. But from what can amour not extract some advantage? Our sentiments were nourished by the hope of seeing one another again, by the idea of not being far apart, by the pleasure of living in the same place, and, finally, by the consolation of one day telling one another about all our suffering.

"Those whose humor torments lovers are unaware of the vivacity they give to amour; that knowledge would be a torment that it is necessary to procure for them. Several years, however, went by in such a cruel situation, which might, perhaps, only have finished with life, for Grondine combined obstinacy with ill-humor. But the doyenne of fays, in consulting her book, perceived that it was lacking a prince and a princess; she asked Grondine, who was responsible for them, to account for them. The first torture that she suffered caused her to confess her sin, which she was obliged to do aloud in the presence of all the fays.

"The Council promptly sent someone to fetch Fidele and me; no one felt sorry for us any longer, because we had nothing to lament. In any case, are not veritable pains always n the heart? We were faithful, and we had not experienced any jealousy. Grondine was condemned, in our presence, to remain an owl for thirty years; the light of her mind and he blackness of her character were preserved, but she was deprived of all power.

"After having rendered that equitable sentence, the fays offered the prince and me a kingdom of our choice; it was even added that I had inherited the one that had seen me born; but with a common accord we did not want to accept any. We assured the fays that we would be sad princes, that we no longer knew society and its usages, and that, occupied with sentiments that were sufficient for us, and with which our hearts were perfectly full, it would be impossible for us to govern others.

"Charmed by an example that seemed so rare to them, but which was only dictated by a sentiment of equity, the fays transported us to one of the Fortunate Isles, where we have found for more than forty years everything that is necessary to us. What do we need? We have amour...."

Belline finished her story thus, and those two veritable lovers, not content with giving Brillant such good examples of the sentiments of the heart, always spoke to him with the frankness of an enlightened simplicity, and enabled him to sense the differences that ought to be necessary between the conduct of a prince on the throne and that of a prince retired from society.

It is time now to return to Bellinette. After having abducted Prince Brillant, Grondine had taken possession of the princess, without all of Sublime's art being able to raise any obstacle to it, for ill-humor has infinite resources and facilities that cannot be foreseen.

As soon as the little queen, who was Belline at that moment—which is to say, old—was in the possession of the evil fay, she transported her into a somber black forest capable of inspiring fear even in people more advanced in age. The cries, terrors and caresses of the princess could not soften the heart of the fay, who told her, after having murmured for a long time without being able to pronounce anything: "Yes, yes, I advise you to want to resemble Belline, I'll teach you...."

"What, Madame! It's for that reason you've abducted me and you're maltreating me?" said the princess, with astonishment.

"I was wrong, wasn't I," Grondine replied, "to make Sublime see that she's only a fool with all her intelligence and great reflection? But we'll see whether you dare to appear again under the form of a princess, whose face will torment me with its old days...."

"Oh, Madame," the little queen interrupted, with vivacity, "if I were never Belline again, how obliged to you I'd be! Heaven is my witness that I have never been by taste."

"I'm annoyed to take away something that gives you so much pain," said Grondine, "but I have to avenge myself on Sublime, and I don't have any other means. No, no, you'll no longer be Belline."

"Dare I ask you, Belline said to her anxiously, "who I'll be now?"

"Who you'll be?" said Grondine. "You'll be you. Haven't you always been? Go, you're nothing but a little idler; travel, roam the world, I don't mean you any harm; however, be assured that your troubles will only end when a portrait in which everyone will recognize you won't have any resemblance...."

The dogs and cats started running then, or flying, for Grondine gave them wings or feet in accordance with her humor. At any rate, the vehicle disappeared with Grondine, and Bellinette remained, charmed to imagine that she would no longer be old before her time. The solitude, the horror of the forest, and all the difficulties and fatigues to which she was about to be exposed were incapable of occupying her; a pocket mirror that assured her that she had ceased to be old and that her charms and her youth were in their full splendor, only left her with an imperfect contentment.

If Sublime had flown to her aid a few moments sooner, she would have put Bellinette in shelter from Grondine's power and would have removed her from her unjust vengeance; but the words had been pronounced and everyone knows that a fay cannot destroy the work of her companion. All that Sublime could do was not to abandon Bellinette. She owed it to her to care for her, as her pupil, but she also owed it to her because the face of Belline was her invention, and that metamorphosis alone had caused the prodigious disorder by which they were tormented.

The helpful fay did not judge it appropriate to appear to the eyes of the little queen, but in order to render the journeys to which she was condemned more useful, she wanted that, although young in her own eyes, she would appear old in the eyes of everyone else until the time prescribed by the injustice of Grondine. It is true that it was no longer under the form or the features of Belline.

As Sublime thought of everything, she gave orders to a little fly not to quit the princess, but forbade it absolutely to make itself known. It is as well to be informed that the fly in question was a former governess; it would not have been becoming for the princess to have traveled, without at least one maidservant.

The young princess, content with her beauty, about which no doubt remained to her, starting walking, with no other concern than encountering Prince Brillant, charmed to imagine that he might love her, and that, for her part, she could please him, every day. For, independently of the solitude that recalls tender ideas, she was very occupied with them when no object of coquetry remained to her.

In order to remedy all the inconveniences of the journey, however, Sublime enabled her to find, at the foot of a tree, a few moments after Grondine's departure, one of those little baskets that girls carry to school; it contained a little snack, a napkin and a pink parasol; the whole thing did not weigh more than an ounce. The little queen picked up the basket, because it seemed to her to be pretty in its form, and kept it because it became necessary to her.

It did not require a considerable time for her to become aware of its admirable properties. She walked for a few hours, and when night fell, the need to eat engaged her to have recourse to the food inside her basket. Cleanliness caused her to lay the napkin on the ground in order to lie down, the fear of rain caused her to plant her parasol over her head, and the habitude of having her head raised obliged her to put her basket underneath it. The napkin became a very good bed, the parasol formed ample curtains and the basket formed the best of bolsters; with such aid, Bellinette passed a very good night.

The sunlight and the song of the birds woke her up, and her first movement was to search urgently for her mirror, to see whether she was still young. She had the satisfaction of finding herself thus and seeing that her hair was not at all unkempt. She then recognized, with surprise, that she did not feel the slightest fatigue, for she believed firmly, in good faith, that she had slept on the hard ground, something that she had feared all her life.

The hope of perhaps having forgotten something in her basket the previous evening engaged her to visit it again; she found a small loaf of bread and milky coffee there; that was her usual breakfast. That visible protection of the fays, and above all, her confirmed youth, gave her a joy very necessary to her travels. She folded up hr little equipage, passed the handle of her basket over her left arm, took her parasol in her right hand, and started walking cheerfully.

At meal times, the napkin became a chaise longue, the parasol a small tent and the basket, having taken the form of a table, presented new, varied and delicious dishes.

The little queen walked for several days in that fashion without encountering anyone; the solitude had not even become tedious, youth and the attractions with which she believed herself to be provided were sufficient for her.

After a few days' march, she heard the noise of a hunt, and saw a young man appear followed by a brilliant court. It was the Prince of Plumes, who, struck by the equipage and the age of the princess, and the encounter, had no doubt that she was a veritable fay. Everyone knows how those ladies have always been respected and feared—respect is often due to dread—so the Prince of Plumes did not hesitate for a moment to dismount. All those accompanying him followed his example. He approached the princess with all possible submission, offered her everything that depended on him, and assured her that he would neglect nothing to merit her good will.

The little queen received these homages as being rendered to her charms; her self-esteem was satisfied by them. *It's not my rank that is being considered here*, she said to herself, *it's me alone, it's my beauty. What a good woman the fay who abducted me is! Her manners are a trifle abrupt and her speech revolting, but her procedures are admirable.*

The impressions she caused, however, were not at all those she imagined. (How many errors are similar to hers!) The little remarks, the little facial expressions, and the childish mannerisms, all things that please or are not noticed in a young person, appeared so ridiculous with her great age that people would probably have burst out laughing but for the respect that they thought they owed to her status. The Prince of Plumes had her given the finest of his horses and conducted her to his apartment.

Without appearing, Sublime took care to maintain that court in the ideas that had been formed there; without that precaution, Bellinette would soon have been destroyed by her vivacity. She appeared to desire nothing but balls, spectacles and pleasures; she would have had entire satisfaction—people only thought of following or anticipating her desires—but those balls and the advances that her natural coquetry enabled her to receive only served to afflict her. The young men of the court surrounded her incessantly, in truth, and sought to please her, but it was in a cruel fashion; they had recourse to her credit, her justice and her authority.

One begged her to render his mistress sensible, another to facilitate a rendezvous—in brief, no one talked to her about herself. What agony for a young person born a coquette only to hear mention of others! She was obliged to retreat a little in her pride, but the more advances she made in order to make someone say something obliging about her, the more the speeches that were foreign to her increased. That humiliating situation reduced the princess to despair, and, finding herself a thousand times more exasperated by all the fêtes than she had desired to be, she made the decision to retreat and to prefer solitude with the feeble resources that she had found in her travels to a court where such scant attention was paid to her charms.

A perfect moonlight caused her to make the decision to depart promptly; she set forth on foot, still followed by the fly that Sublime had ordered to watch over her conduct and pre-serve her from the accidents that are only too common in jour-neys. The fly, which had not abandoned her for an instant, was subtle; thus, when she perceived a few objects that might an-nounce danger, she covered the little queen with one of her wings, rendered her invisible and removed from her sight things that were not suitable for her age and sex.

Bellinette's adventure in the court of the Prince of Plumes caused her to make serious reflections and made her sense the good fortune and the advantage of being loved sovereignly. Those ideas immediately reminded her of Prince Brillant, who did not lose by all those comparisons.

After having traveled for a few days she arrived on the edge of a spring celebrated in the region by virtue of the host of lovers who came to it in pilgrimage, and was known by the name of the spring of roses. That rural and rustic place presented to the eyes and the sense of smell all that nature has of the seductive. Very young as the little queen was, she was struck by the beauties she discovered there, for there are ages consecrated to certain sensibilities.

Bellinette was amused by the quantity of butterflies fluttering in that beautiful place; the variety of their colors, their flight and their agitation animated that beautiful spot. The princess decided to stay there for a while. A secret pleasure, a charm that is not developed, often arrests us without our being able to distinguish the motive that retains us. It is Amour that is speaking to us, him who engages us; the place pleases him and suits him. Bellinette therefore lay down on the edge of the delightful spring, charmed by its shade and freshness; fatigue and reflections soon plunged her into a profound slumber.

Sublime, who desired to take advantage of favorable dispositions of her heart, wanted to occupy her with a mysterious dream. All the butterflies that had amused and dissipated her during the day presented themselves to her imagination, but, by virtue of the power of the fay, those animals, symbols of inconstancy, levity and coquetry, appeared to her with charming heads, which seduced her, with reason, because they all had that of Amour, at all ages. After a long examination, however, she recognized that those beautiful heads, males and female, had the bodies of tigers, ferrets, cats, badgers and other animals of that nasty kind.

Sublime wanted to make her sense, by means of the lightness of the butterflies, that inconstancy and coquetry can have no fixed temple, all their worshipers also having no fixed abode, which becomes the cause of their greatest chagrins. Those ideas sown in the little queen's head became, when she awoke, the material of several reflections, and, already discontented by the scant impression that her charms had made in the court of the Prince of Plumes, she began to have some doubt about their limited value.

That part of self-esteem diminished in a woman is a major point; from then on, constancy and veritable amour, without any distraction, are presented to her with all their merit. Her imagination then presented Prince Brillant to her more forcefully, and made her regret more keenly being separated from him; she was even afflicted by having nothing any longer to sacrifice for him. All the sacrifices in which she had believed herself to be so rich a few days before, those works of self-regard, proofs of a mediocre taste, had vanished by virtue of new ideas. She determined to quit promptly a place that displeased her by reminding her of the idea of inconstancy and coquetry.

Being more delicate and tender, Bellinette abandoned the spring that had given her such great pleasure without any difficulty. It is thus that everything takes hold of the character and submits it to ideas of amour. She departed with vivacity in order to seek the prince, whose attachment she sensed to be necessary to her. The anxiety of his absence, that of his constancy, and the sharing of his pains took possession of her heart.

She did not walk for long before encountering the sea shore; that element caused her to fall into reverie; after having rendered it the tribute of astonishment that is owed to its immensity the first time one sees it, the princess, whose extreme vivacity did not allow her a minute of repose, then completely absorbed in her reflections would have astonished all those who knew her; her very senses were so greatly suspended that she dropped her basket, the basket of such pretty form, which nourished her, which carried everything that was necessary to her—in sum, everything that she possessed, everything that put her in a state to search for Prince Brillant.

She did not hesitate to run after the wave that was carrying away all her treasures. Scarcely had she taken a step into the sea than the basket became a charming boat, into which the princess climbed with so much facility that she hardly got wet. The boat offered her all the comforts that she might need, and conducted her, in the most beautiful weather in the world, to the Fortunate Isles, where it stopped.

Seeing her boat immobile, the little queen stepped ashore, and the boat immediately became the same little basket as before. Bellinette, brought up by fays, was not astonished by all those prodigies, but, engaged by the beauty of the country, she advanced inland.

She had only taken a few steps when Fidele and Belline, who had perceived her, came to meet her. Bellinette, sensible to their offers, went with them and took the path to their habitation. They found Prince Brillant there, who was dreaming at the foot of a palm tree. The little queen blushed on perceiving him, and wanted to run to him, transported by her amour and her vivacity, but Belline stopped her, saying: "Let him dream; liberty reigns in this happy place, he doubtless has more pleasure in dreaming about Bellinette than he would have in seeing us."

Charmed by what she heard, the princess reproached herself for what she had wanted to do, and resolved to preserve the pleasure of surprise for her lover. But her agreeable projects were of short duration; the noise they made obliged the prince to get up and to come and join them. He approached with an expression of interest and amity for the old people, which was converted into coldness and seriousness at the sight of a person unknown to him.

Surprised by such a welcome, Bellinette made him a few reproaches, to which he only responded with mild and light pleasantries. They were not long, because they soon arrived at the habitation. After having visited it, Bellinette remained alone for a moment in the Belline's cabin. She was experiencing the cruelest anxiety.

What? she said to herself. *Am I no longer pretty? Am I unrecognizable, then?* Promptly, she looked in her mirror, and found herself so well that she was flattered by it. The inconstancy that she supposed on the part of the prince and the scorn by which it seemed to be accompanied caused her to fall in a faint.

She remained in that state for some time, but Belline and Prince Fidele, worried by her long absence, came to find her and helped her. They carried her into Prince Brillant's cabin; he consented easily to yield it to her. It was decorated with the spoils of birds with the richest plumage, which were innumerable in that fortunate abode. Brillant, who had a good deal of natural good taste and who drew very well for a prince had not only amused himself giving a marvelous arrangement to the flowers, but he had also imitated the most beautiful flowers that were born at every step in that delightful climate; those designs were arranged in the midst of monograms, and those of Bellinette—in sum, everything there traced his amour.

When the little queen came round, Prince Brillant was the first object that her eyes encountered, but she only saw in his eyes an indifference and a coldness that put her in despair. She thanked Belline and Fidele for their cares and begged them to leave her alone, under the pretext of resting, but in fact to abandon herself to her dolor.

Her beautiful eyes shed torrents of tears; her imagination reminded her in vain of what Belline had said when she perceived the prince; she could only attribute it to a cruel coincidence of names. Her gaze fell upon the monograms with which the cabin was filled.

"Can it be," she cried, "that so many marks of the prince's amour are for someone else?" But how could she reconcile them, if they were for her, with the indifference that Brillant had shown her?

It's necessary to clarify this, she said to herself, getting up precipitately. *A longer uncertainty cannot be sustained. If the prince loved me, he couldn't affect not to know me; in any case, what reason could he have? Let's see, let's examine with*

*care, and above all, let's not name myself; let's hide my shame
and my humiliation from these old people.*

She went out, in fact. The prince had already gone away
in order to dream at his ease; she had the liberty to ask Belline
and Fidele all the questions that could interest her amour. She
learned that the prince, who had often told them his story, only
had Bellinette for an object, that all the trees were ornamented
with her monograms and that his cabin, which he had ceded to
her, was filled with them. She was also told that he had attempted to make her portrait a thousand times, but that his
imagination, always more vivid than his hand, had never been
satisfied and that he had always torn up his work.

It might appear inconceivable that Bellinette had not yet
recognized Belline, whose features she had worn for such a
long time and with so much dolor. But such are the resources
of self-esteem; however convinced one is of one's faults, old
age is only ever envisaged as a diminution of charms; its deformity appears, at the most as a very ordinary ugliness. That
is how we judge ourselves.

Those good old people, however, who were only seeking
to amuse the princess, showed her their portraits, which the
prince had made to distract himself; she was forced to admire
their resemblance. But all those clarifications only served to
augment her disturbance and embarrassment.

The prince joined them then in order to take a frugal
meal with them, which nature presented to them. Bellinette,
without naming herself, said several things during the meal
that astonished Brillant, and although he was far from recognizing her, he was struck by the features of her intelligence,
which had never lost the right to charm him, and with which
he was incessantly occupied. That species of conversation
rendered him more amiable than he had seemed thus far to the
two old people, so their supper was prolonged.

Bellinette, a little more content, but without being satisfied, was only occupied throughout the night with the means
she might employ to have herself recognized; she saw herself
beloved and simultaneously scorned; that situation could not

be sustained. It was necessary to agree that she had changed; that idea, cruel at any age, was frightful at seventeen.

After having examined many means and formed many projects, she decided to ask the prince to make her portrait. She hoped that the attention necessary for that labor would remind him more easily of her features. She could not understand how she could be so deeply engraved in his heart, while his gaze was so scantly impressed.

The next day—for amour is pressing—she made the proposition to the prince; he accepted out of simple politeness and as a relaxation appropriate to their retreat. He began work immediately, with a great deal of facility.

Bellinette, charmed to see her lover, animated by the desire to be recognized and piqued at not being, did not neglect anything that might please, either by means of the face or the intelligence, for loving is a transport but pleasing is a talent.

The head was almost finished when Belline and Fidele arrived and exclaimed at the prodigious resemblance. Bellinette, who had not wanted to interrupt the prince, interrupted in order to judge it.

"What! That's how you see me?" she cried, as soon as her eyes fell upon the work. "I'm doomed!" she continued, fleeing. "Where can I hide?"

She pronounced those words in her natural voice, not altered by age, for at that moment she resumed her graces, her face and her youth.

Brillant was so struck by the sound of her voice that he followed her immediately, and recognized his dear Bellinette in the arms of Sublime and Cotteblanche, accompanied by the fly that had never quit her, and who had resumed her previous form of an old chambermaid.

"It's at this moment that I'm arriving in these Fortunate Isles!" cried Prince Brillant, with a transport that the heart alone can dictate.

The fays explained in a few words what they wanted to know, and, finding them perfectly corrected of their faults and worthy of one another, they summoned Grondine, whom they

391

had taken the precaution of bringing with them, to keep the word she had given. The latter, in accordance with her character, wanted to make a few difficulties, but they threatened her so seriously that she gave her consent to the marriage; it was with an ill grace, in truth, and she took flight immediately thereafter, unable to sustain the sight of people so content,

Sublime and Cotteblanche left Belline and Fidele in the Fortunate Isles and took Bellinette and Brillant to their realms, where they wanted to celebrate their marriage, assuring them that as long as they loved one another, they would find fortunate isles everywhere.

They learned by their experience that the fays were not mistaken.

AUTHOR'S PREFACE to CADICHON & JEANNETTE

Tales of enchantment have been fashionable for a long time, and in my youth one scarcely read anything else. Madame la Comtesse de Murat and Madame d'Aulnoy have made charming morsels in that genre. The translation of Arab and Persian tales by Messieurs Galland and Pétis de la Croix have had a prodigious success, and that success was merited.[48] Thus they have excited the emulation of many men of letters who have aspired to the honor of imitating them. Some have been fortunate; others have been relegated to the dust of bookstores, just before they pass on to the grocer.[49] I was very hesitant to augment the number of those unfortunate storytellers when the societies in which I was involved engaged me to try my hand at the genre.

I resisted, but I finally allowed myself to be seduced, by the natural attraction of works of the imagination and even more by the goal that a sage and honest man of letters ought to adopt in writing. I find in the pages of the illustrious ladies that I mentioned, and in the *Mille et un*, an infinity of moral lessons that are introduced into the heart under the mask of giving pleasure. I sense, by virtue of my own character, sufficiently urged to render virtue amiable, and I do not believe this means to be useless. In any case, it relaxes me, and when I

---

[48] The Orientalist François Pétis de la Croix (1653-1713) published a collection of *Contes turcs* [Turkish Tales] (1707) and a five-volume collection of Galland imitations, *Les Mille et un jours* (1710-12).

[49] In the eighteenth and early nineteenth centuries jam jars in France were usually sealed by sheets of paper; book pages were a convenient size.

had desiccated my brain and fatigued my intellect in divining the meaning of a few ancient hieroglyphs, I found a true pleasure in parading my imagination in the vast field of Faerie.

Nothing, in fact, can exhaust it, and a however skillful and active the reapers are who harvest it, one always finds, not merely gleanings after them, but a whole new crop as abundant as theirs. I therefore amused myself writing tales, for the same motive that engaged me to engrave etchings. I sense clearly that I cannot attain perfection in either case, but it was as much gained over the ennui of idleness, and that was enough for me.

My first tales nevertheless succeeded, and beyond my expectations; that encouraged me; I published a few others that had even greater success. That of the *Féeries nouvelles*, above all, and *Contes orientaux* flattered my self-esteem, and perhaps I would have continued to exercise myself in that genre if more serious occupations had not deflected me away from it, and I was obliged to follow them without being able to permit myself the slightest interruption.

The taste of the century changed. Metaphysical or libertine novels took the place of Merlin and Urgande la déconnue.[50] That was, perhaps to the detriment of mores. In depicting them as they were seen, the more accurate the portrait was the more it spoiled the heart; for it is necessary to make no mistake, there are problems of casuistry in works of the imagination. It is such questions that those who permit themselves, even in the gravest treatises, which, by the manner in which they are exposed, are most likely to provide lures to vice than to make its ugliness feared. The fables of La Fontaine are excellent lessons in virtue; can one say as much of his tales?

I do not have to reproach myself for straying from the subject. Those who have read the faeries that I have published

---

[50] "Urgande la déconnue" [Urganda la Desconocida in the orginal] is the protectress of Amadis de Gaul in French versions of that epic.

must have perceived at the first glance that I have not had, anywhere, and other goal but sweetening the meat salubrious to the child, as Montaigne says. I do not intend to make an analysis of them here; they are sufficiently well-known. I only ought to say why, after more than thirty years,[51] I have dared to write "Cadichon" and "Jeannette."

A respectable lady, who still holds to the old court, had two young grandchildren, one of whom was extremely impatient and the other a chatterbox who never let up. The good grandmother thought that two tales on those subjects might correct them, and begged me to write them; I could not refuse her anything, and I had to applaud my confidence for, by dint of reading them and rereading them, each of the two tales produced the effect that as expected of it, but it was for another cause than the morality of the tales. The impatient one announced in reading that he wanted to be able to tell the story; it was necessary to put in the time necessary to learn it. The loquacious one employed time that he would have wasted chattering or spying, and that was as much silence for him; I will even say incuriosity. At any rate, these tales were profitable, and with whatever eye one looks at them, tales of enchantment always will be.

What reasonable objection can, in fact, be raised against these sort of works? The marvelous? The bizarre? The extravagance of an imagination without rule or brake? What does that prove? Nothing at all. One gladly pardons the marvelous in Homer, Virgil and many other poets. Is it any wiser to suppose gods who are passionate, divided, inconstant, unjust and cruel than to suppose enchanters and fays who have the same views? No, undoubtedly. There is more: it is that enchanters and fays are only given in any tale as powerful beings, it is

---

[51] This figure must have been inserted by an editor; "more than thirty years" did separate the publication of Caylus's second collection from the 1775 collection, but the later was posthumous and the stories were probably written no later than 1760.

true, but subordinate to a superior power to theirs, and no author of faeries has ever failed to give the supreme power to benevolence; but Jupiter, the master of the gods, is sometimes malevolent.

Poets depict the passions and their excess, but they often limit themselves to depicting them. Content to have rendered nature, they do not worry about correcting its deregulated movements. Horace has told us that the poems of Homer contain a healthier morality than that which results from the lessons of Chrysippus, Crantor and other Stoics. If Horace had not had the goodness to want to find in the *Iliad* and the *Odyssey* the moralities that his admirable analysis presents to us, perhaps none of the readers of the divine Homer would ever have perceived them.

It is not that in all tales of enchantment the moral is as striking as it is in "Serpentin vert" or in "Le Prince Souci" and, above all, in "Rosimond," "Alfaroute" and the other tales of the immortal Fénélon, whose name ought to be of the greatest authority here;[52] but for being more veiled and less apparent, the moral is always made evident enough to produce the effect that the author intended. To prove that assertion, I have only to set before the reader's eyes a synopsis of "Le Palace de la vengeance," one if the finest tales that I know.

Madame la Comtesse de Murat supposes a young prince and a young princess who love one another, and are each loved by a fay and an enchanter who promise themselves to

---

[52] "Le Serpentin vert" is by Madame d'Aulnoy, "La Princesse Minon-Minette et Le Prince Souci" is by Caylus, included in the seventh volume of *Oeuvres Badines* with other Oriental tales in a section headed *Le Pot-Pourri*, taken from a volume first published in 1745. Francois Fénélon wrote his fables and moral tales, including "Histoire de Rosimond et Braminte" and "Histoire du roi Alfaroute et de Clariphile" while tutor to the Duc de Bourgogne, the Dauphin's younger son, in 1689-97, but they were only published in 1719; four of his tales feature fays, including the two cited.

render them infidel. In order to succeed in that they abduct them in concert and at the same time. Everything is put to work to make them forget their first amours: vain efforts, nothing seduces them, and each of them conserved dearly the memory of the beloved object. Finally weary of their futile attempts, the fay and the enchanter resolve, in their despair, to heap the unfortunate lovers with the weight of all their anger, or, to put it better, their fury.

Of a thousand means of vengeance between which their power permits them to choose, they decide on the one that will render life hardest for the lovers too constant for their liking. With a thrust of a wand they construct in an instant a superb palace in an immense solitude that forbids its approach to any human effort. It is there that they transport the prince and the princess. By a refinement of barbarity, they endow them with immortality, forbid them all occupation, deprive them of all society and leave them entirely delivered to themselves. Served by invisible hands they only see that they are alone and believe at first that their happiness is complete. Their inexperience prevents them from perceiving that an eternal tête-à-tête must soon become an eternal torture; for, as Saadi says, everlasting pleasure is not pleasure…familiarity soon produces ennui, and when ennui comes to succeed tenderness, distaste and even hatred do not take long to follow.[53]

So Madame de Murat did not think that she could conclude her tale better than by saying that the enchanter who had imprisoned the prince and princess in that delightful but deserted palace: "had condemned them, in that place testament to his vengeance, to see one another forever."

---

[53] It is perhaps ironic that in *Oeuvres badines* this preface comes immediately after "Bellinette," in which the reward granted to Belline and Fidele suggests that Murat's moral had not, in fact, "slipped into his soul." The story is, indeed, one of Murat's finest, but the synopsis given here is slightly inaccurate, the enchanter working his magic alone, unaided by a fay, although two fays feature in the story in minor roles.

I will refrain from weighing the reflections to which that story gives birth; I shall only say that, independently of the interest that the reader takes in those unfortunate victim of jealousy and vengeance, the instruction slipped into his soul, and he learns that it is necessary not to exhaust sensibility if one wants to conserve sensibility. I will cite, on this subject, these beautiful verses by Monsieur Arouet, in one of the moral epistles that he published nearly thirty years ago:[54]

> *Pleasures are the flowers that are divine master*
> *Enables to grow in the brambles that surround us;*
> *There are some for all ages, and by prudent care*
> *One can preserve them for the winter if one's years.*
> *But if it is necessary to pick them, use a light hand;*
> *Their temporary beauty is easily withered.*
> *Do not offer to your senses, overwhelmed by indolence,*
> *All the perfumes exhaled by Flora simultaneously.*
> *It is necessary not to see, sense and hear everything.*
> *Let us quit sensualities so as to be able to resume them.*
> *Labor is often the parent of pleasure, etc.*

That is enough on a subject that is regarded as purely frivolous; I shall not extend myself further in its justification. Sensate individuals, who know how to appreciate things, never proscribe this genre, and if it is necessary to cite a respectable authority, I will say that Monsieur de Montesquieu, finding it necessary, for want of other books, to read the *Mille et une nuits*, found so much attraction in it that I have heard him say, more than once, hat he congratulated himself for having made

---

[54] Editor's [presumably Charles Garnier's] note: "These words prove that M. le Comte de Caylus wrote this in about 1760." M. Arouet is, of course, Voltaire. The quoted lines, sometimes published separately as "Les Plaisirs" are from "Quatrième discours de la modération en tout" in *Discours en vers sur l'homme* (1734).

the acquaintance of the Arab storytellers and that he gladly read something of them every year.

In any case, I do not know whether these two tales will be successful; I do not even know whether I should publish them. I would like to combine them with a few extracts that I have made after manuscripts in the king's library, but that would require leisure that I do not have.

CADICHON; OR, EVERYTHING WORKS OUT FOR HIM WHO CAN WAIT

There was once a king and a queen who had a very small realm to govern. The king's name was Pétaud; he was a very good man, rather abrupt, simple-minded and very limited, but otherwise the best king there was in the world. His subjects were almost as great masters as him, for in the smallest circumstances they gave their opinion very loudly without being asked for it; and everyone wanted his own to be heeded and followed.[55]

The queen's name was Gillette; she had scarcely more intelligence than her husband but she was mild, timid and tranquil, which meant that she did not say much, and often in maxims; she had the submission and deference for the king that one ordinarily has for a husband on whom one's fortune depends.

As Pétaud was the only child that his father and mother, the king and queen, had had of their marriage, they had resolved, at the moment of his birth, to have him marry a little princess, the niece of an old fay named Gangan, who was then the intimate friend of Pétaud's father and mother. It is true that the princess had not yet come into the world, but on the word and the assurances of Gangan that she would one day be an accomplished person, they promised all that she wished, and even engaged themselves by oath not to go back on their word.

---

[55] "La cour de roi Pétaud" became a popular expression in France signifying an assembly in which everyone wants to speak at the same time and for his own views to prevail, thus making collective decisions impossible. Its origin is unknown but it seems to have existed prior to 1760.

Pétaud, having reached the age of twenty-five, judged it appropriate to marry in accordance with his wishes; he was unembarrassed by the promises of his father and mother, and married without their consent an extremely pretty young woman with whom he had fallen madly in love. She was only the daughter of a rich farmer, but although she had married the king's son, her good nature prevented her from being vain—which is to say, stupid.

The king, Pétaud's father, irritated by the prince's marriage, could not refuse Gangan a vengeance for the affront to both of them; he disinherited the prince, forbade him ever to appear at court, and reduced him to his legitimate inheritance, which was fixed as a rather considerable terrain of which his father-in-law had been the farmer. The only grace that was accorded him was to grant him that land in sovereignty, with the permission to bear the title of King and Majesty. A short time after his disgrace, his father died, and his mother, having obtained the regency, was not sorry to be rid of a son who, in spite of his scant intelligence, might have impeded her projects and the desire she had to reign.

Pétaud was neither ambitious nor a conqueror, so he did not take long to become accustomed to his petty state, and was very comfortable there; small as it was, he reigned there as if it had been large; and, all things considered, that was as much as he needed; the titles of King and Majesty took the place for him of a great kingdom. The most limited minds always have their portion of vanity, however; he was soon keen to imitate his father the king and create a seneschal, a procurator fiscal and a treasurer—for in those days there were no chancellors, parliaments or tax-farmers; kings rendered justice themselves and received their income quite simply. He had coins minted and composed ordinances with his seneschal for the policing of his petty state.

His father in law, whose name was Caboche, was the man to whom he awarded the dignity of seneschal; he was an honest, sincere and equitable man; he had received his share of imagination from nature in common sense, so he decided slowly, but almost always justly; he knew the quatrains of Pibrac by heart and loved to recite them.[56] That petty fortune did not render him vain, for he continued to cultivate his farms profitably as before, which gained him the confidence of his son-in-law to such an extent that His Majesty could not do without him.

Every morning, Caboche went to see the king, with whom he had breakfast. Afterwards they talked business, but more often than not the minister said: "Sire, with your permission, you don't know anything about it; let me handle it and everything will go well; every man ought to take care of his own trade, Monsieur Pibrac says."

"But what shall I do, then?" replied the king.

"Whatever you wish," Caboche replied. "Govern your wife and your vegetable garden. That's all you need."

"I believe, in fact, that you're right," said the king, "so do as you wish."

However, in order not to lose anything in terms of his reputation, he appeared on fast days in his royal mantle of woolen cloth, imprinted with golden flowers, a toque of the same fabric, and a scepter of gilded wood that he had bought from an old country actor who had quit the profession.

After his council meetings he had the Almanacs of Liege and Milan brought to him.[57] Which were sent to him every

---

[56] Guy de Faur, Seigneur de Pibrac (1529-1584) was a lawyer and poet whose chief literary legacy consisted of a long essay on the pleasures of rustic life and a series of moralistic quatrains, frequently reprinted in France, often learned by heart by schoolchildren, and translated into English more than once.

[57] The Almanach de Liège, credited to the fictitious Matthieu Lansbert was published annually from the early seventeenth century to 1792, when it became a casualty of the Revolution. It juxtaposed often-gnomic astrological predictions with commonplace household advice. Many of the *philosophes*, including Voltaire, loathed it. The *Almanach de Milan ou le*

year from Troyes in the month of July, and which he had bound in fine marbled paper with gilded edges. From one he learned the times appropriate to sowing, planting, pruning, grafting, bleeding and purging, and he had so much confidence in it that he often had himself and the queen medicated without any necessity. In the other he studied the political predictions, at which he marveled all the more because he did not understand any of them. After a few years, all those almanacs made up a little bookcase for him, which he esteemed as much as if it had been a good one, and only the seneschal and he had a key to it.

In the afternoon he occupied himself in his little royal vegetable garden, practicing what his almanac had taught him in the morning. In the evening, he sent for Caboche in order to play brusquembille or piquet until supper-time, then he supped in public with the queen, and at ten o'clock, everyone went to bed.

For her part, Gillette occupied herself with domestic affairs; she spun with her maidservants, and made excellent cheeses with cow's milk and goat's milk. Above all, she did not fail to knead a little barley-cake every morning, which she cooked under the ashes, and carried it immediately, with a cream cheese, into her little garden, to the foot of a rose-bush, as she had been ordered to do by a dream on the day after her marriage.

The tranquility that they both enjoyed in their little kingdom was only troubled by the desire to have children. The king had consulted, but in vain, physicians, charlatans and seeresses; with regard to fays, he was too piqued against them to have recourse to them. Gillette, by contrast, had a perfect confidence in their power, but she dared not make it known, for fear of displeasing her husband. In spite of that, Gangan, unsatisfied by Pétaud's disinheritance had avenged herself

---

Pecheur fidèle was its principal competitor in France in the early eighteenth century

403

further on the poor queen by condemning her to be simultaneously sterile and fecund.

Gillette had been married for two years without the slightest appearance of pregnancy, and Pétaud was beginning to despair of having children when one day, the midwife of his kingdom, who was the queen's first lady-in-waiting, came to announce that Her Majesty was pregnant. At that news, transported by joy, he embraced her wholeheartedly and, taking from his finger a beautiful ring made of a cat's-eye, he presented it to her.

He did not stop there, for in the evening he gave a great supper to all the nobles of his realm, after which he fired all his artillery personally, which consisted of a dozen wheel-lock arquebuses and six carbines with forks. It is claimed that his immoderate joy caused him to say things during supper contrary to his dignity, and that he replied to the remonstrations of his seneschal, while pouring that minister a large glass of wine: "Thank you very much, father-in-law; perhaps you're right, but after all, one doesn't become a father every day. Anyway, let's not talk about it anymore, and let's rejoice; for, in my place, perhaps you'd be just as sage." Caboche made no reply, and each of them retired, very content with Their Majesties.

As the king was loved by his subjects, there was rejoicing throughout the realm on the same day and at the same hour; and everyone waited patiently for the childbirth. They were very surprised, however, when, after nine months had gone by, the queen having felt violent pains, suddenly became tranquil again. Her pregnancy, however, far from diminishing, only augmented for a further nine months, at the end of which time she felt the same afflictions, but without any success. Eventually, they saw, with the utmost astonishment, an event so singular repeated seven times, to the great displeasure of the king, the queen and the midwife, her first lady-in-waiting.

From time to time the king riffled through his almanacs and consulted their predictions, without finding anything regarding pregnant women, and that made him very impatient.

He often asked the queen when she would care to finish giving birth, but the queen, replied, very tranquilly: "Sire, Everything works out for him who can wait." So no matter how impatient he became and no matter how much the queen wanted to obey him, Gangan's edict was executed, and the princess never ceased to be pregnant for more than five years.

No one knew what to think of such a singular adventure, when one day, when the king was in his orchard with his seneschal, someone came to tell them that the queen had just given birth to a prince and a princess. They ran to her immediately, and had scarcely entered the room than she gave birth to another son and daughter, who were followed a moment later by two more.

"Mercy!" cried the king. "What's this, Madame, and when will you finish?"

Then the queen, uttering a loud scream that announced something further, replied: "I don't know, Sire, but I know that everything works out for him who can wait."

"Wait!" said the king. "Oh, by my scepter, I can't do anything about it; if I stay here any longer I'll have as many children, it seems to me as there are apples in my orchard."

In fact, scarcely had he gone out than the queen gave birth to a fine boy, who rendered his mother the calm that she had desired for a long time. He had the most beautiful eyes that had ever been seen, very white skin and jet black eyebrows and hair. As he was born coiffed, the king and the queen felt more inclination for him than for the others, and the princess absolutely insisted on nursing her little Cadichon—that was what they named him—herself.

After eighteen months, the three princes became so lively and sprightly that the nurses could no longer cope with them. When they complained to the king, he replied to them: "Let them be; when they're my age, they won't be so lively; I once was myself, and it will come." The three princesses, by contrast, were mild, but so somber and so tranquil that they remained wherever they were put—which had the result that the king preferred his sons to his daughters, and the queen liked her daughters better than her sons, except for Cadichon, who, having none of the defects of his brothers and sisters, was the prettiest child in the world. He would soon have been spoiled if a benevolent fay, unknown to Gangan and even to Gillette, had not endowed him at the moment of his birth with an even and invariable character.

When it was a question of weaning Their Majesties' children, a extraordinary council was assembled, composed of the seneschal, the procurator fiscal, the treasurer and the nursemaids. After much argument it was resolved, on the advice of Caboche, to make use of cow's milk for the three boys and goat's milk for the three girls; that advice appeared very appropriate to correct, in a simple fashion, the vivacity of the princes and the sluggishness of the princesses.

When they were more advanced in age, however, and it was necessary to give them more solid aliments, they consumed so much that the king's revenues were considerably diminished. In addition, as the princes had only lost a part of their vivacity by virtue of their first nourishment, and the princesses had acquired a new one, there was a din and frightful arguments all day long. They squabbled and they wailed, and wore out so many clothes so rapidly that there were scarcely sufficient. There was only little Cadichon who was mild and obedient, so his brothers and sisters always made him some niche.

The king often said to the queen: "Your three daughters are growing furiously, and by my scepter, I don't know what I can do with them; for my sons, I can give them the leases on my farms, and the profits will be theirs, but for your daughters, it's different."

To which the queen replied: "Let's be patient, Sire. Everything works out for him who can wait."

While King Pétaud was becoming anxious and Queen Gillette remained tranquil, their children reached the age of seven. All the people making up their court were already voicing their opinions—or, rather, their decisions—as to the establishment of the princes and princesses when one morning, as the queen came to knead her little cake, she perceived on her table a pretty little blue mouse nibbling the dough. Her first impulse was to chase it away, but an involuntary sentiment stopped her. She considered it attentively, and was very surprised to see it pick up the little cake and carry it into the fireplace.

Her tranquility gave way to her impatience and, running after the mouse with the design of taking away its prey, she saw both disappear and only found in their stead a wrinkled old lady about a foot tall. After a few grimaces and unintelligible words, that little figure put the shovel and tongs in a cross, drew three circles and three triangles above them with the broom, uttered seven little shrill cries, and ended up by throwing the broom over her head. In spite of her fear, the queen did not fail to notice that the old woman, while designing the circles and triangles, had pronounced distinctly the three words *confidence, discretion* and *happiness*.

She was seeking to penetrate the meaning of it all when a noise she heard in the next room extracted her from her reverie. As she thought she recognized Cadichon's voice she ran in there immediately, but she had scarcely opened the door when she perceived three huge cockchafers, each of which was holding one of her daughters in its feet, and three huge damsel-flies, which were carrying her three sons in their beaks. All of them flew out of the window, singing in chorus, and very melodiously: "Cockchafer fly, fly, fly."

What touched Gillette the most was to see Cadichon in the middle of them, between the paws of the blue mouse; they were both in a little chariot made from a large pink snail shell, drawn by two goldfinches, perfectly plumed. The mouse, which appeared to be much larger than animals of that species usually are, had a beautiful blue-green robe, a mantlet of black velvet, a headdress knotted under the chin and two little blue horns above its forehead.

The chariot, the cockchafers and the damsel-flies departed so rapidly that the queen soon lost sight of them. Then, more occupied with the loss of Cadichon and her children than fays and their power, she started screaming and weeping with all her might. The king, who heard her, came running, followed by his seneschal, and wanted to know the reason. But Gillette's dolor was so intense that she could only reply with the words: "The cockchafers...the damsel-flies...oh Sire, they've stolen our children!"

The king, who only paid attention to the last words, quit Gillette abruptly and ordered Caboche to fetch two muskets from his antechamber—for he always had half a dozen there, awaiting guards. Then, traversing his royal vegetable garden, he reached open country with the design of pursuing and killing the kidnappers.

About an hour after he had left, the queen, whose tears were exhausted, was no longer uttering anything but sighs at the loss of her children when she heard something buzzing around her and saw a piece of paper folded in a square fall at her feet. She picked it up immediately, opened it precipitately, and read these words:

Calm your anxiety, my dear Gillette, and remember that your happiness depends on confidence and discretion. You have commenced it by giving me cakes and cheeses, and my gratitude will do the rest; but always be convinced that everything works out for those who can wait, and in that regard you ought to have every hope in your friend, the Fay of the Fields.

That note, combined with her confidence in the power of fays, succeeded in calming her fears, and, addressing a little linnet that she perceived over the awning of her bed, she said: "Linnet, lovely linnet, I'll do everything you wish, but give me, I beg you, when you can, news of my little Cadichon."

At those words, the linnet flapped its wings, and flew away, singing, and the queen was convinced that she heard it say: "I consent to that." She thanked it, and bowed deeply.

Meanwhile the king and the seneschal, weary of having run around in vain, returned to the house, and found the queen so tranquil that the king was almost scandalized by it. He asked her several question in order to know the reason, to which Gillette never answered anything but: "Everything works out for him who can wait."

That sang-froid made the king so impatient that he would have become angry with her if his seneschal had not remonstrated with him, saying that Gillette was right and that Pibrac and councilor Matthieu had told him before her in one of their quatrains,[58] which he recited immediately. The king, for whom Caboche was an oracle, shut up, and listened with attention to a fine little speech he gave him on the inconveniences of having children and the chagrins and expense they caused their parents.

"By my scepter," said the king, "father-in-law is right and those seven brats would have ruined me if they'd remained in my house much longer; so, many thanks to whomever has taken charge of them; as they came, they've gone; nothing but time has been lost; so let's rejoice and start again."

The queen, who dreaded taking too much, made no reply, and the king, having nothing more to say, returned to his cabinet to play piquet with his seneschal.

While all this was happening in the abode of King Pétaud, the queen, his mother, wearying of a widowhood that had lasted a long time, resolved to marry again. To that effect, she cast her eyes upon a young prince, a neighbor of her kingdom and the sovereign of the Green Isles. He was handsome, well-made and his intelligence had as many graces as his person. His pleasures were his only occupation, there was no talk of anything but his gallantries, and it was said with assurance that no pretty woman in his realm had resisted him.

The advantageous reputation and portrait of that prince turned the queen's head so thoroughly that she flattered herself with the notion of being loved by him and fixing his incon-

---

[58] Pibrac's quatrains were often combined in volumes with those of Pierre Matthieu (1563-1621), a far more prolific writer and historian.

stancy. There was only one difficulty, which was that she was neither young nor lovable. She was tall and thin, with small eyes and a long dangling nose, a very wide mouth and a passable beard. Such a face might be advantageous to a queen for imposing, but it was hardly likely to inspire amour.

One cannot be entirely blind to one's faults when they are evident to a certain degree; she felt, in moments of reflection, that in the state she was in, it would be impossible for her to please the young King of the Green Isles, and that, in order to succeed in that, it was necessary to have beauty, or at least youth. But how could she achieve that? How could she change her gray hair and homely features into a lovable face with child-like graces and provocative expressions?

It is true that Gangan, her friend, would have been a great help in that instance, if that fay had not pressed her several times to adopt her niece and to designate her as the heir to her crown; thus, there was everything to be feared if she excited her anger by such a proposition. The old queen sensed that, hesitated and debated, but looked so long and hard at the portrait of the handsome Prince of the Green Isles that amour finally prevailed over the regard that she owed the fay. She made her party to her sentiments and implored her, in the most pressing terms, to lend her the assistance of her art and not to refuse her that essential mark of her amity. She even went so far as to show her the portrait of the young prince and demand her approval of her design.

Gangan could not hide her surprise, but she dissimulated her resentment; she foresaw the consequence there would be if she declared herself overtly against the marriage, since the King of the Green Isles, who had almost ruined his estates to subsidize his expenditure, was capable of concluding it out of self-interest, and sustaining it with the aid of a powerful genius, the protector of his realm. Thus, feigning to lend a hand to the affair, she promised the queen to work as soon as possible on her rejuvenation; but she promised herself at the same time to deceive her and to make it impossible for her to carry out her design.

On the day that the fay had marked for the execution of her promises, she appeared clad in a long satin robe, flesh-colored and silver; her coiffure was only composed of artificial flowers and tinsel pompoms. A little amaranth dwarf carried her train, and had a black Chinese lacquer box under his left arm. The queen received her with the greatest marks of respect and gratitude, and begged her, after the initial compliments, not to defer her happiness.

The fay consented to that, had everyone withdraw, and ordered her dwarf to close the doors and the windows. Then, having taken from her box a vellum book garnished with silver locks, a wand composed of three metals and a phial containing a clear green liquid, she had the queen sit down on a cushion in the middle of the room and commanded the dwarf to stand facing Her Majesty. Then, having traced three circles around them, she read from her book, touched him three times with her wand and threw the aforementioned liquid over them.

The queen's facial features gradually diminished then, and the stature of the little dwarf grew in proportion, with the result that in less than three minutes they had changed form without feeling the slightest pain. Although the queen was armed with courage, she could not see the growth of the dwarf without some dread, but blue-tinted flames that suddenly rose up from the three circles augmented her fear so much that she fainted. Then the fay, having finished her enchantment, opened a window and disappeared with her page, who, tall as he had become, picked up his mistress's train again and her Chinese lacquer box.

The first thing the queen did, after having recovered her senses, was to stand in front of her mirror. She saw there, with an extreme pleasure, that her features were charming, but she did not remark that the features in question were those of a pretty girl eight or nine years old, that her coiffure had taken the form of a small cap on top of long blonde tresses, and that her costume had changed into a short dress with dangling sleeves and a lace apron.

All that, combined with her tall stature, which the charm had not diminished, produced something quite bizarre; however, that did not strike her, for, of all the ideas that she had had before her transformation, the only ones that remained to her were those relating to the King of the Green Isles and the amour that she felt for him. She was therefore as content with herself as her courtiers were astonished.

No one knew what had become of her, or what course of action to adopt, when the prime minister, on whom all the grandees depended, overcame his embarrassment and decided that, far from annoying the queen, it was necessary, on the contrary, to flatter her tastes and whims, and he commenced by ordering his wife and daughters to conform to her desires. Soon, in order to please the minister, their example was followed, and in very little time the entire court was dressed like the queen and imitated her in everything. No one, even the men, talked any longer except in a childish manner; they only played madame, give me back my daughter, knucklebones and battle. The cooks were only employed in making baked custards, tartlets and puff pastry. People spent their time dressing and undressing dolls, and in all the games and snacks there was no question of anything but the King of the Green Isles; the queen talked about him a hundred times a day, and always called him "my little husband."

She asked for him incessantly and accepted, for some time, the excuses of which people made use to flatter her, but in the end, the gaiety gave way to petulance; she experienced all the caprices of a child who does not have what she wants, and whose will no one dares oppose. After being amused for some time by such a singular event—for the idleness of a court is such that its members are amused by everything—people became impatient with the puerilities of the overgrown child; they wearied of the constraint and complaisance it was necessary to have. Gradually, they left, and she was on the point of being completely abandoned when it was learned that the King of the Green Isles, who was traveling in the neighboring realms was to arrive imminently in that one.

At that news, courage returned. The queen became so lively and cheerful again that she did nothing but sing and dance while awaiting the prince. That fortunate moment arrived; she ran to meet him, and, although it was represented to her that ceremonial did not permit it, she absolutely insisted on receiving him at the foot of the staircase. While descending the stairs, however, her feet got tangled in her dress, which she had not tucked up, and she fell rather rudely. Although her hands had protected her head and her nose was only slightly scratched, her fear was so great that she uttered loud screams. She was carried to her room; her face was bathed with the Queen of Hungary's water,[59] and they succeeded in calming her down by telling her that her little husband wanted to see her.

The prince did appear, in fact, but the sight of an object so ridiculous made him burst out into such violent fits of laughter that he was obliged to leave the room, and even the palace. The queen, who saw him leave, started shouting with all her might that she wanted her little husband. People ran after him and pressed him to return, but all they said was futile; he never wanted to consent to it and drew away promptly from a court where everyone appeared to him to be insane.

The queen, who learned of his departure, was inconsolable. People tried in vain to calm her down; her ill-humor only became more insupportable. The yoke seemed too harsh even to those who were most attached to her; the others, ashamed of being subjects of such a queen, proposed taking the crown away from her. That party was about to prevail when Gangan, who had only intended to put her off the marriage, disenchanted her and restored her original form.

---

[59] "The Queen of Hungary's Water" was an alcohol-based perfume dating from the fourteenth century, consisting of various herbs dissolved in brandy. Although primarily used as a fragrance it was also employed as a medicament, employed both internally and externally.

At the sight of her natural face, she nearly stabbed her-self in despair; she had thought herself charming with the one she had just quit, but no longer saw in its place anything but a visage more than sixty years old and an ugliness that she had detested. She did not believe that she had been ridiculous in the state from which she had emerged, and she had lost noth-ing of her amour; thus, the loss of her youth and that of the Prince of the Green Isles threw her into a languor which made people fear for her life, and inspired at the same time an im-placable hatred of the fay Gangan. As regards her subjects, they pitied her, but regarded the event as a just punishment for the sacrifice she had made of maternal tenderness and grati-tude to her ambition and her insensate desires.

It was about this time that the Fay of the Fields abducted the children of Pétaud and Gillette; that generous fay was the protectress of those who found themselves obliged to spend their lives in the country; she employed herself in preventing or diminishing the disgraces might overtake them, and was all the more able to protect them because she possessed the amity of the Queen of the Fays.

Bambine Isle, of which that sovereign had given her the government, was the place to which she transported the four sons and the three daughters of King Pétaud and Queen Gil-lette. That island was only inhabited by children under the protection of fays, nursemaids and those destined to serve them. A continuous spring reigned there; the trees and mead-ows were always covered in fruit and flowers, and the soil produced of its own accord, without any culture, everything that could flatter taste and the eyes. The promenades there were charming, the gardens varied and filled with pretty little carriages of all forms, pulled by long-eared barbets.

The nicest thing of all was that the walls of the children's bedrooms were made of sugar-candy, the floors of candied lemon-peel and the furniture of excellent Reims gingerbread. When the children were very good, they had plenty of it to eat, but it only ever appeared then. In addition to that, all kinds of pretty little dolls were found in the streets and promenades, magnificently dressed, which walked and danced on their own.

Little girls who were not proud, greedy or disobedient had only to wish, and immediately, bonbons and fruits detached themselves and came to find them; the dolls threw themselves into their arms and allowed themselves to be dressed and undressed, caressed and whipped with an unparalleled discretion and obedience. When, on the contrary, they had committed some fault, the doll fled, pulling a face, and its little costume became ugly and ragged.

As regards the little boys, when they were not obstinate, deceitful or lazy, they had marionettes, kites and rackets, and all the toys one can imagine; but when their nursemaids were discontented with them, the marionettes mocked them, flicked their noses and told them all the naughty things they had done; the kites lacked wind, and the rackets had holes in them; in sum, nothing worked, and the more obstinate they were, the worse things became.

There were punishments and rewards of these kinds for all ages: for example, fining oneself mounted on a donkey when one thought it was a nicely-harnessed little horse, or hearing people say: "Oh, how ugly she is! How dirty she is! What is that doing here?" while other little damsels were well-dressed and fêted. In sum, nothing was neglected to correct their faults of heart and mind; and, in order to instruct them while amusing them, there were enabled to read the annals of Faerie, which contained the most remarkable stories of that empire, such as those of Javotte, Nabotine, Landore, Jeannette and many others; for the Fay of the Fields was very fond of them, and assembled them with great care from all the kingdoms of the world.

While the children of Pétaud and Gillette remained on Bambine Isle, all imaginable means were put to use to vanquish the obstinacy of the three boys and the pride of the three girls, but those faults, far from diminishing, were only augmented with age. For four years, the particular interest that the

415

governing fay took in those children, combined with the care, attention and patience of the nursemaids, had changed almost nothing in their character, and, sensing only too well that their nature was prevailing over their education, she no longer hoped to change them by means of simple methods and was obliged to have recourse to violent remedies, such as metamorphosis.

That extremity was harsh, in truth, but it was infallible for improving characters. In spite of their changes, the children conserved their ideas and the sentiment of they were and what they had been, but submitted to the laws of their estate. As soon as the fay, who had the gift of penetrating thoughts, believed them to be corrected, she rendered their original form to them, with her amity, and often procured them an advantageous establishment. She therefore changed, but with pain, Pétaud's three sons into polchinels and his daughters into dames-gigognes, and condemned them to be marionettes for three years.[60]

As she was as content with Prince Cadichon as she was dissatisfied with his brothers and sisters, the fay did not want him to witness their disgrace, and resolved to take him away. It was only a matter of finding him a refuge where he would be safe from the malevolence of Gangan; in order not to take anything for granted, however, she thought it appropriate to consult the Queen of the Fays, her friend, and take her advice as to what she ought to do. With that design, she put on her green velvet farthingale, her jonquil satin mantlet and her little blue hood; then, having harnessed six white cockchafers with pink ribbon to her gilded wicker poste-chaise, she departed swiftly and arrived shortly afterwards in the Fortunate Isle where the Queen of the Fays ordinarily resided.

---

[60] Polchinel is the French equivalent of Punch in English puppet shows. Dame Gigogne also features in such shows as a fecund mother, in live comedies the part was often played by a man, and she was the ancestor of the English pantomime dame.

Having dismounted at the end of a magnificent avenue of orange trees and lemon trees, she entered the courtyard of the castle, where she found a line of twenty-four black men six feet tall, with long tucked-up robes and carrying polished steel clubs over their shoulder; behind them were twenty-four black ostriches with red and blue spots, which they held on leashes, and they maintained a profound silence. The black men were wicked fays condemned to fill those posts for several centuries, depending on the quantity of their crimes. As soon as they perceived the fay they saluted her, letting their clubs fall to the pavement; as it was also steel, it rendered a ringing sound and sparks. That honor was due to all those who, like the fay, had a government.

After having climbed the stairs, composed of porphyry, jasper, agate and lapis, she perceived in the first chamber twelve young women, simply dressed but without hoods; they only had a clavier in their belt and half-wands, with which they saluted her, as the black men had done. She returned the salute, for that employment was usually reserved for those who were soon to be initiated into the art of faerie. She traversed a long sequence of magnificently furnished apartments and arrived in the queen's antechamber, which she found filled with fays who had come from all over the world, some on business and others to pay court.

There was almost no one in the queen's cabinet any longer when old Gangan was seen to emerge. But for the respect the fays had for their sovereign, they would not have been able to help bursting into laughter at the sight of a figure as grotesque as Gangan's. Over a corps de robe of green satin, decked with blue and gold lace, she wore a broad farthingale of the same fabric, embroidered with pink caterpillars and pompoms and a demi-girdle enriched with emeralds. Hanging from a silver key were a little mirror on a box of beauty-spots, a large watch and a coin-purse; her ears were charged with two large pendants of pearls and rubies, and she had a yellow velvet hood on her head with a brooch of amethysts and topazes; a large bouquet of jasmines ornamented the front of her

417

body and ten or twelve beauty-spots dispersed over old rouge covered a wrinkled skin the color of a desiccated rose.

If the Fay of the Fields was astonished by Gangan's ridiculous attire, the latter was no less so to encounter her rival at the moment she least expected it. She was not unaware of the protection that the fay had accorded the children of Pétaud and Gillette, but as the place forbade her to let her resentment burst forth she dissimulated it and affected an air of politeness mingled with arrogance.

"What, Madame," she said to her, "you've resolved to quit the calm of the country to come and confound yourself in the tumult of the court? You must have very strong reasons for that...."

"Those that bring me here," the Fay of the Fields interrupted, "don't resemble yours; interest and ambition have never been the motives for my protection, and I only accord it to those who are worthy and grateful."

"I believe," Gangan replied, "that turkeys and geese are good people."

"That's true," said the fay, hotly," and much more so than Gangans, for they are not unjust; what do you say to that?"

The dispute would not have stopped here if the Fay of the Fields had not been informed that the queen was alone and that she wanted to speak to her, so the two fays saluted one another and separated, like women who hate one another perfectly.

The queen, who perceived the emotion that the dispute had caused her friend, pretended to be unaware of it and asked to be informed. The Fay of the Fields, charmed to satisfy her mistress's curiosity, did not hesitate to tell her the story of the unjust reasons that Gangan had had for persecuting King Pétaud and Queen Gillette, and that pity had caused her to attempt to thwart the designs of the perfidious fay.

"Your action in laudable," the queen said to her, "and I like to see that generous ardor to protect the unfortunate, but I fear, however, that Gangan might avenge herself further for the kindness that you have shown the good Gillette and her children; she is wicked, and I often receive complaints about her, but be sure that if she abuses her power against you again, I shall punish her for it in a terrible and striking fashion. I can't say any more than that; it's time for the council. When I come back, we'll consult together about the means of thwarting the designs of your enemy."

As soon as the Fay of the Fields was alone, she could not resist the desire to consult her sovereign's books. All the mysteries of Faerie are revealed there, and one discovers, day by day, everything that is happening in the world; but it is only the queen's prerogative to suspend or prevent events; she has the same power over the fays as she has over humans.

Cadichon's protectress had scarcely opened the books when she read distinctly there that, by the power of grand faerie, the perfidious Gangan was abducting the young prince at that very moment and that she was transporting him to the Inaccessible Isle, where she had retained her niece since the moment of her birth. At that sight, she immediately trembled for the life of her young protégé, and afterwards for his heart and sentiments, for she knew that the wicked fay was more capable of corrupting him than forming him. The disturbance that that incident cast into her soul gave way to reflections, and she was thinking about means to prevent the consequences of that enterprise when the queen emerged from the council and came to rejoin her.

By the sadness the queen remarked on her friend's face, she judged that something had happened during her absence, and spoke to her.

"You wanted to satisfy your curiosity," she said, "and you've learned things that I wanted to hide from your knowledge. It's true that I couldn't refuse Gangan the power of grand faerie, since it's due to her antiquity, in accordance with our laws; but the knowledge that I have of her character made me limit that power to a certain span of time. Be assured, generous fay, that after that, your enemy will be severely punished if she abuses the very power that she holds by virtue of our laws and my generosity. However, to give you proof of my amity today and to shield against attack the other children of Gillette, in whom you are interested, take this phial, rub them with the liquid it contains; it's the water of invisibility, it only hides objects from the eyes of fays, and its charm is such that Gangan, with all her power, cannot vanquish it. Go, my dear friend, remember that your queen loves generosity, that she protects virtue, and always count on her protection and tenderness.

At those words, the fay took the queen's hand respectfully, kissed it and left.

She was no sooner on her island than she made use of the water of invisibility; she rubbed the three polchinels and the three dames-gigognes with it, and only reserved the extremities of their noses, which she left visible, in order to be able to recognize them. Then, having given her orders and consulted her books, she departed to go to the home of King Pétaud, where she had read that her presence was necessary.

In fact, when she arrived, that prince's little kingdom was in combustion, and this was the subject of it. For a long time, already, the house in which His Majesty had lodged thus far, which his father-in-law the seneschal had inhabited before him, had been falling down, in spite of the repairs that had been made to it. He had resolved, in a private council with his master mason, who was also his first architect, to build a new one.

That officer of the crown, having not made anything new or Their Majesties for a long time, had demolished the old building completely, with the intention of beginning a new one, which, according to him, would be far more magnificent than the other. But the king's savings, since the abduction of his children, and his annual income not being sufficient for the execution of the new edifice, he made the decision, on the advice of his treasurer and the procurator fiscal, to impose a tax in order to furnish the expense of the building.

His subjects, who had not yet paid taxes, murmured very loudly and swore not to obey. They even threatened to complain to the queen-mother and render her the arbiter of their complaints. Their discontentment was combined with Caboche's remonstrations; he claimed that it was ridiculous to make others pay for something that could neither be useful nor profitable to them; that His Majesty was only, fundamentally, a man like any other; that, having his own property and income, he ought not to take those of others in order to spend more; that, in consequence, when one only had the means to have a house, it was necessary not to have a castle; and that anyone who only had one écu should only spend one écu.

All these arguments seemed very good to the king, but at the same moment, the procurator-fiscal and the treasures cried to him that he was the master, and that it was not worth the trouble of having subjects if one could not make them pay for the care that one took in governing them; that they were made for paying and kings for spending; and that only the head of a seneschal was capable of thinking otherwise and advising the same.

The king found that they were reasoning very accurately, and concluded that the tax should be levied; however, everyone else came to his own conclusion and made his own decision.

"They'll have to pay," said some.

"They won't pay," said the others.

"It won't be thus," said Caboche, "for I've made up my mind."

"It will be," said the procurator-fiscal, "or I'll lose my Latin."

In sum, there was a great racket, in which no one could hear themselves speak.

The king, who no longer knew what to think, did not know which side to take. When he was with the queen, he sometimes said to her: "Oh, by my scepter, if this goes on, I'll drop everything, and then anyone can be king who wants to be; for I'll go far way, so far that I won't her any mention of the kingdom, the people or the house."

"Don't be impatient, Sire," the queen replied, tranquilly. "I've already had the honor of telling your majesty that everything works out for him who waits."

"Eh? What the devil do you want me to wait for?" replied the king. "If whoever took away our children had left us a house in their place, we wouldn't be where we are, but doubtless Gangan has put them in good order, and if this goes on, we won't have any more houses than we have children." Then he driveled on against the fays, so much that the good Gillette lost her patience with him.

The fay, who had been a witness for some time to what was happening, and the anxieties from which the queen was suffering, finally showed herself to her under the form of a linnet, which she had already used once before, and tranquilized her by assuring that she would soon give her convincing proofs of her amity and her protection.

Transported by joy, Gillette kissed her a thousand times, after having asked for her permission; begged her to stay, and promised her, in order to engage her to do so, to make her a little cake every day for as long as she remained with her, composed of millet flour, hemp-seed and milk.

The fay consented to that, and her promises did not take long to be accomplished.

A fortnight after her arrival, the king, who ordinarily got up early in the morning, was strangely surprised to see that he was in a brand new house, very comfortable and solidly build. I say a house, for that is all that it was, in no way a palace; it had no architecture, painting, sculpture or decoration. On the ground floor there was a kitchen, a pantry, a dining room and an audience hall, on the first floor an antechamber, a bedroom, a cabinet, a wardrobe or the queen and a large cabinet in a wing for the king, in which the aforementioned bookcase was already placed. Up above were fine grain-lofts, nicely paneled, which had the most beautiful view in the world. A milking-shed had not been forgotten, with all the utensils, but what was most admirable was that the entire house was well furnished and equipped with everything that was necessary. The furniture was all perfectly similar, in form and fabrics, to Their Majesties' previous furniture, and could have been mistaken for it if it had not been new.

It is easy to imagine Pétaud's astonishment on finding himself in an unfamiliar house, but it was something else when, having opened one of the windows of his bedroom, he perceived, instead of his little royal vegetable garden, a large grass lawn, at the end of which was a rather fine pond, terminated by a wood of tall trees. To the right of the lawn there was a vegetable garden filled with all the different legumes, and to the left an orchard planted with all sorts of fruit trees.

He considered all that for some time, but, his surprise giving way to joy, he ran to the queen's bed, where she was still asleep, and woke her up, exclaiming: "Wife, wife, get up! Come and see a brand new house and magnificent gardens. Do you know what all this is? I don't understand any of it myself."

The queen hardly had time to pick up her skirt, her indoor jacket and her slippers before she was at the window with the king, who immediately took her to the whole apartment, and from there to the ground floor, where they found the kitchen and the pantry equipped with everything that they might need. All those marvels did not fail to alarm the good Pétaud, but the queen, who had no doubt as to where it had all come from, had not the slightest fear, although she dared not say anything about it.

They were both in that situation when the seneschal, who had been looking for the king's house for an hour, entered that one, more out of the duty of his responsibilities than in the hope of encountering Their Majesties. He did not know what to think of a house built overnight, and although he was less fearful than his son-in-law, he only began to be reassured when he saw that he was still in the country. The king, for his part, was very glad to see him arrive, and, still holding on to the queen's arm, they went over the house for a second time from top to bottom, and all the gardens.

Everyone argued a great deal about that adventure; some thought that Their Majesties were very bold to live in a house built by the fays, at the risk of being teased; others, by contrast, claimed that they were doing the right thing, and that it was to be hoped that all the old houses in the kingdom might be rebuilt in the same way.

As one adapts easily to wellbeing and novelties, after having talked about it a great deal, they did not talk about it any longer, and in a short time, the king was as accustomed to his new house as if he had been living in it all his life.

By that means, there was no more talk of taxes; tranquility returned to the state, and union between the great officers of the crown. There was only the poor architect who thought about hanging himself, but he contented himself with sending genii and fays to the devil and calling them magicians and sorcerers a hundred times over.

While the Fay of the Fields was producing all these marvels, she remarked in Gillette so much respect for the fays and gratitude for her that, sensing herself increasingly attached to the interests of the queen, she could not refuse to make a longer sojourn in her court than she had projected. She reassured her as to the fate of her children, and told her about their punishment and the reasons she had had for taking them to that extremity; but as true and tender amity makes a mystery of the most interesting things when they can be afflicting for the beloved individual, she carefully concealed the abduction of her dear Cadichon and the alarms that she felt on that score herself. Then, having recommended her to confidence, patience and discretion, if she wanted to achieve happiness, she quit her, with regret, in order to return to her government of Bambine Isle.

As soon as she arrived there, she was informed urgently of an event unprecedented since the establishment of the island. The senior nursemaid, who had fulfilled the functions of government during the fay's absence, told her that a few mutinous, stubborn children, who had been pardoned several times, supported by dolls, their friends, had revolted, in the design of no longer obeying their nursemaids; that the spirit of revolt had gained ground so rapidly that it had been very difficult to stem its course; that, to that effect, making use of her authority, she had commenced by imprisoning the dolls in their boxes, and with regard to the children, she had condemned some of them only to have dry bread to eat for a fortnight, and others to night coiffure for a month, or to be enclosed between four chairs for two hours a day, until they asked for pardon publicly.

The governing fay approved of the conduct of the senior nursemaid, and praised her abundantly for her zeal; but as an example was required without setting aside the general law, she condemned the most mutinous of the rebels to be marionettes for a hundred years, and obliged them to serve in different kingdoms of the world, for the livelihood of fairground performers and the spectacle of the people. She let herself go to that rigor all the more because she learned that her six protégés had had no part in the rebellion. Charmed by the change that was beginning to take place within them, she summoned them to appear before her and, addressing the tips of their noses—for she could not see any more of them—she made them a reprimand more gentle than severe, and sent them away promising them her amity and recompenses, if in future, she had reason be satisfied.

Although that event and her duty did not permit her to absent herself from a place where her person seemed so necessary, she could not resist for long the interest she felt for Cadichon and the impatience she had to learn news of him. Thus, as soon as she thought herself less useful to her little people, she departed promptly with the design of satisfying her curiosity and tenderness for the young prince.

In order not to be perceived by the genii and fays who were continually traveling the median region of the atmosphere, she took the little poste-chaise, which she sealed exactly on all sides, equipped herself with the utensils of faerie, and above all, did not forget the water of invisibility. Then, having ordered her six lizards to fly at top speed, she arrived in the vicinity of the Inaccessible Isle in a few minutes. There she got down, made her vehicle appear, and, having rubbed herself with the aforementioned water, surmounted without being seen all the obstacles that might have opposed her passage.

In order to forbid genii and fays access to her island, Gangan had surrounded it with a triple barrier, formed by a rapid torrent that rolled stones and tree-trunks in its waters. The shores of the island were defended by twenty-four dragons of enormous size, and the flames that they vomited at the sight of fays or genii rose up to the clouds and formed, in coming together, an impenetrable wall of fire.

Scarcely a quarter of an hour after the Fay of the Fields sought to inform herself, without being seen, of the fate of Cadichon, hazard furnished her with the moist favorable opportunity. She saw Gangan, accompanied by a diva—for she only made use of malevolent genii. Her face appeared to be inflamed by anger, and she was speaking with a great deal of gesticulation. The Fay of the Fields, profiting from her invisibility, resolved to listen, and heard Gangan speaking to her companion in approximately these terms:

"Yes, my dear Barbaree, you see me in despair; I'm losing forever the greatest kingdom in the world; Pétaud's ingrate mother has died without ever wanting to be reconciled with me. That's not all; she had engaged her subjects by oath never to receive any successor from my hand, and even to render the crown to her son or to one of her grandsons. I've tried to regain the people by mans of my benefits, but I found an inveterate hatred against me; they've refused my gifts, regarding them as so many perfidies and treasons, and by virtue of a unanimous and authentic deliberation to follow the intentions of the queen they've succeeded in stealing from me a throne on which I had counted on putting my niece.

"But those ingrate subjects won't be long delayed in experiencing my just wrath; and to begin with those who are the principal causes of my disgrace, take one of my strongest griffins from the stables, fly to Bambine Isle, seize Cadichon's brothers and sisters and bring them to this island. I'll take charge of abducting Pétaud and Gillette, and when I have them all assembled, I'll change them into rabbits and their children into basset hounds.

"If a residue of pity that I still have for Cadichon abandons me, I won't answer for him not experiencing my anger as well; let's go and prepare everything for the execution of my designs, and let's think, my dear Barbaree that, having quit the laws of peris to follow those of divas, we have become the enemies of fays and humans, and that we ought not to neglect anything to overwhelm them with the weight of our hatred."

The Fay of the Fields could not hear that discourse without shivering; she remained motionless for some time; then recalling her reason and sensing what consequence there was in not remaining any longer in his terrible abode, she made the decision to leave and to go as soon as possible to implore the power of the Queen of the Fays.

She went back to the other side of the island, but she had scarcely descended to the ground when the sky darkened, the earth trembled and frightful roars, mingled with thunder and lightning, seemed to announce the imminent destruction of the world. A few moments later, calm returned to the atmosphere, but as the daylight darkened more and more, it gave way to a new spectacle as terrible as the previous one. The twenty-four dragons, uttering frightful howls, launched torrents of flames against one another, and formed a combat of fire that ended up by consuming them.

Daylight returned, and in place of the torrent and the island, all that appeared was an arid rock. A that moment, a black ostrich took flight from its summit, carrying on its back Prince Cadichon and the little princess, Gangan's niece.

All those prodigies had not astonished the Fay of the Fields as much as she was touched by the situation of those lovable children, her tenderness having counseled her to follow them, she made her vehicle reappear immediately and departed with so much diligence that she had on caught up with the black ostrich. Her initial design was to remove the prince and princess from it, but, having perceived that it was taking the route to the Fortunate Isle, she contented herself with following it and observing it closely.

In fact, after a few minutes, the ostrich landed on the island and directed its steps toward the Queen of the Fays. That sovereign, seated at the entrance to her palace on a golden throne enriched with precious stones, was surrounded by her twelve fays, the twenty-four black guardsmen mentioned previously, and a numerous court. As the ostrich approached the throne the Fay of the Fields seized the prince and the princess and cried them to the feet of the queen. Then the ostrich resumed its original form and character; confusion, chagrin and despair were painted on her face by turns, and she was in the cruelest expectation of what was about to happen to her when the queen addressed her in these terms:

"The malignity of your intelligence and the perversity of your heart have not permitted you to make a good usage of your power; far from repairing your injustices by means of the power of grand faerie that the laws and my bounty have accorded to you, you have, on the contrary, abused them, and that abuse finally demands my justice. Receive today, then, the punishment for your sins, in losing for two hundred years any power of faerie and resuming the form of an ostrich, under which you will remain for the time destined to the service of these guards."

With those words, the queen touched her with her scepter, and, all the fays having raised their wands toward her in a sign of applause, pronounced a few words, during which the unhappy Gangan became an ostrich again and immediately went to place herself among the other animals of her species.

Meanwhile, the queen, having summoned the fay Judicieuse, confided the care of the young prince and the young princess to her while they remained in her court, and recommended them above all to form their hearts while cultivating their minds. Then she embraced Cadichon and Feliciane—that was the name of the princess—and those lovable children, penetrated by joy and gratitude, only quit the arms of the queen with difficulty in order to render themselves to those of Judicieuse.

They profited so well from the two years of education they were given while they remained in the home of the Queen of the Fays that they attracted the amour and admiration of her entire court.

When one of them attained the age of fourteen and the other of twelve, the sovereign of the fays resolved to unite them and to return them, with Cadichon's brothers and sisters, to King Pétaud and Queen Gillette, but she declared to the Fay of the Fields that, in order to serve as an example to Cadichon and Feliciane, the other children—although perfectly corrected of their defects—would only resume their original form in the presence of the young spouses and when they had arrived in the home of the king, their father. Then, having rendered her visible and having determined the moment of departure, she confided to her the conduct of the six children of whom she had taken care, and ordered her to choose husbands and wives for them. Then she summoned Judicieuse and charged her to accompany the prince and the princess. Those amiable children shed tears on quitting the person to whom they owed their happiness, and the generous queen, embracing them tenderly, promised them her amity, and saw them depart with regret.

They did not take long to return to the court of Pétaud, where that king had been in a state of extreme embarrassment. The queen, his mother, after having languished for several years, had left her throne vacant and delegates of her kingdom had come to invite her son to mount it. They had asked for a audience and no one knew in what fashion it was necessary to accord it to them. Pétaud was uncertain as to whether he ought to be standing or seated, on foot or on horseback. For that purpose, the council had been assembled where, as usual, everyone decided.

The seneschal Caboche claimed that the king ought to be standing and sustained that he had heard it said that the Emperor Charlemagne and the twelve peers of France were always standing, and that they only sat down in order to eat and to go to bed. The procurator fiscal opined that His Majesty ought to be seated; he said, for his reasons, that kings and judges ought always to be at their ease, and that after a bed, there was nothing as comfortable as an armchair. The treasurer, by contrast, was of the opinion that the king ought to appear on horseback, and alleged that the posture in question was the noblest for kings, since their statues always represented them thus.

Each sustained his sentiment; they shouted, they quarreled, and might perhaps have gone further if the king, raising his voice above all the rest, had not said: "Will you stop it, then? That's a lot of noise for one chair more or less. As I am, they'll see me, and as they find me, they'll take me, that's all that I can do. But as for being their king, thank you very much, but I'd go mad with all the bother of royalty that they tell me I'll have in my hands. Long live my petty kingdom; since I'm comfortable here, I'll stay here. So, let them get used to it. However, since they want to have an audience, it's necessary to give them one, so let them come in."

Everyone retired, each murmuring loudly that the king had not chosen his advice, and criticizing him for always wanting to have things his own way.

While someone went to fetch the delegates, His Majesty, believing that he thought much better than his council members, put on his royal garments and sat on the foot of his bed, the curtains of which he had raised in festoons around the spiral columns. He held his scepter in one hand and his cap and fringed gloves in the other. The queen was to his right in a blue serge chair garnished with big gilded nails, and her chambermaids were behind her. To the king's left were his grand officers, who were almost all laughing behind their hats at the singular figure of their king.

When everything was arranged, the door was opened and the delegates came in, followed by all the people of Pétaud's realm; they made him three profound reverences, to which the king and queen responded with three others, and they were about to commence their harangue when they saw a woman with a majestic face arrive, holding a young man of fourteen or fifteen by the hand. Addressing Gillette, she spoke to her thus:

"Queen, everything works out for her who can wait. Your misfortunes are over and your destiny has changed face; it has been possible to remove from the wickedness of Gangan the prince you see here; that perfidious fay can no longer harm him and her malice has been confounded; recognize him, therefore, as Cadichon; and you, delegates, render homage to the legitimate successor of your estates."

Then the king, recognizing his son, took him in his arms and kissed him a thousand times; then, throwing his arms around the fay, he embraced her without any regard for her age or her character; he did the same to his wife, to Caboche, to the procurator fiscal, the treasurer and everyone he found around him. After that, taking off his royal mantle, he put it over Cadichon's shoulders, gave him his scepter, sat him on the foot of the bed and started shouting with all his might: "Long live the King!"—which was immediately repeated by the grandees and afterwards by the people, to whom the king said, several times: "Shout then, the rest of you!"

Meanwhile, the queen, penetrated by joy and gratitude, had fallen at the fay's knees, which she embraced, weeping. The fay, after having lifted her up, made a sign that she wanted to speak.

Everyone fell silent except the king, whose joy was so great that, so to speak, he could not see or hear anything. Finally, running out of breath, he shut up, and the fay continued thus:

"What you see is only a part of the benefits of the Fay of the Fields, your friend; she also combines it with the choice of a young and lovable princess, whom our queen has destined to the prince for a wife; if the qualities of intelligence of that princess and the graces of her figure are a feeble guarantee of the happiness of these spouses, the mildness of her character and the kindness of her heart, which I have taken care of forming, can assure its duration; confirm that union, then, and thus merit the powerful protection of the Fay of the Fields and that of...."

The king did not want to hear any more, and, immediately taking the hand of the prince and that of the princess, he said: "Done! I'll marry them and give them all my kingdoms and all my farms; as for my other children, I'm no longer embarrassed, and the good Madame of the Fields won't let them lack anything; so let's have the wedding and rejoice. You'll all dine with me, although I don't know what I can give you—but as my wife says, 'Everything works out for him who can wait.'" To Caboche he said: "Meanwhile, Father-in-Law, go to the kitchen, have everything in my farm-yard killed—and above all, eat well, for I want everyone to talk about it!"

The seneschal obeyed, but as he traversed the dining room he perceived a table with twenty-four place-settings, served with the finest dishes. He went no further, and returned promptly to tell the king and queen what he had just seen. Everyone wanted to witness it; they went there, not without some fear, and, in consequence, without ceremony. The spectacle was astonishing at first; they hesitated to taste the meats, but they finally became accustomed to it, and the king, for whom all of it cost nothing, set the example; he ate wholeheartedly and drank his share exactly. It is said that he did not stint himself on his old stories and his old jokes, for the fellow repeated them frequently, always in the same terms.

They had been at table for nearly two hours when they heard violins in the audience hall; as they had eaten and drunk well, they quit the table willingly, and the king, who was cheerful, unable to ask for anything better than dancing, wanted to open the ball with the queen and asked for a courante. The violins obeyed, and he commenced it, but, no longer remembering it, he did not finish it, and told the young prince and princess to dance a minuet, which they did with an admirable grace.

They had reached the final reverence when six marionettes were seen to enter the room, prettily dressed, three as Roman knights and three as Roman ladies. Each of the six marionettes had an empty space alongside it, in which the tip of a nose was perceptible, and all of that was led by a woman to whom little attention was paid, so much did the spectacle attract the gaze. Everyone stood aside to make way for them, and immediately they performed a dance, in which each of the six nose-tips figured marvelously.

When the ballet was finished, they arranged themselves in a circle, in the same order they had observed on entering. Their conductress placed herself in the center, applied the extremity of her wand to the extremities of the six noses, and caused three polchinels and three dames-gigognes to appear in their stead.

"Good, good!" said the king. "All that will be for my grandchildren, provided that they cost me nothing to nourish and dress; I'll keep them and enjoy them in the meantime."

"Gently, Sire," said the woman. "Have patience. Everything works out for him who can wait."

At the same instant, the twelve marionettes resumed dancing, and everyone was utterly astonished to see them visibly changing, and gradually resuming other faces and new costumes.

"Mercy!" cried the king. "There's Toinon, Jacquot and Chonchon, wife! It's Toinette, Jacqueline and Chonchette! No, I don't believe it...oh, by my scepter, that's admirable." Then, addressing their conductress, he said: "Why , I'll wager my cap and my royal mantle that you're Madame of the Fields, our friend; my word, you're worth your weight in gold, and here are the children all warmed up, all dressed and as tall as their father and mother. But who will marry them?"

"Me," replied the Fay of the Fields—for it was her—"and it will be right away."

At those words, the king, feeling nothing but joy, took her by the hand, made her I know not how many compliments in his fashion, and made her sit down next to Gillette, to whom he cried; "It's Madame of the Fields; at least, it's our good friend."

But the queen, only listening to her sentiments, yielded to all her gratitude for the fay and all her tenderness for her children. The fay introduced her then to the three princes and the three princesses who were unknown to her, and proposed their marriage with her six children. The king and queen consented to that immediately; all those present applauded the choices of the fay, and the delegates proclaimed Cadichon and Feliciane to be their king and queen.

The seven marriages were celebrated in a manner worthy of the sagacity of Judicieuse and the noble simplicity of the Fay of the Fields.

Cadichon gave each of his brothers and brothers-in-law one of the great governments of his kingdom in sovereignty, and the seven princes departed with their wives, accompanied by the two fays, who only quit them when each of them had arrived in his capital. There they gave them new instructions for the conduct of their families and their estates, and, after having heaped them with marks of their benevolence and their generosity, they departed, in order to take care of their own affairs.

As for Pétaud and Gillette, the fortune of their children caused them neither ambition nor jealousy, and did not change their way of thinking at all. The majesty and representation of a great queen did not suit Gillette's simplicity; the character and genius of Pétaud were unsuited to the cares of a great kingdom, and the latter would not have exchanged his seneschal, his piquet and his vegetable garden, nor the former her spinning-wheel, her milking-shed and the amity of the Fay of the Fields, for all the grandeurs in the universe.

JEANNETTE; OR, INDISCRETION

There were once two good people whose house was near the castle of a benevolent fay. They had often heard mention of her power and her generosity, but they had never implored her aid; perhaps their natural timidity prevented them from doing so, or rather, according to what others have assured me, the contentment they had in a simple estate to which they had been able to limit themselves is a happiness that one has no need to ask of the fays, and which we can all grant ourselves.

Those good people had a daughter of their marriage who really was very pretty, but, pretty as she was, they thought her a thousand times prettier. In fact, they brought up their little Jeanette—that was what they named her—as best they could, and did not perceive, either because of the blindness that is only too commonplace in fathers and mothers, or because they knew no better, one great defect, which was that of always talking and always reporting what she had seen and what she had heard. The good folk regarded as vivacity or prettiness the first indiscretions that Jeannette committed; they repeated before her the little tales that she had told them about her companions, they applauded them and almost always laughed at them. That paternal complaisance authorized Jeannette in her faults.

As I said, those good people had never asked anything of their neighbor the good fay, but one often does for one's children what one would not do for oneself. They finally decided to present themselves to the fay, and they appeared before her, one turning his hat and the other presenting her with a little basket of fresh eggs, but both with a very embarrassed countenance, and begged her to grant them a favor.

As soon as the god fay perceived them, she approached them with as much kindness as if she had been their equal. "What do you want of me, my good people?" she asked them.

"We've come," they replied, "to ask you for a favor, which is to be kind enough to take in and care for our little daughter Jeannette; she is, in truth, a pretty child."

"Well, bring her here in a week," the good fay said to them, mildly.

A week later, the good folk returned to the fay's castle, wearing their best clothes, leading Jeannette by the hand, whom they had dressed as well as they could. She had brand new clogs, a very white bonnet and a little scarlet dress decorated with blue ribbons. The fay thought her very pretty, and did in fact take her into her service; that very day she was dressed and adorned with the greatest magnificence, and she was not given any other occupation than playing with seven or eight little princesses, whom kings and queens had put in the hands of the fay, and of whose education she had kindly taken charge.

Jeannette's employment was not difficult, so she acquitted it very well from the first day. But as a talker does not reflect on the propriety of what she might say, Jeannette, not being able to talk about the castle, the custom of which she did not know, Jeannette talked, sometimes to one and sometimes to another of the little princesses, and often to all of them, about her father, her mother and her village. The subject-matter was not very interesting, so it did not amuse those whom she had been expressly commanded to divert. On the contrary; they said in low voice: "Those really are fine stories that Jeanette is telling us; it's necessary to hope that she catches a cold, she needs a sore throat," and a hundred other remarks by which they turned her to ridicule.

The day after her arrival she made all the little princesses confidences in which she told them everything that she could imagine to please them and to insinuate herself into their affection. She confided to one that another had said that she was not pretty, to this one that that one accused her of having wet the bed, and a hundred other things of that species, very disagreeable to hear said. She did it so effectively, in brief, that all those pretty princesses, who, until her arrival, had lived in great harmony, were soon all quarreling with one another, without wanting to make up, so annoyed were they.

The fay was informed of that division, and discovered the source of it very easily. She scolded Jeannette, and threatened to send her back to her village. That reprimand had its effect for a few days, at the end of which she obtained permission to go and see her father and mother to show them her fine clothes. The fay recommended her to great secrecy about everything that happened in her bode. Jeanette promised that, but, the desire to talk and to relate what she had seen being the true motive or her journey, she told everything she knew at home—or, rather, what she thought she knew. She talked recklessly about the fay, and often without employing the truth with exactitude, but as it is not worth the trouble of lying unless one lies to one's own advantage, she said that the fay had made her a princess and that she would soon be going to her beautiful kingdom. She told a hundred stories, each as ridiculous and inappropriate as one another.

Those stories almost made Jeanette's parents' heads spin; they could not understand how they had been fortunate and clever enough to have made a princess. "For," they said, "the fay is very powerful, but if we hadn't made our daughter, she would never have been able to make her a princess."

It was not only to her father and mother that Jeannette told those fine stories, it was also to all those of her acquaintance that she found in the village, and the fine clothes she was wearing authorized those assertions. The next day, all the peasants in the village, dying to see their daughters become princesses, came one by one to ask the fay for that little favor. If it had been granted, there would never have been such a great promotion of princesses, for they all came to the castle, without exception, to request that bagatelle.

The fay obliged Jeannette to go and take them her response, which, as one might think, was an honest refusal, but she carried the message while experiencing the utmost despair, for that pretended princess appeared in clogs and all the attire in which her parents had taken her to the castle. Jeannette appearing in a costume so different from the one in which they had seen her, and so inappropriate to the dignity that she had given herself so liberally, giving the lie to herself, responded easily to the request of all the peasants, who, in order to compensate themselves for the futility of their journey, made a great many pleasantries and mocked Princess Jeannette as much as they could. All he inhabitants of the castle, princesses and others, did the same.

Such a good correction ought to have rendered Jeannette less loquacious and more discreet, inasmuch as she was infinitely sensitive to it; however, in spite of her tears and the advice that the fay gave her about her faults, with as much kindness as reason, she made further confidences to all the princesses, and told them that there was one of them who, out of jealousy of seeing that she was so pretty, had indisposed the fay against her and had engaged her to make her appear as she had before the peasants. She told that fine story to all the princesses individually, without taking any other precaution than changing the name, depending on the one to whom she was talking—for great talkers and liars are subject to making very few reflections.

However, the lie had no more success in the castle than the one she had told in the village, for all the princesses, having made their reciprocal confidences in their turn, turned her to ridicule, saying: "It's me who is jealous of Jeannette."

"No, it's not you, it's me," said another.

Finally, all of them, making horns at her, cried while dancing around her: "It's all of us who are jealous of Jeannette's clogs."

They fay, in the depths of her heart, was not displeased by that public reprimand, for two reasons; firstly because nothing corrects faults like examples, and that Jeannette would learn better from all the little princesses how necessary it was to avoid loose talk and gossip than punishment and the whip can teach others, or anything she could say herself on that subject. Furthermore, she was eager to see whether she could corrected the child of such an inconvenient fault; she desired it all the more because she found her charming in every other respect.

Jeannette, having quarreled with all the princesses, who no longer wanted to talk to her, was constrained only to associate with the nursemaids and governesses, something that she had already commenced long before, because, in order to render herself necessary to them, she reported to them all that the others had said and done.

That procedure is unpardonable, so it was not pardoned; it brought the hatred borne against Jeannette to its culmination, and the fay, who, as I said, wanted to correct her but did not want to cause pain to the little princesses, because she was good, was obliged to send her out of the castle and shut her up in a pavilion that she had named "the Solitude." It was there that she retired to meditate on the mysteries of faerie; it was also there that she sharpened her wand and where she retired from society in order to dream at her ease and relax from her great occupations. It was there that she took Jeannette in order to make her forget a fault that can only be put into practice in society.

The pavilion was in the middle of a plain that only produced heather, and which extended as far as the eye could see; the horizon of the plain was not terminated by any mountain, and the fay only ever went there by air, no road leading to the retreat. Its apartments were furnished with the most agreeable panted canvases that have ever been seen; a delightfully planted garden surrounded it, and the most superb aviary, filed with the rarest birds of all the countries in the world, complete the charm and delights of the pretty garden. It was in that Solitude that the fay locked little Jeannette, giving her everything that might be necessary to her.

Jeannette had some difficulty accustoming herself to solitude, but she could not suffer without weeping the silence to which she was condemned. She had recourse to lamentations, and then to songs; that aid was all the more consoling because one cannot employ them and still maintain silence, but the consolation as slight, for, after all, she was deprived of the satisfaction of being indiscreet.

Jeannette was curious; that is a fault necessary to those that have just been reported, and when one likes to talk, it is necessary to be attentive in order to have something to talk about. Jeannette therefore gave herself so much trouble and took her measures so well that during the fay's absence she went into her cabinet. She examined all the instruments of faerie with great care, but what struck her the most, and with reason, were the regulations of the fays.

She read there how it was recommended to each of them to be careful of her wand, from which she ought never to be separated, and to beware, above all, of sleeping in the presence of anyone; her power was absolutely attached to that attention, and even more to that essential mark of the fay, for it was said positively in the book that anyone who took possession of her wand could not only do anything they wanted, but that the fay herself might become their slave.

Jeannette, very occupied with that discovery, but being unable to make any use of it, because the fay never slept in the pavilion of the Solitude, and having no one to whom she could confide that important secret, felt the greatest pain that an indiscreet subject can suffer, which is that of knowing something important and having no one to whom to confide it.

In that cruel state, after having meditated for a long time, she came up with an expedient to satisfy herself. As I said, in the garden that surrounded the fay's pavilion there was an admirable aviary, which was filled with all sorts of birds, known and unknown. There were, in consequence, parrots. It was on one of those birds hat Jeanette cast her eyes, in order to make it her confidant. She took it in amity, and taught it to talk much better, because it was necessary to talk to show off. As it had learned a hundred thousand useless things, she enabled it to recite, in a very short time, this rhyme of sorts:

> *If you take her wand while a fay is asleep*
> *You have only to command in order to reap.*

When the parrot was well instructed, Jeanette implored the fay to permit her to send it to one of one of the little princesses in her castle. The fay regarded that mark of attention as evidence of her natural good nature, and therefore consented to it. Putting the bird in her carriage, she gave it to the princess for whom Jeannette destined it; but imagine the fay's astonishment when, in the midst of all the little princesses, after having obtained from the parrot all the words it knew, after having repeated a thousand times "Bonjour, Jeannette," "My little friend," and a thousand other similar things, she heard it say, in the manner of advice:

If you take her wand while a fay is asleep
You have only to command in order to reap.

She shivered at the risk she had run, and, immediately having her carriage harnessed, she ordered her griffins to go and fetch Jeannette. She was obeyed, and in less than a quarter of an hour, in spite of the prodigious distance, Jeannette was brought to the castle.

Immediately, she reproached her for her indiscretion, and, what was more, her ingratitude; and without giving her time to employ the poor excuses that she might have alleged, with a stroke of her and she turned her into a magpie, and gave by that means a terrible example to all little girls, in order to prevent them from talking too much and repeating what they have seen and heard.

To punish her further, she did not want to leave her, as they say, "the key to the fields." She put her in a large wicker cage, on which was inscribed: *Princess Jeannette's Palace*, in order that it could not be mistaken anywhere, and that the lie she had told would be an eternal source of reproaches and pleasantries.

In that equipage she sent her back to her parents, informing them that it had not been possible for her to make anything worthwhile of their daughter, but that she advised them to be careful what they said in front of her, because the whole village would immediately be informed of it.

In order to console them a little, she pointed out that they had at least gained her upkeep and her dowry, and that a piece of cheese would suffice henceforth for her nourishment. All the hopes of those good people vanished on seeing the cage, and Jeannette, of whom they had hoped for so much, became an insupportable torment for them.

It is thus that naughty children, who are not corrected, in making their own misfortune, often make that of their parents.

All indiscreet persons are curious;
Be careful with whom we converse.
One thinks talking necessary to live with people;
To know how to shut up is much better.